The Doctor's SECRET

A NOVEL by TINA K. FUNT

MARBLE HOUSE EDITIONS

Published by Marble House Editions
67-66 108th Street (Suite D-27)
Forest Hills, NY 11375
elizabeth.uhlig7@gmail.com
www.marble-house-editions.com

Funt, Tina
The Doctor's Secret/by Tina K. Funt

Summary: A novel that traces the social, emotional and intellectual
journey of a woman growing up in midcentury New York through her
adult life as a doctor, wife and mother.

ISBN 978-0-9966224-7-9
LCC Card Number: 2019943839
Production Date   October, 2019

Printed by WESP in South Korea

To my father, who always believed in me,
to my husband, who believed in me when
I did not always believe in myself,
and to my son, who gives me reason to believe.

Tina K. Funt

THE DOCTOR'S SECRET

PROLOGUE

Arainy early October morning. The trees were changing color, creating a tapestry of burgundy, orange, gold and cinnamon. The slow downward drift of the leaves and the crisp rustling underfoot created a nostalgic atmosphere.

This was always a season of reminiscence and reevaluation for Dr. Julie Kent. Maybe it was the quiet after a summer that had been filled with outdoor activities and parties. Or perhaps it was the start of the school year, which had always presented new projects and goals. The images of autumn appealed to Julie's romantic nature—the thought of being wrapped in a woolen blanket in front of a crackling fireplace on a misty afternoon. A novel and a cup of hot apple cider would bring on the mood of an English novel in which the young heroine steals across the fog-laden moors to meet her lover.

At this moment, though, Dr. Kent was not in front of the fireplace. She was sitting at her desk in the consultation room, preparing for the morning's flood of patients. She had been practicing dermatology for more than twenty years in the tony Long Island suburb of Manhasset, and even after so long, she loved treating patients, still deriving the same satisfaction she had during her first year as a community physician. The days were filled with patients of all ages who had an array of ailments and concerns, not all of them physical.

There might be an elderly man or woman complaining of psoriasis, then someone coming in for a skin cancer screening. Next there would be a mother with a toddler scratching his arms and legs. Different time slots in the day brought different groups—the teenagers who came after school to get help for their acne, and young children with warts. The early evening brought the wave of professionals with demanding careers, and scattered throughout the day would be women seeking skin rejuvenation—Botox, fillers, the eradication of brown spots and lines.

In addition to their skin care concerns, patients shared their personal stories. Over the years, Julie had developed a wonderful rapport with many of them. She chuckled as she thought about how she had known some of them during childhood, their teen years, through marriage, childbirth and sometimes divorce. The gratification she enjoyed came from treating generations of patients—grandparents, parents and children. The close relationships she cultivated had earned her the families' trust and respect, which she treasured. As she often said, "This practice is my second child."

And in a sense, it was. Her first child was Drew, her remarkable 20-year-old son, born just six months before Kent Dermatology was founded. Julie would say that her practice and her son were "Irish twins," and whatever tensions came into her life would dissipate when she was in "doctor" or "mom" mode.

For reasons beyond mere taste, Julie had cultivated a keen sense of serenity and beauty. Ever since childhood, she'd had a need for routine and consistency, and as an adult, she made sure these elements were always present in her life. At her practice, each room was lined with soft beige wallpaper and furnished with off-white chairs. Framed prints of Impressionist paintings adorned the walls, and classical music wafted through the rooms.

On Julie's desk, everything had its place. A leather blotter was surrounded by Post-it notes reminding her of patients to call or diseases and their latest treatments to read up on. There was a vase that held a small bouquet of fresh mums, red, gold and purple. Opposite the desk hung a print of Monet's Water Lilies, providing her with a soothing, restful dose of blues and lavenders.

Julie took a deep breath and experienced the sense of pure safety and well-being that she always felt in her office. Sitting with a mug of coffee, she sifted through some pathology reports. Before long, she heard the voice of her nurse, Lisa, chirping, "Good morning! I'm here!" She glanced up to see Lisa in neatly-pressed scrubs, her dark hair tied into a ponytail. After this quick greeting, Lisa bounced down the hall to set up the treatment rooms.

Julie stood up, gave her own hair a quick brush and dabbed on some lipstick. Slipping her white doctor's coat over her simple, chic clothes, she made her usual upbeat announcement to the nurses: "Ready, girls? Let's start the morning's festivities!"

◊ ◊ ◊

"Good morning, Mrs. Schwarz. What brings you here today?" Julie asked her first patient.

"It's the rash again! The itch won't stop, and I keep scratching," complained the elderly woman.

"Well, let's have a look." As Julie lifted Mrs. Schwarz's blouse, she saw the patient's dry, flaky skin dotted with crusts and long scratch lines. "It does look like you have been scratching away," Julie noted. "Let's look at your lab tests." Sure enough, Mrs. Schwarz's thyroid levels were very low. "That explains it," Julie said. "Your skin is very dry, and that is causing the itch. You will need to visit your primary care doctor to get medicine for your thyroid. I'll get you a copy of the lab report. In the meantime, I am giving you a prescription for some strong moisturizers." Mrs. Schwarz nodded gratefully.

"How is your family doing?' Julie inquired.

"Everything is wonderful. May I show you our latest addition?"

"Of course!" Mrs. Schwarz proudly displayed a photo of a healthy-looking baby wrapped in a pink blanket. Next to her stood a little girl in a flowered dress.

"How absolutely precious," Julie remarked with a smile.

Mrs. Schwarz smiled warmly. "And how is Drew?" she asked.

Many of the patients had known Drew since he was a child. They had heard about his accomplishments over the years, including how he was now attending one of the famed Ivy League colleges. Julie described her son as "a Renaissance man" because he was an excellent student, musician, outdoor enthusiast and skier.

"Drew is doing great," she beamed. "Working hard and maybe playing too hard!" she added with a laugh. "So different from when I was a student. All I remember doing was studying and working in the shoe department at Macy's. I took time off to date, go to the movies and have a little ice cream, but it seems that now the kids major in two subjects, one academic and the other partying," she joked.

Handing Mrs. Schwarz the prescriptions, she told her to make a follow-up appointment. "And make sure you see Dr. Larson for your thyroid evaluation," she added. As she shook the patent's hand, Julie smiled warmly and left the exam room. She entered the next room to find a new patient, an attractive 40-year-old woman whose complexion was dotted with blemishes. She scanned the chart, briefly reading the medical history.

"How can I help you today?" she asked.

"Just look at my face!" the woman exclaimed.

"How long has this been going on?"

"For about three months. I'm so frustrated. My skin is

worse than when I was a teenager! Why do you think this is happening?"

Julie looked into the patient's eyes. "I'm going to ask you a few questions, and I will help you. I do treat adult women with acne all the time," she continued. "I'd like to obtain more medical history. Did you start or stop and medicines or birth control?"

"No."

"Are your periods regular?" Julie asked.

"Fairly regular. I can't understand this!" The patient's eyes began to well up with tears.

Julie nodded. "Of course you're frustrated. But we will get you better. Now, let me examine your skin closely." Julie checked the patient's scalp for thinning hair and examined her back and abdomen and breasts for signs of increased hair growth but found nothing. "I'm going to prescribe some topical medication and give you a daily skin care routine. But while you're here, let's work on some of these breakouts."

After the brief treatment, Julie said, "OK, start with the topical medicines and if they don't help within three weeks, we'll add oral medicines. Please come back so I can see how you're doing. I'll reevaluate at that time." The patient, looking relieved and comforted, thanked Julie, and the two women said goodbye.

Julie was glad to offer her patients a compassionate ear and a soothing environment in which to address their problems. She knew that along with her gentle and knowledgeable manner, she was providing something of a haven for them. When they allowed her to examine them, they were baring not only their bodies, but their emotional vulnerability.

The next patient was Jennifer, a pretty woman in her mid-forties whom Julie had known for some time. Although usually good-humored, today Jennifer was visibly upset.

"Jen!" Julie greeted her, "Good to see you, but why the tears?"

"Oh, Dr. Kent!" Jennifer replied. "Things are not that great."

"Why is that?"

"Well, it looks like I might be single again. My husband doesn't want to be married anymore—at least not to me. You know how it is: late-forties finance guy making big bucks now needs a 28-year-old secretary." Her voice was tinged with bitterness. "It's so unfair! I'm home with four kids, striving to be just what he wanted me to be. I gave up my career in fashion! What did I do wrong? I got older!"

Julie had no problem understanding Jennifer's pain. She had heard countless stories like this: a man in midlife, usually a successful one, equating his monetary worth with power, which usually included the conquest of women. When his achievements should have given him a sense of well-being, he'd instead turned away from his wife's devotion and felt a sense of entitlement. Perhaps the sexual routine had become just that—routine—and a bit of boredom had set in, so he would look outside the marriage for more excitement.

The sad thing was that other women were happy to have an affair with someone else's husband. The man would tell the "other" woman that his wife didn't give him adequate attention or didn't appreciate him. Or he simply said his wife was perfect, but he wanted a change of scenery. And if the wife didn't know, then who cared? Even worse was the man who peddled the myth, "My wife and I have an understanding."

"Well, you have great kids," Julie said encouragingly. "You're pretty, energetic, and kind. You'll get through this and in time, you will find a better man who will cherish you," she added with a hug.

Jen smiled weakly. "How about some Botox to make me feel better?"

Julie laughed. "Of course! Nothing like a little rejuvenation for the soul."

Jennifer relaxed on the examining table, and Julie injected her face, making sure to rejuvenate in a natural style. She made sure that her patients never ended up looking like clowns and ducks.

◊ ◊ ◊

After a morning of visits and treatments, Julie sat down at her desk to eat lunch. Always the same lunch: a mixed salad and grilled chicken, and sparkling water with lemon. That morning, she had started her day with her usual spartan breakfast of oatmeal and fruit. Julie had devised her strict food regimen not only for health reasons but, as with everything else, to maintain order and a minimum of change in her life, and it served her well. Not to be too strict, however, she allowed herself a 3 p.m. break to enjoy tea with cookies or chocolate.

Julie picked up the phone and dialed her husband, Dr. Doug Stone. As was often the case these days, his secretary told her that he was consulting with a patient or was in the middle of a procedure.

Julie and Doug had been married for more than twenty years. A successful ENT surgeon, Doug was the epitome of an accomplished Type-A personality. Everything down to his shiny, dark-blond hair was perfectly in place. Six feet tall with a lean, sculpted physique, he weighed the same 170 pounds he had when they got married. His piercing blue eyes absorbed every nuance of a situation, and he had a razor-sharp mind that jumped easily from one topic to another. There wasn't anything that Doug didn't perform without excellence and attention to detail. A brilliant surgeon and a fabulous hiker, biker and skier, he was also a terrific chef, handyman and techie. It seemed as though he knew just about everything about anything.

However, like a coin, Doug had two sides. What made him so meticulous and capable often made him critical and impatient. If Julie spent one minute more than necessary talking to a server in Dunkin' Donuts, Doug would stomp away from the counter complaining about how slowly she moved. He needed to be in complete control, and there was no discussion with Doug. If you disagreed with him, you were being "argumentative" and just plain wrong, as he believed he was always right.

But although she would get angry with Doug, Julie knew she was terribly insecure without him. During their dating days, Julie had been quite impressed with him. She had been raised to be frightened of the world and so found Doug to be a source of strength and stability. She needed him, and he filled those needs, taking care of everything. Back when they'd first met, Julie did not even know how to write a check or fry a chicken cutlet. True, she did become a doctor, but the fact is that medical school had been a refuge from the very frightening world where, she had been taught, she should be dependent on a man. Julie remembered many discussions with her mother that were punctuated with, "Why don't you ask 'blank?'," and the blank would be filled in with the name of Julie's current boyfriend.

For the past six months, Julie had been sensing that something was terribly wrong between her and Doug. They had always argued, as Doug liked to have his own way. In the beginning of the relationship, Julie capitulated to his opinion, but as time went on and she became successful, she gained more confidence. She would disagree with him, but somehow they always got back on track.

Lately, though, he was constantly snapping at her and seemed to be distracted and impatient all the time. She found it harder and harder to reach him after work. At 5:00, the answering service took phone calls, and if Julie called Doug's cell, he didn't answer. When she'd question him about this, he would use the excuse that he was still seeing patients or was in the gym, where there was no cell service. Intuitively, she knew that something had changed, and it was confirmed when, on this particular afternoon, he did answer the phone.

"What's up?" he said curtly.

"What time are you done today?" Julie asked.

"I'm done when I'm done."

Quietly seething, Julie maintained her composure. "Do you want to have dinner at The Grill, and at what time?"

"How can I tell you what time?" he snapped back. "I'll call you when I'm done. Stop calling me!"

She hung up, feeling alone and despondent. She needed to trust Doug. Should she check up on him, sneak over to his office and see if his car was still there? She didn't want her world turned upside down as it had been with her father. Maybe if she just let this go, it would disappear on its own. She felt her cheeks flush with humiliation. Here she was, a well-respected doctor sitting in her office, shaking with anxiety.

She stared at Monet's beautiful landscape, trying to take in its peace and stillness. You will be OK, she told herself. Everything will remain stable and return to normal. Then she said this aloud, but in the inner confines of her heart, she knew she was deceiving herself. It was just another secret that the doctor kept.

Tina K. Funt

— PART 1 —

SHELTERED LIFE

CHAPTER 1

In 1960s America, the postwar traditional values were still intact. For young people, the excitement of the decade was the Beatles, Twiggy, and "The London Look," which came out of Carnaby Street. For both young and mature men, especially those with an education, an array of professions was available. Women, however, educated or not, were faced with only two options: get married and have children or have a career. Professional choices for women were limited: teaching, nursing, office work, and not much else. There were rumblings of political and social change going on, but since women were not in power, there was no parity in their work status, not just with respect to salary, but also no prestige, esteem and prospects for future career growth.

The Kent family lived in Ditmas Park, a neighborhood in central Brooklyn that comprised large, early 20th-century houses on wide, tree-lined streets. It was a quiet, upper-class district inhabited by families of professionals and well-to-do-businessmen. Julie's father, William, had inherited and ran a jewelry company in Manhattan that designed and produced earrings, rings, brooches and cufflinks. The business provided the Kents, a family of five, with a comfortable lifestyle.

William always stressed the importance of education and professional goals and made sure all three of his children got the message. He was a child of the Great Depression, whose parents had come from Czechoslovakia. As a young man blessed with a brilliant mind and a love of learning, he was on his way to a practical career in engineering. But at the behest of his father, he left City College and joined the jewelry company along with his brothers. This was a step he would regret daily for the rest of his life because despite earning an excellent living in business, William always knew that his heart was in the academic and scholarly world. He lamented having not followed his plans to finish college and maybe become an English professor or doctor. That would have suited his character and temperament and satisfied his soul. For as long as Julie could remember, her dad, whom she admired and emulated, could recite poetry and quote Shakespeare.

Julie had inherited her father's curious mind and quest for knowledge, delving into mathematics, poetry, music and literature. She relished mastering new academic subjects and in fact went on to be valedictorian of every school she attended. Her motivation to study so assiduously was borne out of a pure love for learning and a desire to please her father. In addition, time spent studying protected Julie from the outside world, which she regarded as a scary place. As a highly sensitive child, she found solace in working at her desk or at the piano, where the threatening forces beyond her front door could not reach her. One source of comfort was a newly-opened box of Crayola crayons, so predictable, so knowable, so soothing with its assortment of colors, always in order inside the box. And the smell, the waxy smell, always provoked the same reaction— pleasure. The magic inside the crayon box was literally and figuratively a safe island for Julie.

This timorous view of the world was something she had inherited from her mother, Lara. Lara's fears arose out of her experience as a Jewish child in Russia, a place that was not friendly to Jews. Unable to live in peace, her family emigrated from Russia to Canada when Lara was seven. Later, as the little girl grew into a teenage beauty, the family immigrated to the U.S. There, at age nineteen, Lara met 24-year-old William, an airman who was about to leave for his wartime assignment in India. They got engaged in just six weeks, and he did not return for two years.

Julie was an admixture of her parents' stances toward the world. She had her father's keen intellect tempered by her mother's cautious nature. As immigrants, Lara's parents brought with them the after-effects of the trepidation they had suffered in Russia. This led them and, by extension, Lara to live by such axioms as "Don't draw too much attention to yourself," "Don't stand out," "Danger is lurking in every corner," "Watch out for the gypsies, who steal children." In Lara's adult life, these anxieties morphed into fears of the physical world: "Don't swim in the pool right after eating," "Don't go in the ocean—there might be an undertow!" "Don't stay out late," "Be careful crossing the street." Curiously, however, Lara had no anxiety about emotional matters. When it came to the ups and downs of relationships, she usually had confidence that things would "work themselves out." Almost fatalistic in such situations, she never invested time worrying about that which she could not control.

Julie was the youngest of the Kents' three children. Charles, ten years Julie's senior, was the oldest. He was the school athlete, captain of the baseball and basketball teams, and, though never a dedicated student, he excelled in the schoolyards of the neighborhood.

The second child was Elizabeth, three years older than Julie and the beauty of Ditmas Park. With a heart-shaped face and thick, blondish hair cascading past her shoulders, she was a picture of sincere grace and sweetness. Julie was the "smart" child. Skinny with black wavy hair and big brown eyes, she was Daddy's girl. William would joke that Charles and Elizabeth were Lara's children and Julie was his, as he saw in her what he would have wanted for himself. She was intelligent, stubborn and driven to complete a task once it was started. Where William's thirst for knowledge had been limited by the conditions of the Depression, Julie, fortunate to be born in the postwar generation, was able to exploit her curiosity about the world.

Julie's values, while influenced by those of her parents, were also shaped by those of the community. Grade school served as a safe cocoon for young girls, who clung together in tightly-knit groups. The elementary school years that included treasured toys like Chatty Cathy and Barbie gave way to middle school years in which girls developed similar ways of talking, dressing and even studying. In their plaid skirts and sweaters, knee socks and loafers, they strode along the avenue after school to the corner candy store or went back to the Kent house, a gathering place for friends. Lara loved having her children close by and welcomed all guests, who knew that in the Kent kitchen there would be cookies, cupcakes or charlotte russe. Once homework was done, the kids stretched out on the floor of the den and played Monopoly or Clue. As they became teenagers, they spent time dancing to vinyl "45s," sometimes with boys, or being so bold as to play Spin the Bottle. It was a safe, happy childhood and youth.

Home was a place of love and respect, where some of the best traits of the Old World were combined with modern American standards. The Kent children lived in an atmosphere that nurtured education, support, good manners and reverence for elders. There was a predictability and meticulous organization of the house, its routines, its meals. Each night of the week had a set menu of main dishes: Monday—cutlets, Tuesday—meatloaf, Wednesday (dairy night)—salmon croquettes with noodles and pot cheese, Thursday—lamb chops or steak, all served with vegetables and potatoes or pasta and followed by small glass bowls of fresh fruit.

Friday night's meal was different because it was Shabbat. Lara would light candles, recite prayers and serve a traditional meal: challah, chicken soup (brimming with matzah balls and noodles), roast chicken, potato and noodle kugel, and kasha varnishkas. And everyone knew to leave room for sponge cake and mandel bread.

Like the meals, the children's schedules were regular: on Wednesday afternoons, a piano teacher came to the house and gave lessons to Elizabeth and Julie. Thursday afternoons the girls went to Miss Ricki's dance studio for ballet lessons. And every afternoon there was homework. Lara never had to nudge the girls to do that. In fact, it was difficult to pry Julie away from her books. Not so with carefree Charles, who could not get enough of sports.

"He's an athlete!" Lara would say with a laugh. With her accepting nature, she looked for the good in everyone.

Although Lara and William were strong advocates for the importance of education, they did not believe in pushing their children beyond their individual capabilities. As parents, they achieved a delicate balance, knowing when one of their children, despite making a true effort, could not excel in a subject, or if he or she was simply being lazy.

Like so many mothers of her generation, Lara saw education for women as a gift, a bonus, that would make her girls cultured wives of professional men. They might aspire to being professional as well, but not *too* professional. Their careers would be a second priority. No, they should be homemakers, putting the family first. Lara thought a good career choice for her daughters was teaching or nursing. She imagined that Julie, especially, with her laudable study habits and grades, could become a high school English teacher. This would be the perfect career for her, as it would afford her time to be a devoted mother.

William, on the other hand, hoped Julie would become an English professor or a doctor, as he had dreamed of being. Julie remembered how, when she and her father would drive by NYU School of Medicine and Bellevue Hospital, they would see only a few female doctors hurrying along in their white coats, stethoscopes swinging from their necks.

"That's you," her father would say, as he pointed to them. "One day you too will be a doctor." But at the time, Julie had no intention of studying medicine, for in the 1960s, no woman she knew was a doctor except her family doctor's wife. Well, she had time…

Woven into the fabric of upper middle-class life in 1960s New York was the women's Saturday afternoon outing to B. Altman, a posh department store on East 34th Street and Fifth Avenue. Lara and the girls would travel by train into Manhattan to enjoy Altman's quiet elegance, where unhurried shoppers browsed through fine apparel, accessories and cosmetics. Farther down the street at Macy's Herald Square, there was a more chaotic, lively atmosphere that some preferred, but B. Altman had a certain panache that was all its own.

After sifting through racks of clothing and peering into glass cases of fine scarves, kid gloves and other trifles, the three Saturday shoppers would go to lunch upstairs in the Charleston Garden, the store's faux-Deep South dining room, where they would enjoy tea sandwiches and scones. If they were in a less formal mood, they would venture out to Chock Full O' Nuts for the unique specialty—sandwiches of cream cheese on date nut bread, followed by powdered donuts and hot chocolate.

Then it was back to the stores for more shopping, until 5:00, when William would sail by in his navy-blue Cadillac, ready to ferry everyone to dinner at Oscar's Salt of the Sea on the Upper East Side. Charles, being the athlete, did not come along for this; he was either playing sports or out on a date, so it was just William and his three ladies.

The Sunday dinner ritual was different. Frequently, the whole family ate at Lundy's in Sheepshead Bay. The large, cavernous restaurant, with its soft lighting and Moroccan-style stucco ceilings, could hold huge numbers of patrons and was a popular gathering place for Brooklynites on Sunday afternoons.

On these occasions, Lara was always beautifully dressed in one of her fashionable ensembles, and the two girls wore pretty party dresses. To see Lara with her daughters was like seeing one of Renoir's pastel paintings of a mother flanked by her affectionate and lovely children.

William always ordered a chilled martini for himself and an apricot sour for Lara, and each girl got a Shirley Temple, a harmless mixture of ginger ale, grenadine syrup and cherries. The food was over the top and generous: high platters of clams, shrimp and oysters to start, followed by clam chowder with cornbread and salad. The main course might be fillet of sole, scallops or lobster tails. And if one had any appetite left, there was warm apple pie topped with vanilla and chocolate ice cream.

If the Kent family was not at Lundy's on Sunday night, they were at the Chinese restaurant, the standard choice for Jewish families in the neighborhood. (The Italian and Irish families would already be dozing after their own huge Sunday afternoon dinners.) The Kents, like so many of their Jewish neighbors, would feast on spare ribs, shrimp in lobster sauce, vegetable lo mein, wonton soup, egg rolls and fried rice. The meal always ended with pistachio ice cream and, of course, fortune cookies.

◊ ◊ ◊

There were facets to life that extended well beyond Brooklyn. Being a family that valued time together, the Kents had ample exposure to culture—museums, Broadway shows, travel. During two weeks in the summer, they rented a cabin at Lake George up in the Adirondacks. The girls would swim or play shuffleboard and ping pong, and Charles would spend hours perfecting his shots at a basketball hoop. At night, after dining in a small country inn on the lake, they would all go to Gaslight Village Amusement Park or play miniature golf.

In the winter, they went to some of the grand hotels up in the Catskills: Grossinger's, the Nevele, the Concord. This was the heyday of life in the "Jewish Mountains," where vacationers could ice skate, ski, go sledding, practice archery and see movies. The food was abundant and sumptuous, yet it had an Old World *geschmack*: matzah ball soup, creamed herring, blintzes, stuffed cabbage and brisket. Guests went from a meal to an activity, to a meal to a snack to an activity, happily getting a little bit fatter.

"Are we rich?" Julie asked Lara one day.

Lara smiled. "We are not rich, but we are extremely fortunate and privileged. Your father works hard. But remember," she added, "always give to charity and treat everyone with equal respect." No matter how secure or pampered she was made to feel, Lara never forgot her loving but poor immigrant background.

One would think that a young person growing up in such a family would never feel anything but sheltered and safe. But it was Lara's worried nature that added something of the opposite to the chemical mixture that made up Julie's view of the world. Lara's generation of women had gotten the message—and accepted it—that they needed a husband for emotional and monetary support. Lara had worked for only two years before getting married, and once she became William's wife, she took on a new role, putting herself fully in charge of all domestic tasks: preparing meals, organizing the children's activities, decorating the house and entertaining William's business associates. This was her domain. The world outside her home, she felt, could be a sinister place, where one needed to always be on guard.

"Julie, be careful when you walk to the store alone to meet your friends," she would warn her daughter, adding, "Have the friends meet you at home and all go together."

"It's only 3:00, and I am going twenty minutes away!" Julie protested.

"You just never know," Lara insisted. "You're so thin, and anyone could grab you and take you away. You know in Europe the gypsies stole children, and we must be careful."

"But it's not Europe! It's the United States."

But despite such protests, Lara's fearful immigrant mentality seeped into Julie's consciousness. Julie never quite felt at ease being alone and imagined danger lurking nearby. As a result, she chose to spend much of her time in a museum or library, where she could find stimulation yet feel safe. Nestled in an edifice of knowledge, she could further her learning and, at the same time, be secure. At least she could try to, because although she wanted to dismiss Lara's words from her head, the world and its dangers were still there, either real or imagined. Always expecting something bad to befall her, Julie resolved to find someone to depend on who would take care of her. That would solve two problems: she would be protected and would never have to be alone.

CHAPTER 2

C hildhood flowed into adolescence and the teenage
years. As an exceptionally bright child, Julie had
skipped kindergarten, and in grade school she was academically
tracked into a "Special Progress" class. This step allowed her to
skip 8th grade, and so at age thirteen, she started high school.
She had not even menstruated yet.

The school population comprised an array of cliques.
There was the corps of sharp but nerdy students and the artsy
kids who joined the drama guild, school newspaper and literary
clubs. Julie felt at home with both these groups because of her
academic excellence and love of the arts. As in every school,
there was the "cool" crowd, which attracted the male athletes
and their cheerleader girlfriends. When Julie and a couple of
her friends tried out for and made the baton twirling team, they
were immediately linked with the cool crowd, no matter that
these girls had no idea about the rules of football.

There were girls who were already smoking cigarettes and
pot and even dabbling in sex. Some were more promiscuous
than others and boasted of having gone "all the way." But Julie
was not part of that crowd. Her recreational activities with
friends were rather wholesome: walking on Flatbush Avenue, the

girls would go out in groups to window shop for clothes, shoes and other niceties. Then there was Friday night ice skating in Prospect Park, followed by ice cream sundaes at Jahn's. If she was not home by 10 p.m., her mother would telephone her friend's house to make sure she was safe.

Her first boyfriend, a high school senior, came along when Julie was just fourteen. A typical, contemporary-looking '70s guy, he had long, dirty-blond hair and usually wore a blue denim work shirt. Emulating James Taylor in his looks and in guitar playing, he could frequently be heard humming such popular favorites as "Sweet Baby James" and "Fire and Rain."

So naïve was Julie that the first time the young man kissed her and touched her breasts over her shirt, she sat frozen and frightened.

"Am I supposed to like this?" she asked, which left him a bit cold. He might have dropped her then, but he liked Lara and hung around the Kent house for good meals. By the time Julie decided that she liked him, he left for college and that was that.

In January of her senior year, Julie, only fifteen-and-a-half years old, graduated as valedictorian. Afraid to leave home just yet, she chose Brooklyn College, where two of her best friends would also be going. This was a good choice for someone who had been sheltered, and Julie felt secure being on familiar territory. She was going to major in English literature and enrich her studies by minoring in music and art history.

The campus of Brooklyn College was not immune to the kinds of drama and problems that abounded in the 1970s. It had its share of riots, war protests, free sex, and plenty of drugs. Brash, popular music was everywhere. The Grateful Dead, Fleetwood Mac, and Led Zeppelin were heard along with the softer sounds of Carol King, Joni Mitchell and the Moody Blues.

While the college's political and social life whirled around her, Julie took refuge in her studies, usually engrossed in her books and ignoring everything else. She had set herself a goal of becoming an English professor. She knew the course of study would be stimulating and rewarding, and she felt that helping others was a way to satisfy her passions. At the same time, taking this route would fulfill her father's dream of the intellectual life.

Now and again, though, her father would tap into his other dream and bring up the idea of Julie becoming a doctor. She was simply not interested.

"I'm not smart enough to be a doctor," she confided in him.

"Yes, you are. You can be anything you want," he would say encouragingly.

Then her mother would chime in, "But she has to consider how she will raise a family and be a good wife!"

The feminist movement might have been underway, but not for Lara or Julie.

◊ ◊ ◊

Everyone needs a mentor, a role model, and Julie found hers in a thirty-something female English professor. Dr. Nevins embodied everything Julie aspired to be. A true bohemian with straight black hair that reached her waist, Dr. Nevins dressed in long, flowing, printed skirts, black jersey tops, beaded earrings and clogs. She and her professor husband and their young child lived in a Park Slope brownstone, where they would hold Friday night poetry readings. Every bit the New York art scene, these gatherings were attended by poetry-loving students who sat sipping wine on Persian rugs that covered gleaming parquet floors. A baby grand piano was nestled in one corner near the bay window, and a fire sputtered in the fireplace. The guests took turns reading the works of Lawrence Ferlinghetti, Robert Frost, T.S. Eliot and Elizabeth Barrett Browning. Dr. Nevins served crackers, cheese and cookies, and her four-year-old son scampered around after the cat. The cozy setting, where Julie could bask in the intellectual life she craved, provided much-needed nourishment. And with Professor Nevins as the host,

Julie felt she had entered the community she had been seeking. This scenario and the players in it encouraged Julie to pursue all aspects of the artistic and literary life.

During Julie's college days, she dated on and off, but compared to other sixteen-year-olds, she was sexually conservative. She loved dating, but free love, smoking pot and having casual sex were not for her. Julie wanted sex to be blended with romance and love, and she quickly weeded out guys who were looking only for a quick encounter. After rejecting their crude advances, she would not hear from them again. Just as well. She'd made a vow to herself to wait until she was engaged before losing her virginity.

During the fall of her senior year, Julie realized that she had not fulfilled the science credits required for induction into Phi Beta Kappa. She enrolled in basic chemistry and biology courses and found, to her surprise and delight, that these subjects were actually quite enjoyable. This got her wondering if perhaps one of the health science professions might be a good choice. She accepted the notion that being a doctor was out of her reach, but what about physical therapy or speech therapy? Maybe…?

Chemistry was challenging, but Julie was keen to get that A she aimed for. Since all the students at Brooklyn College who were taking chemistry were either pre-med or pre-dental, the competitive atmosphere was tough. Luckily for Julie, her friend's cousin, a pre-med student, was also a part-time chemistry tutor.

Robbie, so handsome and brilliant, was a modern Orthodox Jew who intermittently embraced and rejected Judaism. Once the tutoring began, it did not take long for him to fall for Julie. By the third session, he leaned over and kissed her. Julie did not resist as his hands travelled to her full breasts. Panting with anticipation, Robbie pulled her onto the couch and rolled on top of her.

"I really want you," he whispered into her ear. Julie didn't know what he meant by "want you," and she did not protest. Robbie fumbled with the hooks on her bra and in seconds, Julie was naked from the waist up. She breathed heavily, and her head spun with confusion as she realized that an Orthodox young man could be so sexually aggressive. Continuing his advances, Robbie fondled and kissed her breasts and, with one quick move, unsnapped her jeans.

"Wait!" Julie whispered, "I'm not ready for sex!" She could barely speak. "I just can't do this! We don't even know each other."

Robbie rolled over on his back. He lay there quietly and then said hotly, "I'll wait, but not too long." Julie, who would normally have left the room, found that for the first time in her life, she was genuinely aroused.

Despite the awkward, strained start, Julie and Robbie started dating and found that they had a tremendous amount in common. Robbie loved rock music, his favorite band being the Grateful Dead. The two of them attended concerts in the city, went to the light show at the Hayden Planetarium and always had much to talk about. But more than these, Robbie loved to get high on pot. One Saturday night as they were on their way to the city, Robbie convinced Julie to get high with him.

"No," she said firmly. "I tried that in high school, and I didn't like it. I get kind of paranoid."

"With me you won't!" he said as he passed the joint to Julie. Her resolve weakened, and she inhaled the weed. Within twenty minutes she felt lightheaded but not euphoric. As Robbie drove through the Brooklyn-Battery Tunnel, Julie had the sensation that they had both fallen down the rabbit hole and was suddenly gripped by a claustrophobic terror.

"Robbie!" she cried, "We've been in this tunnel for an hour!"

"Oh, shit! You're getting paranoid!" was his less than compassionate response.

Julie was panicking. "Pull over and ask for help!" she implored.

"Oh, shut up!" Robbie exploded. That was the end of their communal pot smoking.

Robbie's mean-spirited and impatient ways did not derail the relationship. The young couple continued to go to movies and concerts, although they refrained from pot-smoking. Spending time with Julie in the basement of his parents' house, Robbie increased the pressure on Julie to give herself to him.

"OK," Julie said, negotiating, "Everything but…"

Julie found herself behaving with Robbie as she never had with anyone else. She enjoyed being naked with him, heavily petting and touching. Robbie seemed satisfied with this and for the moment, the issue of having full-blown intercourse was put aside.

With Robbie, Julie had her first experience of oral sex. It captivated her so much that between dates, she would find herself daydreaming about it. She smiled secretly to herself upon hearing the song "Miracles," as the Jefferson Airplane sang, "I had a taste of the real world when I went down on you…"

Julie's sexual connection and her infatuation with Robbie's looks and bright mind blunted her ability to see how rude and cruel Robbie could be. She would push aside her thoughts that he was mistreating her and told herself that all he needed to do was grow up a little and then he would appreciate her. But one night, the lies she told herself did not hold up, and she could tolerate his behavior no longer.

It was over a dinner of pizza and falafel that Robbie remarked, "You know, my friends all think you are very pretty." She batted her eyes and smiled at him. Then he continued, "But I don't really see it."

Julie thought she would choke on her pizza. "Too bad for you," she muttered, and changed the topic. "Well, I'm doing really great in chemistry, so thanks for the tutoring. Lately I have been thinking about being pre-med."

"You'll never do it!" he laughed. "Look how hard you're studying for this course! You'll screw up organic chemistry and physics."

She took a deep breath. "Just because it takes me longer to catch on to concepts in chemistry doesn't mean I can't achieve my goal. Anyway, I had to write essays for your literature course, and I didn't demean you. Everyone has different talents and strengths," she said calmly. "I'm a hard worker and I'm diligent, so if I have to study harder, then I will." Then she felt her cheeks flush with anger as she added, "You know, I don't waste hours getting high on pot, so it'll work out for me." Robbie just looked away. Julie knew she was almost done with him.

That night, she sat with her mother and recounted with indignance what had happened. Lara shook her head. "He's a nervous boy. Just ignore him."

"Ignore him?!" Julie exploded. "You make excuses for the devil! You taught me to be kind and caring. You always tell me to be sweet and ladylike, but what about strength and self-respect? Robbie is downright rude, and if he's nervous now, how'll it be when life's problems get bigger?"

Despite her seeming conviction, Julie was not ready to completely finish with Robbie. She continued to date him and tried, as her mother had advised, to ignore his caustic remarks. Once again, Robbie tried to coax Julie to have sex with him.

"No," Julie stated, "Unless we are going steady and in love, I'm not sleeping with you."

"I'm not in love with you and never will be," he told her.

Julie consoled herself by saying that at least Robbie was honest. Did she love him? True, he was handsome and had a sharp mind, and while she valued those traits, she would never confess that to him. To be honest with herself, Julie had to acknowledge that Robbie was an angry, confused young man rebelling against the restrictions of his Orthodox upbringing. Sooner or later, however, he would surely want to marry an Orthodox girl. Too many issues and too little kindness, she thought. Julie vowed to herself that she would never run after a man who didn't love her. She remembered her grandmother Jenny's words: "A bought love is worthless." She also recognized that if a shoe hurt in the store, it will kill you when you get it home. From this moment forward, she would only let herself be loved by someone who loved her as much. Her need for romance and deep affection would surmount unrequited love.

She broke up with Robbie, telling him, "You bore me. You're a ball of anger, and I deserve more." Robbie didn't protest or fight for her, which only validated her resolve to never waste time on a guy who didn't treat her well. New beginnings for education and for her love life.

When January came along, Julie got A's in both chemistry and biology. She was proud of her achievement in the science courses, but her heart was still in the humanities. New York University's graduate school was where she would pursue a master's degree in English literature and education. Although plagued by some doubts, she took the path of least resistance and considered that perhaps her mother was right and things would work themselves out.

Tina K. Funt

—— PART 2 ——

EMERGING BUTTERFLY

CHAPTER 3

In 1977, Julie was in her glory. She was attending NYU in the heart of Greenwich Village, a lively neighborhood where students, locals, street musicians and drug dealers congregated in Washington Square Park. Still extremely conservative by 1970s standards and immune to the proliferation of drugs all around her, she was totally immersed in her studies. After all, what could be better than losing herself in the world of English and American literature? In addition to adding to her already rich storehouse of knowledge, Julie was acquiring educational techniques that she hoped to use in the future to help her students enhance their readings skills. When she was not in class or studying, she liked to frequent the Village's small cafés that served flavored coffee, and there, while listening to jazz, she made notes in her journal.

In the spring of her first year, Julie felt the surge of energy that New Yorkers always feel after the long winter. The city was coming alive again, with tulips and pansies blooming in the square wrought iron fences that bordered the trees. The days were mostly sunny, and the night rain did not diminish the feelings of renewal and anticipation. Julie's birthday would be coming soon, a reminder of her true Taurean nature: a bit stubborn and fiercely loyal. With Taurus being ruled by Venus, Julie was quite sensuous, and her curiosity about sex had increased.

Lara was thrilled to learn that Julie had begun dating a law student she'd met in the library. As a mother, Lara felt the satisfaction of knowing that all her children were on the right track. Elizabeth, now a teacher, was married to Billy, a law student. Charles, married to Bibi (also a teacher) had joined William in the jewelry business. Julie was ensconced in graduate school and dating a law student. What more could a Jewish mother ask for?

Julie was at home one night, studying for her upcoming finals, when she suddenly heard Lara say loudly, "Will, are you all right?" She walked rapidly down the hall to her parents' bedroom and found her father panting and sweating, the color gone from his face.

"He doesn't feel well," Lara said, looking frightened. "His chest is tight."

"Let's get him to the hospital now," Julie urged.

Despite William's protests, they drove to the local hospital. In the emergency room, he was diagnosed with angina, a closing of the coronary arteries. The doctors prescribed medicine and insisted that William stay overnight. He cooperated, and to Lara and Julie's relief, he was discharged the following day, feeling somewhat better.

But about a week later, the symptoms resumed while he was at work. This time the family insisted he be admitted to NYU Medical Center. Julie felt totally helpless. Her father, her hero, might be very ill or die. She sat in his hospital room with her mother as the doctors performed tests confirming that William had angina. But while the situation seemed dire, the doctors were optimistic. William had responded well to the medicines, and they assured Lara and Julie that the patient would be fine.

Lara glanced at her daughter. "Go study in the library downstairs," she suggested. "We got a good report from the doctors, and I know you have so much work. All will be well."

Julie was encouraged by the doctors' prognosis, and feeling relieved that her father was stable, she headed downstairs to study. The library was a large room with long wooden tables where students sat either staring at their textbooks or gazing around during a momentary break. She plopped down on a chair and buried her face in a book. With the recent ordeal, she had left her curly hair unbrushed, and the strain of the emergency visit had drained her of some of her usual robust color. But she didn't care.

Looking up for a moment, she found herself peering into the blue eyes of a student staring intently at her from across the table.

"What is a pretty girl like you doing in this library? I've never seen you before, and I always recognize good-looking women," he said with an arrogant laugh. "You're not a med student, so are you looking for a doctor to date?"

"If you really must know, and I truly don't owe you an answer," Julie replied, "I'm here because my father was admitted to the hospital with heart disease. I'm trying to study for an exam."

Smiling sheepishly, the young man said, "I'm so sorry. I didn't mean to offend you. I just couldn't stop looking at you. You're a welcome distraction from studying. My name is Rick. Can I take you for a cup of coffee?"

Julie paused, noticing Rick's deliberate manner of speaking. "Sure," she replied, "but I drink tea." She smiled shyly. "By the way, I'm Julie." They stood up, and Julie could feel Rick's eyes fixed on her body, sending a bit of a frisson through her. As they walked toward the cafeteria, Julie observed Rick, taking in all the details. He had straight, dark brown hair that fell softly on his neck, and a beard. In his gray T-shirt and jeans, Julie could see the outline of his broad shoulders and narrow waist. He seemed to be about her height, and she liked that, because as they walked, their eyes met.

After getting their drinks, Rick directed them to a quiet area of the cafeteria. "So, what are you studying?" he asked.

"English literature and education in the graduate program at NYU downtown. I plan on becoming an English professor," she told him proudly.

"Wow! I love literature," he said, seeming impressed. *Or was he putting on an act?* Julie thought she'd test him.

"Really? Which authors do you like?"

He rose to the occasion. "Oh, Hemingway, Faulkner, Fitzgerald. But probably my favorite is Somerset Maugham."

"*The Razor's Edge?*" she exclaimed. "That is my favorite book! Larry Darrell and India!" Rick grinned broadly. He knew he was making his mark.

"Where did you do your undergrad?'" he asked.

"Brooklyn College. You?"

"City," he replied. They shared a laugh.

"Guess we are city kids," she giggled.

Rick seemed to like her giggle. His unabashed, direct stare made her feel shy and excited at the same time. She had a feeling he was undressing her with his eyes.

"So, you want to teach?" he asked.

"Yes, I do. I love literature, and I want to impart that love to young adults. You know," she continued, "a part of me really liked basic science very much, and sometimes I think I want to do pre-med and become a doctor." Julie had no idea why she was sharing this information with a stranger.

"I get it," he said. "Like me, you enjoy studying."

She nodded emphatically. "Isn't it your favorite thing in the world?"

Rick laughed. "Oh, I can think of something better than that!" Julie squirmed in her seat.

She glanced to the side, feeling her cheeks flush as she batted her long eyelashes.

"You are very pretty," Rick blurted out.

Again, she blushed. "Thank you," she replied demurely.

"And I can't believe you love *The Razor's Edge*," he

added.

Julie was impressed that Rick was a medical student and also liked literature.

"I love the arts," she told him. "I go to museums whenever I can."

"Do you like Impressionism like—"

She finished his sentence: "Monet, Manet, Degas, Renoir?"

Rick reached for her hand. "You and I seem to have a lot in common. How about I walk you to your dad's room and take your phone number? I'll call you this week and take you to a museum."

Julie felt her body tremble a bit. "Yes," she said softly. *Did she have a choice?* Rick walked her upstairs, and Julie scribbled her number on a scrap of paper.

"Great!" Rick said. "I hope everything goes well with your dad. I'll call you."

"Thank *you*," she replied. "You helped me to stop worrying for this past hour."

Rick smiled. "Thank you. I really needed a break from studying. Now I think I'll concentrate even better. Or maybe not."

Julie laughed lightly. "We'll go to a museum."

Rick thought for a moment. "Did you ever go to the Frick?"

"The Frick on Fifth and 70th is my favorite. Really!" Julie gushed.

Rick took her hand again. "I can't wait to go there with you," he said, his blue eyes riveted on her. They both knew that somehow they had made a connection, but neither one knew how strong a bond they would forge for a very long time.

Rick did call Julie, and a week later, she was getting ready to meet him at the Frick. She had slipped on a lacy white silk blouse and tight blue jeans, and because it was a mild May afternoon, only a light cotton sweater was needed. Letting her dark, wavy hair hang loose around her face, she applied eyeliner and mascara and daubed on pink lipstick and a soft blush. To complete her alluring look, she chose large gold filigree earrings that her father had given her. After a quick spray of Chanel No. 5, she slipped into her flats, grabbed her black pocketbook, and dashed off.

Her mood was joyful. William had been released from the hospital and was at home now, recuperating. For Julie, the thought of losing her father had been terrifying. He was "the rock of the family," as her mother said, always working hard to provide for her and the children. He was generous with his in-laws and factory workers, and everyone knew that they were equal in his eyes. The loss of such a man would have left a huge abyss in the lives of many people. But that had not happened, and for the moment, Julie relaxed and felt free to go out and enjoy herself.

Promptly at one o'clock, she arrived at the Frick, a Gilded Age mansion that was once the home of business titan Henry Clay Frick. Now it was a small jewel of a museum that housed Frick's extensive and varied art treasures. It had a wonderful permanent collection and also featured exhibitions on loan from other famous museums.

Rick was already waiting for Julie on the front steps. She liked his punctuality, a trait that reminded her of her father. He wore a pale blue button-down shirt with blue jeans and brown loafers. He smiled when he saw her and winked. "You look very pretty and much more relaxed than you did the other day."

Julie smiled coyly. "Thank you."

They walked slowly through the museum, admiring the vast array of artwork by El Greco, Renoir, Monet and Titian, and the huge canvases by Turner, among others. With no break in the conversation, they eagerly discussed different genres and concepts: the Renaissance painters' emphasis on proportion, humanism, and the revival of classical Greek/Roman style and mythology. They examined El Greco's paintings, noting his trademark twisting and elongated figures, intense colors and vibrant landscapes. Julie sighed wistfully over the Impressionist paintings, with their muted hues and shapes interspersed with reflections of light. Rick pointed out that Turner's paired works detailed 19th-century maritime trading.

By the time they left the museum, they were spent with talking but felt like kindred spirits. They crossed Fifth Avenue and walked into Central Park, feeling the warm breezes as they strolled along, each enjoying a large Bavarian pretzel and a Coke.

Then the topic of heritage arose. "Tell me about your background, Rick. What's your full name?" Julie inquired.

"Rick Wind," he replied. "I'm German-Jewish and grew up in Queens. My family emigrated from Germany in the late '30s, at the time of the Holocaust. My grandfather was a prominent surgeon, but the Nazis didn't care. How about you?"

"I'm Julie Kent. My mother and her family left Russia when Mom was just a child. They originally went to Quebec City, but when my mother was sixteen, they came to the States. My father was born in America; his parents were Czech immigrants."

"You're *Jewish?*" Rick asked with some surprise.

"Yes, is that a problem?"

Rick shook his head. "I thought that, you know, with your dark hair and dark eyes you must be Italian."

She laughed, "You mean Jewish women can't have dark hair and eyes?"

"I don't know. You have this little nose and ass. I stereotyped and thought you were Italian or maybe French."

Julie didn't know what to make of this but continued, "I come from Brooklyn. Ditmas Park. Do you know where that is?"

"Not really. People from Queens don't know too much about Brooklyn neighborhoods. Anyway, go on," he urged her.

"I went to Brooklyn College. Like I told you, I'm in

NYU Graduate School to get a dual degree in literature and education, but I'm starting to wonder if I shouldn't have gone into the health professions."

Rick listened intently. "How old are you?"

"Nineteen."

He looked startled. "What? Nineteen? In *graduate* school?"

Julie smiled. "I know, I know. I skipped third and eighth grades. Then I graduated high school in January and completed college in three years. I'm a bookworm," she chuckled.

"Well," said Rick, "You're so young, you should go back to college and do the pre-med studies. That'll only take two years. Then you could start med school. Obviously, you're really smart," he added with assurance.

Julie paused. "How do I know I'm smart in the sciences?"

"You won't know until you take the courses. If you don't do well, you can go back to your original plan of teaching." Rick seemed logical and supportive, and Julie liked that about him.

"That's what I needed to hear," she said, smiling.

He grinned, pleased with himself. "Now maybe you can fix *my* problem. I just don't know if medicine is the right career for me. I was always the top of my class in high school and college. I kind of goofed off for first two years of med school and didn't do very well. Actually, I don't really like medicine," he said, sounding depressed.

Always craving an opportunity to be of comfort, Julie looked him straight in the eye. "You don't have to punish yourself for not being at the top of the class. It sounds like you just weren't focused, so of course you fell to the bottom. It's like the champion horses of the Kentucky Derby. They're all amazing, but if one isn't focusing on the track, that horse will fall behind."

He laughed. "I know. But maybe medicine is boring for me."

"Well," Julie continued, "there are so many aspects of being a doctor. You have to see what suits you. Start fresh this year. Study hard. Forget that you didn't do well the first two years and see what happens when you *do* focus." She started to giggle. "It's funny that you're talking me into going to med school while you're thinking about dropping out."

"You gave me good advice," he said. "I think I'm feeling depressed because I didn't do as well as I'm used to doing. It'll be a new start for me this semester."

She nodded. "Exactly. People go through many phases in their lives. Sounds like you were burnt out and needed the time off."

"I *was* going to ask for a leave of absence, but now I'm not going to. Instead of worrying, I'm going to concentrate on doing well. Besides, I might really like surgery. I like using my hands," he said, grinning.

The day was waning, and it was now four o'clock. The late afternoon sun was still shining, so they walked to a quiet place in the park and sat on a large rock hidden beneath the trees. With the leaves making a canopy over them, Rick leaned over and kissed Julie's small delicate lips, circling his tongue against hers. His hand cupped her breast over her silky blouse, and as he began to rub his thumb slowly over her nipple, Julie let out a sigh. He kissed her more ardently and slid his hand under her blouse. Within seconds he unfastened her bra and fondled her with plucking and stroking motions. They slid down the rocks onto the grass, Julie straddling Rick. She felt the firm bulge in his groin as he pulled her face toward his and covered it with long, hot kisses. Within minutes he rolled her onto her back and unzipped her jeans, deftly sliding his hand under her panties. It was clear that he knew exactly what he was doing as he reached for the spot he wanted, stroked her core with his thumb and inserted his middle finger past her wet curls. She groaned loudly and tried pulling away, but couldn't.

"Someone likes this," he whispered.

"I do, but we are in the park, so you must stop."

"OK," Rick agreed. "I'll stop."

"No, don't!" Julie begged as she pulled him back toward her. She didn't want him to stop, and he knew it. He kept up the rhythmic movement inside her as the base of his palm rubbed against her moist sweet spot. She breathed out hard against his warm chest, arched her back and shuddered in his hand.

It was late afternoon and time to leave the park. They made their way down Fifth Avenue, Julie barely able to focus as Rick held her hand and smiled broadly.

"You know, I think you'll be a good surgeon," she remarked with a laugh. "You're very good with your hands."

"You think so?" he chuckled, "Just wait till I get you alone inside." She knew he wasn't kidding.

From then on, Julie and Rick met every Saturday afternoon. They had a regular routine that included a visit to a museum, a walk in the park (rain or shine), followed by lunch. They liked to have sandwiches and coffee and finish with a chocolate eclair for Rick and a Linzer tart for Julie. Afterwards, they would go to their favorite spot in the park and cradle each other among the rocks, where they would kiss and touch breathlessly. But as the afternoon gave way to nightfall, Julie always insisted on going home to sleep.

On their fifth date one warm, slightly rainy evening in June, they were having dinner at a local Italian restaurant when, over spaghetti, meatballs and red wine, Rick revealed to Julie that he had never dated a Jewish woman before. Julie was surprised and asked why. His reply was that embedded in his strict German upbringing, which stressed perfection and performance, was his parents' assumption that he would marry a Jewish girl. Perhaps, he mused, by dating only Gentile girls, he was rebelling against his parents' wishes.

By contrast, Julie told Rick that she had been raised in an environment of unconditional love. Although she strived for academic excellence, she knew her parents would be proud of her as long as *they* knew she'd tried her best. Rick admitted that his parents had always been extremely critical and demanding, even to the point of punishing him for soiling his underpants when he was a child. This was all very foreign to Julie, but despite that, she could see that they had a common denominator. It was their European upbringing, which valued education, culture, literature, and a love of classical music. Rick loved Mozart and Beethoven with their Austrian/German dramatic influence as much as Julie loved Rachmaninoff and the Russian romantics. And they both agreed that Springsteen was the boss and the Rolling Stones and Fleetwood Mac held a close place.

That night, Rick took Julie to his apartment in Turtle Bay. She found it to be a typical student apartment, with posters on the walls and no-frills decorating. But it differed from other student apartments in that it was extremely neat and organized. Nothing was on the kitchen counters and the linoleum was spotless. In the living room, books were shelved in perfect size place, and cassettes were arranged in alphabetical order. He led her into his bedroom and as she suspected, his desk was immaculate, with pens arranged by color and books stacked in a straight line, their spines touching. Julie glanced at the pages of notes written in precise, small handwriting, definitely underscoring Rick's need for discipline, organization and neatness. *He is really meticulous*, she thought to herself. *He wasn't kidding about his Teutonic values.*

As organized and compulsive as Julie was when it came to her studies, she could be messy and leave a cup in the kitchen sink or papers strewn on her desk. Order and discipline were imperative in schoolwork but were much less important in her personal space. She could see that Rick would never get up from his desk and forget to push in his chair, whereas Julie could have a sweater on the back of a chair for days before hanging it up.

As she was gazing around the room, Rick swiftly pulled her onto his bed and slid his hand under her blouse. In no more than a moment, her bra was loose, and her blouse came off.

"We're alone now, not in the park," he whispered. "I have been waiting to see you undressed," he added, caressing and kissing her breasts. Julie moaned softly as his mouth came down masterfully on hers. Wanting to be everywhere at once, Rick let his lips graze Julie's nipples, and as her body responded, he unzipped her slacks and yanked them off. A moment later, her panties came down, and as Rick's thumb skillfully circled her firm pink bud, his fingers penetrated her.

She was completely naked, but Rick was still dressed, and she could feel his huge erection against her thigh.

"You're so hot," he repeated in a hoarse whisper. Her voice trembled in her throat as he kept stroking and kneading her soft flesh. Then he abruptly stood up, ripped his clothes off, clasped her buttocks and lay her face up on the bed. With one deliberate move, he spread her thighs and buried his head between them. Julie felt his tongue moving inside her, and in what seemed like seconds, she reached a boiling point, spasmed and came. Satisfied that he had brought her to ecstasy, Rick was then ready to reap his own pleasure and prepared to enter her.

"Wait," she cried out, "I'm not on the pill!"

"I'll use protection," he said, reaching for a condom on the nightstand.

"No, there's more," she gasped. "You need to know that I never did this before."

"You're a virgin?" he asked incredulously.

"Not *technically*. I don't have a hymen. My ex kind of broke it with his hand, but I never did *this*."

Still confused, Rick asked bluntly, "*This?* Look, it's simple. Did you ever fuck?"

Julie stiffened defensively. "What?"

"Did any guy ever put his dick into you?"

"No!" she answered, starting to cry and feeling humiliated.

Rick softened. "No, no, baby!" he soothed her. "It's not a problem at all. It's good in a way. I'm going to show you everything, and then you'll do it how I like. I kinda had the feeling you didn't know what you were doing," he laughed. "I'll be your teacher."

Julie took a breath and tried to relax. Slowly, but with determination, Rick plunged his hard member into the smooth, satiny folds between her legs. He kissed her firmly on the mouth, and she could taste her scent on him. As he cupped his hands under her bottom, Julie wrapped her long legs around his back and crossed her ankles. Rick lifted her and thrust deep inside her, relishing the way her body stiffened and then released as he moved vigorously. Then once again, he felt her shudder and contract as she cried out his name. A moment later, he surged inside her and collapsed on top of her.

For a few minutes, they lingered, gazing into each other's eyes. Fully satiated, Rick smiled and murmured, "You're going to be a great lover, Julie."

"Yes, if you are my teacher," she cooed.

CHAPTER 4

The hot, steamy summer in the city gave way to fall, and once again, autumn displayed her glory with blazing, colored leaves. The days flew by rapidly, and Julie and Rick were always together. Within six months, they had formed an incredibly close bond rooted in affection, desire and respect.

Following up on Rick's advice to apply to medical school, Julie had enrolled in post pre-med courses. Every day she commuted to Brooklyn College for her chemistry and biology classes and then drove back at night to Rick's place in the city. As a third-year medical student, Rick was required to be on call every third night during clinical rotations, but when he was at home, he would cook dinner for the two of them. Julie never cooked a single meal, as she barely knew how to boil an egg, so when Rick was on call, she would visit her parents in Brooklyn and sleep over there.

Additionally, although studying furiously, Julie took a part-time job at a doctor's office to earn some money. Between studying, working and commuting, Julie's days were full to the brim, but she was never too tired for lovemaking. Rick loved sex. They started their day with a quick romp and looked forward to hours of passions in bed at night.

Rick was enjoying medical school more and was encouraged as he gained momentum. With the new wave of studying, he was able to focus for hours at a time. As a means of memorizing a large volume of material, he would walk around the living room reciting differential diagnoses and pharmacological treatments for diseases.

Although very ambitious, Julie and Rick were driven in different ways. Rick wanted to be a highly prominent success and earn lots of money, and Julie wanted to save the world. She was eager to become a medical student for its own sake and was also happy that her father would be thrilled, vicariously living his dream through her.

The small apartment in Turtle Bay did not feel cramped. Jazz played on the radio as Julie and Rick studied in the evening. Rick would cook chicken and vegetables in the wok, or they would go out for pizza. At night they would lie in each other's arms, dripping wet after having sex. They would talk about the day when they could afford an apartment with air conditioning and how they would have Champagne and steak instead of Chinese food and pizza. But while living the American dream of financial success, they would still hold onto their European heritage and travel yearly to Europe.

Julie laughed mischievously one evening and asked, "Can we make love on an overnight train in Europe?"

"Baby, we *can* and we *will* make love whenever and wherever you want."

They had found in each other a devoted friend and advocate. Although Rick could be difficult with his compulsive neatness and insistence on having his own way, he was nonetheless totally supportive of Julie. When she cried that science courses didn't come as easily to her as the humanities did, he would encourage her to just keep studying, unlike her last boyfriend, who took pleasure in making her feel incompetent and inadequate.

"You're so bright, sweetie. Accomplishing something easily is not proof of success," he reassured her. "Unlike me, who you think absorbs information so quickly, you're very analytical, kind and patient. You would be a great pediatrician or psychiatrist. I have zero patience for people and could not do what you can. Everyone brings something different to the table."

She went over to kiss him, and he ran his hands through her dark hair. "Tell me, Jules, how much do you love me and need me to be inside you?"

"More than I can say," she groaned.

"How much do you love me?"

"Too much for my own good."

He rolled over on top of her, and after they shed their clothes, he slid inside her and felt her catch fire. "Let's make love like it's forever, baby," he said biting her ear. "Never forget how good this feels. Promise?"

She snuggled into his chest. "I promise you everything."

The radio was playing Bruce Springsteen's "Sandy Fourth of July." "Hey, Sandy girl, my, my baby," Rick sang. "That's your song, Julie. You're my Sandy girl."

The months flowed into one another, and a new routine evolved. Now that Rick was working with patients in the hospital, he had cut his hair and trimmed his beard. Julie appreciated this more mature look. During the week, they would dress conservatively, but on weekends they wore their jeans and jaunty caps and walked in Washington Square Park. Along with other city dwellers, they would peruse the outdoor art displays or would sit on a bench near the arch to do some people-watching. Sometimes they poked around the Village's small shops that sold trendy clothing or browsed stores crammed with shelves full of books. And all the while, they felt totally sexy and cool and in the rhythm of life. This was what Julie had imagined in the days of Professor Nevins' gatherings—a vibrant life filled with a variety of people, cultural stimulation and new experiences.

But with all of this, Julie was still haunted by her longstanding fears and insecurities. She confided in Rick, for now she knew that he was not only her lover and a best friend, but also her adoring protector. She admitted to being afraid to walk alone after dark or worrying that she'd hurt her friends' feelings by spending so much time with him, or that she wouldn't be a good wife because she'd never learned to cook.

Rick laughed at her for being raised so sheltered. He bought her cookbooks and pulled her into the kitchen. "Baby, if you're one percent as good in the kitchen as you are in the bedroom, I'm a lucky man," he stated with great gusto. "You're a lady, and I love your ambition and love of learning. I love our long, intellectual conversations, and I love loving you," he proclaimed one night. But more important to Rick was that he and Julie shared a common passion, and that was their intimate life. It could be sweet and gentle, both of them crying out their deep love as they held each other tight, or it could be kinky.

One night after sex, Rick grinned at her. "You know what I love about you?"

"What?" she asked.

"There are two sides to you."

"How so?"

Rick beamed at her. "There's the lady you were when I met you and the slut that I created."

They roared with laughter as Fleetwood Mac's "Gypsy" played in the background.

"You're my gypsy,'" he whispered.

"You make loving fun," she whispered back.

Rick paused. "Our passion is the glue that will always keep us together. We must always remember this, even if things get rough."

"Of course we will," she assured him, gazing into his eyes. They fell asleep in each other's arms. Heaven. Sheer bliss.

Julie had completed her first year of pre-med studies. Thrilled that she excelled in basic chemistry and biology, she was ready for the more advanced physics and the dreaded organic chemistry courses. Once she got over that hurdle, she would be facing the MCAT (medical course admission test) in the spring. Julie was resolute in her decision to become a doctor, but like anyone hoping to get into an American medical school, she was plagued by doubts and insecurities. In 1978, securing a place in med school was an extremely competitive goal, as only the brightest students were accepted on the path to this prestigious, lucrative profession. Julie only hoped she could make the mark.

It was better not to think too far ahead to avoid getting overwhelmed, so during the break in July and August, she planned to work in a summer school program, tutoring students in reading skills. It would be a nice change from the intense academic schedule she had been keeping. Rick would be occupied completing his third-year clerkships. He was on a roll now, and with Julie having a clear picture of her plans, as a couple, they were in a groove.

A warm breeze, redolent of springtime, floated through the apartment as they sat on the couch listening to soft jazz. They had enjoyed a dinner of chicken and noodles, and now they sipped tea from small Chinese teacups that Julie had bought in a shop in Chinatown. Rick sat shirtless, staring into space, listening to the rhythm of drums, saxophone and piano. Julie looked with deep longing at his strong physique, the hairy chest and muscular biceps. He smiled back at her, flicked his finger affectionately on her upturned nose, and ran his hands through her hair. The whole evening lay before them.

They had many flavors in their sexual repertoire. Rick could be in the "Let's fuck" mode one night and in the "You're my angel" mode the next, and Julie would play along. Sometimes the mood was tender, with classical music, a flickering candle and sips of Champagne. Other nights were purely titillating, with Rick wanting Julie to wear a garter belt, fishnet stockings and stiletto heels. Intermittently, there were nights driven by raw emotion, with tears that felt almost spiritual.

This late spring evening was a romantic one. Rick was playing Santana's "Europa," with its tones of yearning urgency. He slowly undressed Julie and poured Cointreau on her breasts and abdomen and began to lick the brandy off her pale, soft skin. He circled her nipples with his tongue and inched his way down, over the curve her stomach to the seething cove between her thighs. She felt the warmth of the brandy as he licked and sucked her sweet spot over and over. Undressing quickly, he thrust himself hard into her steamy warmth as she lifted her torso off the bed and called out his name.

"Julie, I love you," Rick whispered. "I love your strength, your mind, your beauty, your needs and your fears. I love dressing you and undressing you. I want to spend my life with you and make babies. Marry me, baby."

Julie gasped. "Yes, yes I will!" she cried out with him deep inside her.

They exchanged long, soulful kisses. She knew that Rick was her soulmate, the love of her life, her true companion. They fell asleep in each other's arms and awoke in the morning completely in love. No, it had not been a dream.

◊ ◊ ◊

When Lara and William got the call with news about the marriage proposal, they were thrilled. There would be a fall wedding, dovetailing with Rick's graduation from med school, when he would become a surgical intern. All of Rick's doubts about becoming a physician had dissolved, and now he was intensely focused on becoming a general surgeon. Also worth celebrating would be Julie's completion of her pre-med studies. For the following year, she planned to work in a lab doing research while awaiting acceptance into medical school.

As a team, they made arrangements day and night for their wedding and their future. The ceremony would be in the reform Jewish temple in New York, and afterwards there would be an intimate reception on a Sunday afternoon. Of course, the honeymoon would be in Europe, with plans to travel by overnight railroad so that Julie could fulfill her fantasy of making love aboard a train. They vowed to make love nightly, kiss each other good morning and good night, and always be loyal to one another.

Julie knew in her heart that Rick was a one-woman man. Prior to her, he'd had a girlfriend for four years and had never strayed. His father was very much in love with his mother, so he had great role models for marriage. Unlike so many men who were players, Rick never flirted with other women when he was with Julie.

Grandmother Jenny's advice for a good marriage came to Julie's mind: "Make sure the man loves you a little bit more than you love him." Over lunch with her mother, sister, Aunt Thea, and cousins, Julie discussed the engagement. These women were a team known as "Jenny's girls," in memory of their beloved matriarch. All of them valued education and hard work, but placed family as the top priority, and knew that their men protected and provided for them. Jenny's girls agreed that every marriage had its ups and downs, but trust and loyalty were key to success, as was having common goals and interests.

"How do you know if a man will be loyal to you?" Julie queried.

"Well," said Lara, "if he has a good role model, that helps."

Cousin Rachel said, "Remember what Grandma Jenny said. He should love you more than you love him."

Then Aunt Thea chimed in, laughing, "Never go to bed angry."

Julie admired her Uncle Joe, her mother's brother, and Aunt Thea's husband, too, but her heart belonged to her dad. Brilliant, cultured, ambitious and protective of his children, he was the man Julie had always adored. Rick reminded her of William in that he, too, was brilliant and ambitious and had a bit of a renegade in him. She loved that he was zany and was probably the only medical student who played the harmonica in the halls on the way to class. She trusted these two men in her life who would always keep her safe, buoy her, look out for her best interests and take care of everything for her. In this way, she could preserve and prolong the sheltered, charmed life she had enjoyed as a child.

The summer passed, and autumn was back with the turning of the leaves. Warm nights surrendered to the chilly air of late September as Julie and Rick were busy with engagement party plans. Rick presented Julie with a ring with a bright round diamond that he ceremoniously gave to her with a glass of Champagne and a bouquet of roses. The bride-to-be gazed lovingly at her ring and dreamed of her wedding and marriage.

Soon Julie's desk was laden with organic chemistry and physics notes from the last of her pre-med courses. She was lucky to meet and befriend a fellow student, Sara, who would play an essential role in her academic success. A blonde with cat-green eyes, the daughter of Hungarian immigrants, Sara was not only striking, but intensely goal oriented. Like Julie, she had grown up pampered and privileged. Sara was as assiduous in her studies as Julie, so it was no wonder that the two of them struck an immediate bond. They became inseparable, studying and reviewing notes at all hours of the day.

Organic chemistry was known to be the most challenging course in the pre-med program. It was the one subject that separated the men from the boys, so to speak, because any competitive medical school would require an A for acceptance. Knowing this, Julie and Sara plowed through the stereotactic molecules with equations to memorize. "Orgo," as it was called, wouldn't be relevant to any course in medical school, but it was an important prognostic factor because it comprised a tremendous number of equations to memorize and organize. Thus, the course served as an indicator of a student's ability to manage massive amounts of information.

Julie sometimes stayed at her parents' house in order to study into the late hours with Sara, who lived nearby, and Rick was happy that she had a study buddy. The girls had different styles, but studying together reinforced the knowledge they needed to retain. Like a sponge, a virtual study machine, Sara absorbed information with speed and accuracy. Julie, who also studied very hard, needed an occasional break to play the piano or listen to classical music.

Rick was busy with his rotations and welcomed Julie's attachment to Sara, knowing the girls would be together even on Friday nights when he was on call. Frequently, they drove to Bleecker Street to relax in a coffee house for a few hours after hitting the books. While other young women were hanging out at the bar, flirting with men, Julie and Sara were sitting together, sipping cinnamon-topped cappuccinos. With youthful enthusiasm, they discussed how terrific it was for them to become medical students at a time when few women, let alone attractive ones, were going into medicine.

Sara had dated a few guys but didn't have a steady boyfriend. She liked Rick and thought he was cool. Julie figured it out: "We will work part time in clinics or private practice and marry doctors. Rick will become a general surgeon, and for sure he'll find you a fellow resident. And we will live in adjoining brownstones!"

"Julie," Sara grinned, "I know you'll organize this for me!"

——— PART 3 ———

SHATTERED DREAMS

CHAPTER 5

How it began to unravel was really a series of unfortunate events. The first of these events occurred on a Friday night, when Julie and Rick traveled to Brooklyn to have Sabbath dinner with Julie's family. This was a regular ritual, with all the Kent couples, including Charles and Bibi, Elizabeth and Billy, and now Julie and Rick, gathering to enjoy a festive meal. Afterwards, the guys would hang out in another room while the girls cleaned up, then chatted around the dining room table.

Sabbath dinner had always been an evening of happy and peaceful celebration, but on this night, the feeling in the room was tense and uncomfortable. Recently, William, now in his late fifties, had been pondering everything from his career to his personal life. He seemed distant and reeked of alcohol most of the time, which was a complete departure from his normal behavior.

The initial explosion came during the meal. Noting William's strained demeanor and uncharacteristic way of speaking, Lara asked, "Are you drinking?"

He retorted harshly, "No! Are you?" a clearly ludicrous question, as Lara could nurse a glass of wine for three hours.

"Maybe I should just leave this family and start a business in Puerto Rico!" he vented.

"Why Puerto Rico?" Lara asked, baffled and embarrassed in front of her children.

"It's not so boring. This Jewish bourgeois atmosphere stifles me!"

The family members cast glances at each other. Always the strong, steady husband and father, William seemed to be unraveling, now repeating daily that he should have been an English professor instead of a jewelry manufacturer. His words were slurred tonight, as they had been on multiple occasions. He turned to Julie. "So, you think you're going to med school?"

Julie stayed calm. "Of course," she said assuredly, hoping to assuage his excited manner.

"Nah! You'll never do it! You don't have it in you!"

Julie recoiled. "What?" she cried out. She barely recognized her father and was horrified that Rick was seeing this side of him.

"Seems like a real midlife crisis," Rick muttered in her ear.

But the crisis had only begun. Later, Julie would reflect on the clues that were already apparent. It was clear that something in her father's behavior was totally out of sync with the status quo. It might not have become such a problem if her mother had not behaved like an ostrich, shutting her eyes and ears to the obvious. Why Lara ignored the clues was an enigma to Julie. Perhaps she needed to keep everything in order, maintaining the family routine, looking the other way just to avoid change. Or true to her nature, she may have hoped that if she just waited it out, the problem would resolve on its own. Staying put and hoping for the best instead of confronting the situation was its own kind of paralysis. And unbeknownst to Julie, what was presently her mother's predicament would soon become her own.

Lately, William was coming home at night disheveled

and smelling of alcohol. Whereas he had always been immaculately dressed, with a jacket and tie even to Sunday lunch, now his shirts were wrinkled, and his face was always flushed. He was continually harping on the idea of abandoning his middle-class existence and going to live in Puerto Rico. He sounded like Gauguin leaving France to live among the natives in Tahiti to relate to people with basic values. The behavior escalated daily. He would get home at 10 p.m., glazed and angry. Lara, in total denial, blamed his drinking on the frustration of working with his brothers at the factory. She made excuses for him, saying that he was stressed, and maybe even one drink was too much for him. Julie was desperate to find out what was behind this.

"Mom," she pleaded, "He needs help! He's an alcoholic."

Lara sighed. "Jewish men are not alcoholics. This will pass. He's just going through a difficult time at work."

"But he drives a car!" Julie screamed. "He might kill himself, or worse, an innocent victim!"

"Don't be so dramatic," Lara answered, annoyed. "God will protect us."

Metaphorically, Julie felt as though until now she had been dining at a posh restaurant with beautiful china, fine linen and a bouquet of roses on a table laden with the best food and wine. Then suddenly someone had come up and yanked off the tablecloth, sending the china, the crystal and the flowers flying and crashing to the floor. Her once luxurious, snug and well-ordered life was shattered.

The tipping point came in December, when she was studying for her final in that most pivotal course, organic chemistry. She had decided to study at her parents' house, in order to have some of her mother's home-cooked food. She sat down for last-minute studying that morning, as Lara left to go to the store. William entered her bedroom, already smelling of alcohol. He had not gone to the factory that day, claiming to be ill. Julie never remembered her father missing a single day of work. He had always been a stoic man and would work even if he felt feverish.

"What are you doing?" he shouted with a drunken slur.

"I'm studying for my Orgo final," she replied, noting his foul mood.

"Then you'll go to that guy who is using you for sex!" he ranted.

She gasped. "Dad, you're talking about Rick. You love him!"

"You're all a bunch of shits," he blasted, "and you'll *never* become a doctor."

Julie exploded. "Get out of my room, you stinking drunk!" William left but returned moments later wielding a steak knife. He held it up to her neck.

"Go ahead, I dare you," Julie said coldly. Somehow, she knew he would never hurt her. Inside, though, she was seething with hatred for him, her role model and source of strength. He left the room, beaten down, defeated by his own impotence against liquor.

Julie left the house within an hour to take her exam. She sat down for the final and silently told herself, *We're going to ace this test.* Shutting out the morning's horrid events and focusing only on the subject matter, she completed the test and felt she had done well.

As she walked out into the daylight, the last scene from part one of *Gone with the Wind* popped into her mind. She saw Scarlett O'Hara, haggard and exhausted, desperately pulling radishes from the earth. Scarlett holds them up, tilts her head back and, looking heavenward, vows, "As God is my witness, I'll never be hungry again!" Like Scarlett, Julie had once lived the life of riches, safety and privilege. And like Scarlett, her world was turned upside down. But Scarlett had gotten through the Civil War and rebuilt her life, as she had promised herself. And Julie would do the same.

She swore then and there that she would be a professional woman, be it a doctor or a professional of equal stature in a field that would allow her to be self-sufficient and never have to depend on a man. Having been betrayed by her father, Julie now knew that her confidence in men was obliterated. It was doubtful that she would ever regain full trust in any man.

A week later, Julie and her friend Sara learned that they had each received an A in organic chemistry. Julie experienced the initial elation of success, but her high spirits were quickly dampened when she thought of the situation at home.

To add to the tension of late, the relationship between Julie and Rick was becoming erratic. True to his perfectionistic nature, Rick was constantly, neurotically trying to maintain order, demanding, for example, that after every meal the floor be mopped. If Julie brought home a blueberry pie, he'd criticize both the bakery and the pie.

"Why not an apple pie?" he'd complain. "Why the French bakery? Why not the German bakery?"

"Rick, you know I'm under stress," Julie replied with a sigh of frustration. "I'm finishing up pre-med, but I also have the MCAT exam. Who knows if I'll get into medical school?" she wailed.

Rick had the answer ready before she could finish her sentence. "Well, Julie, then you won't go to med school. Be a speech therapist or to go back to becoming an English professor. Wasn't that the plan?"

"But Rick," she persisted, "I really want to be a doctor. And I don't want to disappoint you or my dad."

Knowing that Rick could be judgmental, she had been doing her best to shield him from the true extent of William's alcoholism. She feared his reaction if he learned his future father-in-law was a rampant drunk. Fortunately, whenever the family got together, William kept things under control. He still worked and was a high-functioning alcoholic, so Julie was able to protect what was left of her father's reputation.

The qualities that Julie had tolerated in Rick were now becoming impossible to live with. Trying to groom her to be the perfect wife, he wanted her at his beck and call. He insisted that they have dinner at the same time every night and was compulsively straightening up the apartment. If he wasn't on call both in the morning and the evening, he expected to have sex twice a day. And while their sex life had always been a source of pleasure, the joy and satisfaction of making love was diminishing now, as Julie's nerves were fraying.

One particularly cold, rainy night in January, Julie drove to Brooklyn to visit her parents. The wind was howling, and it seemed that the dismal weather conditions portended the scene that awaited her. She came in the front door and heard loud voices in the living room.

"Then *leave* for Puerto Rico if that's what you want!" Lara yelled at her husband.

William kept repeating, "You guys will take care of each other."

He was about to push Lara, but Julie ran between them and shoved her father out of the way. She fell on top of Lara, screaming, "Get out of here! What do you want from us?" Seeing William out of control, she was frantic, sure that whatever problem had been percolating all these weeks was more far gone than she knew. Why the Puerto Rico comments all the time? She waited for the commotion to die down as William collapsed and fell asleep on the couch.

"I need space!" Julie said. "I have to leave. You're not dealing with the situation by just ignoring Dad's drinking."

She left the house and drove back to Rick's apartment, her throat tightening, her heart palpitating and her mind racing. Pulling into a parking spot, she began to sob uncontrollably. It would be the first of many panic attacks she would experience. Finally, she collected herself enough to go inside. She walked in, carrying a small box of butter cookies from the Viennese bakery in Brooklyn. Rick was glad to see her.

"Baby, here you are!" he greeted her with relief in his voice. He hugged and kissed her and then noticed that she was upset.

"Sweetie, what's wrong? You look as though you've been crying."

"No, everything's OK," she lied. "I'm just anxious about the MCAT. And we have to make our wedding plans. It's January, and the wedding is in September," she whined.

"Baby, please! Stop worrying! I'm going to take care of everything. We booked the temple already. I'm going over the menu, and I think I found a band. We want a small wedding, right? I'll speak to the florist. All you need to do is get a wedding gown. And enough with the med school shit! We've been through this. If it works out, great. If not, forget it! You'll do something else."

"That's *it*?", she shrieked. "*Forget* it? Med school *shit*? I worked so hard these past semesters to accomplish this goal. I want you to be proud of me, and my father is counting on me becoming a doctor," she exploded, shaking like a leaf.

Rick wouldn't relent. "What does your father have to do with this? Isn't this your life? Our life?" This would have been the moment to tell Rick the truth, but she was still adamant that he not know the extent of William's drinking or the emotional burden she was carrying. Secretly, she felt that if she succeeded as a doctor, her father's alcoholism would magically stop. It was a kind of private bargain she had made with herself, and she was not going to try to explain it to Rick.

She handed him the box of cookies. "Here, I bought you cookies," she said, smiling faintly.

"I don't get it!" he roared. "You know I like the *German* bakery, so why did you go to the Viennese shop?"

She grabbed the box of cookies and flung it out the open window. "There," she smirked. "You won't have to suffer eating the Viennese cookies."

His blue eyes darkened. "What did you do?"

She knew that he would never understand the dilemma she faced. She loved Rick and wanted to be a devoted and loving wife. If it meant not becoming a doctor, she might accept that for herself and for the sake of their life together.

But her father wanted this, and she could not rid her mind of that obligation.

Rick and Julie went to bed angry that night, one of the rare nights that they didn't have sex. In the morning, they didn't talk but succumbed to their carnal needs.

Every young woman looks forward to being a bride, but Julie's ability to enjoy her engagement was clouded. Her need to mask William's drinking from Rick and his family weighed heavily upon her. Rick had taken charge of all the wedding plans. On the plus side, his looking after so many details of their lives enabled Julie to concentrate on her studies. But on the minus side, he didn't allow her the freedom to express or assert herself. He micromanaged every detail of her life, including what dress she should wear. Now he was determining her career path, discarding her dream of becoming a doctor if it didn't work out easily.

"You were so easy-going when I met you," he lamented.

She responded in a tense tone. "Maybe I had less on my mind."

"You aimed to please me. Now you don't."

"You didn't pick out every pair of shoes," she retorted.

The bickering was incessant. What was happening? Her nerves were jangled from trying to maintain the façade that William was still the man they had known. The family stress was increasing, but Julie wondered if her disturbed state of mind might be exacerbated by Rick's domineering behavior. Perhaps if Rick weren't so self-righteous, she told herself, she would have revealed to him the extent of her family's problems.

Julie knew she just had to finish the semester, take the entrance exams, and then she'd be done. Rick had arranged for her to work in a research lab at NYU Medical Center in the summer, before their September wedding. It would all work out, she promised herself and decided to once again soften her campaign for independence and yield to Rick's needs.

Despite all the recent upheaval, the Friday night Sabbath ritual was unchanged. Lara prepared her splendid dinner of vegetable soup, roast chicken and potatoes, noodles, kugel, and vegetables, and everyone gathered around the table as they had always done. Over an array of desserts—mandel bread, rugelach and apple strudel—the family made a toast to Julie's grades, Rick's success and, most of all, the wedding plans. Lara was in heaven that Rick was managing all the wedding arrangements and relieved that William had been strangely calm and not drinking. With the good mood prevailing, Julie and Rick retired to her bedroom. They collapsed on her bed and fell into each other's arms. After intense lovemaking, he held her tightly, nuzzled her hair and murmured, "I love you baby, always. Don't worry about anything. I'll always take care of you." With those comforting words, Julie fell asleep.

The next morning, Rick left, and since Julie was off from school, she and Lara had a quick breakfast and dashed out to look at wedding dresses. They were bundled up against the frigid February day and headed to Kleinfeld's in Bay Ridge.

Stepping into the warmth of the store, they beheld racks and racks of glittering satin and lace gowns. Of course, Julie was drawn to the romantic ones with lacy sleeves and beaded bodices. There were so many to choose from that after the initial perusal, she and Lara took a break at a local coffee shop. Over tuna sandwiches and hot chocolate, they made notes about the various gowns, listing the ones they liked best. They were laughing with joy, as everything seemed to be falling into place. William's drinking had abated, and he seemed to be returning to his old self. His litany of complaints about Jewish-American life had disappeared, and although there was no explanation for his ranting about Puerto Rico, Lara did not demand one. She was just glad he had stopped. True, there were still arguments between William and his brothers, but that did not adversely affect him.

Now Julie felt she could focus on her wedding plans, and she was so excited that she even calmed down about the pre-med journey.

"What will be, will be," she confided in her mother, who of course agreed that whatever was "*bashert*"—the old-world term for "meant to be"—would happen.

Like many mothers of her time, Lara was more concerned with Julie obtaining her MRS than her MD. She emphasized that even if Julie did become a doctor, she should work only part time and focus on family, as Rick would be a very busy surgeon. Julie imagined such a scenario and figured that if she was going to have only a part-time career, there was no reason to make herself crazy. Perhaps the stars were aligning after all.

Upon arriving home, they found a large yellow envelope protruding from the mailbox. Lara took it, and they went into the kitchen, where Julie made some tea and put out a coffee cake. She reflected on the afternoon's shopping trip and pondered which of the gowns was her favorite. It had been a pleasant outing, she thought, looking at all that beautiful, elegant bridal wear. Now she and her mom just had to make some choices.

Suddenly there was a shift in the energy in the room. Lara had opened the envelope and was scanning the enclosed papers. Within moments, her face turned ashen white and her eyes widened. Julie grabbed the papers and began reading the legal document addressed to William. Her mother just stared ahead, expressionless.

It read: "William Kent, you are hereby summoned to appear in court in the custody case involving Maribel Perez, the daughter of Maria Perez and yourself."

Julie didn't read any further. She stared at Lara. "Well, this explains his drinking, doesn't it?" she blurted out, stunned and devastated.

"I am in disbelief," murmured Lara. "This cannot be true!"

Julie shook her head. "We have to confront him, Mom. This must be the reason he's been so distraught. Maybe he ended whatever was going on and that's why he stopped drinking, and now this woman wants revenge."

"Well, let's not jump to conclusions," Lara said softly.

"Maybe we should just ignore this and it will pass over."

Julie shrieked, "*Ignore* this? He's being summoned to court! Should we just casually put these papers on his pillow and pretend that we never saw them? You've got to be kidding, Mom! You can't be an ostrich with your head in the sand. It's bad enough that you denied that he was even drinking!"

About 7:00 p.m., William came home. For the past few years he'd been getting in at 9:00 p.m., saying he had meetings with businessmen. Now something had changed. As he entered the house, there was a deafening silence.

"Why is everyone so somber?" he questioned.

Lara looked away. Julie handed him the papers as she and Lara watched his complexion change from a red flush to white.

"Oh, no," he moaned. "I dreaded this. Men do stupid things in haste and repent in leisure. I tried to avoid this."

"So, it's true," Lara whispered.

He nodded his head. "In some ways. It was nothing, really. It happened about three years ago, and it meant nothing. When I said I wanted it to end, she blackmailed me, saying she'd call you. I kept sending her money for the child she claimed was mine, but she kept asking for more. I thought she would stop. But why would she? I started drinking from the pressure of keeping the secret from you. Finally, I told her I was done with her ridiculous demands for money. It was quiet for a month, and now *this*." William kept shaking his head. "I'm so sorry."

"Why didn't you tell me the truth?" Lara demanded. "Even if the child was yours, I would've understood that you needed to pay for support."

"I was ashamed, and I didn't want to hurt you. I thought I could meet my responsibility and never have to confront the issue. She was selfish and vengeful."

"But the drinking was hurting us all!" Julie said, raising her voice with rage. "We were petrified that you'd kill yourself or someone innocent. You fought with everyone constantly. The truth would've been better."

William shook his head. "I made a terrible mistake. All I can say is that I'm sorry. I want to make this up to all of you."

"You've been a good husband and father all these years," Lara continued in a soft voice. "I'm so hurt, but I will forgive you. But I will never forget."

Julie went to her room, needing a few minutes to process the shock and to decide if she should tell Rick. Secrets could definitely destroy trust. She reflected upon how William's secret had hurt all of them so terribly. More than ever, the point was driven home that she would *never* depend on a man to support her. Maybe her mother would have left her father if she'd had some means of supporting herself. Or would she have? Probably not, as Lara placed traditional family values above her own happiness.

Julie decided not to tell Rick about her father's affair. This was the second secret. First, she minimized his drinking, and now she completely avoided the issue of infidelity. No, she would not let Rick know there was the slightest blemish on her father's character.

Although Rick was as demanding as always concerning the apartment being perfectly neat, Julie was not giving in to him any longer. She was furious with men and had no more tolerance for bullying. Rick was still a loyal and devoted fiancé, and she didn't doubt his monogamy, but the loss of trust she'd experienced blurred her sense of reality. One thing was clear, though: she had reached a threshold with Rick's uncompromising behavior. Of course, William's deceit had nothing to do with Rick's controlling nature, but the bizarre issues surrounding *both* men ignited an anger that blazed inside her.

"You didn't fold the bathroom towels like I told you," Rick criticized one Saturday afternoon.

"So I didn't!" she snapped. "Are you perfect?"

"Noooo," he said arrogantly, "but I do like neatness."

"And I suppose you'll tell me which sweater I should wear tonight?" she retorted.

"Listen, sweetheart," he continued abrasively, "you never needed my advice. What's up with you, anyway?"

She quipped back, "It's not advice, it's control. And what if you change your mind about me if I don't look pretty or if I gain weight when I'm pregnant?"

"Julie what's wrong? Where is this coming from?" Rick looked genuinely hurt.

"I just feel you men care for women in a superficial way. The woman gets older and then you have affairs with younger, manipulative ones."

Rick looked bewildered. "Sweetie, please believe me. I'm not a player, and I love you."

Julie noticed the shift from "sweetheart," a term of endearment he used sarcastically when angry, to "sweetie," his real term of endearment. Resigning herself, she accepted that his plaintive tone was sincere, and she cuddled up to him. *If only he knew my secrets*, she thought.

With the ebb and flow of stresses and problems, arguments broke out throughout the month, and the couple's growing pains got sharper. The irritating habits and traits that Julie had easily accepted in Rick during the first year had now become intolerable to her. She appreciated that he was kind and caring, but she was always on edge, knowing he had a quick temper if crossed. It did not help that he had no patience with her fluctuating moods.

One night after her shower she put a short, black nightie but no panties. Naturally aroused by her provocative look, he clutched her and put his hands under the lace, caressing her bottom.

"Stop!" she said.

"Now what?" he asked with exasperation. She had never rebuffed his sexual advances.

"Not in the mood," she quickly replied.

"Oh, something new to fight about!" he shouted as he

stalked out of the room.

She thought he was acting like a child, sulking because he didn't get his candy. She stomped after him, glaring.

"Julie," he said in a nasty tone, "if you're going to dress sexy, then at least give it up."

She just couldn't tell Rick what was whirling around in her mind—her fear, her anger, her sense of betrayal. It wasn't only that her father had an affair and then lied about it. It was also the consequences of his foolish behavior that led to his being blackmailed and his lack of judgment in business. And all of this he'd thought he could obliterate by drinking! He had stopped talking to his two brothers and then took a leave of absence from work, blaming all his frustrations in life on working with them. Was it their controlling nature that made him tense and ultimately turn to another woman? What was he trying to escape from? Or was it their knowledge of the affair that led them to being controlling? Was it both? If so, which came first? Julie's head was ready to explode.

Julie would never fully understand everything she was feeling. All she did know, though, was that her faith in marriage was shaken. Rick was a demanding man. Could she satisfy him in the long run? Maybe he'd become frustrated and have affairs too. That night after dinner, she confronted him with a suggestion.

"Rick, maybe we need a break for a while," she said quietly.

"What?" he exclaimed.

"We keep bickering."

"All your fault. You are a brat," he countered.

"And why is that? Because I want to buy pastry from a Viennese bakery and you only want it from the German bakery? Or maybe I want to wear the red sweater and you only want me to wear the black one? Don't you see how controlling you are?"

"Well, sweetheart, you never minded it before." She noted his use of "sweetheart."

"I've become more independent now," she said. Rick just shrugged.

Julie was finishing her pre-med coursework and had started applying to medical schools. She was more determined than ever to become a doctor, and with or without a life partner, she would never live in a man's shadow. Rick, who had once embodied some of her father's best qualities, was now reminding her of his worst ones—the arrogance, self-absorption and disdain for Jewish middle-class values. She remembered that on their first date, Rick told her that he had never dated a Jewish woman before. Why negate your own background? The two men resembled each other more with every passing day.

"I need to leave this," Julie said in a barely audible voice. "If it's meant to be, we will come together again. We need to call off the wedding."

The wedding was set for the fall, and it was already late spring. Julie's friends had thrown her a bridal shower, and the gifts of linen, china, housewares, appliances and lingerie were stacked in boxes in her room back home. Thankfully, invitations had not been sent out yet, although Lara had her heart set on the ivory linen paper with formal calligraphy. Now every arrangement, every detail and every plan would come to a halt.

"Julie," Rick said, looking into her tearful brown eyes, "you are changing too much for me. We can't go on with this." His blue eyes were red rimmed from crying.

"I can't be who you need me to be," she choked on her tears. "You're my best friend and you mean the world to me," she sobbed, "but I can't see living with you, and I don't know how I'll live without you."

Rick held her tightly. His voice cracked as he said, "Oh, Julie baby, we would've had the cutest kids." He held her face in his hands. "OK, maybe we just need time."

Julie left the apartment late that afternoon in May. She walked to her car, got in and started driving back to Brooklyn.

She sobbed softly the entire way, her makeup forming rivulets as it flowed down her cheeks. Slowly, she climbed the steps and entered the house.

"What are you doing here?" Lara asked. She saw Julie's tear-stained face and disheveled hair. "Is everything OK?"

"It's over," Julie whispered. "Rick and I broke up."

"Oh, nonsense," Lara replied. "you're both just nervous and headstrong."

"No, Mom, I can't do this. He doesn't let me have an opinion. I can't breathe." She was rambling furiously. "He criticizes everything I do. It's never precise enough. If I wear one dress, he tells me to wear another. If I bring apples, he wants oranges. Remember what we went through to find black suede boots that were over the knee with the kitten heel? I'll never make him happy."

"Look," Lara said, soothingly, "you both have great ambitions. He does like to have his way, I know that. But he also adores you. I see the way he looks at you. You need to be more diplomatic, work around him. He's going to be a surgeon, and they always need to be right!"

"But," Julie protested, "I'm going to be a doctor, too. What about *my* needs?"

"He *wanted* you to be a doctor. He *encouraged* you. But he wants a wife. He takes care of so much for you, so maybe you could be the more accommodating one."

Julie disagreed. "If he wants a traditional wife and a 'yes' girl, then I'm not the one. I'm not going to play games. I need a partner. He acts like he's the father and I am his child," she continued.

"He could be wrapped around your finger if you'd only act sweet," Lara suggested.

"No," Julie argued. "In some ways he's so giving. He cooks for me, he shops and does the laundry. He doesn't care when I read and study. But he must pick every restaurant, every movie, every piece of clothing. It's too much."

Lara sighed. For her it didn't seem so bad. She was

a much less determined and ambitious woman than Julie. "You two share so much in common. You come from similar backgrounds. You enjoy culture and value education, and I see love between you."

"He will smother me." Julie knew that she was treading in dangerous waters, and the last thing she wanted was to hurt her mother's feelings, but she had to ask. "How can I trust that he'll stay loyal?"

Lara, unperturbed and unoffended, continued, "He comes from a good family. Everyone in his circle is well educated. His father worships his mother, and there's no better role model." Still, Julie was not to be swayed.

The following weeks were hellish for her. She wandered in a daze from her house to Brooklyn College to finish her classes. It was some consolation knowing that she had made a decision and acted on it, but that did not mean that it felt good.

Soon came July. The temperature in New York was sweltering, and it was oppressively humid. After a stifling subway ride with the screeching of trains grating on her nerves, she walked to NYU. She felt abysmal. She was supposed to be living with Rick a few blocks away from the medical center instead of making this miserable commute.

Steam appeared to rise from the sidewalks, and the soles of her feet ached. Her neck muscles were tight with pain, but she kept telling herself to put one foot in front of the other and just get through the day. For now, Julie wasn't living, she was merely existing. *Why doesn't Rick call me?* she wondered. She went home to Brooklyn each night and stared at the phone on her desk and was barely able to eat the meals Lara lovingly prepared for her.

Lara knew that Rick was working as an intern at Bellevue Hospital and NYU Medical Center and hoped Julie would cross paths with him. "Did you see him?" she would ask.

Julie would snap back, "Of course not! It's over. If he really cared, he would come after me."

"Well, he may have felt that you turned on him for no good reason. You never did explain everything about Dad."

"He's too rigid," Julie retorted. "I need someone who is more easygoing. He makes a ridiculous fuss over a blueberry cake."

Lara understood that her youngest child was kind, honest and extremely intelligent. But she knew that Julie was book smart, not street smart. "Men like to be catered to," she stated quietly.

Julie retorted, "Well, a lot of good that did you!" She gasped as she heard her own words.

Lara was unruffled. "Just because Dad made mistakes, you can't hold that against Rick. They are two different men. Dad is a good man who made a stupid mistake. And Rick is a good man, too. He just wants what he wants."

"I need someone I know is flexible and will never betray me. Rick is a fussbudget! And if I disagree with him, he snaps. He needs someone he can dominate and control," she pressed.

"Julie, he may want his way, but I'm telling you again that he adores you. If you were diplomatic, you'd get whatever you want. You just have to know how to handle him."

Julie remarked slyly, "Let him figure out how to handle *me*."

Truth be told, it would be many years before Julie would understand the good advice Lara gave her. She would later learn that from her mother's point of view and experience, many men were like boys who had never grown up. A man would love a woman not for who she was, but how she made him feel.

Julie knew that she had no choice now but to succeed in medical school. She had sacrificed her personal time and suffered a broken engagement and a broken heart because in her mind, her father's continued sobriety rested on this goal of hers. She hoped and prayed that her efforts would pay off because the price had been high. *This had all better be worth it,* she told herself.

That summer, Julie began dating a few medical students she met while working in the lab. Though they were nice, intelligent men, she rejected their advances, feeling totally numb. She couldn't get intimate with anyone because no matter how she tried to turn away from the memory of Rick, her mind always drifted back to him and their smoldering sex life. In vain, she would compare every man to him and everything to the relationship that had failed.

CHAPTER 6

Julie was walking to the subway late one Thursday
night when from behind she heard someone call
her name. She immediately recognized the voice, hoarse and
deliberate. It was Rick. A lump rose in her throat as she turned
to look at him. No words came to her.

"I've been thinking about you," he said. His tone was
casual, but his stare was intense. "How're you doing?"

It was hard to speak. "Oh, you know, busy at the lab,
and I'm working on finishing up my med school applications."
She paused, giving him a moment to say he would help her
with them, but he did not offer. He looked tired after what
must have been a long night on call, but she could sense his
hunger for her. "Come to my apartment," he said.

She smiled softly. "OK," she replied. The open wound
Julie sustained as a result of their breakup had not healed at all,
and in this encounter, she was rendered completely vulnerable.
She had no buffer, so whatever resolve she'd had about
distancing herself from Rick was blown away like dust by his
invitation.

As they walked, Rick took her hand, and she felt her
pulse quicken. Once inside the apartment, he wasted no time

in walking her over to the couch, pulling her down onto his lap. Kissing her hard, he sensed her body acquiesce to his touch, and within moments, he lifted her light cotton shirt over her head, unfastened her bra and leaned down to kiss her nipples. Slowly, and then with urgency, he caressed the soft contours of her breasts as he pulled off her jeans. His mouth was drawn to that warm, alluring valley between her legs, where he hovered over the moist opening. She could feel him breathing, teasing her with his tongue, until at last she surrendered, letting out a small cry. Then all at once he was inside her.

"Julie baby, I missed you," he murmured. "You belong here."

She did not know if she belonged there or not, but the heady pleasure of the lovemaking she had known with him swept over her. She clasped his back with her small hands as her hips swiveled rapidly beneath his. Fiercely he pumped her until he felt her climax, and then he released his nectar inside her.

As they lay motionless, time seemed to be suspended. Everything bitter and ugly that had passed between them evaporated. She looked deeply into his eyes, and a song came to her. Humming Maxine Nightingale's "Right Back to Where We Started From," she asked, "You know this song?"

"Yes, I do, baby."

"Well," she purred, "that's us, and we are right back to where we started from." Now completely relaxed, she chuckled.

"Not that it's my business," he said, "but have you been with anyone else?"

She laughed and replied, "Of course not, Rick!" She knew he wanted to hear this.

"I thought by now you would've slept with someone else," he responded bluntly.

"Why?"

"What do you mean, why? You're a sexy girl and I see you talking to guys in the cafeteria, so I just figured…"

With a jolt, Julie was hurtled back into the present. She looked incredulous. "Are you following me?"

"I'm working at the same place you are, so since I'm sleeping with this chick I'm dating, I imagined you were doing the same thing."

She shook her head. "I am *working* at the hospital, and I do need lunch and a cup of tea sometimes. These men are basically friends. But it's good to know you're sleeping with someone else. Thanks for telling me that. I can't even imagine anyone touching me."

"Well, you wanted this!" he barked brusquely.

They were fighting again. Just moments before, they had been in some kind of Nirvana, with all bad memories shut out and only their pleasure masquerading as reality. It had been so brief. She sighed and slowly explained, "Rick, I didn't *want* this. I was under pressure, and you were demanding." She knew there was more to the story, all the horror she'd lived through with her father, but she was not going to tell him.

"Rick," she continued in a soft voice, "do you really think now was a good time to tell me about a woman you're sleeping with? We just made love, didn't we?"

"You were so quick to give all this up, weren't you?" he said, glaring at her.

She felt the tears welling up in her eyes. "Did you fight for me?"

He bristled and shouted, "Oh, so this was a test to see how much I cared?" As his characteristic ego and pride emerged, the few minutes of rapture they had lived were ruined. There was no answer to his accusation, and Julie did not want to fight anymore. Anyway, what difference did it make now?

"Let's go get something to eat," he said in a resigned tone. They got up from the couch, threw on their clothes and went out to a local Mexican restaurant. There was a table in a quiet corner, and when they sat down Rick ordered a pitcher of sangria and chips with guacamole.

Sipping her sangria, Julie peered over the glass and steadied herself enough to ask, "So who are you dating?"

He quickly replied, "There's this really cool social worker named Linda at the hospital. Comes from a very rich family in Connecticut. She wears these long flowery dresses and floppy hats. *Really* cool," he emphasized.

"Oh," Julie replied, "sounds great." She nearly choked on the drink, barely believing how easily Rick had moved on to someone new.

"She is so sure of herself, such confidence," he said.

"So good to know you're happy," murmured Julie, draining her glass. Rick, whose appetite for food was obviously not dulled by the emotions between them, wolfed down enchiladas as Julie toyed with the tacos on her plate.

They left the restaurant and walked through Washington Square Park, stopping to listen to street musicians, as they had in the early days of their relationship. Rick draped his arm around Julie's shoulder, and for the moment, whether she wanted to or not, whether she understood her own feelings or not, she felt a shiver of excitement. Could Rick's talking about Linda, who might not even exist, be a ploy to make her jealous? Maybe he was trying to rekindle their love affair.

They walked back to the apartment, and Julie felt herself shaking with anticipation. "Come to the bedroom, baby," he whispered, opening the door. He led her to the bed, the place they had made love hundreds of times before.

He seemed to be in a more playful mood now and said, "I want to watch you undress for me."

She complied, slowly removing her clothes while keeping her gaze fixed on him. Then she lay down seductively on the bed.

"Go ahead. I like to see you pleasure yourself."

"No, you do it, Rick," she murmured.

"No, baby, let me watch you."

Julie nodded, closed her eyes and begin to stroke her own soft crevice. Quickly aroused, she begged, "Rick, come to me."

He watched her intently. "No," he began with a note of sadism in his voice, "you were too difficult. Now I want you to picture me with Linda, doing everything I did to you."

Julie stopped, horrified, and sat up abruptly. "Keep going, Julie," he coaxed. "You know I love watching you finger yourself. Now imagine Linda has me touching her."

"You bastard!" Julie exploded. "How can you be so cruel?"

"Cruel? You fought with me! You ruined us. You were so coddled by your parents and thought I'd kiss your ass."

Coddled? Was she to explain to him what it was like living with an alcoholic? She'd been anything but coddled for the past few years. Could she to reveal to him the ordeal of her father's paternity suit and divulge all the heartache the family endured watching William fall to pieces? No! She needed time to heal before she dared share that secret.

She got up quickly, feeling his eyes locked on her. "I cannot and *will* not do this!" she shrieked. "I am leaving, and I'm going to find someone who is kinder than you!"

"Well, sweetheart, good luck finding someone who will love you and care about you like I did! You will regret this your entire life!" he ranted, as if cursing her future.

Julie left the apartment, slamming the door behind her. She was breathless by the time she reached her car. Why did he do this? To test her? To punish her? What a naïve fool she had been! He had played her, and she fell for it.

Home within the hour, she ran upstairs to her room. Her mother called after her, but she didn't answer. Closing the door, she fell on the bed and buried her faced in her pillow. This humiliation, this isolation, was worse for her than the first time they broke up. She had harbored some hope at that time that they might reconcile one day, but now she knew beyond a doubt that "they" were over. *At least I'll be independent,* she reassured herself. And then, exhausted, she fell asleep.

In the days that followed, Julie threw herself into her work at the lab and, in the off hours, sought solace in her piano playing and her books, delving into everything she could, save the topic of romance.

Julie kept her secret and the shame of her father's alcoholism to herself. She was, on some irrational level, haunted by the idea that she would replicate her father's pattern, not with drinking, but with finding success and then losing it. And if that happened, would she be disgraced, abandoned by her husband? If she failed in life, would that husband forgive her as her mother had forgiven her father?

William's collapse signified for Julie that the Rock of Gibraltar in her life had crumbled. Her father may have been in recovery, but she had seen that he was merely human, not superhuman. It had all been an illusion. Coddled? Sheltered? Innocent? All forever gone.

CHAPTER 7

Julie had entered the season of her life that was dominated by the task of applying to medical schools. Between working in the lab and sitting down with reams of paper to fill out, her days were pretty much booked. Periodically, her mind returned to the notion that if things had been different, Rick would be nearby, assisting her in this arduous, tedious process. But on the other hand, doing it without him gave her a feeling of independence. She had been on a difficult journey with Rick, and the end of that relationship had left her confused and sad. It was some consolation that she and Sara were going through this together. One thing she knew: whatever happened in her life, Julie was going to be a doctor, even if she had to study overseas. Her determination to reach this goal galvanized her, and by the end of July, she and Sara had applied to all the medical schools where their chances of acceptance were the best. One very positive aspect of the situation was that neither of them viewed the other as competition.

"Maybe we will go to the same medical school and be each other's support system," they reassured one another.

Sometimes Sara tried talking about Rick to Julie, but

Julie would just shut her down. She was on a mission that did not include Rick and was trying her best to go forward instead of looking back. Sara, who thought there might still be hope for them as a couple, pleaded with Julie to confide in Rick about the crisis with her father. But she also acknowledged that if Julie couldn't be totally honest with Rick, he was probably not the right man for her.

One cold afternoon in October, Julie was working in the lab, drawing up material from Petri dishes, which was part of her research on adrenal gland activity in guinea pigs. Suddenly, she felt Rick's unmistakable presence nearby and glanced up to meet his eyes.

"Hi, Rick," she said softly. "What brings you here?"

"Why do you think I'm here?" Three seconds into the visit and he was already being abrasive.

Julie maintained her composure. "I guess you wanted to say hello."

"How's the application process going?" he snapped.

Despite his curt tone, Julie could not help but feel touched at his concern for her. "It's all good," she said." Just waiting to hear from all the schools for interviews."

"No, not good enough, Julie! You have to call and ask if you're being considered for an interview. Especially with Downstate Medical School because it's affiliated with Brooklyn College. Show interest!"

"But," she persisted, "won't I appear presumptuous and pushy?"

"Just do what I'm telling you to do."

Face to face with him, she could see that her need for his advice had never left her. For a moment she had the impulse to jump into his arms for reassurance, but then she thought the better it. He had been so horrid the last time they were together, and she needed to remember that he was capable of tremendous cruelty. *Someday*, she thought, *if he wants me back, he is going to have to beg.* This was false pride, but it was the best she could do at the moment.

She did take Rick's suggestion and a few days later called Downstate Medical to check on her application. Her efforts paid off, and she was granted an interview. Once she found the courage to make the first call, the others were not so intimidating, and she was able to schedule additional interviews at other schools in New York.

Julie and Sara spoke on the phone each evening to boost their spirits and to practice for their interviews. As it turned out, the role playing they did was helpful, and the interview process proved to be not too daunting. Most of the physicians were polite and friendly, and Julie found it easy to just speak from her heart. She told them sincerely that she wanted to help people, had a true love of learning and a keen desire to be of service to the community.

The exception was the doctor at Mount Sinai Medical Center, who was rude and goading. He asked Julie why she even wanted to become a doctor since she had been an English literature major who had already started graduate school.

"Do you just like school, or are you a dilettante?" he asked, thereby trivializing her ambition. He had tried to put her on the defensive, but she stayed cool and resisted being provoked by speaking honestly. Upon leaving, she assured herself, *I'll be a doctor—and he'll always be a miserable human being!*

A few weeks after the interviews were completed, Julie called her mother to chat during her lunch break. Lara answered the phone in a voice filled with enthusiasm.

"Mom, "Julie asked, "you sound like you're bubbling over! What's going on?"

Lara begin to laugh and cry at the same time. "Julie, you've been accepted to Downstate Medical School! I'm so happy for you! I just called Dad at work, and he's beside himself with joy!"

Julie paused and said, "Mom, read it to me."

Lara read the letter, and Julie screamed, "Yes!!" so loudly the people in the cafeteria turned around. Though bursting with excitement, she decided to hold off on telling Sara until *she* was accepted, too. But maybe Sara had been accepted and not yet told *her*.

Her mind drifted to Rick. She wanted to call him but was afraid he might not be kind in his response. It was hard to predict what he would say because their breakup was so complicated. She sensed that they still loved each other but were they *in love?* He had totally deserted her during the application process and shamed her with details about his dating and sex life. Then he checked in on her to make sure she was getting interviews. Unable to read him, she felt terribly conflicted.

Julie convinced herself that for a change, it would be nice to have a man she could dominate. She had started dating Donnie, who was much more mellow. For now, anyway, she didn't want a complicated man like her father or Rick. They were good men, but they were self-centered and cynical and at times restless and dissatisfied with life. That kooky quality that she once loved in Rick and her father now terrified her because she had seen its dark side. But the news of her acceptance was too good not to share, so to be fair, she called both Rick and Donnie and left messages.

That evening she practically skipped home from the subway, hugging Lara as she entered the house. They sat down to a cup of tea, and at 7:00, the doorbell rang with a delivery of flowers. Not one bouquet of roses, but two – one from Donnie and the other from Rick, who had included a card that read, "To my baby, Julie, and to the future Dr. Kent." She kissed the card with tears streaming down her face.

"He'll always love you," her mother said sweetly.

The doorbell rang again. "What now?" Lara said, and asked on the intercom who it was.

"It's me, Rick." Julie and Lara glanced at each other. As Julie went downstairs to meet Rick, Lara, ever in Rick's corner, stashed Donnie's bouquet in the closet.

Rick flew up the steps and grabbed Julie, kissing her

long and hard. "I knew you would do this, baby. I'm so proud of you!" Julie's heart fluttered. Rick did care! Now she knew he had distanced himself because he was guarded and hurt. "Now you have other schools to hear from!" he exclaimed.

Julie paused and said, "I don't care. I want to go to Downstate. It's close to home and it will cost less."

Rick immediately got in the driver's seat. "No, no, sweetie," he persisted, "NYU is a better school, and if we get it back together, we will both be in the city, so that's where you should go."

"I'm not smart enough for NYU," she answered back. "I always have to work harder than you, so I won't do well there."

"There you go with that lack of confidence," he said.

Julie felt her throat tighten. *Here he goes again, taking over the situation.* So unlike mild-mannered Donnie. She had once loved Rick's ability to take charge because it addressed her need to feel safe. Why did she resent it now? Was she conflating Rick with her father again?

If her father had been more complacent and accepting of his life, if he hadn't had an affair, if he didn't drink, everything could have been easier. Now, with gold at its highest price in decades, he'd left his family business and impulsively opened his own jewelry factory.

Of course, this new venture wasn't going well. As usual, Lara said little, but Julie and her siblings urged their father to return to the family business. His response was to explode. This arrogant, know-it-all attitude was a trait William shared with Rick, and Julie had had enough of it.

Despite all the rhetoric in her head, though, Julie conceded to Rick's sleeping over and even to their making love that night. Afterwards as they lay there peacefully, she told him that she loved him but needed time to sort things out.

"So," he said, irritated, "I brought you to this place of being a medical student. Now you need to *think*?" Somehow, he must have felt he was owed something for the advice he had given her. And since Julie was not about to pay him with a commitment, he left angry and confused in the morning without saying goodbye.

Within the week, Sara was accepted at Downstate. The two best friends rejoiced over cappuccinos at Café Ferrara, their favorite haunt in the Village. They had a clear plan: they were going to Downstate, close to home. It would cost less than other schools and they would be roommates. There was a lot to look forward to.

Financially, things would be tough for the Kents, as William's new business was on rocky terrain. Julie did not care what it would take to make it through medical school. She would put on blinders, putting one foot before the other, with no distractions. She would think about Rick again once she was in medical school, not now. He'd just have to wait, and she assumed he would.

—— PART 4 ——

JOURNEY TO MD

CHAPTER 8

September 1980 marked the start of Julie's medical school experience. With a strong sense of partnership, she and Sara decided to take a place together in the dormitories across the street from the school. Their room for two was about the size of a shoebox with two beds on either wall and two desks near windows facing the noisy street. Each of them had a small closet, and they managed to squeeze a table into the miniature kitchen that was, amazingly, equipped with every appliance needed. It was cozy, and since neither one of them knew the first thing about cooking, they would be taking their meals in the cafeteria. They warmed the place up with matching bedspreads, hung up some Impressionist prints and felt that as long as they were together, the setup was perfect.

The first days of school were taken up with orientation. Sitting at attention in the large auditorium, they noticed that out of 200 students, only 40 of them were women. Everyone appeared a bit nervous, but the professors spoke to them with enthusiasm, saying that they expected everyone to graduate. They reminded the students that if they had come this far, they were the cream of the crop, but they also warned that those who were at the top of their college classes might not find that to be the case in medical school.

After orientation, the real schedule began, with classes in anatomy, biochemistry, microbiology and public health. The textbooks were huge, and Julie was overwhelmed from day one.

The anatomy course would be a full semester, with daily sessions needed to complete the extensive curriculum. Dressed in short skirts, white jackets and clogs, Julie and Sara reported to the anatomy lab, a large room filled with the acrid odor of formaldehyde. Cadavers with their heads covered lay face down on steel tables. Four students were assigned to each table. Julie and Sara were partners, along with two male students, Rob and Peter. None of them were particularly squeamish when confronted with the cadaver, as it seemed less like a human and more like a rubber model.

As they stood around the table, the men immediately took charge of the dissecting. Julie didn't mind, but Sara was not going to be pushed aside. She immediately told both guys that she was going to do the dissecting as well. With the lab manual propped up on a stand, they were busily engaged in labeling the organs and surrounding blood vessels and nerves.

The amount of information to take in was mind-boggling. Students were required to memorize the main arteries, veins and nerves as well as the smaller tributaries arising from the major structures. The organs were of course to be dissected, along with the bones, tendons, ligaments and muscles. Julie felt ridiculously inept as she struggled with the three-dimensional aspects of anatomy. As the organs were dissected, one had to visualize the cross-section as slices of a fruit that were part of the whole object. She berated herself because she just could not grasp it as quickly as the other students did.

"Sometimes I feel so stupid in anatomy," she confessed to Sara. "I feel like I slow down the group."

Sarah reminded her, "You were an English literature major. Most of us were biology majors, so we've had more exposure to the sciences. Just be patient with yourself."

Julie sighed. "It really does seem that Peter despises me. I can't even ask an extra question. He just wants to dissect at a very fast pace."

"I know," Sara agreed. "Just focus on yourself, and screw him."

The following weeks brought a flood of schoolwork, and sticking by one another made things somewhat easier. Always seen side by side, Julie and Sara quickly became known as Betty and Veronica, the *Archie* comic book characters. During the first month, they were running on all cylinders, barely even taking time to eat. They gulped down most of their cafeteria meals or sometimes microwaved food that Lara prepared for them. But there was never enough time for a real meal, and it did not take long before they were each about 10 pounds lighter.

Sara's study style was to aim for perfection, memorizing every fact with complete accuracy. For the moment, Julie was happy to survive, and being average was good enough. Both girls were meeting their goals, but to achieve them meant they had to lead extremely narrow lives. Between the workload and their zealous study habits, they barely had time to socialize.

One afternoon in anatomy lab, the dissection lesson was on male genitalia. At this point, the students were already emotionally detached from the cadaver, which, in a sense, was no longer even regarded as human. Peter, as usual, decided he would be in charge, and quickly detached the penis, which was going to be further dissected.

Julie clipped her long hair back with a large barrette she kept in the pocket of her lab jacket. At the end of the dissection, she unclipped her hair, but when she placed the barrette back in her pocket, she felt something elongated and spongy in her hand. Lifting the cadaver's penis out of her pocket, she shrieked and threw it in the air. The anatomy professor, who had witnessed the event, walked over to Julie and, putting his arm around her, said, "I'm sorry, dear," in a comforting tone. Then with a stern face and loud voice, he asked the class, "Who is responsible for this?"

Of course, it was Peter, who only admitted to his prank because Rob and a few other students had advertently glanced in his direction.

"I'm sorry, Dr. Hunter," he said, red-faced and stuttering.

"Peter, you not only disrespected your fellow student, but you also disrespected this person who is now your cadaver," Dr. Hunter stated.

Peter stammered and uttered, "I…I don't know why I did that."

"Well," bellowed Dr. Hunter, "you will write a letter of apology to Julie, humbly asking for forgiveness. Do you understand?"

Peter, completely embarrassed, replied, "Of course."

If Peter disliked Julie to begin with, he now resented her, although she could not fathom why. She and Sara left the lab, Julie shaking and Sara trying to console her.

The extent of the girls' social life was attending a few Thursday night parties. "Shit Night" or "So Happy It's Thursday" were gatherings in the student union's social hall, where beer, soda and snacks were served. It was a relaxed gathering that was fun for exhausted medical students and was the one place where Julie and Sara, who were among the few attractive female students, got some attention from the male students.

"Why do you think we're not dating?" Sara queried one night.

Julie smiled smugly. "Why do you think? We are already going steady with our textbooks. We barely give any guy the time of day. We are neurotic. I'm studying nonstop to keep my head above water and you're obsessed with getting perfect grades, so of course no one likes us."

"I kind of agree with you," Sara nodded. "Why are we like this?"

Julie paused and continued, "We have no real role models. A lot of the women here had fathers who were doctors, but you and I are from traditional immigrant families. Our mothers imbued us with a sense of danger and worry, so we approach our work seriously, maybe too seriously."

It was true. Sara's mother was a survivor of Auschwitz, and Sara had always felt the need to spare her any worry. Julie's mother was a loving presence, but her provincial immigrant background was the source of her insecurity, which she passed along to her children. That insecurity, coupled with the link Julie created in her mind between her success and her father's sobriety, gave her a sense of panic about achieving. Both young women were plagued, not only by a quest to soothe and assuage their parents' worry, but also the obligation to right the wrongs of their parents' lives. It was a huge psychological burden from which there seemed to be no escape.

They were having lunch one day around the end of the first semester, noting that finals would be starting in three weeks, and their tension was increasing. They choked down the usual turkey and cheese sandwiches with cups of coffee. With their spotty, rushed eating habits, they had both grown thin and pale.

"Do you think we will ever return to normal?" Sara asked.

"Yes. They say the first semester is the worst, and honestly I can't imagine it being harder than this or us looking worse than we do now!"

By pulling together and encouraging each other, Julie and Sara did jump the first hurdle successfully. Julie got two A's and two B's. Sara got straight A's. They hugged each other when their grades arrived, and then each went home to their parents for rest and recuperation.

The next semester brought its own challenges. The torture of anatomy was to be replaced by neuroanatomy. They would also be continuing with biochemistry, psychology and cell biology. But just knowing they had completed the first round propelled them forward with a degree of confidence.

They made a decision to go to every "Shit Night" party, just to be more social.

"We have to work on our MRS degree as well as our MD," Sara reminded Julie during their allotted coffee break.

Julie nodded. "You know, we're surviving the first year and are getting out a bit more. Let's face it, we look really good next to most of the other women, but we're like vampires hidden away all day, only coming out only on Thursday nights."

It was a huge commitment to become a doctor, starting from college and striving for high grades, especially in the pre-med courses. And for the duration, years of intense studying awaited Julie. She didn't doubt her decision to go to medical school, but she was beginning to fully comprehend the enormity of that decision. It was overwhelming and lonely.

Julie knew that she could not survive four years of living like a nun, but she had not yet met a guy that she liked. Many of the students were sleeping with each other out of convenience, but it was neither Julie's nor Sara's style to have casual sex. Even kissing and touching would lead them to develop emotional attachments, so they avoided that.

Compounding the stress and isolation was the problem of expenses, because where money had once been plentiful, it was now scarce. William's decision to leave the family business and go out on his own when newly sober had definitely been a mistake. The business went bankrupt, and he wouldn't reconcile with his brothers. Julie felt constantly strapped for money but wouldn't pressure her parents for help.

Skinny, drawn and anxious most of the time, she couldn't even walk around the neighborhood for some diversion, as Downstate was in one of Brooklyn's poorest, meanest ghettoes. She felt sad for the community, which was riddled with the urban cancers of drugs, gangs and violent street crime. For the very first time in her insular life, she was living in "the hood." There were constant warnings to the students to be vigilant, as there were muggings, and everyone had heard about the horrific rape of a female medical student that left her comatose.

Sitting in her room one night, Julie burst out crying. For the very first time, she felt sorry for herself and realized that she might have bitten off more than she could chew. Had she stayed with Rick, life would have been easier. Had she chosen to become a speech therapist or a social worker, the academic demands would have been lighter. After she sniffled a bit, the tears stopped flowing, and she said aloud, "No, I'm going to stay on course and succeed."

By and by, the first year came to a close. The two good friends were in a permanent state of exhaustion but thrilled. Many of the students were going on vacation abroad, but, of course, Julie had no choice but to work. She didn't mind, though, because at least it was a break from studying. She landed a spot in the gynecology clinic at Kings County Hospital, helping to provide wellness care for local women. Uneducated about health and always short of resources, these women never went for routine health exams. Julie would be performing Pap smears, screening patients for venereal disease, and monitoring blood pressure and blood glucose levels. She was extremely excited to be treating actual patients.

But the circumstances were less than ideal. It was brutally hot in July, and neither the dorm nor the clinics had any air conditioning. The dorm windows could not be left open for fear of break-ins. Additionally, summer was a more dangerous time, with street fighting and the possibility of a stray bullet entering the dorm room.

Remembering her youth, Julie had a new appreciation for having grown up in a safe neighborhood, never wanting for decent food or good health care. She was raised in a cohesive and loving family and had the benefit of education. Many of these women at the clinic, who were desperately trying to change their lives, did not know who their own fathers were or which men had sired their children. Most of them were struggling single parents who had never lived in ease or comfort. Julie realized that, as a student confined to the classroom and library, and even enduring the rigors of school, until now she had been sequestered in an ivory tower, removed from the horrors of these drug-infested neighborhoods, where women lived with the threat of rape and violence. In a strange way, working in the clinic made Julie see that whatever she'd suffered with her family's reversal of fortune, she still had privileges in life.

This first fleeting summer after year one of medical school was a bridge between academics and the real-life experience of being an inner-city doctor. Julie grew up more in that one summer that she had in twenty-three years. She came away from it feeling that she was fortunate to have a strong family foundation that had allowed her to weather many storms. Now she was more determined than ever to be a doctor and contribute to society by healing others, both physically and emotionally.

CHAPTER 9

Julie had barely had time to recover from the relentless demands of the first year of medical school when the second year began. The new curriculum was going to be intense and would include pathology, microbiology, pharmacology and introduction to clinical medicine. It was daunting, but having done well at the end of the last semester, Julie was fully confident that she would perform even better this year.

It was a very warm September morning when Julie and Sara, dressed in shorts and light tops, had breakfast together before their morning session. The first lecture was going to be in histology, where they would learn about the microscopic structure of animal and plant tissues. But before facing such technical material, they had a talk about more everyday matters.

"You know," Julie said as they downed corn muffins and tea, "this year we need to focus on all areas of our life, not just school. I want us to take better care of ourselves and also have some kind of social life."

Sara agreed. "Well, I did start dating Scott, and he's trying to get me to exercise."

"I need to find a guy too, but I can tell you, with or without one, I'm going to the gym!" she declared.

Sara, always her best friend's advocate, said, "Julie, you could date anyone you want."

Julie shook her head. "Sara, you always think that. But things haven't gone all that well for me. First there was Robbie, who behaved horribly toward me, and Rick, who after such deep involvement, didn't even fight for the relationship! Do you realize that he never checked on me during the first year of med school?"

Sara disagreed. "Julie," she said softly, "you never let Rick know what was going on in your life back then. He must have felt that you rejected him."

"OK, let's not talk about those two. They are *over*. I've moved on," she stated with certainty. "They were both *way* too self-centered and high-strung for me. I'm going for someone calm next time."

They finished breakfast and made their way to class. The histology lab was laid out with tables that accommodated six students. On each side of the table were three equally spaced microscopes. Julie, Sara and another female student found their places on one side, and three male students were opposite them. Julie arranged the slide set in front of her and concentrated on adjusting the microscope. As she looked up from the lens for a moment, her eyes met those of her lab-mate, Kevin McCormack. He looked away, embarrassed that she'd caught him staring.

Julie vaguely knew Kevin, having met him briefly at a Thursday night party. Standing at 6 feet 4 inches tall, he towered over her. She noticed then that he was a quiet and handsome man and appreciated how he smiled broadly when he looked at her with his warm hazel eyes. Kevin seemed different from the conceited, arrogant guys he hung out with, but since they were all athletes, she figured that sports was their common ground. *Hmm*, she thought to herself, *I wonder what Kevin is all about.*

As they left the lab, Sara whispered, "Boy, was Kevin gazing at you!"

"I know," said Julie, "but if I dated him, my mom would freak out. He's not Jewish."

"Right," Sara said, "neither is Scott."

Julie laughed. "Maybe we need to shake it up and date some non-Jewish guys. They're calm, and we're nervous wrecks."

The girls proceeded to the auditorium, where they would sit for four straight hours of lectures in microbiology, pathology and histology. It was riveting and fascinating, and the two eager students wrote copious notes.

After they left, Julie went back to the dorm to change into workout clothes. She was determined to start a routine at the gym, and slipping into a tight T-shirt and pink nylon shorts, she headed out. Once there, she thought it would be a good idea to start with the treadmill, but after stepping onto the platform, she had no idea how to start the thing.

Kevin, a regular at the gym, noticed Julie's bewilderment and walked over to her. "You look confused," he said with a light laugh. "Let me show you how to adjust this." He turned on the treadmill and then hopped onto the adjacent one. Julie smiled and thanked him, noticing his incredibly muscular arms and legs and perfectly shaped calves. He was so good looking but didn't seem aware of it.

"I'm really not in shape at all," she confessed. "I never exercise."

He laughed again. "You're in amazing shape, just probably not in *aerobic* shape. I could show you some easy exercises, but first get used to the treadmill. Take it nice and slow," he encouraged her.

Usually Julie would have been mortified for anyone to see her so inept and breathless, but she felt comfortable with Kevin, and his easy manner dispelled her self-consciousness. Following his instructions, she walked at a slow pace for thirty minutes, then stopped and rested.

"Let's try some weights," Kevin suggested. He handed her three-pound weights and showed her how to do bicep and tricep curls. Julie followed his example, and after an hour of hard work, she turned to Kevin and laughed.

"I feel like Cinderella, whose coach is waiting. I have to start studying, or I'll turn into a pumpkin."

Kevin smiled. "Julie, the semester just started!"

"You don't know me. I have to study a little bit every day because I'm terrible at cramming."

"Well," he paused, "then maybe you want another exercise session?"

She smiled up at him. "Oh, I do. This is my goal for this year. To exercise and have a more balanced life."

"Tell me whenever you want to work out," he offered.

They waved goodbye. Julie liked him. He was pleasant, mellow and very attractive. But he was also Irish Catholic, and she could not avoid thinking how upset her mother would be. Lara's entire life was centered upon Judaism and the family, and she viewed any man Julie dated as a potential husband. Though very kind and non-judgmental, Lara was, nonetheless, steadfast in her conviction that her children marry in the Jewish faith. Charles and Elizabeth had done so, and Julie was expected to do the same. *I have to keep this friendship casual,* Julie said to herself, *or he'll ask me out and then what will I say? I can't date you because you're Irish?*

Meanwhile, Sara was busy dating Scott, whom she fit into a three-hour slot each Saturday night. This schedule allowed her to study nonstop during the week. Sara was less emotional than Julie and could put the brakes on her feelings. Julie, always eager for romance, would plunge headfirst into a relationship and regret it later.

It was October, and the leaves were starting to turn color in downtown Brooklyn. Julie felt she was keeping up with the second-year curriculum, although there was a plethora of information to absorb. During the week she had a good study routine, alternating with time at the gym after class.

She had also started dating two men. One was a fourth-year medical student and the other, a young academic infectious disease doctor. John, the medical student, was a mystery to Julie because after five dates, he still hadn't made any sexual advances. They had kissed and touched but that was the extent of it. Compared to the behavior of other men she had dated, this lack of libido seemed very odd.

Finally, one night after dinner he asked Julie if she would like to stay over. She was encouraged that he seemed to be leaning toward intimacy. They watched a movie and kissed, but to Julie's dismay, her companion didn't even get an erection when she touched him over his jeans. In fact, he brushed her hand away and snapped, "You're too impatient!" She recoiled, a little confused, and when she looked at him questioningly, he said, "You're tugging at me!"

"Oh, don't think about it," she replied. "You're probably just tired."

But he didn't stop. "No, it's *you*, you're pushy." Her cheeks flushed with embarrassment, but she was not going to be intimidated.

"You know, when you can't dance, you blame the music!" she shouted, and got up to leave. He did not protest. Outside, she hailed a cab and went back to the dorm. Both the evening and the budding relationship ended on a sour note.

Julie then turned her attention to Mike, the infectious disease doctor and professor. He was TV-actor handsome, and although she was nervous dating such an attractive man, he seemed kind and sincere enough. He was ten years older than she, but he was very hip, and after the impotent medical student, Julie felt she had nothing to lose.

As before, the relationship began to unravel on the fifth date. They were dining at an Upper East Side Italian restaurant, and Julie was contemplating sleeping with him that night, regardless of what he felt for her. It had been a long time since she'd had sex, and the fiasco with the medical student certainly didn't bolster her confidence, so a new experience with this new partner would be welcome.

The dinner started out fine, but after the doctor had a second glass of wine, he started staring at other pretty women who passed the table. Julie knew this type —frequent eye contact with women was an affirmation to him that he was irresistible. By the fourth time he pulled this stunt, Julie decided to call it a night. She reached into her purse, slapped a $50 bill on the red checkered tablecloth and promptly stood up.

"I'm leaving," she stated.

The doctor grabbed her arm. "What's wrong?" he asked.

"What's wrong?" she replied in an even but sarcastic voice. "You may be a handsome doctor but guess what! I am a pretty medical student, and actually I am a rare commodity. You take me out," she continued breathlessly, "and you stare and flirt with every skirt that passes by! You're not even subtle about it."

She pulled her arm away and left, amazed at having spoken so plainly. Jumping into a cab and heading home to Ditmas Park, she sought the comfort of her mother's arms.

In December another semester of medical school came to a close. Julie was confident about her performance in school, but once again, she was very lonely. She spent New Year's Eve at home with her parents watching *Casablanca* and *Breakfast at Tiffany's*.

"I don't understand this," Lara said, "You're in medical school with so many men around, and you're so pretty. Isn't there anyone you can date?"

Julie shook her head. "There are many men who would like to date me, Mom, but look at what just happened! One blamed me because he couldn't get excited enough have sex, and the other one flirted with strangers the entire evening. I need someone different. I need a guy who is bright but kind."

"Don't be discouraged, Julie," her mother said. "You just need to give it more of a chance."

Julie nodded. "I know, Mom, but I don't think I have patience right now. If I met a guy like Robbie or Rick, I wouldn't put up with their stuff. I need someone gentle, someone laid back," she said.

"Time will tell," Lara continued. "I am not worried." And then, reverting to her ever-important goal of her daughter's marriage, she added, "Soon enough, you'll have both an M.D. and an MRS."

Julie was sure about the M.D., but not so sure about the MRS.

CHAPTER 10

With the latter part of year two of medical school starting, Julie knew that a milestone was approaching. At the end of this semester, she would not have any more classes but instead would be doing clinical rotations in the hospital and clinic.

As polished as she had become in her one and half years as a medical student, and as much as she had had to rise to the demands of her academic program, Julie was still dealing with some unresolved issues. Her social life had not really evolved, and despite her efforts, she was still without a meaningful partner.

One Thursday night, she went to the usual social gathering at the student center. Always striking and stylish, she wore snug-fitting jeans with a tight red sweater and her over-the-knee black suede boots, all of which created a sleek and sexy silhouette. Within moments, she bumped into her old college boyfriend Robbie.

Robbie had already graduated from Downstate and had just begun a residency in the emergency room at Kings County Hospital. He had come to the social that night, and when he spotted Julie, he wasted no time putting his arm around her and giving her a light kiss on the lips.

Julie introduced Robbie to Sara, who was standing nearby, and after a brief conversation, she gave him her new phone number. She couldn't quite understand why. She had not forgotten that he was a terrible boyfriend. But maybe, she thought, having no one else at the moment and feeling lonely and vulnerable, she considered re-exploring her relationship with him. She always thought Robbie was brilliant and handsome, so why not? Maybe now that she was studying to be a doctor, he would have a new respect for her.

A week later they were sitting together in a Mexican restaurant in Greenwich Village. Julie had taken two hours and great pains to prepare for the date, showering, blowing out her hair and applying makeup. She chose a fitted black knit dress with knee-high boots and put on her glossy red lipstick. Confident that she looked sharp, she admitted to herself that she was excited about seeing Robbie.

The restaurant was dimly lit but very noisy. She and Robbie were busy chatting about medical school and specialties they were interested in pursuing. Robbie discussed what it was like to be an emergency room doctor, which Julie thought suited him just fine, given his acute and quick mind. He was totally lacking in bedside manner, so the "strictly business" nature of the ER would be perfect for him.

True to form, Robbie, never big on compassion, had much criticism for the ineptitude of the city hospital staff, labeling the nurses "lazy."

"Robbie," Julie countered, "they are overworked. Why do you call them lazy?"

He just sighed. "Here goes Pollyanna. You never see things as they are."

"What's wrong with Pollyanna? I'm happier than you."

"It's not reality. You know, Julie, fools are the happiest people."

She laughed. "You always knew how to give a compliment."

"Anyway, Julie," he continued, "I have something to ask you."

She peered over the rim of her margarita. "Yes? What?"

"Well," he replied quietly," it's kind of awkward to ask you this in a crowded restaurant."

"Oh, don't be silly," Julie smiled. "Anything you ask is fine. We've known each other a long time." She brushed her hair back, glancing at Robbie and thinking that he was getting up the nerve to propose.

Robbie smirked. "I don't know what you'll say."

"I'll probably say yes," Julie winked, her eyes sparkling.

"OK," he said. "Do you mind if I ask Sara out on a date?"

Julie laughed. "No really, Robbie, what do you want to ask me? Be serious!"

"No," he said firmly. "I mean it. I took you out because I didn't know how to ask you on the phone for Sara's number."

Tears started to roll down's Julie's cheeks, but at that very moment, the waitress tripped, and a tray of margaritas landed right on her. Julie sat there, cold, immobile, miserable and disillusioned. The splattered strawberry and lime drinks trickled down her hair and face, blending with rivulets of mascara and eyeliner already staining her cheeks.

"Robbie, what kind of a man are you?" she asked, incredulous. "You asked me out to get my best friend's phone number? Are you kidding? That's insane! If you want to ask Sara out," she ranted, "find her fucking phone number yourself! I'm done with you, Robbie. You're a loser!" She stood up, shivering, soaked and sticky, but proud of herself as she made for the door.

As she'd done after so many other terrible dates, Julie hailed a cab and went straight home to Ditmas Park. She got in the shower and let the stream of hot water rinse all the disappointment and humiliation from her. Then wrapping herself in a soft nightgown and robe, she nestled under the covers in her familiar bed and cried herself to sleep.

When she awoke the next morning, it was clear that she would never deal with Robbie again. She related the evening's scene to Sara, who, like any good and loyal friend, was nothing short of indignant that Robbie even considered asking her out. And although Julie felt bruised by the unfortunate exchange, she knew now that she was free of this man who, in both the past and the present, caused her so much pain. She was free at last.

◊ ◊ ◊

It was February—freezing, dark and gloomy. With only one more semester left of the basic science curriculum, Julie sat alone in her dorm room poring over pictures of diseased lungs. The phone rang and when she answered, she immediately recognized the voice.

"Hey, Julie, it's Rick."

"Rick." She smiled widely as she spoke. "How are you? I can't believe we haven't spoken in almost two years."

"Yeah, it's been a long time. What's happening?"

"Well, I'm almost done with the basic science course work. Rick, I did it! I survived this past year, and I did well!" she gushed.

There was silence at the other end of the phone. "Julie," he paused, "I'm getting married."

Julie quietly gasped. "Really? That's great!"

"Yeah," he continued, "she's an Asian American medical student. Really so beautiful and smart. She barely has to study! Just absorbs like a sponge. She's really amazing."

Julie held back snapping at him and asking why he called. If things were so perfect, why was he contacting her? Did he hope she would plead with him not to marry this woman? Did he want her to beg him to reconsider the two of them again? Was he telling her that he moved on?"

"That's such wonderful news," she said kindly. She really

was happy for Rick. A part of her would always love him and would regret that they didn't marry. They chatted about Rick's residency in surgery and how he wanted to settle in North Carolina.

"Why North Carolina?" Julie asked.

"I just need to get away from the aggressive New York Jews," he said.

Always the voice of reason, Julie reminded him that not every surgeon in New York was Jewish. She hated his prejudice, as nothing was worse than a self-loathing, anti-Semitic Jew. They exchanged a few more pleasantries and covered some safe topics, and then the conversation came to a natural end. There was a loud silence between them as they ran out of things to say. Julie said she had to get back to her books and hung up.

The conversation left her feeling confused and blue. First Robbie asking her for Sara's number, then Rick calling to tell her he was getting married. What next? Valentine's Day was less than two weeks away. She thought she could celebrate with her mother and father. *One day my prince will come,* she told herself.

Drained by the conversation and in no mood for any more studying, Julie retreated once again to her bed and buried herself under the covers.

CHAPTER 11

It was blistering cold the next day when Julie bundled up and went to class. Despite the disturbing exchange with Rick the previous night, she put her full attention on the lecture and diligently filled several pages with notes. Afterwards, as the sun started to disappear, she headed to the cafeteria for her mid-afternoon snack.

Sitting at a table sipping tea and nibbling a Kit Kat, she thought about Rick's phone call. What did Rick want from her, anyway? She had spent a lot of time trying to get over their painful, wrenching breakup, and that call gave her a setback. She was trying to think about something else when McCormack passed her table and sat down across from her.

"Hey, pretty lady," he said in his mellow voice, "why are you looking so blue?"

She didn't hold back, "Oh, Kevin, last night my ex-fiancé called to tell me he's getting married. Our relationship wasn't meant to be, but his news still stunned me."

Kevin laughed. "Well, I hate to take advantage of the situation, but this just may be my lucky day. Julie, I've been wanting to ask you out for a long time and maybe you'll say yes. I'll cheer you up."

She grinned over the rim of her cup. "Yes, Kevin, I'd like to go out with you."

"Gee, that was easier than I thought! OK, this Saturday night! We will go to a restaurant in the city and get to know each other better."

Julie's frame of mind suddenly shifted, and she felt a new kind of giddiness. Their brief conversation seemed to open a window, allowing her to see a way out of the dark mood that had been hanging over her. Kevin was tall and handsome and in great shape, she reflected. He was the epitome of masculinity, yet he had an outwardly gentle nature. Julie had never dated anyone like him before.

Mentally, she enumerated her romances of the last five years. First Robbie was a total creep. Miserable, sarcastic and arrogant. Then there was Rick, whom she adored, but who was totally controlling and too demanding. Then came John, the impotent medical student, and then Mike, the conceited infectious disease doctor.

She thought about how this year had started out giving her a double whammy, with Robbie asking her out in order to get Sara's number, and Rick calling to tell her about his upcoming marriage. These two guys had had such a strong impact on her, and the other two, who meant nothing but had still hurt her, her were all Jewish. She had, in fact, never dated any guy who was not Jewish. Well, that wasn't working. Maybe it was time to try dating this Irish hunk just to see what would happen.

Despite her considerable experience with men, Julie was a little nervous about going out with someone new. When Saturday evening arrived, she was excited to see Kevin, who showed up wearing a blue sweater that emphasized his huge biceps. From the look of him, Kevin seemed pretty excited and happy too. He smiled approvingly at Julie, who looked fetching in her black jeans and pink wool sweater.

They drove to the city and parked near a Japanese restaurant that Kevin had chosen. The mood inside was romantic, with dim lighting, the subtle trickling of a fountain and the faint plunking of a koto somewhere in a corner. They decided upon a table by the wall, where translucent Japanese screens offered privacy and they could talk.

The conversation started on general topics. As Julie already knew, Kevin was an athlete who loved everything that had to do with sports and outdoor life. He'd played football in college and enjoyed working out, hiking and skiing. She characterized herself as a nerd who liked reading, playing piano and visiting museums. She reminded him about what she had told him in the gym that day: she could barely climb a flight of stairs without feeling exhausted. She had never hiked or skied. In fact, the extent of her experience of the great outdoors did not include much more than a love of gardens.

As things warmed up a bit, they moved to exchanging information about their family backgrounds. Kevin had grown up in Poughkeepsie in a large, close-knit Irish Catholic household with six kids: three boys and three girls. It was a middle-class family with no extra luxuries. His parents were both educators, and the kids had part-time jobs to help chip in with the finances. Kevin was very close to his siblings but was especially close to his mother, who, he told Julie, was a very kind woman. Julie appreciated that Kevin loved his family and spoke of them with affection. He admitted that he had never dated a Jewish girl before. Likewise, Julie told him that she had never dated a Catholic or Protestant man. These personal revelations did not inhibit the relaxed feeling between them, and they both laughed easily.

As they continued to chat over sushi and saki, it became clear that professionally, they had the same goal: to be doctors who would serve the community. Their avocations and personal interests, however, were completely different. Julie was passionate about the arts and culture, and Kevin was devoted to sports and outdoor life. But differences being what they were, both young people shared a pivotal value: family and friendships. These were extremely important to both of them and created a common thread.

"Well," Kevin said as he took Julie's hand, "we can learn a lot from each other," and he smiled. Julie could feel the chemistry stirring. Kevin didn't take his eyes off her for one moment. He also didn't have that nasty habit of perusing the restaurant for other women, as Professor Mike had done. "You know," Kevin said, "I have wanted to ask you out for the past year."

Julie wrinkled her nose and giggled. "And why didn't you?"

"I'm shy, believe it or not," he said. Julie loved his candor. The 6'4", 225-pound athlete was telling her he was shy. "You're so pretty," he continued. "Everyone wants to be with you."

She smiled demurely. "Kevin, you're handsome too."

"Well, here we are," he said. "I've learned a lot about you tonight. You know, Julie, some people may think you are aloof, but I see a different side of you."

"Thank you, Kevin, for saying that. I really need to study very hard, so I can't socialize that much. I think people may mistake my quietness and anxiety for being conceited. By the way, how is it that you're always so calm?"

He paused. "Growing up in a large family forces one to go with the flow. Even if I was nervous, no one could pay that much attention to me. Anyway, I'm Irish. We'd rather put pins in our eyes than complain about something. You know, stiff upper lip and that type of mentality."

"We're Jewish," she laughed lightly, "We live to complain."

The last few hours had given Julie and Kevin a deeper experience of their new friendship. The mood was good, and when they went back to Brooklyn, Kevin kissed her gently on the lips. "I had a great evening with you," he said. "I'd like us to go out again."

She felt a shiver of excitement. "Yes," she winked. "Of course!" It felt so comfortable. No game playing, no pretense. Just sheer pleasure.

The following Saturday night, they went to a movie and then to dinner at a quiet Indian restaurant. Sitar music created a soothing backdrop as they discussed the movie in depth and enjoyed shish kebab. But as Julie was talking in an animated fashion, she felt a chunk of lamb lodge itself in the back of her throat. Embarrassed to spit it out, she tried swallowing it. Suddenly, she felt her entire airway blocked. Panicking, she quickly stood up and flung the small table over, sending the food flying off the plates and the dishes clattering on the floor.

Kevin stood up behind her, his arms engulfing her frame as he pumped rhythmically with his fists on her upper stomach. The food flew out of her mouth and she breathed in with relief. Gratefully, she looked up at him.

"Well," he said, "it's a good thing I learned the Heimlich maneuver. For a second I got nervous that I'd lost you," he laughed.

She nodded. "Thank goodness you have grace under pressure. I'm so embarrassed."

"Why? These things happen."

Julie was impressed with Kevin. He was even-tempered and capable, and it seemed that nothing fazed him. They finished dinner with Julie afraid to eat, let alone eat and talk.

The following week would bring Valentine's Day. Kevin planned an evening that included time at a jazz club and then dinner. In the meantime, he called Julie every night to say hello and gently smiled at her in class each day. Knowing that med school was a small community, they decided not to discuss their relationship until they were sure which way things were going. But trying to avoid looking at each other during lectures was becoming increasingly difficult.

That Saturday night, Kevin arrived at Julie's dorm with a red, heart-shaped box of candy. Julie hugged him. It was only their third date, and he already knew she loved chocolate and was sure she would appreciate such a thoughtful, romantic gesture.

When they arrived at the club, Kevin ordered a beer for himself and a white wine for Julie. The music played softly as they talked quietly and held hands. Julie, not usually a drinker, was on her third glass of wine when she looked up at Kevin and saw the room spinning. A wave of nausea swept over her.

"Kevin," she whispered, "I'm feeling really sick. I never drink."

Kevin stood up and helped her out of her chair. "Don't worry, let's get you some fresh air." He led her outside just in time for Julie to lean over and throw up on his shoes.

"Oh, my God!" she said, gasping, "I'm so sorry! I can't believe I did this."

Kevin laughed. "You certainly are a lightweight when it comes to drinking. Let me go get a towel."

He returned with paper towels to help Julie clean up and then put his arm around her and walked her to the restroom. He splashed water on her face and brought her a glass of cold water.

Julie was mortified. "Kevin," she whispered, "I'll understand if you never want to date me again. I was trying to be cool, so I drank too much. First choking on the Indian food, and now this. I am so sorry. You've been so kind, and I really like you," she went on, "but I do understand why you wouldn't want to date me again."

"What are you talking about?" he exclaimed. "I'm in love with you."

Julie looked up at him, tears streaming down her face. In that moment, feeling utter trust and adoration for this man, she buried her face in his chest. They left the club and said nothing in the car on the way back to Brooklyn, but only held hands and smiled at each other.

Kevin tucked Julie in, kissed her head and then fell asleep next to her in her small single bed. In the morning, she woke to a cup of hot coffee. She showered, gulped down the coffee and didn't need to say too much. She knew they would be lovers and best friends. The following Saturday night, they went to a small Italian restaurant. Kevin suggested that they share a bottle of wine.

"Wait!" Julie blurted out. "You saw my drinking tolerance last week!"

"Well, I'm not much of a drinker either," Kevin replied. "Bad family history. You know the Irish. My mother was an alcoholic, so it left me hyper-vigilant about excessive drinking." Julie was astonished that Kevin shared this rather personal information in such a matter-of-fact way. She had harbored so much shame about her father's drinking.

"You know, Kevin," she said with some hesitation, "my dad had a problem with alcohol about three years ago. It devastated me. In the Jewish community, alcoholism isn't very common."

Kevin took her hand. "Julie, it's nothing to be ashamed about. Among the Irish, alcoholism is known as 'the Irish curse.' Some people just have an extreme sensitivity to alcohol. It's a physiologic trait, and they can't drink."

"But Kevin," she whispered, "my dad left his family business and made rash decisions. He lost the new business he'd started and then went from riches to rags." Julie could hardly believe that she was sharing this so openly. She had hidden this from Rick, who had been her fiancé! But Kevin was just different. He could be strong and tender at the same time.

He held her hand lightly and he said in a soothing voice, "That was your Dad, Julie. That's not you."

Tears filled her eyes. "Oh, Kevin," she murmured, holding back her tears, "I've been so ashamed of what happened. My dad was my hero, and then it was a disaster."

"People don't understand or tolerate alcoholism. It's a disease like diabetes or cancer. Patients need their treatments," he continued.

"But it's a disease that doesn't engender sympathy. My dad was rough and ill-tempered when he drank. I hated him," she emphasized.

"Well, my mom would black out on the kitchen floor, and I had to take care of my younger siblings." He stopped to take a sip of water and continued, "You know, Julie, I couldn't even have friends over because I didn't know if my mother would be sober or drunk."

She cradled his hand in both of her small palms. "Thank you, Kevin, for listening to me without judging. It's as though bricks have been lifted off my shoulder. You've made me feel free just unburdening my secret." They smiled into each other's eyes.

When their serious mood passed, they finally looked at the menu. They ordered real comfort food: spaghetti and meatballs and chicken cutlet parmigiana and decided to split a half carafe of red wine.

Over espresso and cannoli, Julie, returning to the topic they'd discussed, asked, "Can you believe we have this in common? I've never talked out this stuff with anyone before."

Kevin laughed, "We probably have more in common than we realize."

Julie laughed lightly. "Really? Well, we're both medical students and we are committed to helping others. But we already went over this on our first date. You're an athlete, you're laid back, and you love being out in nature. Now me. I love to read and go to museums. I can barely walk up a flight of stairs without losing my breath. And I never hiked, but I like gardens."

"And I told you," he continued "we are going to learn a lot from each other."

"I love old movies," she volunteered.

"I love working on old cars."

"I love libraries."

"I love mountains," he countered.

"Ice-skating with pom-poms on my skates makes me happy."

"Nothing better than skiing," he replied.

"I love kissing," she whispered.

"Now *that*, pretty Julie, we have in common."

After dinner, they headed back to Julie's room, still in a cloud of euphoria. There had been no doubt that tonight was the night. Kevin reached over and flicked on Julie's desk lamp and turned off the other lights in the room. He pulled Julie on top of him as he lay down on the single bed. He gently kissed her and ran his long fingers through her hair. Rolling her on her side, he snuggled her into him, then slowly pulled her sweater over her head and removed her bra.

Kevin was mesmerized by the beauty of her naked breasts. "Julie, you take my breath away," he said huskily. Then he lowered his soft lips and let his tongue slowly circle her firm nipples. He stroked her mound but then inserted his long fingers into the inviting portal. Julie purred as he continued rubbing while smoothly but firmly moving his fingers inside her. Bringing his mouth down between her legs, he lingered there, licking her slowly and gently.

She moaned with delight and ran her hands through his thick, sandy hair. When he felt her whole body erupt with pleasure, he lifted his 225-pound frame on top of her and rested himself on his elbows so as not to crush her. He entered her slowly, kissing her adoringly. He was a powerful, undulating force inside her, and he could tell that she was eager for his thrusts.

"Julie, Julie," he whispered. The momentum continued to build until he burst with bliss. He held her tightly as he rested upon her. "You are amazing," he said as he left tiny kisses all over her face. Julie kissed his cheeks, his lips and his eyelids. She felt gratified and safe in his arms. They fell asleep together.

In the morning, she felt Kevin's hardness nudging her backside. She smiled and rolled over.

"Looks like someone's up again," he said, with his slow, relaxed laugh.

"Hmmm," she replied. "Why not?"

They were quickly joined, Kevin moving more

vigorously than he had the previous night. He was pleased that she enjoyed their lovemaking and appreciated how her body moved in sync with his. Julie, totally enveloped by his strong, muscular frame, relished how he swooped her in his grasp, creating a shelter. In just moments, he came hard, calling her name aloud.

Sated from the early morning activity, Kevin went out foraging for breakfast at a local McDonald's and brought back hot chocolate and Egg McMuffins. Feeling newly fortified, Julie was ready to start studying, but Kevin felt impelled to go to the gym and work out.

"Don't you think you should study for the pathology quiz this week?" she asked.

He laughed. "Yes, Nervous Nellie, I will, but I feel the need to switch gears after all the excitement around here."

She chuckled. "I know I'm a nerd. I just like to study a bit each day. I'm sure I told you that I'm a terrible crammer."

"That's all right. Do what works for you. I do best when I cram a little."

Julie lost all sense of self-consciousness with Kevin. She was at ease, sitting at her desk in flannel pajama pants and a sweater, her hair up in a ponytail. Her head was buried in her textbooks, and as he leaned over and kissed her on the nose, she heard him say, "You are so beautiful."

"I look like a wreck! I'm busy studying and my flannels and you think I'm beautiful?"

"Yes. I think you're amazing. I'm a lucky guy."

During the ensuing weeks, they were inseparable and let it be known on campus that they were a couple. They sat together in the lecture hall, sometimes holding hands. Kevin would stay over in Julie's room a few nights a week, going back to his place just to grab a change of clothes.

Now that they were "an item," they fell into a routine of attending a lecture, going to the gym, and then heading back to Julie's room. Sometimes they would make love before eating dinner in the student cafeteria. Even better, though, was when they had one of Lara's prepared dinners in Julie's room. From the time Julie had started medical school, Lara always made her hot meals that she packed in small aluminum pans: chicken, turkey or brisket with vegetables. She would bring them over to the dorm on Sunday afternoon. It made life easier for Julie, and of course, the homemade food was far preferable to the cafeteria fare. And now Julie could share these meals with Kevin.

Julie told her mother about Kevin and was honest about his not being Jewish. At first, Lara was flummoxed. "How did my Jewish daughter manage to find an Irish fellow in a predominately Jewish medical school?" she asked, almost amused. But she could see that Julie never looked happier or calmer and started preparing dinner parcels for two.

Their sex life became a focal point in the day. Some afternoons, they sacrificed eating a "proper" lunch to have a quickie back at the dorm and would then compensate by gobbling sandwiches in the lecture afterwards. Julie thought about it. She and Kevin had sex every day, sometimes three times a day. Now that Kevin was no longer afraid of hurting his little china doll, their escapades became more animated. Kevin might pull her on top of him and hold her in his arms as he stood up and carried her around the room. They experimented with every conceivable position, Kevin always whispering in her ear how great she felt.

They had been dating for only two months, but Julie felt as though they were true friends. The comfort and security she had had with Rick, she now felt with Kevin, but without the element of control. Kevin never dictated to Julie what to wear or what to do. On the contrary, he asked her for advice and treated her as an equal partner. Rick may have loved and respected Julie, but he had treated her like a child. Kevin saw her as a partner, friend and lover.

Julie was still awed by Kevin's equanimity. "Are all non-Jewish men this calm?" she asked him one afternoon.

As usual, he laughed out loud. "I told you, Irishmen are

taught to keep a stiff upper lip, so you never know if we are calm or nervous," he told her.

"You're strong and grounded, she remarked. "I wish I could be like that."

Kevin fixed his gaze on her. "You're perfect. I love that you're so talkative. I'm never bored."

Julie laughed out loud. "When I was a young child, my brother and sister would constantly tell me to stop talking. Even my mom would cry out that I had talked enough! I just always had lots of questions."

Kevin nodded. "When you grow up in a large family, no one really wants to hear everything that you have to say. I was busy helping raise my younger siblings, especially when Mom was drinking," he continued.

"Were you terribly embarrassed that she drank?" Julie quietly asked him as she peered over a cup of tea.

Kevin was pensive, then spoke. "You know that drinking is not uncommon in Irish culture and sadly, neither is alcoholism. I kept my mother's problem from my friends, but it wasn't that I was embarrassed as much as that I felt bad for our family. We didn't have lots of money, so I didn't get the exposure to cultural events like you did," he noted. "But my dad introduced us to skiing and sports and hiking, and that was great."

Julie looked at him with admiration. "Kevin," she sighed, "you always see the good in every situation. I'm optimistic, but I'm such a worry wart, especially with school. You're so balanced," she told him as she jumped into his lap and kissed him.

"You're the most interesting girl I've ever been with," he replied. "I like that you're chatty, and even your anxiety doesn't bother me in the least. Sometimes, I think it's funny."

Julie pretended to be annoyed. "Oh, I see, my quirkiness is funny. As I suffer, you laugh," she said wryly.

He grabbed her, stood up carried her over to the bed. "I not only find your anxiety funny, I know the perfect antidote for it." He laid her down and started kissing her long and hard. Within seconds, he pulled her clothes off and dived down to that warm spot he loved so much. His tongue circled around in a fast, fluttering rhythm and he didn't stop until he felt her come in his mouth.

"Feel any calmer now?" he queried. She gazed into his eyes. "Well, doctor, you do know your medicine."

Together they were an excellent couple, mitigating each other's weaknesses and enhancing each other's strengths. Julie would get Kevin psyched up to study, and he would help her relax. They complemented each other emotionally and physically, and they shared a powerful and flexible bond. Kevin may have appeared shy, but he was sexually very uninhibited and loved it when Julie talked dirty to him. He told her that most of his Catholic girlfriends had been sweet, but rather quiet and inhibited in bed.

"You are my exotic Jewess," he said one night. "You love sex. Every position is good for you, and I like when you whisper naughty things in my ear," he said seductively.

Julie stared at him in amazement. No matter what she did or wore, he was hot for her. "You know, Kevin," she confided one night, "I've never seen you not erect. Every time you take off your clothes near me, you're hard," she giggled.

"My sexy girlfriend does this to me," he said as he kissed her neck. "You were like a porcelain figurine to me when we first started dating, so charming and shy. Now I can't keep up with you. You're wearing me out," he said with a grin.

Julie loved teasing him. He could be so easily amused. Unlike Rick, who was a strong lover but needed to be in charge of everything, Kevin was putty in her hands. If he was sitting at the desk studying and Julie sauntered by and wrapped her panties around his eyes, he couldn't control himself. "You little vixen!" he'd exclaim, grab her and throw her onto the bed.

They resolved that they were going to enrich each other's interests. Julie wanted Kevin to be more culturally aware, and Kevin insisted that Julie be in better aerobic shape. They sat down and made a schedule and implemented it immediately. One day out of every weekend, they would take the subway to Manhattan and go to a different art museum. As they perused the collections, Julie did miss Rick's knowledge of art and literature, but keeping their mission in mind, she explained the different artistic techniques and styles to Kevin. She told herself regularly that no one is perfect. *Who am I to judge him?* she asked herself. *So what if he is not well read in literature and history and doesn't know who Monet, Manet or Cezanne were? I can barely walk uphill, and he's so patient with me.*

Kevin was, indeed, very patient with Julie and her lack of physical stamina and vowed to help raise her tolerance for exercise. Julie was in awe of his dedication to sports. *He's a total athlete,* she'd remind herself. *He ran the Boston Marathon, played college football, hiked mountains in Maine and New Hampshire with his buddies. And he's a skier.*

"I think we are best friends," she told Kevin one evening during a study break. They were sipping tea and Julie was snacking on cookies while Kevin crunched an apple. "We're like Yin and Yang. One of us is so serene; the other, beyond nervous. One of us loves art and culture, and the other one loves the great outdoors. One of us is quiet, and the other is a chatterbox. We both are determined people, and we really care about each other."

Kevin nodded. "Opposites attract, they say."

"Well," Julie replied, "opposite personalities, like outgoing and shy, or calm and anxious. But not opposite values. People who are in sync with their goals and ethics form strong bonds."

Kevin looked at her lovingly. "Julie, whatever we do or don't have in common, I know we have extraordinary chemistry. I just love being around you." He wanted to take her hiking during the summer. It was April, and he was talking about traveling up to New England in August.

"We have four months to get you in shape," he said over lunch one afternoon. "We will start today after class." At 5:00

p.m., they changed into workout clothes and went to the gym. After walking for about fifteen minutes on the treadmill, Julie was panting.

"Kevin," she gasped, "I really am in terrible shape."

Kevin just grinned. "What do you expect? You just started. Let me organize a program for you. We'll go day by day. We'll start with some light weights. We will exercise for thirty minutes four times a week, OK?"

How could she refuse? Kevin was in phenomenal shape, jogging five miles a day. His large biceps were bigger than her thighs. Julie had confidence in him as her coach. She knew that whenever she set her mind to completing a task, she'd succeed, so she just repeated the mantra, "Sound body and sound mind."

Kevin also wanted Julie to stop smoking. Like most medical students, she did smoke, but not much, only five to seven cigarettes a day. She decided to cut down to one cigarette after dinner. Within a few weeks of their regimen, Julie was able to jog one mile on the treadmill. Her goal was to jog four miles, but she was proud of herself and appreciative of Kevin's encouragement.

"We're going to have a great time hiking this August," he said with anticipation. Julie did not want to burst his bubble by telling him that she hated insects. She was squeamish about hiking in the woods, but there was time enough to tell him.

On a warm Saturday afternoon in April, when spring buds were just beginning to appear on the trees, Julie and Kevin decided to shake up the study routine and go to the main branch of the library in Grand Army Plaza. They planned to hit the books for a few hours and then visit the Brooklyn Museum. Julie slipped on jeans, a white angora sweater and a navy blazer. Kevin wore his usual jeans and hooded sweatshirt. Julie made a mental note that handsome Kevin needed to add some style to his wardrobe but didn't share that with him yet.

They ate a quick breakfast of bran muffins and coffee

and set out for their day of study and recreation. The Brooklyn Public Library was an imposing Beaux Arts building with marble floors and multiple rooms replete with books. The main reading room had long tables with slotted wooden chairs and that aroma of books that Julie had always found to be as soothing as lavender soap.

The two students concentrated for three hours straight and then took a well-deserved study break in the museum. Kevin was eager to learn about art, not just for its own sake, but also to please Julie. They walked in the quietude of the galleries, holding hands and pausing to look at the works of Winslow Homer and the Hudson Valley painter, Thomas Cole. This brought a wide smile to Kevin's face.

"I love the nature scenes. I've hiked these mountains in the Catskills, and I plan on taking you with me," he told Julie running his hands through her hair.

Julie looked up at him and smiled. "I don't think I could hike thirty feet."

"Yes, you will. I'll help you improve your stamina. Besides which, you have great stamina when you want it," he laughed and winked at her.

She felt herself blushing. Yes, she did have stamina in bed, but Kevin did the lion's share of the rigorous work. "I'm up for the challenge," she cooed.

After some time soaking up the American painters, they went downstairs to the cafeteria for coffee and snacks. Then it was time to return to the library. With this combination of activities, Julie felt that Kevin was helping her learn how to balance work and play. Even her sister remarked how much more settled she seemed of late. Kevin got the credit for this, as he was a great example of someone who could juggle work responsibility and leisure, reminding Julie that a battery needs to be recharged.

"We will follow the wisdom of the Greeks: Sound body and sound mind," she remarked. "You know, before med school I was much more balanced. I exercised, played piano and read all the time. Maybe I made a mistake becoming a doctor," she pouted. "Maybe I'm just not smart enough."

Kevin turned toward her as he spoke. "Julie, stop this talk now. Yes, med school is a challenge for you, but you're doing fine. If you could spend the time exercising instead of fretting during your breaks, you would better off. You don't have to be the valedictorian of the class. You're swimming in a bigger pond now. It's OK not to be the biggest fish."

She felt love singing in her heart. "Oh, Kevin, you are an amazing gift. You put everything in perspective for me."

He shrugged. "You don't give yourself enough kudos for how much you are accomplishing. Not everyone who climbs Mount Everest can be the fastest. It's just enough to make the climb." She pulled his head down to her and smothered him with kisses.

The following Saturday was another beautiful day, and the young lovers headed to the Brooklyn Botanic Garden. They strolled along the path, admiring the various spring flowers and the French, English and Japanese formal gardens. Julie felt a particular affection for the pansies and tulips, and Kevin took photos of the spring foliage.

"I want to take you to my parents' home for Easter," he exclaimed. "You'll flip over the flower arrangements my mother makes for the table."

Julie nodded, her eyes opening wide. "Are you asking me to meet your family?" she asked tentatively.

"I most certainly am asking you," he asserted.

Julie continued, "And I want you to come to Passover Seder at my parents' home!"

And so it was settled. They would meet each other's families and would experience their respective religious holidays and traditions.

For the Easter outing, Julie wore in a light pink wool dress with a narrow black belt, accentuating her small waist.

She kept it simple with sheer stockings and black patent leather pumps and played her makeup lightly, finishing with a light pink lipstick. When she opened the door for Kevin, he gasped and exclaimed, "You look so pretty!"

"I bought some chocolates for your family, and I have a small Easter gift for you," she said as she handed him a stuffed Easter bunny.

He laughed out loud. "You're too cute, Julie."

They drove up to Poughkeepsie to the McCormack family home, a 1950s split level furnished in traditional American style. The rooms were decorated in shades of burgundy, hunter green and gold, and the walls were elegantly papered in a beige damask with floral borders. There was a holiday spring wreath on the living room wall, and the dining room table was set with china and crystal. In the center was an arrangement of pansies, tulips and daffodils.

Kevin's family, including his parents, five siblings, and two unmarried aunts, were warm and welcoming to Julie. Kevin kept a strong arm around Julie's shoulder to make sure she felt comfortable, and she did. As they sat down for the Easter Sunday meal and recited the prayers, Kevin squeezed her hand, knowing this was Julie's first Easter dinner. Mrs. McCormack had baked a glazed ham with pineapple and vegetables and served it with a huge bowl of mashed potatoes. Around the table, everyone chatted about school and their interests as the parents beamed.

Before dessert, Kevin took Julie's hand and led her outside for a stroll with the family dogs. They walked to a small park at the end of the row of houses, as the dogs scampered ahead on familiar terrain.

Kevin held Julie in his arms. "My family really seems to like you. My sisters told me you're pretty and sweet. Julie, I'm very proud to be with you." He kissed her strongly on the mouth, his tongue intertwining with hers and his hand caressing her breast through her dress. "I would like to undress you right now and make love," he whispered. She felt his hardness press up against her, and she softly moaned in his ear. They knew they would enjoy each other later.

Back at the house, the table was set with cookies, apple pie, chocolate and a bowl of painted Easter eggs. After more conversation and coffee, the very pleasant and meaningful day came to a close. Kevin and Julie said goodbye to everyone and drove back to the dorm. After sweet lovemaking, they fell asleep in each other's arms.

The next day it was back to class, but a busy night lay ahead because Kevin was going to attend his first Passover Seder. In his khaki slacks, light blue shirt and wool blazer, he looked sharp and appealing. They took the subway to the Kent home, and after introductions, they sat down to the traditional dinner.

A cheerful participant, Kevin read in English from the Haggadah and took part in the rituals of tasting the bitter *maror* and sweet *charoset*. He followed the directives, dipping his pinky in the wine after naming each of the plagues. He tried gefilte fish and matzoh ball soup for the very first time and had more than one helping of Lara's kugel and brisket.

After the long and lively dinner, everyone sat in the living room and chatted in little groups. Kevin was talking about sports with Charles, and that gave Elizabeth a chance to sidle up to Julie and confer.

"He's a catch, Julie," she said with a smile. "So handsome and polite."

"I know," Julie agreed, "he is such a pacifying influence on me. He is the proverbial 'strong, silent type,' and not to brag, but he a fantastic lover," she admitted. "We share each other's passions. He's going to museums with me, and I'm exercising with him. I don't shut up, and he's a great listener when I get nervous. He just makes me laugh."

"He's perfect, except he's not Jewish," Elizabeth said, stating the obvious.

Julie shrugged. "Look, Elizabeth," she told her with

determination, "Robbie was a jerk, and Rick the know-it-all was extremely demanding. John the med student couldn't get his dick up, and he blamed me, and Mike the professor was a conceited idiot—and they were all Jewish! Kevin and I are just having a great time. We're best friends and great lovers, so I'm not going to worry about what will be. I'm sure if we get serious we'll respect and observe each other's religions. Let's not even talk about that now."

"You are right," Elizabeth agreed. "He's gorgeous and very sweet. It's good to see you so happy."

CHAPTER 12

As the weather in New York was turning hot and humid, the second year of medical school was winding down. With test-related pressure building, Julie and Kevin were holed up in the cloying dorm room, poring over mountains of notes to memorize.

"I need a break!" Kevin declared and pulled Julie onto his lap. His sandy hair was falling onto his forehead, and he gave Julie his irresistible "I need you now" look.

Perspiration dotted their foreheads and streaked down their cheeks as they looked into each other's eyes with ardor. Having each other close was a relief from the arduous study regimen. Kevin kissed and nibbled Julie's ear and ran his hands through her ponytail.

"Julie" was all he needed to say in his deep soft voice. She felt his hardness against her thighs and breathed rapidly as he ran his hand under her T-shirt and onto her breasts. A moment later he unzipped her jeans and was soon gently moving his hips and rapidly dancing inside her. They came hard, kissing each other wildly. Kevin looked at her and for the first time, whispered, "I love you."

Julie knew that he loved her, but he had never said it

aloud before. Now it was more real than ever. For a second, her heart leapt with joy, and then she echoed his words.

"Kevin, I love you too." With that declaration, she felt a release, a surrender and a greater degree of comfort.

He leaned his head on her hand and said, "You know, I've never felt this way about anyone before. Julie, if you ever leave me, I think I will just wander into the woods for weeks." She didn't take her eyes from him.

"Kevin, I am not going to leave you. I think you're my soul mate. With you, I feel safe and free to be myself. You boost my strengths and soothe my insecurities. You cheered me on to exercise, to believe in myself. I'm evolving so much since we are together."

He leaned over to kiss her. "You're my amazing lady. I didn't know classical music from jazz, and I'd never even been to a museum until I met you," he said, shaking his head.

"So, are we an item?" she asked in a soft voice.

Kevin laughed loudly. "What do you think? I spend every second of my time with you. The guys tell me I'm whipped, but I told them they're just jealous!"

Julie continued, "I was thinking, we have to set up our clinical rotation schedules. Should we try to get the same one, or will that be too much time together?"

He grinned widely at her. "Nothing, sweetie pie, would be too much time for me to be with you."

"Kevin," she persisted, "we're from such different worlds. I mean, a Brooklyn Jewish girl and an Irish Catholic country boy? Can this ever really work out?" she asked and then added a nervous but hopeful giggle.

"Of course it can! We add new dimensions to each other. I love that you're so artsy and smart, my little neurotic princess," he responded.

"Maybe," she said teasingly, "I'll get so calm you will miss me being neurotic."

He burst out laughing. "I assure you, Julie, you'll never be too calm for me."

She nodded her head in agreement. "Different genetics. We Jews are always worriers. It's in our DNA because of all the centuries of having to run from persecution."

"And we Irish are stoic, even if we're dying."

"So we are Yin and Yang. A little up and a little down," she said contentedly.

"But Julie," he exclaimed, "I'm always up when I'm with you!" And there, on the floor of a sweltering dorm room in a Brooklyn ghetto, they smiled and snuggled together and felt as if they had reached Shangri-La.

They submitted their requests for the clinical rotations and were granted permission to have identical schedules. In addition, Julie's application for a studio in the dorm was approved, which meant she would have no roommates. She and Kevin planned to purchase a double bed and live together.

"We are going to be near each other nonstop," she noted over a lunch of turkey sandwiches and apples. Kevin had insisted that she have one wholesome snack during the day.

"Enough junk food for you," he'd snapped as he traded her Kit Kat bar for an apple. "You'll get this later," he promised.

His caring, protective gestures were so sincere that she didn't mind. "Oh, I know I'm getting that Kit Kat, or you're not getting your treat," she added with a coy smile.

"You win every time," he said as he grabbed her tightly. "I can't resist you. You're my temptress, my little sex kitten and my love."

They could hardly wait to begin their rotations and start living together. But first, Kevin planned a two-week vacation in New England for the end of the summer. He assured Julie that it was going to be the best time of their romance so far, as he knew New England inside and out. Apart from Cape Cod, Julie had never been anywhere in New England, and she was anticipating a fabulous trip. They would both have a change of view and a refreshing break from the intensity of their everyday lives.

Back in 1978, during the steamy dog days of August, Kevin was a college student in Massachusetts and traveled throughout New England with his football team. He was well acquainted with the places that offered stunning views and good hiking trails, and he couldn't wait to share all of this with Julie. The itinerary he planned began in Vermont and had them heading north to Quebec City, then south to New Hampshire, and ended in Maine.

"What if I can't hike for long periods of time?" Julie said, expressing her fears.

Kevin just laughed. "You're even worrying about vacation! You'll do what you can. Besides, your stamina has greatly improved since I've been making you climb stairs."

"I just don't want to ruin your fun hiking," she admitted in a shy voice.

He shook his head. "Go on, Honey, you could never ruin my fun. I've hiked enough in my life. This is for us to enjoy and my watching you experience the thrill of being out in nature," he added proudly.

Kevin was like a giant eraser, Julie mused. He blotted out her fears. She couldn't believe how lucky she was to have a handsome, bright, athletic, strong, gentle man in her life. She looked at him and beamed with admiration.

"What are you looking at?" he grinned.

"I admire you," she whispered.

He stared at her long and hard. "You mean the world to me. I'm growing in so many ways because you're in my life."

She laughed. "Let's see if you feel that way after being on the road with me for two weeks!"

They started out, aiming for Manchester, Vermont. The drive took them through hilly green countryside that was dotted with white churches. Stopping for a break, they sat in the fresh air and enjoyed donuts and coffee beneath blue skies and billowy clouds. Everything having to do with Brooklyn, medical school and the dorm was now far away, and there was nothing here to remind them of that life. Gradually adjusting their pace to the pressure-free days that lay ahead, they got back in the car and continued their journey.

When they arrived in the quintessential New England town of Manchester, they checked into a quaint inn on a side street. Leaving their bags in the room, they went out to explore. Manchester's central village green, which had not really changed since the town's early days, offered a peaceful vista of wide-open space surrounded by small shops and restaurants. Julie and Kevin walked hand in hand through novelty stores full of candles, ornaments, knickknacks, books and cards. They bought fishermen's sweaters in one shop and Vermont cheddar and wine in another. Later that day, they rented a rowboat and went out on the lake, and while Kevin rowed them along the surface of the still, glassy water, Julie served him cheese and crackers and a paper cup of Chardonnay. Kevin was definitely in his element. Julie looked with wonder at his muscles as he rowed the boat and felt herself flush with excitement as she imagined the evening ahead.

Her romantic fantasy was fulfilled later as they made love on the flowered sheets of a queen-size bed. Kevin devoured her until her head spun and then placed her on top of him. He gazed lovingly into her eyes while gently rocking her back and forth, then gasped and shouted her name in his moment of gratification. With so much fresh air, physical pleasure and soft quilts, they slept soundly and awoke to another beautiful day.

In the morning, they walked through a meadow and appreciated the landscape, which reminded Julie of those in some of her favorite Impressionist paintings. Lunch was cheddar cheese and ham sandwiches followed by Ben & Jerry's ice cream cones in town. Satisfied with their visit to Manchester, they decided to start their drive north. The next stop was Stowe, a ski resort in winter and summer getaway in the warmer months. The mountains were steeper there, so Kevin made sure to choose gentler hiking trails that would be less taxing for Julie. They put in a full three hours exploring the paths through the woods and enjoying the scenery before settling into a bed and breakfast for the night. Totally satisfied, but spent from their mountain adventure, they collapsed on the bed and slept deeply.

The high point of the trip would be the next destination: Quebec City. Julie was a true Francophile who had always loved the language, music, fashion and food of France, so Quebec City, known as "Little Paris," was perfect for a romantic interlude. They entered Old Quebec and stumbled upon a small bed and breakfast that looked inviting. They checked in quickly and went out meandering the narrow cobblestone streets. The small 19th-century houses with their slanting roofs and dormers had facades of sturdy grey stone that were brightened up with colorful doorways and baskets of flowers. Uniquely shaped signs in Old World style jutted out over the entrances of shops, cafés and bars.

The two travelers decided to have their first meal in a cozy bistro. There, at a corner table, they started with French onion soup and red wine, followed by duck à l'orange and a small portion of chicken and French fries. So much for their shoestring budget. This jewel of a town was a place to splurge.

When they finished dinner, it was not quite dark outside. In the mild evening air, they strolled the Old Quebec Funicular walkway that overlooked the Saint Lawrence River. They paused now and again to share deep, ardent kisses, and Julie felt herself swoon as Kevin clasped her in his strong, gentle arms. As the evening turned to night, they stopped into a jazz club and sat for two hours sipping wine and listening to a saxophone blending with the rhythmic jolts of horns and drums. It had been a day filled with exquisite food, stimulating sights and sounds and enduring images of beauty.

The next day, when they explored the center of town,

they went into the historic church, Notre-Dame-des-Victoires. Kevin kneeled in the pew and pulled Julie down next to him.

"Pray with me, sweetie," he whispered. Julie was comfortable praying, and the building, be it a church or synagogue, made no difference. To her, God was the ultimate source of strength and love, and religions, she felt, were like the individual colors of one magnificent rainbow.

For Kevin, the more nature, the better. He never tired of seeing the grandeur of mountains, rivers and forests. And so they had to see the waterfalls of Sainte-Anne-de-Beaupré and walk over the extension bridge that spanned the churning waters below.

Then back in town, they ended their full day of sightseeing at another bistro for more onion soup and chicken cordon bleu.

Later that night, as they lay in bed, Julie started re-reading Hemingway's *The Sun Also Rises,* a book she'd loved in high school. Kevin was reading his own copy of the same novel. Just as Kevin had taken Julie walking on mountain pathways, Julie wanted Kevin to read good literature and to be more aware of world politics.

"You can't just read the sports section of the paper," she gently chided. "You've gotten me to exercise, so now I have to expose you more to different facets of culture."

Kevin nodded in agreement. "I've always said we were a perfect pair. We each have something to offer, and we are learning from each other."

"And you are laid back, and I'm the chatty Nervous Nellie," she added.

Kevin laughed. "You're not as nervous as you think. Really, Julie, you're in medical school, which is pretty impressive! You have to give yourself more credit."

"Kevin," she continued, "It's not that I'm insecure. I like myself well enough. I'm just afraid of the world!"

"That's part of being a neurotic, raven-haired beauty," he winked. "I'm going to infuse confidence into you so you'll stop being a scaredy-cat!" He rolled over on top of her. "Are you ready for an infusion?"

She laughed lightly. "When am I not ready for an infusion?"

After three days in Quebec, they pointed the car toward New Hampshire's White Mountains. Kevin knew this region well, as he used to hike there with friends every year. Driving up to the cabin they had rented, they breathed in the clean scent of evergreens and took in the pleasant gurgling of a mountain stream that ran alongside the road.

The cabin was rustic, but clean and cozy. They dropped their suitcases on the bed and changed into shorts, T-shirts, hiking boots and thick socks. Kevin swung his camera over his neck, and they headed off to the hiking trail. Noticing the apprehensive expression on Julie's face, he smiled and said, "We will be doing easy hikes, I promise you."

"OK," she nodded, "I just don't want to cramp your style because I know you're accustomed to more challenging routes."

He shook his head. "I thought you understood. I can hike the advanced trails with my friends anytime. Right now this is about you and me."

Julie appreciated Kevin's ever-optimistic, upbeat spirit. He rarely complained about anything and always saw the glass half full. Even though his mother's alcoholism had had an impact on his childhood, he had grown up to be a confident, capable man who could accept life's challenges. Before Kevin, the men Julie had known were cynical and arrogant, and those men had worsened her feelings of insecurity. The refreshing change that Kevin brought to her life had been, at first, a novelty, but despite the time they had already invested in their relationship, that novelty, that delight, that wonder had not worn thin.

She liked to consider herself an optimist, but knew she had to fight against the tendency to worry about living in a dangerous world. She was aware that her view had been inherited from her mother and accepted that it would still take time and a lot of work to change it. Being with Kevin was having a positive effect on her, helping her to relax more and face the world with less trepidation.

They hiked easy to moderate trails in the White Mountains, and when Julie became winded, Kevin instructed her to take deep breaths. When she cried out that her fingers were tingling, he warmed her hands and had her drink water and slow down her pace. She chuckled when he took pictures of her climbing so that he could "brag" to his family and friends about how athletic she was.

At dinner over chicken sandwiches, fruit and beer, Kevin beamed and told Julie how proud he felt. "You're really pushing yourself out of your comfort zone," he complimented her. Then he fixed his gaze upon her and asked, "What made you push yourself out of your comfort zone to become a doctor? You told me how easy it would have been for you to be an English professor and educator, so I am guessing that you really do love a challenge."

She paused and replied slowly. "It was so many different things, Kev. First, I was surprised at how much I enjoyed the science courses and how well I did in them. Then there was the appealing idea of being a doctor who would help others. But to be honest, a huge part of my decision was wanting to please my father. I know I told you that he had an unfulfilled dream of becoming a doctor, so when Rick kind of pushed me to apply to medical school, I took up the challenge. I also liked the prestige. It was a good path to take, but frankly, it has been a tremendous sacrifice."

Always boosting Julie's ambitions, Kevin replied, "But you're doing it, Julie, and you do get satisfaction from helping people and gaining their respect. But, Julie, most important, we would not have met if not for med school."

"Well then, it was all worth it." She smiled demurely and snuggled into his lap.

The next place on their itinerary was Maine. Kevin said Acadia National Park was a special kind of paradise for nature lovers and a must-see. Set outside of Bar Harbor, Acadia was a park that offered numerous hiking trails, bike paths and scenic overlook spots. This was true rugged New England, with the salt air and jagged cliffs that plunged into the ocean. They chose a small hotel in Bar Harbor and poked around the tourist-friendly town for a day, where they sampled authentic Maine chowder and blueberry pie.

The next morning's plan was to take along lunch and snacks and hike a route that would include the Thunder Hole, where waves crashed against the rocks to create a dramatic spray of water. Having crossed the rocks, they built up a good appetite and settled down on a promontory jutting out into the ocean below. Julie was completely at peace sitting between Kevin's thighs, resting her back across his strong chest. They unwrapped their turkey and cheese sandwiches, which tasted great as they inhaled the fresh ocean air and took in the striking view along the horizon.

Taking a sip of lemonade, Julie commented, "You love this, don't you? And I can't believe how much this Brooklyn girl loves it too." She held his hands in hers and felt the sheer gratification of the place, the food and the good solid friendship they had created.

He kissed the back of her head. "Nature is always been my sanctuary, and when we have kids, I want to fully immerse them in the outdoors—hiking, skiing, biking, you name it."

Julie gasped. Kevin was picturing their future and putting it into words. She brought his hand up to her lips and softly kissed it. He understood the effect his words had had, and he reinforced them as he whispered, "I meant what I said." She turned her face toward him so she could receive his kisses.

They left Bar Harbor after three days and, en route back to New York, stopped off in the charming town of Camden, Maine. Emotionally, they were in a new place in their relationship. Kevin had discussed a future and told her he loved her, not only in bed, but throughout the day. She could never hear it enough.

Soon they would start the third year of medical school and cross the threshold to the next phase of their professional training and the next chapter of their love affair.

CHAPTER 13

On the first day of clinical rotation, Kevin and Julie donned their short white medical jackets and reported to the obstetrics and gynecology ward in Kings County Hospital. At some time in the future, when they would reach the status of attending physicians, they would wear the long white medical coats.

"Well," the attending addressed the eager third-year students, "it goes like this: you see one, you do one, and you teach one."

Julie took a deep breath and glanced at Kevin. She had some concerns about the new stage of their academic life but was confident that they would be a team no matter what. They entered the delivery room, where a young black woman was giving birth to a baby girl. Despite the mother's having shrieked in pain during the birth process, she smiled tenderly as the infant was placed in her arms. Kevin and Julie stared in awe as the doctor held the umbilical cord that protruded from the birth canal. Using a large surgical scissor, he cut the cord, and in seconds the baby was physically separated from her mother. Soon enough, the bloody remnants of the placenta, or afterbirth, were expelled. It was a miracle to watch, and there was no adequate way to describe the experience.

"OK," the delivery nurse signaled. "there's another delivery next door. You two go in there. Call us if you need help."

Julie squinted at Kevin. "Am I hearing right? Are we going to deliver this baby by ourselves?"

Kevin laughed lightly. "You heard what they said. Unless there's a problem, we are on our own."

Thank goodness Kevin is with me, she thought to herself. *I could never handle this myself.*

They stood side by side in the delivery room as a thirty-five-year-old Hispanic woman wailed in pain during heavy labor. On the stretcher beside her was her eighteen-year-old daughter writhing in labor with her first child. According to the midwife, the patient was fully dilated, and the baby's head was crowning in the birth canal. Kevin and Julie stared in amazement.

The two young students were about to perform their first delivery. The woman was wheeled into the delivery room, crying out at the top of her lungs, and within twenty minutes the baby's head began exiting the canal. Once the baby was delivered, Kevin carefully took hold of it, ensuring that he didn't drop the slimy, wet little newborn. Julie held onto the umbilical cord and, having just observed the doctor, clamped it and cut it as Kevin lay the baby on top of its mother.

There was a moment of silence, and then there were cries from both the baby and the mother. Julie looked up at Kevin to see that like her, he had tears in his eyes. There was nothing she had done in her life so far that compared with bringing a new life into the world. It was incredible.

"We did it, Kevin!" she said with relief as she smiled into his eyes. "We delivered our first baby!"

Kevin looked intently at her. "One day we will experience the joy of our own baby being born."

The next three deliveries were uneventful, and the

babies arrived without complications. But the fifth delivery was a challenge. The fetus was not progressing, and its heart rate was degrading. The mother's energy was depleted, and she could no longer push.

As instructed, Julie told the nurse to inform the attending physician. Within moments, the mother was prepped for an emergency C-section. Drapes were placed upon her as the anesthesiologist cupped a mask over her face. The woman was given a spinal block, and when it took effect, the surgeon carefully drew his scalpel across her abdomen. A short time later, he lifted a tiny wailing baby out of the uterus and placed it on a small table. Apgar scores were calculated to determine whether the newborn was thriving after the unexpected C-section.

On rounds that evening, Julie and Kevin checked on the new mothers, making sure that none of them was running a fever or had developed an infection or excessive bleeding. They were especially concerned about the woman who had the C-section.

As they walked from room to room with their clipboards, they were stopped by a nurse.

"Just look at you two!" she said. "I can see you're a pair and you're going to make such pretty babies together!"

Julie blushed as Kevin asked, "How do you know this?"

The West Indian nurse had an easy smile and a warm voice. "Doesn't take a genius to see that you two are stuck on each other like peanut butter and jelly."

It had been a very long first day in the obstetrics ward, but they felt they had acquired a voluminous amount of knowledge. As they were on call and sleeping in the residents' room, they collapsed on the bed with the beeper beside them. It was possible they'd be needed in the next few hours to deliver another baby. This shift would last until 5:00 p.m. the next day, totaling thirty-four hours.

Exhausted or not, Kevin pulled off his and Julie's scrubs and slid inside of her.

"Julie, I love you," he whispered as he orgasmed quickly. He rolled off her and fell asleep.

Julie laughed to herself. *Oh well, I didn't have to do anything. Let's just spread my legs. We're both so overtired, it's amazing he could get erect.* They slept for about an hour until the beeper went off because another baby was on the way. Jolted awake, they scrambled to pull on their scrubs and ran to the delivery room. Fortunately, it was an easy birth, and they caught a few hours of sleep until 7:00 a.m., when they had to do morning rounds.

The gynecology inpatient ward was filled with women admitted for surgical treatment of cervical or uterine cancer or for abortions. Unfortunately, some women decided to terminate their pregnancies as late as five to six months, as state law still permitted. It was horribly painful to witness such an abortion because the dead fetus had to be delivered. These tragedies were largely the result of the women having little education and lack of routine health care. Most of them had never had access to any care at all, which lead to delays of diagnoses and the need for more risky or complex surgical procedures.

The outpatient clinic offered basic, routine healthcare and treatment of venereal diseases such as gonorrhea and syphilis. It was rewarding to be part of a system whose goal was to treat women in desperate need of medical care. Julie and Kevin learned how to perform internal gynecological exams and obtain Pap smears. Once again, it was the lack of proper and timely medical care that led to severe cases of venereal disease with compromised outcomes. Patients who, if they had known the gravity of their conditions, could have been cured with simple injections of penicillin, ended up hospitalized with sepsis, which can be fatal. In the case of syphilis, they might develop heart problems or deterioration of their mental status.

Kings County had a large psychiatric inpatient ward, with many patients admitted because of an acute change in mental status or because they'd suffered a psychotic breakdown.

Some patients were severely mentally ill, schizophrenic or suffering from a drug-induced psychosis. Julie quickly learned the difference between psychosis and neurosis. Psychosis is characterized as a break from reality, in which patients can't separate fantasy from the real world. They might hear voices or imagine that they are a bird or Jesus Christ. Neurotic thinking, on the other hand, is characterized by a mood disorder like depression, excessive anxiety or obsessive thinking.

Julie found herself extremely interested in psychiatry. The study of the mind and human thought processes was fascinating. On her first day at the hospital, she was assigned to a patient admitted for drug-induced psychosis. She and the physician were on rounds when her patient started to kick in the air, karate-style. Julie was stunned, but the attending physician just calmly scanned the patient's chart.

"Oh, he does this all the time," she commented casually, while continuing to work on her progress notes.

Julie was terribly frightened. She feared that the patient would grab her or the doctor and hurt them. She meekly asked, "Are we safe here?"

The doctor laughed. "Of course. I'm holding a panic button. If it gets tough, I'll press it, and the guards will come."

If it gets tough? Julie thought to herself. *How much crazier can it get?* They left the room as two nurses entered to administer a sedative to the patient. *Poor soul,* Julie could not help thinking.

"Can he be successfully treated?" she murmured to the doctor.

The doctor paused and then in a matter-of-fact tone said, "Probably not. After taking so many drugs, his brain chemistry is permanently altered. That or he'll overdose or get murdered in a drug shootout." Julie stared at the physician. She seemed so emotionally removed from the situation. "Drugs do terrible things, and the ghetto is flooded with them. It's just the way it is," she added, sensing Julie's shock.

In the harsh and wretched world of the inpatient

psychiatric ward, Julie met with some patients who were not acutely psychotic from either drugs or schizophrenia. Many of them were severely depressed, and some were suicidal. Never before had she encountered people who had lost the will to live. The blank expressions on their faces, the disheveled hair and vacant stare said it all. Depression, whether it was intrinsic to the patient or brought on by external hardship or loss, was a dreadful disease. These patients, however, were often responsive to medication and also behavior modification and talk therapy.

Julie felt deep a sadness within her when she was assigned to the substance abuse ward. Watching a patient withdraw from drugs or alcohol, even with the help of sedatives, was wrenching. She was thankful that she never witnessed her father's withdrawal from alcohol. Nevertheless, it stirred up bad memories.

Many of the psychiatric outpatients were being treated for depression, anxiety and substance abuse, conditions that were not severe enough to warrant inpatient treatment. The prognosis for many of them was good, and their problems were treated with a combination of medication and counseling. These patients' cases were not as desperate or frightening to Julie as the far-gone cases had been. She could see that it might be uplifting to help a patient regain control of his or her mental health and lead a full life, not paralyzed by anxiety or weighed down by the emptiness of depression.

There were varied and diverse approaches to treating psychiatric diseases. Some clinicians believed strictly and exclusively in drug therapy, dismissing any talk therapy. Others were averse to drugs other than for psychosis and felt patients needed to change their thought processes. But most psychiatrists believed in a combination of medication and therapy. Julie saw that treating mental illness was not as straightforward as treating an infectious disease or removing a gallbladder. It was much more difficult to quantify the extent of a patient's condition, and there wasn't standard testing or treatment protocols. She was grateful to see that at least psychiatric medicine had progressed since the days when mental illness was attributed to possession by the devil or innate evil. True, many of the patients were unkempt, and some had to be restrained and put in quiet rooms, but they were treated with compassion by the doctors and nursing staff.

The next rotation was surgery, which would prove to be rough and taxing. Julie was miserable from the first moment, for myriad reasons: the rounds started at 6:00 a.m., the mask was uncomfortable, the surgeons were harsh and the operating room made her feel tense. Kevin, on the other hand, was happy as could be. He had always loved fixing things, doing carpentry and tinkering with old cars, and he found surgery to be like a more sophisticated level of those kinds of activities. He didn't mind the early morning rounds and wasn't ill at ease with the rough manner of the residents, so surgery was right up his alley.

One morning, as they drove to the community hospital to start their surgical rotation on the cardiovascular unit, Julie lamented, "Kevin, don't you hate the stupid mask?" He laughed in his slow, easy way. "Julie, there's not a chance in hell that you'll be a surgeon, so just get through this rotation." Everything with Kevin was balanced. He just kept his "grin and bear it" attitude.

Quickly changing into scrubs, they met with the rest of the surgical team. Julie observed that for some unknown reason, most of the heart surgeons were very tall, like Kevin, and next to them, she felt like Thumbelina. This did nothing for her confidence but did not impede her efforts. After rounds, in which they meticulously assessed each patient's vital signs and inspected the wounds from open heart surgery, they entered the operating room. It was cold and sterile, with huge, overhead crystal white lights. Each member of the team took his or her place at the table. The head surgeon was a southerner who loved operating to the sound of blasting, intrusive recordings of Tammy Wynette's heartfelt voice. But once in the operating theater, there was no escape from it.

The atmosphere was controlled chaos in which Julie and Kevin, whose only job was to hold a surgical instrument called a retractor, were basically observers. Open heart surgery involved placing a patient on a breathing machine and stopping the heart while the heart valve was replaced or the coronary arteries were repaired. Each cut of the surgeon's knife had to be precise and efficient, and time played a critical role.

After six hours in the operating room, they went home. Julie was mentally and physically exhausted, but Kevin was energized. So energized was he that he decided to go for a run on the treadmill. Julie fell dead asleep for an hour and then, somewhat refreshed, had dinner and spent two hours with her textbooks. The next day would not be any easier. They were due at the hospital at 6:00 a.m. and would not leave until 6:00 p.m. the following day. Hopefully they would get some sleep during the thirty-six-hour shift.

Somehow Julie survived the first surgical on-call, managing to get about four hours of sleep, but she felt stressed, strung out and miserable. *Only two more weeks of the cardiovascular surgery rotation*, she thought, *and then we'll be back in Kings County for the rest of the ten-week rotation.*

In the environment of a community hospital, hands-on experience was limited. The medical students were observing the surgeries and being questioned on rounds, and they were also helping the interns do the "scut work"—obtaining lab results, drawing blood, taking cultures and changing dressings on wounds. The situation would change, though, in Kings County Hospital, where students would be suturing wounds, draining abscesses, applying casts and assisting in surgery.

Julie was assigned to assist in an operation known as the Whipple, an extremely complex procedure to remove a cancerous growth. This kind of operation usually lasted about nine hours, with no break. Julie knew what she was in for and was willing to carry out her assignment, but at the start of the day she felt weak and warm. She made the mistake of telling the chief surgical resident that she wasn't feeling well.

He snapped at her, "Well, I guess you'll do anything to get out of this case!"

She stood stunned. "Dr. Hoffer," she replied almost tearfully, "I think I'm running a fever. I feel awful. I really need to go home."

"We all want different things," he retorted. "There's a carnival in Rio that I'd love to be at now, so scrub up. You're in the case."

There were six people surrounding the table: the surgeon, assistant surgeon, operating room nurse, anesthesiologist and the two medical students, all draped in sterile scrubs. The patient, who had been scrubbed with Betadine, was lying on his back, and green sterile drapes covered his body, leaving the abdomen exposed. The first incision was quick and meticulous. With the next few cuts, the abdominal cavity was open, and the two medical students held retractors to keep the area clear. Julie stared into the bloody opening as surrounding yellow globules of fat and white strings of fascia were pushed aside. As fast as dark red blood splattered from the area, it was mopped and cleared with sterile gauze and sponges.

The surgeon was approaching his target organ, the pancreas, like a dog hunting for a fox. Any oozing blood vessels in the path of the organ were tied off with sutures. To remove the cancerous tumor, a portion of the pancreas was going to be cut and the remaining part reattached to the small intestine.

This surgeon's choice of music was hard rock. The blaring noise blended with the sucking sounds of blood being cleared out of the abdominal cavity. It seemed like forever that the shining scissors and scalpels were cutting tissue and connecting blood vessels to one another. The bright light shone into the abdominal cavity, and the temperature in the room seemed to be steadily increasing. The surgeon was intermittently calm as he diligently performed his work, and then would curse and scream at the assistant surgeon, and at one point he even tossed a scissor across the room.

Julie was standing at the operating table with a retractor in her hand when the room suddenly appeared very dark. Within moments, she felt herself sway, blacked out and keeled over. When she came to, she saw the kind face of one of the Jamaican nurses.

"What happened?" she cried out, as she felt a cool compress being applied to her forehead.

The nurse peered into her eyes and gently said, "You fainted, my dear girl, and you're burning up."

"I'm so sorry," she whispered. "I caused a scene here."

"Oh, don't worry," she said, nodding towards Dr. Hoffer. "He didn't miss a beat. He just kept going. Now we have to get you home."

The nurse called a security guard, who accompanied Julie back to her dorm. Unable to do anything else, she lay in bed, shivered and slept. When Kevin came back that night, he brought soup from the cafeteria and fed her. "I guess surgery is not your deal," he said gently.

"I hate it," she replied weakly. "I'm counting the seconds."

At long last, the ten-week cardiovascular surgery rotation was completed. Kevin had found his calling as a surgeon, but Julie had yet to find hers.

Their next rotation was pediatrics at Kings County Hospital. There was a large inpatient service and very busy outpatient service in the clinics. This time, Julie was in her element, participating in the health care of adorable children who tugged at her heart.

The care of children in reasonably good health included routine visits, vaccinations, nutrition and safety counseling. Most of the patients were extremely poor and received government assistance, yet despite their difficulties, they were very good parents and appreciative of the care provided. Julie pondered how the cycle of poverty could ever end. Some of the mothers were very young, just teenagers who had gotten pregnant and were now busy taking care of their young children, having squandered their potential for education and decent jobs.

The in-service ward was for more serious issues. There was no oncology unit in the hospital, so Julie and Kevin did not treat children with cancer, but the ward was overflowing with young patients admitted for infections, asthma, surgical procedures, congenital diseases and trauma. At first it was difficult to see children who were so ill. Their large, sad eyes set in drawn faces conveyed fear and discomfort. The important mission was to get them well quickly and alleviate their pain as much as possible. Mercifully, most of the children did well with the treatments.

Julie read voraciously about pediatric disease and well-care of children and told Kevin she had now found her calling. She wanted to not only help sick children, but be intimately involved in preventive medicine, nutrition and education for them.

"I can see how much you love the children," he noted. "I can't wait for us to have our own." He had been talking a lot lately about their future together. She liked hearing him say, "We are an item."

When he said it yet again over burgers and fries one evening, she asked, "Are we?" projecting a casual and innocent air as her heart danced.

"Yes, we are. I think we're ready to get engaged after this third year, and we can get married in the fourth year. We don't even have to wait until after graduation."

Julie climbed onto his lap and kissed him. "We haven't even talked about where we will live or what will do about our different religions or how many kids we want," she said.

He smiled and added, "It doesn't matter, as long as we're together."

They took a break from dinner to jump into bed. Kevin was easy. It didn't matter to him if she was freshly showered or groomed.

"Kevin," she stopped him, "I didn't even clean up after work."

Never to be deterred, he noted, "Julie, I can't help it, I must have you. He ripped her scrubs off and as usual, he was rock hard. He held her gently as he moved inside of her. They orgasmed quickly. The release was good medicine after working the arduous shift.

Changing gears swiftly, they both finished dinner, took quick showers, put on bathrobes and sat down to study. Julie had always been assiduous about studying, but for Kevin this was a new way of life. He himself was amazed at how many hours he spent poring over textbooks and was thrilled with his grades and evaluations.

"You have made me into a real bookworm," he admitted.

"And you have made me semi-normal," she laughed.

The final rotation for that year was internal medicine. In many ways, it was considered the most difficult of all the clerkships. Obstetrics and gynecology, pediatrics, and psychiatry were not considered to be as in-depth or complicated fields. Surgery was the most technical and high-stress of medical practices, but the "Brainiacs" of the class were the internists. Julie was up for the challenge.

She and Kevin were assigned to Long Island College Hospital for the first part of the rotation and then to Kings County Hospital. Many of the patients were admitted for diabetes, cardiac disease and the resultant complications of renal/kidney disease and strokes. There was also a cluster of patients treated for infectious diseases, asthma and lung disease. It was a tame beginning, as the attending doctors had full control of all medical decisions. The students were merely an accessory to the patient care, responsible for checking lab results and starting intravenous drips.

This was not the case at Kings County. The students there worked alongside weary, overtaxed interns and residents.

It was chaotic and frenetic, and students were grilled constantly by the academic professors, who demanded differential diagnoses of an assortment of diseases.

Julie was drained and stressed. She was on a grueling schedule, being on call overnight and then performing at a demanding pace during the day. She grumbled to Kevin, "How are we going to read and do well on exams if we are so exhausted?"

Kevin shrugged. "We will do it. It's not like we're running out to parties or into the city."

"But Kev," she persisted, "this is considered a really important rotation. We must get A's."

"Stop wasting time worrying. We will stay in and study all of the time," he proclaimed.

On this rotation, the patients they worked with had complicated lives. They were poor and didn't get routine care or check-ups. Upon arrival at the emergency room, they were usually already very ill. A diabetic patient's blood sugar would be sky high, and the patient might be in diabetic coma. Many of them had kidney disease, failing eyesight or gangrenous feet. Patients with heart disease were already in heart failure or had suffered strokes. Some had infections accompanied by uncontrolled fevers or were in septic shock, fighting for their lives.

There was also a group of patients, many Haitian and gay, who had high fevers and enlarged lymph nodes. The attending doctors were baffled as to the origin of their condition. It was given the name GRID (gay-related immune deficiency). Young men were dying, unable to respond to standard medications. Recently, the group had expanded to include drug addicts of both sexes. In addition to the swollen lymph nodes, other symptoms presented, such as weakness, fever and purple lumps on face and extremities. This condition became known as Kaposi sarcoma, but it would be years until the final diagnosis of AIDS (acquired immune deficiency syndrome) would be recognized and named. It was a plague not just for gay men and drug addicts, but also for gay and straight people who had received unscreened blood transfusions and for people with Hepatitis C.

The wards at Kings County were dark, and the poorly lit patients' rooms reeked of urine and feces with an overlay of acrid, industrial-strength disinfectant. To serve in that ward was a nightmarish experience, and Julie could barely wait for it to be over.

Finally in August, the third year was complete. Julie and Kevin both got A's in medicine and surgery. Julie got an A in pediatrics and a B in ob/gyn. She was thrilled to have gotten only one B. Kevin got a B in pediatrics and in ob/gyn. They received almost identical grades and were ecstatic and ready for the fourth year of medical school.

CHAPTER 14

J ulie was in the fourth year of medical school, the easy year, as it was called, because students could choose electives that interested them. Julie knew that she was going to be a pediatrician, so she opted for courses in subspecialties such as emergency room, adolescent psychiatry, well-child health and nutrition, pediatric neurology and endocrinology. She was also slated for electives in radiology and dermatology. Kevin, on the other hand, wanted to be an orthopedic surgeon and signed on for four relevant electives that would broaden his knowledge.

The couple had decided to apply to residency programs in New York so that they would continue to be together. Over lunch at a local pizza parlor, they discussed their plans, which included getting married at the end of the year. Ideally, they would get an apartment close to the hospital and hoped they'd be interning together.

"Kevin, can you imagine how great it would be to do our internships at the same hospital? We could meet for lunch sometimes."

"I agree," he said, "but I'm thinking more of meeting for a quickie," and he winked at her.

"Or that too," she nodded.

Julie was really enjoying the electives, and in addition, her schedule was more humane, with hours from nine to five. Kevin's hours were longer, as he was doing a surgical rotation, but being Kevin, he didn't complain. Julie was glad to be done with the grueling, exhausting hours and shifts. Unlike Kevin, she had never found those schedules energizing. Now in a new stage of her education, her favorite elective was pediatric well-child care. Also gratifying, though emotionally challenging, was treating young patients with neurological and endocrinological diseases. Some of the children had incontrollable seizures or gait and balance disorders. There were young children who had Cushing's disease, caused by an imbalance of cortisone. Their backs had humps and their faces were abnormally wide, a condition known as "moon faces." There were children with diabetes who could not manage their blood sugar, rendering them prone to infections and putting them at risk for uncontrolled diabetes later in life.

Perhaps the most upsetting cases were those of children born with ambiguous genitalia, caused by a mistake of nature. A baby would be born genetically male with an XY chromosome, but because the body didn't recognize testosterone, the baby was born with a vagina instead of a penis. It may have been biologically male but appeared female, at least on the outside. Internally, though, the baby lacked ovaries, which meant it would never develop the ability to menstruate or conceive. The psychological toll on these children and their parents was heartbreaking.

Julie and Kevin took the radiology elective with Sara and Scott. Sara was brilliant in this field and decided it was going to be her career. Scott, like Kevin, was going to be an orthopedist, which made sense, since both guys had such a strong athletic bent. With their new schedules, the four friends would be able to spend more time together. This might have been a plus, except that it came along too late, as the nature of both relationships had evolved to an unforeseen place.

Sara and Julie were getting increasingly frustrated with the guys' constant emphasis on going to the gym.

"You know, Sara," Julie confided as they strolled through the mall one Saturday, "it's starting to sink in that Kevin is really very limited in his interests. Despite all our time together and everything we have shared, his scope has not widened beyond football, jogging and tinkering with old cars. He is reluctant to do anything other than that, and I can barely get him to go to a museum." She shook her head in annoyance. "When we first dated, he seemed so enthusiastic when it came to learning about art and music. He used to say that he loved how we brought out different sides of each other. You remember, I was the culture buff and he was the jock. I kept up my end of the bargain—I went to the gym, tried hiking and all that, but he's not looking to go to museums or even read the newspaper. He's getting kind of...I hate to say it: boring," she admitted in dismay.

"Oh, I get it," Sara concurred. "Scott is also only interested in going to the gym! He doesn't even want to take in a movie or go to the city."

Julie sighed out loud. "Sara, you won't believe this, but Kevin never heard of Chopin or Monet. I can't deal with this! How did I miss this? Am I exaggerating the importance?" she asked, dunking her biscotto.

"Julie, what I think is that we were like ostriches with our heads in the sand. We were so busy studying that we were happy when the guys worked out and left us alone. But now that we have time again, we want real companions."

Julie nodded again, but with sadness. "It seems all it would take for Kevin to be happy is to have a good meal, watch football with pretzels and beer, read about orthopedics, and work out. Truthfully, life has gotten pretty humdrum." She felt like a fountain of frustration, gushing full force, but it was good to say it out loud. "I keep telling myself that Kevin is so relaxed and good-natured, and we have fun in bed. But it's not enough. Every time I mention a good book or an artist or even current events, he is totally in the dark and not even curious to know more. And when I suggest he read something to expand his knowledge, he gets really annoyed," she complained.

Sara listened intently. "Hah! I'm not even getting as far as discussing anything! Scott is always prepping for a race, a marathon and now a triathlon! It's too much!" she exclaimed.

"Kevin is talking about getting engaged and married in June or even during our internship. I don't know about this." She widened her eyes. "I'm thinking you and I should take a step back and start dating some other men. Wow! I'm really confused."

"Look, there's no rush to get married if you're still uncertain," Sara added.

When Julie got back to her dorm room, a call came in from her sister. Elizabeth was sobbing so much that Julie could barely make out what she was saying.

"Elizabeth, slow down!" she said. "Tell me what's going on!"

"It's insane here," she blurted out. "I just found out that Billy has been having an affair with a law clerk!"

"What?" Julie shrieked. How could this be? Elizabeth and Billy were high school sweethearts and had been together forever. Julie couldn't believe that Billy would be unfaithful to her beautiful, devoted sister. "How do you know?" she quietly asked.

There was a long pause. "I got a phone call from the woman! I can't believe how much I trusted him. I feel so stupid!" She continued crying inconsolably, both from sadness and shock.

Julie was glad her sister had confided in her right away and found some words of support. "*You're* no fool, Elizabeth. You were there for him financially and emotionally when he was going through law school. You worked so hard, never missing a beat. *He's* the fool."

"He keeps saying that we grew apart, and he's confused about being married! He said maybe this is just a seven-year itch. Can you believe that??"

"Really not funny at all," Julie felt her cheeks flush with rage. "He becomes a lawyer while you work your tail off, and some kiss-ass law clerk probably tells him he is perfect because she has set her sights on having a lawyer."

"I didn't feel us growing apart!" Elizabeth cried in exasperation. "We ice skated, played tennis, loved going to the movies." She seemed to be trying to justify the marriage. "Can you imagine, he told me that *she* is a better skier than *I* am! Like that matters!"

"How would he know, anyway?" Julie asked.

"Because remember when he said he was going on a ski trip with the firm? Well, he really went with her alone," she said in a hushed voice.

"That dirtbag!" Julie hissed. "When he was studying nonstop, you could have said that he was boring, and *you* could have had an affair. What an ingrate!" At that moment, Julie despised Billy.

A thought flashed across her mind—first, about her father's indiscretion and now, Billy's lies and his affair. Maybe it was not uncommon. Maybe lots of men were dishonest. Did everyone find long-term relationships unexciting after a while? Even if they did, did they have to act upon their temporary dissatisfaction? Maybe she shouldn't be dissatisfied with Kevin. After all, he was consistently devoted and grounded and was definitely not a cheater. Billy, like her father, had a restless, irritable edge to him. They both seemed cynical much of the time. Come to think of it, Rick could be like that too. Julie had no idea to why Rick popped into her thoughts, but he always seemed to be hanging around the background of her mind.

Julie finished her conversation with Elizabeth, who was heading to their parents' house. She needed time away from

Billy. "Call me if you need to talk," Julie said. She felt bad for her sister. Where would her life go now?

That night, over dinner, Julie told Kevin what her sister had told her. He seemed surprised that Billy would not only cheat on Elizabeth, but that he would actually jeopardize the entire marriage, and he added that he would never be unfaithful to Julie. A month later, in the bleakness of January, Elizabeth and Billy separated. Billy, perhaps to justify his infidelity, continued to berate his wife and say that he was still confused about being married at all. For her own well-being, Elizabeth knew she had to get away from him and found herself an apartment in Forest Hills, Queens.

The schedule for the fourth year of medical school was quite easy, with routine hours. Julie had electives planned for dermatology, rheumatology and pediatric cardiology, and she planned to finish out the year in the pediatric emergency room.

Much as Julie felt that pediatrics was the right field for her, she found dermatology fascinating. It was a visual discipline and appealed to her love of art and attention to detail. One could look at a rash for a few moments and arrive at a diagnosis. She read about it constantly but set aside time on weekends for her beloved cultural pastimes. As Kevin seemed more intent on just working out and watching football, Julie went off on her own to enjoy these leisure activities. With each passing weekend, though, she felt herself getting more frustrated and resentful, and as her spirits waned, she began to lose interest in sex. It was impossible to ascertain what was going on with Kevin, as he was never one to express his feelings.

One February afternoon, as he sat watching the Super Bowl, she decided to confront the issue that had been palpably brewing between them.

"What's with you?" she asked.

"Will you shut up?" he barked. "I'm watching the game. Bad enough we are not at a Super Bowl party," he scoffed.

Julie was stunned. "Sorry, I have a bad cold. I told you to go to your brother's house."

"Yeah, right! My brother's house! Why aren't you sharing this with me?"

"Oh? Like how you share current events and the theater or museums with me?" she retorted. It was only one year ago that they were at a Super Bowl party, Julie cuddled into Kevin and cheering for his favorite team. Now they were fighting about going to a museum or watching football.

As everything came into focus, Julie realized that she couldn't imagine living the rest of her life with Kevin and his provincial attitudes. True, he was a hard worker with a very stable, kind disposition, but he had such limited interests. His latest idea of a perfect life was to move to a remote area of upstate New York and join a practice in Poughkeepsie or join one in western Connecticut.

"Are you kidding?" Julie asked. "There's not a Jew in the entire area! You know I love everything about city life," her voice rising with annoyance.

Kevin's jaw clenched. "Well, guess what! I don't want to live in a brownstone in Brooklyn where it's hot and dirty. I like the outdoors, or did you forget that?" he asked in an uncharacteristically sarcastic tone.

Julie was not going to escalate the argument. "Then we could get a country house in the Berkshires," she suggested, "and spend weekends in the mountains. I'd even be happy to live in the suburbs of Westchester, a place like Scarsdale, or Ardsley."

"Of course, any place where the Jews live," he muttered.

She looked at him, stunned. "Kevin, where is this coming from, this new aversion you're expressing? Didn't we agree we would raise our children in both the Jewish and Catholic faiths? You know, Judeo-Christian theology. The religions are not that different."

"Look, I've been thinking about it, and I don't ever want my son to have a bris."

"Kevin, you yourself are circumcised. It's a health issue."

He nodded his head emphatically. "Just my point. Health issue is totally different from religious ceremony. My son will not wear a yarmulke."

"So funny you say that," Julie shot back. "Your pope does."

Julie felt her throat tightening. She couldn't believe how Kevin was completely transforming before her eyes. Everything they'd discussed in their time together had totally evaporated, at least on his side. Suddenly they seemed to be city mouse and country mouse. Julie knew deep in her heart that Kevin had not been lying to her all along about his willingness to compromise on religious values, lifestyles or goals. He had been sincere at the time, but now, with graduation upon them, they were at the threshold of a new life. Now they had to seriously consider the importance of their persuasions, their vision of what their lives should be. As the current reality set in, it was clear that the differences between them were too great. It had been easy to fool themselves when their focus was on medical school, with little time for leisure, except for great sex. Back when the future loomed on the horizon as an unknown, they clung to each other like shipwrecked passengers grasping onto a common float for survival. But now they had the luxury of time to really think about their needs, and they found the abyss between them to be too great. The truth was surfacing, and Julie, terribly sad, knew the romance was ending.

Kevin and Julie applied for internship and residency at Montefiore Hospital in the Bronx. When March rolled around, they both received confirmation that they would be working there. As planned, Julie was going to do her residency in pediatrics, and Kevin would be doing his in orthopedic surgery. As they opened their envelopes and read the respective decisions, each of them grinned with satisfaction. Kevin, smiling tentatively, asked Julie where she was placed, and upon hearing the news, he kissed her cheek, not her lips. He then showed her his letter. Only one year ago they would be delirious with joy, but so much had changed since then.

Over in the other corner of the auditorium, Sara and Scott were experiencing a similar situation. Sara's request for a placement in radiology was granted. This was a fortunate outcome because Sara had a real gift for reading films and making quick diagnostic decisions. She was brilliant but insecure about her own powers of decision making, and knowing this, Julie had urged her to apply in that direction. Both women were pleased with the results. Scott, like Kevin, would be going in for orthopedic surgery, and, like Kevin and Julie, this couple would be together at the same hospital in New York.

As the four friends congratulated each other, Julie and Sara exchanged side glances. Once alone, Julie asked, "Are you happy that you'll be together?"

"Yes and no," Sara confessed. "He's really on my nerves lately. All he does is work out and swim."

Julie nodded. "Don't I know? All Kevin does is work out and play around with old cars up at his house. How did life get so small?"

"There's another problem. Scott keeps wearing a bigger cross around his neck each week."

Julie's eyes widened. "Same with Kevin! And he's lost his usual good attitude. He's sulking all the time. What's with that?"

"Yeah, Scott, too. I wonder if they are in cahoots. Looks like we are both headed for a breakup."

Julie looked directly into her best friend's eyes. "You're going to be a radiologist. I know you're going to marry a man about fifteen years older than you, and you're going to live in the city in a penthouse. For sure you're not going to be with Scott. Mark my words!"

"That sounds like a plan. What about you? Anything in the crystal ball?"

Julie thought for a moment. "I'll probably marry a surgeon, but it won't be Kevin. Let's see…we'll live in Park Slope or Brooklyn Heights, but we'll also have a country house. Maybe one or two kids, too."

April showers were at their peak the second week of the month. As Julie had expected, Elizabeth left Billy for good and filed for divorce. She was only twenty-nine years old. and it was still early enough for her to recreate her life. Everyone who knew her agreed that she deserved someone who adored and appreciated her and that she would not have difficulty finding that person.

Julie had moved in with her sister for the last year of medical school and would drive from Forest Hills to her electives at hospitals in Brooklyn and Queens. Elizabeth lent Julie her tiny sportscar, a Mercury Capri, which was perfect for city driving, as it was easy to park.

One dreary, wet weekend, despite their recent trend to drift from each other, Julie and Kevin had plans to meet up with friends to go to a dance club. Julie knew that the relationship was over but didn't have the strength to formally break up.

Kevin got to Forest Hills around 8:00 and found Julie dressed to the nines in a short black dress, fishnet stockings and black heels. She had applied her usual seductive touches: red nail polish, red lipstick and plenty of smoky eyeliner and mascara. But when she opened the door and looked at Kevin alluringly, all he said was, "You look pretty." At one time, this kind of scenario would have sent him straight into a state of arousal, but now it only produced lukewarm results.

Not sure what to do next, Julie paused and softly said, "Should we meet the friends or stay here?"

Kevin sat down on the bed. "I don't want to be here. Really, I don't."

"Why not? Can't we just have fun, even as friends? We have a trip planned for Mexico in May after graduation. What should we do?"

Never one to feel comfortable with confrontation, he seemed unsettled and awkward.

Irishman, Julie thought to herself. She leaned into him and he started kissing her hard on her mouth. He pulled her on top of him and began peeling her clothes off. She laughed quietly to herself and thought, *He can't resist me,* as he flipped her over onto her back and entered her fervently, coming quickly.

He rolled off of her and stared at the ceiling. "I'm going to leave now," he said.

"Are you freaking kidding me?" Julie shrieked. "Wham! Bam! Thank you, ma'am?"

"Now you know what it feels like to fuck with someone's head." Julie stared at him in disbelief. This was not like the Kevin she knew. "Yeah," he snapped. "You criticized me nonstop because I didn't like museums or classical music. You nagged me to read *The New York Times.* You got pissed when I watched football."

"Kevin," she gasped, "I was trying to make you well-rounded. I took your cue and begin to exercise because you wanted me to."

He was ready with his response. "But I *encouraged* you. I didn't put you down for being out of shape. You never really developed any interest in things that are important to me. Heck, you don't even know football rules! *Football!* The fucking most popular game in America!"

"Why did you not tell me I was hurting you? My intentions were good."

He held her tightly as he hissed, "Because Miss Perfect thought she could just say whatever she wanted and get away with it.

Julie knew she had lived through a scene like this once before. It was with Rick, when he'd come back into her life after their breakup. She remembered walking back to his apartment, where he had asked to watch her undress and fondle herself, and then he hit her with the hammer, telling her about the woman named Linda. She had told him he was cruel, and he attacked her with words: "You fought with me! You ruined us. You were so coddled by your parents and thought I'd kiss your ass." In this moment, Kevin seemed just as angry as Rick had been, just as vengeful, just as resentful.

"You know, Julie, I used to be a confident person until I spent enough time with you." Painful as it was, she listened intently as he rattled off comments she'd made during the past two years. "It's not within me to fight or defend myself," he said. "I thought you loved me."

"I did. I do. I just felt you wouldn't allow yourself to grow. It was frustrating. I never meant to hurt you," she continued, "but I wanted you to share my world, my interests."

Kevin narrowed his eyes. "Well, baby, go find yourself some intellectual who will impress you with his style, his money, his level of culture, his desire to live in Brooklyn Heights. But only time will tell if he loves you as much as I did." He stood up, walked out of the apartment and slammed the door shut. Julie lay motionless in bed, tears pouring down her cheeks. She felt alone and scared. Had she just made the biggest mistake of her life not appreciating Kevin? He was totally unintellectual, but did it matter?

She cried herself to sleep and woke to a rainy Monday morning feeling totally drained. She got into the Capri and started out for Kings County Hospital. When she reached the Brooklyn Queens Expressway, the rain was increasingly heavy, and the visibility was bad. Despite the hazardous conditions, the drivers of cars and trucks were in a terrible hurry, and the roadway was crowded and chaotic. Suddenly the car in front of hers jammed on its brakes. Julie stepped on her brakes and stopped quickly enough. There was a split-second of silence. And then a loud boom.

A crash thundered as a large truck rear-ended her little sportscar. Julie felt the car fly up and crash against the metal guardrail. She heard herself scream "Mom!" and then... nothing.

The ambulance crew arrived, pulling her out of the car, which had folded up like an accordion. She could barely speak, her knee was pulsating and her neck muscles were in a spasm. Blood trickled down her dress from the cuts on her hand as it had smashed against the steering wheel. She remembered little after the moment of impact.

"Where am I?" Julie cried out to the emergency room resident.

"This is Long Island College Hospital. You've been in a car accident," he said in a soothing voice as he cut her dress off of her.

She stared into his warm eyes, "Am I badly hurt?"

"You've been jostled around a bit," he offered quietly. "We're going to check you out, but I think you'll be just fine."

"Was I unconscious? I don't remember anything." Her mind was going haywire, imaging the worst of what might have happened.

The resident shook his head. "No, according to the ambulance crew you were fully awake, just very frightened, almost panicky."

When she was somewhat calmer, Julie called her sister. After hearing what happened, Elizabeth was amazed and grateful that Julie was alive. She reassured Julie that she would call their mother and break the news to her gently. In the interim, Bibi and Charles showed up at the hospital.

After a series of x-rays and blood tests, the orthopedic surgeon examined Julie and determined that nothing was broken, but she did have whiplash and was badly bruised. He suggested crutches and told her to rest, use ice packs and elevate her legs. He also gave her a soft collar for her neck. Her brother and Bibi brought her home to Brooklyn.

Lara had been distraught when she heard about the accident, but once Julie was home, Lara could see that there was no cause for alarm. She breathed a deep sigh of relief.

As dusk arrived, Julie, feeling wistful and fragile, looked out her bedroom window. Life, she once again realized, could so easily be shattered and ruined. She knew she was lucky to be alive. Hesitantly, she called Kevin at his apartment. "Kevin," she murmured quietly, "I've been in a car accident."

"Are you OK?" She heard genuine concern in his voice.

"Sort of," she replied. "It happened this morning, A truck hit my car and I was taken by ambulance to the hospital."

"Julie," he gasped, "it's my fault! I upset you last night and just left you. Oh, my God! If anything had happened to you, if you hadn't survived, I'd find the driver and kill him. I'm coming over now."

Kevin arrived and went swiftly to Julie's room. He cradled her in his arms as she buried her head against his chest. "Julie, where are we?" he said sadly. "I love you, but we've got to face it—we're from two different worlds."

"I know," she softly agreed. "But you do love me, don't you, Kevin?'

"Of course, Jules, I will always love you. That's the truth."

They fell asleep to the sounds of Phil Collins's "One More Night" with its very heart-wrenching words: "…just give me one more night." And it was, indeed, their last night together.

◊   ◊   ◊

A few weeks later, when spring was in full bloom, the time came for the medical students to get their well-earned degrees. This chapter of life was over, and every graduate stood on the brink of a new adventure. They all clapped loudly as each of their classmates was called up to the stage to receive his or her diploma.

Standing in caps and gowns, Julie and Kevin smiled at the flashing cameras.

Although their once-solid relationship and their plans for the future had dissolved, Julie knew they would both be fine, but the feelings between them were bittersweet. They kissed tenderly and vowed to love each other as dear friends.

The month of June felt like the calm before the storm of internship. Knowing that her schedule was going to be hectic, Julie put aside some time to be with her sister to enjoy the kind of girl stuff they had always liked—shopping, dining, chatting, getting massages. They were living together now. All of Julie and Kevin's plans for doing their internships at the same hospital were for naught. She could never have predicted that they would not be together at this stage of their careers. But she was resolved about the way things had turned out and was happy to be with Elizabeth in the cozy one-bedroom apartment in Queens.

One evening they went out to dinner on Austin Street, the quaint shopping street in the center of Forest Hills. Julie was picking at her eggplant parmigiana and salad when she said, "You know, I thought I would be more upset over Kevin. But it seems I have just kind of moved on."

Elizabeth laughed. "When something is over, it's over. Look at me, I just regrouped after being married to Billy for seven years."

"But you've always been practical. You're like my friend Sara. She's done with Scott and is not looking back. I am the helpless, hopelessly romantic one in the bunch," she added, devouring a mouthful of eggplant.

Elizabeth nodded. "You couldn't have said it any better." She raised a glass to toast with Julie.

"Here's to new beginnings! Move forward!"

When they got home, Julie noticed the blinking light on the answering machine. She listened to the message and gasped. *Julie, I got your number from your mom. She said you were living with your sister. It's Rick, in case you don't recognize my voice. Call me if you want to. Congrats on finishing med school.*

"Elizabeth!" she cried, "did you hear this message?"

"I thought he was married! Don't call him back." Elizabeth said in a guarded voice.

"Are you kidding? I'm calling right now." She smiled as she reached for the phone and within seconds heard Rick's husky voice on the line.

"Hey, Julie, how are you?" he asked.

She felt a strange twinge in her stomach, hearing him speak. "I'm doing great, Rick. I graduated. I did it!"

"I know you did, sweetie. I heard you were living in Forest Hills. Maybe we can have lunch when I go to visit my folks in Queens. Maybe this Saturday? I'm going to be there."

"Sure," Julie exclaimed, unable to hide her excitement. They made a date, and she quickly got off the phone.

"Julie," Elizabeth said in a serious tone, "did you ask him if he is still married?"

"No, that would be awkward. I'll find out soon enough. Anyway, he's probably just curious as to how I am getting along, don't you think?"

"Uh-huh," Elizabeth said. "You're kind of slow on the uptake. He obviously wants to see you for a reason."

"Well, we shall see," Julie replied.

Saturday rolled around, and Julie put together an ensemble of tight blue jeans and a white lacy blouse. She carefully applied makeup and clipped on small gold hoop earrings. Slinging her pocketbook over her shoulder, she went out to the street to wait for Rick. As she saw him walking toward her, she felt a small nervous quiver within her.

Approaching her, he placed a kiss on her lips. A small kiss. They walked to a local restaurant, and Julie told Rick about the car accident and how her knees still hurt.

"I'll check it out later," he offered. He was staring at her as intently as he always had.

Over dinner, Julie chatted on mostly about medical school and told him she'd recently broken up with her boyfriend. She glanced down at his left hand, noting the wedding band. Finally, she just asked, "How is your marriage?"

"Fine. My wife is in Atlanta doing her residency. She

wanted to be in a great family medicine program, so she's down there."

"And you?" Julie cut in, "Will you move down there?"

"Well, I have to finish my surgical residency this year, but yeah, I think I'll look for opportunities in North Carolina or Kentucky. Great programs. Got to get out of New York. Sick of the competition here."

"But Rick, you're coming *out* of a great program! Why not take advantage of New York? You love the culture and the vibe, don't you?"

He shook his head. "Nah, Julie, not anymore. There's going to be a revolution here. Things will change. Medicine will change. Better to be the big fish in a small pond."

Julie paused. She had always loved Rick, but his cynicism dismayed her. He always had an angry edge. Or was it insecurity? Like a rebel without a cause, Rick always seemed uncomfortable in his skin. Julie had never wanted to leave New York. She loved the mixture of ethnicities and cultures, and certainly after her father's reversal of fortune, she was not going to gamble with security.

They left the restaurant and walked to her apartment. At the door, Julie nervously fumbled with the keys, anticipating what might happen once the two of them got inside. But it was not what she had thought. Rick guided her to the bedroom and gently pulled her onto the bed.

"Let's see that knee," he said, placing his hands on the bruised area.

"Oh, it hurts!" she groaned.

He slowly massaged her knee and looked in her eyes. For one moment, Julie thought he might lean over and kiss her, but she glanced down at the wedding band and felt a lump form in her throat. Rick was always a one-woman man, so what was he doing here with her? In fact, he had not talked about his wife at all. She stood up from the bed and walked to the stove.

"How about some tea or coffee, Rick? It'll only take a minute." She felt his eyes on her back.

"I should get going," he said.

She slowly walked him to the door. "You know, we like to go dancing with some friends I have. Maybe one night you'll want to join us?"

"Yes, I would like that," she said.

He flicked her gold hoop earring and said, "You always looked so pretty in gold." He kissed her quickly on her pursed mouth. "I'll call you, Julie. We'll go dancing."

For weeks, she waited for him to call, more out of curiosity than desire. He was a married man, and perhaps naively, she assumed he was happy that way. If not, he would have told her so. She thought about what she would do if he called her to go dancing. But it didn't matter, because he never did.

—— PART 5 ——

HAVING IT ALL

CHAPTER 15

The summer of 1980 was one of the hottest on record. Power failures were common, and heat waves emanated from the pavement. It was at this time that young Dr. Julie Kent begin her pediatric internship at Montefiore Hospital in the Bronx. She was incredibly proud and scared at the same time. She had heard it said that no one should get sick in July, as that was when the new interns were "thrown into the fire." Entering the hospital on July first, she hoped to be able to fulfill all the tasks required of her. Although medical students had four years of formal education and clerkships, a residency held new responsibilities and professional challenges.

Julie wore her brand-new white medical jacket over a crisp navy-and-white shirt and navy slacks. Many residents wore chunky athletic shoes, but Julie had chosen rubber-soled flats, which were both practical and stylish. With a stethoscope around her neck, a copy of *The Harriet Lane Handbook* (a manual of pediatric medicine) and a slew of index cards in her pocket, she took the elevator up to the pediatric wing.

As she walked down the corridor, Julie could hear children crying. She had already done multiple clinical rotations in pediatrics during medical school, but on this day, she felt totally unprepared to be attending to sick children. She kept reminding herself that she was an intern and that there would be senior residents and attending doctors present. But she also knew that she was going to be scrutinized and criticized.

Each intern was given a list of patients for whom they were responsible. On small, colored index cards, Julie had written each patient's name, age, date of admission and presumed diagnosis. Beneath that, she logged their temperature, pulse and critical laboratory counts for the day. Also listed were the patient's medications, which left space for proposed medical plans and treatments. The whole packet of cards was attached to a metal ring and was tucked into the pocket of her lab coat.

The hours were grueling. Interns on call were expected at the hospital at 8:00 a.m. and would work through the night until 5:00 the next afternoon. There were times when they could sleep in between patient admissions or after taking care of patients who'd already been admitted. But on some shifts, there was absolutely no time to sleep. Residents had to draw blood from the patients, label the specimens and deliver them to the laboratory at all hours of the day and night. At this time before the computer age, interns had to go to the laboratory and manually look up the results. The lab could be a ten-minute walk through the long corridors, which is why this task was called "scut work."

Pediatric patients were often brought to the emergency room in the wee hours of the morning. It was not unusual for a panicky parent to bring a barely breathing child in at 3:00 a.m. One could not help but think, *What was going on until 3:00 a.m.?* It would be years later, when Julie became a mother, that she would understand how much more terrifying everything seems in the middle of the night.

Some children were taken to the emergency room after having fallen out of tenement windows. The windows of the old Bronx buildings had no railings and were frequently left open because of the oppressive heat in the city. Miraculously, some of these young accident victims survived, albeit with multiple broken bones. Car crashes were also common on the hot summer nights. An accident victim brought into the emergency room would be designated "MVA DOA," which "meant motor vehicle accident, child dead on arrival." Again miraculously, some children could to be shocked back to life.

Montefiore Hospital was part of a University Hospital Center where children with every serious disease were admitted. Tragically, there was a particularly large number of cases of pediatric malignancies. Cancer in adults was terribly upsetting, but in a child, it was devastating. Yet these young children handled it with aplomb. Little heroes, they were. Unlike many of the adult patients who had severe chronic conditions and diseases, most of the children with acute illnesses could be cured. It was rewarding to see a child recover from a serious illness such as pneumonia, and it was a great moment when they were well enough to be discharged.

There were specialty clinics for various diseases. An intern could be assigned to the cardiology clinic, and each day they would work with senior residents who were doctors in training with more experience. All the interns and residents were supervised by attending physicians who were full-time academics. These doctors were very bright and dedicated not only to patient care, but also to research and lecturing. Thus, the schedule was extremely varied for an intern. They could be assigned to the inpatient hospital ward or emergency room or scheduled for a daily rotation in a well-child or specialty clinic.

The drama, bloodshed and split-second decision-making in the ER contrasted sharply with Julie's experience in well-child care. In this clinic, she performed routine exams on children and discussed preventive care, vaccinations and developmental issues with their parents. Engendering healthy habits in young families made Julie feel accomplished.

It was said that internship was the hardest year and the

first month of internship even harder. Julie loved her work, but the 90- to 100-hours-long week was physically, mentally and emotionally exhausting. Most other twenty-five- and twenty-six-year-old women were teaching nursing or had forty-hour-a-week jobs. They could have a social life, pursue hobbies and pamper themselves. Julie looked drained, was rail thin and had dark circles under her eyes. But her ambition and determination bolstered her stamina. She had to succeed. For years she had devoted herself to studying hard to get excellent grades and accomplish her goals.

There were many moments when Julie questioned why she had pursued the path of becoming a physician. *Am I smart enough for this?* she would ask herself. *And am I strong enough?* These kinds of haunting thoughts usually surfaced after she had been up all night. She'd feel irritable and full of self-doubt as a result of sleep deprivation. But there was an antidote for when the negative thinking reared its ugly head. She would tell herself, *If I got through my first year of medical school, I can do this.* She just needed to remind herself that she had come this far, and she *could* and *would* complete the journey.

Montefiore Hospital had a craniofacial plastic surgery and an ENT care center that was quite renowned, and children from all over the world were referred to it for reconstructive surgery. One patient, baby Rodriguez, with a severe cleft palate, changed Julie's life.

In August 1980, the second month of her internship, Julie was assigned to a general pediatric ward, where some of the patients had been through surgical procedures. She was sitting at a workstation, writing progress notes in her patients' charts, when she heard the young chief of ENT surgery say, "There you are. I've been looking for you."

"Huh?" she said, looking up from her notes.

"Funny! I thought you were a secretary," he laughed.

"Huh?" she responded again.

"Well, I thought you were far too pretty to be a doctor. Guess I was wrong," he said, as his sharp blue eyes met hers.

"Well, I guess you were wrong," she replied.

"You know, the first week of July, I was looking out the window and I saw you. I actually looked around for you. I never thought I'd find you here," he volunteered.

Julie was skeptical, as she could see that he was coming on to her.

"Which patient are you taking care of?" she asked.

"Baby Rodriguez. I repaired her cleft palate."

"Oh. I'm taking care of baby Rodriguez also," Julie said.

"You know, you have perfect features," he grinned.

"Huh?" It was the third time she'd answered this way.

"I'm the chief resident of ENT. We study facial proportions all the time. Your features are perfectly aligned with each other. The tip of your nose matches the tip of your chin."

Good God, she thought. *What a line! Not only do I not want to date a doctor, I'm not dating another surgeon.* She knew that surgeons in general had the reputation for being highly perfectionistic and arrogant, surpassed only by cardiovascular and neurosurgeons. She smiled sweetly. There was no sense offending him, as he was a much senior resident.

"Well, it was nice to meet you," she said, as she stood up and quickly left the desk.

Her colleague Sue, the second-year resident, caught up with her in the hallway. "So, you were talking to Doug Stone. Keep away from him. He can be a real dick," she warned Julie. "He threw a fit one day because I didn't follow his orders perfectly."

"What did you do wrong?" Julie asked.

"I made a mistake and gave a cleft palate repair patient red Jell-O. He freaked. He said he couldn't see if the baby was bleeding. Then he told me to follow the orders and said that I was incompetent," she seethed

"Oh dear, I'd better be careful," Julie commented.

The next day Julie was writing her notes when Doug Stone approached her workstation.

"Good morning," he said. "May I have a word with you in private?" She got up and followed him to a small nook that housed an ice machine.

"What is it that I did wrong?" she snapped. Sue's words rang in her head and she figured she'd go on the offensive. "I did not give the baby Rodriguez red Jell-O. I made sure to rinse out her mouth and clean the sutures. So what is the problem?"

"Absolutely nothing," he said. "I wanted to ask you out to dinner."

"Oh," she said, and took a moment to regroup her thoughts. "That would be lovely."

Julie spent Saturday afternoon preparing for her first date with Dr. Doug. She decided to wear a short black dress with black patent leather high heels. At 7:00 p.m. sharp, the doorbell rang, and she answered it. There was Doug, looking perfectly groomed. He was wearing white jeans and a pale blue tailored shirt with the sleeves rolled up. Everything was neatly pressed.

They got into his sporty Datsun and made some small talk. Julie was filling Doug in about growing up in Brooklyn and how she was a English literature major and then decided to become a doctor. He told her that he grew up in Manhattan and was the son of German-Jewish immigrants.

Hmmm, she thought to herself. *This is familiar territory, and it explains the perfectionism of a pressed outfit on a steamy August evening.* Doug told her that he went to Dartmouth College and the Perelman School of Medicine at the University of Pennsylvania and that he'd worked his way through both schools. Julie was impressed, as she had barely managed the medical school workload without having a job. She had worked only during the summers.

There was no question that Doug was an overachiever. Like many descendants of German Jews, he'd grown up in

Washington Heights, where immigrants had settled and
subsequently attained success in the United States. Doug's
family was middle class, devoid of luxuries but big on
ambition. Julie found herself surprised that she could be
attracted to another son of German-Jewish immigrants and
was wary that Doug might be controlling and arrogant, like
Rick. Her concern was not unwarranted. It was known that
German Jews absolutely considered themselves above Eastern
European Jews. They were more educated and had not lived in
small ghettos in Europe, as the Polish, Czech and Russian Jews
did. In America, they maintained that proud, exacting and
even somewhat snobbish attitude and passed it along to their
children. Julie took this into consideration as she approached
this new relationship.

Julie and Doug drove to a trendy, noisy Mexican
restaurant on the Upper East Side. Doug took charge of the
food and drink choices.

"We will each have a margarita," he told the waitress,
"and bring some guacamole, and make it spicy." As was her
way, Julie didn't say that she preferred sangria and couldn't
tolerate spicy food.

She started the conversation. "How is work for you?"
she asked.

"No problem at all. I just do what I have to do,"
he stated, exhibiting an air of confidence that Julie found
intoxicating. He did not ask her how work was for her but,
rather, went ahead and ordered their dinner: chicken fajitas,
beef enchiladas, fish tacos and another round of margaritas.
When the food arrived, he ate everything with great gusto and
did not notice Julie's cautious approach to the piquant dishes.
She managed to nibble on a few of the tidbits, but with little
food in her stomach, she felt the margaritas go straight to her
head.

When they finished dinner, Julie looked up and saw the
room spinning. She did not seem to mind. "I'm buzzed! Lucky
I don't have work tomorrow."

Doug drove her home and came into the apartment with her. She was still dizzy and plunked herself down on the couch. Doug, encouraged by Julie's acquiescent state, started kissing her and touching her breasts. She gently pushed his hands away.

"We need to go slowly," she advised him. He ignored her words, continuing to caress her, despite her efforts to discourage him.

"You're so pretty," he said.

"Thank you," she demurred, "but I need to know you a little more."

"You will!" he promised with confidence. He did not insist on going any further but simply gave her a kiss and left. Later that night, Julie lay in bed and stared at the ceiling. *What am I getting myself into?* she mused.

When Monday morning rolled around, Julie hummed to herself as she recollected her date with Doug. She got dressed for work, all the while reviewing how that night had unfolded. It was not what she had anticipated. It had all happened a bit soon, perhaps, but there were no regrets. She looked approvingly at her reflection in the mirror, where there stood a pretty young woman in a red cotton blouse and black slacks. It was still important to her to look attractive, even in the obscurity of the hospital wards.

As she entered the neonatal ICU, it was clear that she was in for a rough ride. A nurse handed her scrubs, winked and said, "Darling, you will need these." Around the room nestled in bassinets were premature babies, some born at twenty-four weeks of the normal forty-week gestation period. Most of them were sick, having been born to crack-addicted mothers. Nurses would swaddle them in blankets and hold them tightly in their arms during withdrawal. Some babies, barely the size of a hand, had tubes emanating from their little limbs and plastic tubes down their throats. Each baby was hooked up to an IV apparatus containing electrolytes and medications to sustain them as cardiac monitors recorded their heart functions. Watching them struggle to survive was heartbreaking.

Three babies with critical problems were assigned to Julie. One, born to a mother with gestational diabetes, weighed more than twelve pounds and had an electrolyte imbalance. The second was born to an HIV-infected, crack-addicted mother. The third, born at twenty-five weeks, had underdeveloped lungs and was struggling to breathe. The parents were a loving couple who had tried to conceive a baby for five years. The situation was devastating for them.

Night call in the neonatal unit was another scene altogether. An intern was left in charge of all the newborns, and a senior resident was there to discuss cases. Blood samples had to be drawn constantly from tiny babies' threadlike veins, and sometimes a sharp lancet was used to draw blood from the heel. Try as she might, Julie could not get the hang of inserting the IV into a baby's vein. Tears cascaded down her face as she patiently kept re-sticking the infant. Then, to her relief, came the voice of Doug Stone.

"Here, let me help you," he said in a relaxed, capable tone.

"Oh, my goodness, I can't get this," she tearfully confessed.

Doug took the IV and, in seconds, inserted it and taped it to the baby's hand.

"You owe me another date!" he laughed. "How about this weekend?"

"Great! I'm off Friday night and not on call till Sunday," she answered.

"Sounds good. I'll pick you up at your place at 7:30."

Doug showed up that night to find Julie in a short purple dress and gold sandals. Always glamorous, she had applied eyeliner, mascara and red lipstick. She was not sure of the effect this would have on Doug but felt sexy and alluring. Doug drove them to Chioki, a swanky Japanese restaurant decorated in black and red lacquer. On one wall, a huge aquarium filled with glistening tropical fish lent an element of mystery and romance to the softly-lit room.

Doug ordered a vodka orange juice for himself and a white Russian for Julie. Having barely eaten all day, Julie felt the rum and Kahlua produce in her a pleasant lightheadedness. Doug was talking about his day at work, but she barely heard him. Any inhibitions she may have had melted away as she slowly slid her foot up his leg, reaching his groin. He stiffened beneath her foot as she circled his crotch with her toes.

Then came the food, pungent and tangy: shrimp with peanut sauce, steamed pork dumplings and wok chicken with steamed broccoli, peppers and plum sauce. They devoured the dishes, and then each had another drink. When Julie stood up from the table, she could barely walk. Doug held her arm tightly as they left the restaurant. He drove her home to Forest Hills, and once inside, they replayed the scene from the first date. His hands were everywhere as he kissed her long and hard. When, predictably, he unzipped her dress and slipped his hands under her bra, she did not resist.

"No wonder you can start IVs so easily," she laughed. "Your hands are lightning quick." Julie felt as though she was nineteen, lying under the trees in Central Park. It was so good to be excited again. But despite her deliberately playful and provocative behavior, Julie heard something tell her that she was going too fast. So when Doug started running his caressing fingers up her thigh, she firmly grasped his hand. "No, not yet," she said. Doug did not protest, but he knew it was only a matter of time before he would have her.

A week later, Doug asked Julie to accompany him to a surgery dinner at Stella's, a restaurant in the Bronx. After her shift, she went to the on-call room and changed into a tight red dress with white, high-heeled pumps. She applied her usual seductive makeup and lip gloss. Although she was tired, with youth and natural beauty on her side, she looked hot. She met Doug outside the hospital.

"Get your car and follow me to the restaurant," he instructed.

At the gathering, Julie mingled with the residents, sipped white wine and nibbled pizza wedges. Doug was busy circulating. Julie did not know what he had planned for the rest of the evening or even why he had invited her. After an hour, he nudged her and said they should leave. She drove behind him up to his place in Riverdale.

Doug's apartment was a typical well-off bachelor's pad, immaculately done in tones of soft gray. The only touches of color were in the modern art posters that adorned the few walls not covered in smoky mirrors. The gray carpet matched exactly with the sofa, which was artfully strewn with zebra-skin pillows. It was all very masculine, confident and understated.

Doug opened a bottle of white wine, and they settled onto the couch.

"This place is really pretty," Julie said between sips.

"Thanks. I built this couch myself."

"Really?" she said in surprise.

"Yes. I grew up somewhat poor, so I learned to do everything myself."

"Really?" she said again. "I grew up so sheltered. I never even learned how to cook."

"Well, I'll make you dinner. My mother worked from the time I was eight years old. She wasn't exactly a traditional woman. I was the one to prepare dinner for the family."

"What? You actually turned on the oven?"

"No big deal," Doug responded. "Mom would give me directions over the phone. It made me very independent," he said with pride.

Julie didn't know whether a childhood filled with that level of responsibility was good or bad. Doug may have learned to be extremely capable, but hadn't he been robbed of his carefree years? She considered briefly her young life with her own doting parents. Was she better off than Doug?

He poured two more glasses of wine.

"Doug," she whispered, "I think I'm drunk. I'll stay right here tonight," she said, patting the couch.

"No, I'll make you a strong coffee. You're better at home," he said.

"Oh, no! Right here I'll sleep!" Again, she patted the couch.

"OK, if you want to. Let me at least go get some milk and juice for the morning," he said, scooping up change from the kitchen drawer. He left the apartment for about twenty minutes and came back with a bag of essentials for breakfast.

"You know, I agree. It's too dangerous for you to drive. Stay here tonight." He led her into a small bedroom, where she promptly collapsed in a state of pleasant intoxication. Years later, she learned that Doug's hesitancy with her staying over was because he had not yet totally broken with his former girlfriend. When he went to get "juice" he was also calling her to say that he was going to sleep early.

Doug started kissing her over and over, pulling her closer to him. She was aroused and yielding, yet a part of her said that it was their third date and way too soon for sex. But she reasoned, *To heck with the moral principles! I am an overworked intern!* She was hopelessly attracted to the self-possessed young doctor who had come at a time when she was lonely. And so she let go of all restrictions, mental and physical. Within minutes, the pleasure flowed, peaked and ebbed, though she was not conscious enough to fully enjoy it.

In the morning Doug gently woke her with a tray of juice and coffee.

"You'd better get up. You'll be late for work." Her head was spinning as she gulped down the coffee. "That was fun last night," he winked.

"Yes, it was." She couldn't remember all the details but knew it must have been great.

"I'll come visit you later in the ward," he promised.

Julie and Doug dated during the rest of the summer. He would visit her in the neonatal unit, helping her start the IVs on the babies and sometimes reviewed her notes. She was always relieved when he appeared, as he seemed to know everything about everything. Doug was truly a brilliant young doctor, and Julie appreciated his vote of confidence in her. As a result of his tutelage, she was more assured of her tactical and diagnostic skills.

Summer came to an end, and in September Julie was assigned to the emergency room rotation. During the day, children were brought in for asthma attacks, diarrhea, vomiting, strep throat and lacerations from accidents. Julie found that she was becoming adept at managing children's illnesses, learning the dosages of antibiotics required to treat infections. She learned how to perform spinal taps on children to rule out meningitis and how to suture a laceration. By now she could start an IV within seconds and was able to generate the diagnosis to determine a medical problem.

On weekdays she would return to Doug's apartment, tired and exhausted, and he would have dinner ready. The food was simple but beautifully prepared: chicken cutlets with steamed vegetables, or shrimp and chicken with broccoli and cashews tossed in a wok. Occasionally he would broil chops or steak. No matter what he made, Julie relished it. Then, relaxed and satisfied, they would retreat to the bedroom for a night of lovemaking.

On those nights when she had to be in the ER, she would call Doug to check in and say good night. Hearing his voice was a comfort, particularly on the evening weekend shift, when the ER was overflowing with young asthma victims or children running dangerously high fevers. There was always a senior resident present, but in a busy surgical ER, the intern had to make quick decisions and act on them right away.

Julie and Doug fell into a routine of spending weekends off with Doug's friends. One of them had a thirty-foot powerboat docked at a marina in Mamaroneck and would take the group out to enjoy the mild, early autumn days. One Sunday afternoon, Julie and Doug took the boat out by themselves and went on the East River, under the Throgs Neck Bridge to the Long Island Sound. It was thrilling, romantic and refreshing.

Julie, quite impressed, asked, "How long have you been boating?"

Doug grinned. "I never did this before. I watched a captain once or twice in the Bahamas."

"Wow, you really can do everything!" Julie exclaimed.

"*You can do anything you put your mind to*, is my motto!" he said proudly.

Julie could not argue with that. Doug's life was certainly a testament to his words.

On a rainy Sunday, for a change of pace they went to the Metropolitan Museum of Art. Julie was happy to be back in one of her favorite settings with some of her best-loved works. They walked through the Impressionist wing, slowly taking in the masterpieces.

"Do you know what Impressionism is?" she asked Doug.

"Of course. The real meaning of Impressionism is 'the playing of light in the paintings.' There are early Impressionist painters, Manet in France and Mary Cassatt in America. Notice how the images in their pieces are not discrete but blurred."

It was like a dream come true to be with someone so well-versed in this field. Julie was used to being on the *explaining* end rather than on the *learning* end.

"What about Monet?" she asked.

"Monet painted after Manet. Come look at how he gives an illusion of light in the garden and the sun setting through the fog over the Houses of Parliament. There's even more blurring of the images and more play of the light." Julie was in awe.

After the museum visit, they found a small French bistro and had a meal of onion soup, duck breast and red wine. Julie knew Doug was deferring to her taste for quiet, romantic restaurants, as he preferred loud, lively places and going out in groups. She wondered if that preference came from a desire to avoid real intimacy. But then she acknowledged to herself that he was able to spend time alone with her and appeared to enjoy it.

Julie liked the time they spent together before going out to meet the friends. Doug would start off the evening with Champagne, caviar and Frank Sinatra. In the small living room, he would dance with her to her favorite Sinatra song, "Witchcraft." Then they would head downtown to meet up with the group and go clubbing, dancing for hours. Julie found his friends to be wild with their heavy drinking and snorting of cocaine in clubs that were crowded and filled with blasting music. She tolerated it, knowing that afterwards they would return to the apartment totally exhilarated and would make love intensely.

Doug was highly sexed and could have strong, pumping intercourse for an hour. He had to have full control of the choice of position and never spoke while making love. Not a word, just intense movement. Julie could not help but compare him to Rick and Kevin, who emitted a steady stream of words as they made love to her. Somehow, Doug's silent, serious approach excited Julie, yet at the same time made her feel safe, which was something she always craved.

Doug was quite a bundle of contradictions. He was an educated Ivy Leaguer, meticulous and perfectionistic with his work and personal space. An intellectual who could appreciate nature and the outdoors, he was also a party boy who liked drinking and clubbing into the wee hours. Julie valued the gentle, cerebral, caring side of him. As for the rest, the pace of life with Doug was getting a bit out of control. He did not understand that she was not nearly as high energy as he and needed to rest from her hectic schedule.

"Why can't we spend more time alone?" she complained one Saturday night as they headed out to meet friends at Ernie's, a trendy Upper West Side restaurant.

"We can be alone when we're old," he responded glibly. "Now it's time to party."

"But isn't it more romantic to be together, just the two of us?" she pleaded.

"We are a couple. That's romantic. Anyway, we do go to small intimate places sometimes, don't we?" The discussion began and ended there. It was no use arguing with Doug. To his mind, he was always right.

Julie had lived this scenario before and knew that in getting involved with Doug, she was taking a calculated risk. It was a delicate balance, being frustrated but willing to put up with the terms of the relationship because he made her feel secure. She tried to look at the plus side of a romance that did not exactly meet her criteria, telling herself that if not for Doug, she could never afford to go to fashionable, hip places. After all, she was still an intern. And Doug took care of everything from cleaning to cooking, leaving Julie to concern herself only with work and her personal needs. It certainly reminded her of her arrangement with Rick, who had looked after the details of their life so she could concentrate on school. It was a bargain she had struck willingly then and was doing the same thing now. Would the end result be any different?

Much as she rationalized all of this, Julie could not escape the fact that her romantic sensibility was not totally satisfied. *I'll change him to my ways,* she would tell herself. She still had not learned the painful truth that should have been clear to her by now: how the relationship is forged at the start is how it is going to be.

CHAPTER 16

October arrived, bringing the vibrant foliage that Julie loved. With autumn, she started her assignment in the hospital's well-care clinics. She was more than happy to be working with infants, toddlers, and youngsters up to age eighteen, making sure they had their routine health examinations, vaccinations and good nutrition. The schedule in the clinic was a nice, comfortable nine to five, with every third night on call. Those overnights were not so exhausting now because the workday schedule was not as stressful as before.

In an eight-hour day, Julie saw twenty patients, giving each one between twenty and thirty minutes. When she got home, she still had energy left over to enjoy dinner with Doug and even have some time to relax afterwards without immediately falling asleep. The years of training had been so arduous that by comparison, life was now extraordinarily easy.

Julie and Doug had been in a relationship for two months, with Julie dividing her time between her own apartment in Queens and Doug's apartment in Riverdale. The romance had grown fast and was quite intense, so a mere two months seemed longer and deeper. And as the relationship deepened, inevitably, Julie saw Doug's dark side emerge. Many of the traits that affected her negatively were those that reminded her of Rick's demanding nature. When Doug didn't get his way, he became petulant and unable to compromise. Julie found herself capitulating to his choices and needs more than she liked. He was also critical of Julie's lax standards for neatness when she stayed in his apartment. His meticulous habits were obsessive and to her mind, unnecessary.

Perhaps the most difficult trait for Julie to accept was Doug's constant pursuit of the adrenaline high, which made him impatient when *she* needed extra rest. She defended herself by saying, "You're German, a Virgo and an ENT surgeon, so of course you're a type-A personality! But I'm not, and I can't keep pace with you all the time!" This had no effect on Doug, but Julie expected that eventually he would try to meet her halfway.

In November, they took a mini-vacation to Coconut Grove, Florida, where they relaxed on the beach and went boating on the serene, warm waters. In the mild evening air, they dined at outdoor cafés, sipping margaritas and crunching spicy shrimp. Afterwards, they indulged in the local dessert, key lime pie. It was a much-needed respite from the demands of the medical world.

One evening, after watching *An Officer and a Gentleman*, they lingered over drinks and discussed the movie. Julie's tender mood was tinged with sadness because she was aware, ever more in this setting, that Doug had never told her he loved her. She decided to probe a bit.

"It's fun being away, and romantic, don't you think?" she asked. He did not respond. "You know," she continued, "what I've learned from work is that there are only a few things in life that matter: your health, your contribution to the world and love."

"What is love?" he answered with a note of dismissiveness.

His words hurt her. "Well, obviously after being with me for four months, you still don't know," she snapped.

"I just mean that love can come and go so easily," he said, in an effort to explain. "Is love a *feeling* or could it be great sex or just having fun?"

He was digging himself deeper with each word. Julie felt betrayed, not so much because he never actually *said* he loved her, but because she thought he *did* and simply would not say it. A lump settled in her throat, but she didn't want to show her dismay.

"Well, either you know what it is, or you just don't feel it," she offered.

He took her hand, which by now had gone stone cold, but still said nothing to mollify her feelings. She began to ponder if the origins of his attitude would be found in his upbringing. Would he be capable of really loving her? Doug saw the doubt in her eyes but did not speak.

Julie reflected how, despite all the pain her family had endured during her dad's spate of drinking, there had always been a solid base of love. It seemed to her that Doug had no inkling of this kind of love. They had never spoken in depth about his parents' marriage. Doug just said they were ill-suited, owing to his German-Jewish mother's perfectionistic standards. His American father was unable to meet his wife's emotional or intellectual expectations and, in time, she left him.

This limited profile of Doug's parents was enough to set Julie pondering whether Doug's arrogance and perfectionism, the traits he shared with his mother, would create unavoidable obstacles between them. She had trodden this ground before with Rick and knew its pitfalls. By entering into this arrangement, was she making a huge mistake?

"Julie, let it go," he insisted. "I meant nothing." She wanted to believe him, and clasping his hand tightly, she felt reassured. But that night, she did not sleep soundly. Her mind raced, and the tightness in her stomach and throat remained.

The next day, she was due to leave Florida because of her work schedule, but Doug was going to stay on for another few days. They drove to the airport, and as she opened the car door, he leaned over to kiss her goodbye.

"See you soon!" he said with a smile.

On the plane ride back to New York, Julie mulled over the events and conversations of the past few days. She created in her mind a checklist of Doug's qualities, good and bad. He was intelligent, cultured and accomplished. She loved asking him questions on any topic from medicine, to the arts, to politics, to how to cook a turkey. Undeniably, he had courage and energy, and she felt physically safe with him, enough to step outside her comfort zone. As a Brooklyn girl who could barely swim, she was pleased now to be able to enjoy sailing and powerboating. And when in the right mood, Doug was fun to be with. But emotionally, he was walled off and made himself completely invulnerable. He didn't like discussing or revealing his deepest fears or desires. He may have been a sexual animal with tremendous endurance, but he never held her tenderly or uttered an adoring word in bed. Ungenerous with hugs, he was, in fact, the least affectionate of all her lovers.

She had known better treatment. Rick and Kevin were much more physically engaging. They never seemed to get enough of her touch, scent or taste. Kevin's relaxed nature and his acceptance of her imperfections made life pleasant and easy. But, then, he was not very developed and left her bored. He was always late for everything and could be imprecise, yet, ironically, he expected to become a surgeon. Julie had to wonder how that would work out for him.

Then her thoughts turned to Rick. He was a fuss-budget, like Doug, but he was also affectionate and playful in bed. She felt like a sex kitten when he made love to her, always desirable, always cherished. But in in the light of day, he needed to escape the demons that plagued him and masked his insecurities by voicing cynicism and criticism of New York life and Jewish people. He exhibited quick anger and resented his own heritage when he should have been proud of it. His parents had been forced to flee Nazi Germany, yet he spoke like an anti-Semite. The paradoxes in his character had always been unsettling to Julie.

So now here she was, involved with someone who, to her mind, certainly had some shortcomings. *Maybe*, thought Julie, *I'll be able to change Doug and teach him how to be affectionate and tender.* It would be a challenge, but she wanted to embrace it. She was optimistic that with enough love, Doug could overcome his fear of intimacy.

As she came out of her deep train of thought, the plane landed. She caught a taxi to Forest Hills and got ready to settle back into her New York life. The next day, she resumed her work routine and relaxed in the evening, looking forward to Doug's return. That Friday night, when he was expected, she took a long bubble bath and poured herself a glass of wine. At 7:00, the phone rang.

"Oh, I missed you!" she exclaimed. "Did you miss me?"

"Yes," he said. "but I had a lot of fun going to clubs with some cool people I met at the hotel. I know how much you hate the noisy clubs! Anyway, what time are you coming over tonight?"

Julie paused. "I'll call you back in five minutes." She hung up and took a deep breath. *He had a lot of fun going to clubs.* She felt as if she had been slapped in the face. How clueless could the man be, actually telling her what a great time he had without her? *That's it*, she said aloud to herself, and she slowly dialed Doug's number.

"You know what?" she started, in a soft voice, "I'm not coming over tonight. In fact, I'm not coming over at all. I'm disappointed that you don't know what love is. I'm sad to hear that you had a great time in Florida after I left. And you know what else? I'm sick of hearing about your time with friends at the gym when I'm on call the hospital. Furthermore, I have had enough of running around with you and your friends on weekends, watching them snort cocaine on their coffee table. We could be going to quiet, cozy restaurants, just the two of us, and building our relationship. Maybe all of this activity with groups of people is a way to shield you from intimacy. I don't know. What I *do* know is that you're brilliant and exciting and can be fun. But Doug, you're a boy, and I'm ready for a man! A *grown* man." She could not believe she had the presence of mind to deliver this monologue. When she finished, there was a moment silence.

"Please, Julie," Doug pleaded, "let me come over and talk."

"I'm not sure," she said. "I need to be alone and think about this."

About an hour later the buzzer of the apartment sounded. She opened the door to see Doug, who was holding a huge bouquet of roses, daisies and lilacs.

"These are for you," he said in a tone of repentance. "I am an ass, and I am so sorry. I have not been showing you that you really do mean the world to me."

Julie wondered if he had rehearsed these words on the drive to Queens. It could not have been easy for him. Her dark eyes glistened with gratitude as she took his words to be the long-awaited declaration of love. She put her arms around Doug's neck and kissed him. Relieved by Julie's acceptance of his apology, Doug put the flowers on the coffee table and kissed her with a new and perceptible tenderness. A rhythmic patter of a rain shower on the windowpane made the room feel like a safe haven where the two of them were embracing. Julie's anger evaporated, and she welcomed Doug's caresses.

"I'm happy you came by," she said.

Doug, clearly contrite, said, "I'm happy you opened the door for me." For the moment, peace had returned.

CHAPTER 17

By the time the first year of internship was halfway completed, Julie was ecstatic and confident. She knew for certain that she was well on her way to becoming a doctor.

But she had a dilemma. She enjoyed working with children, but she also missed seeing adult patients. To create more balance in her work life, she considered completing her pediatric residency and then going on to do a dermatology residency so that she could be double-boarded in both disciplines.

"What do you think I should do?" she asked Doug one night over dinner. She knew he was able to see things from a practical standpoint. His views were useful because they offset Julie's tendency to make decisions based on emotions.

"If were up to me, I would complete the pediatric residency and be double- boarded. It would give you access to a greater number of patients, and you'd be more credentialed for private practice." Doug was a big believer in private practice. He was almost finished with his residency in ENT and planned to enter a surgical practice with a colleague. Julie didn't see herself going that route.

Julie's conflict about doing another year of training arose from her thoughts about marriage and having a family. She didn't want to bring up the notion of engagement just yet, so instead she attributed her ambivalence to being undecided about her specialty.

"Well," she said, "I don't know if I want to do an extra year of residency. After all, how can I be sure I want to specialize in pediatric dermatology?"

"Because, I just told you—it further credentials you when you go into private practice."

"But I may want to just work in a clinic," she stated.

"That's ridiculous!" Doug snapped. "You did all this training, and you should earn good money for it." Julie knew that money played a key role in Doug's decision-making, not just at work, but in all areas of life.

"Well, I'll think about it. I just don't know. A part of me always dreamed of being an academic and working in a teaching institute, like where we are now, working with residents. It would be like being a doctor, a professor and a researcher all in one.

"You could still get that academic experience as a voluntary doctor. In a practice, you'd be at the forefront of medicine and would be making much more money," he repeated.

"Why are we arguing about this? I'm only going to work part time anyway. Don't we want to have a family? With children, I believe in quality and quantity time."

She had broached an important subject, but Doug did not take the bait. He obviously disapproved of her reasoning and turned silent and sulky. Julie thought to herself, *This is going to be my decision.*

Julie and Doug had been a couple for six months. The frenzied pace that had originally characterized their life had slowed down somewhat. After their mini-vacation, when Julie confronted Doug about her areas of discontent, they had cut back on socializing with Doug's gang of friends. Life had become more serene. They would go out with couples for dinner or visit cultural spots in New York. Julie did not miss the explosive energy of Doug's high-rolling friends, but she knew he probably did.

Now Valentine's Day was here. In the spirit of the holiday, Julie came to work wearing a bright red sweater and her signature red lipstick. While doing paperwork, she hummed her favorite love songs, "As Time Goes By" and "Moon River." She thought about Ilsa Lund, the female character in *Casablanca* and Holly Golightly in *Breakfast at Tiffany's*. Didn't she have some of the traits of those two women? One was caring, grounded and sensitive; the other, kooky and vulnerable. Both of them were deeply loved by the men in their lives. *How nice it would be to be loved like that*, she thought.

She and Doug had plans to go out to dinner that night, and Julie hoped it would be at one of the smaller, more intimate places. She smiled to herself, wondering what he might bring her when he came home. He knew she loved chocolates and flowers, and, like most women, she loved shiny trinkets. Apart from the bouquet he brought her after their trip to Florida, Doug had never given her anything. But tonight would be different, she hoped.

Although temporarily absorbed in thought about the evening to come, Julie was completely involved in her work with the children. She found them to be adorable, and she felt deep affection for each patient. She particularly enjoyed the tasks not connected with serious illness, like checking their charts to see if their height and weight had increased and if they were current with their vaccinations. She'd examine their ears, throats, skin, teeth, hair and nails and would softly palpate the abdomen to see if the stomach, liver and spleen were normal, not enlarged. Gently feeling the skin under the neck and groin, she could tell if there was any swelling in the lymph nodes. Using the stethoscope, she would listen to the breath, check that the lungs were clear and listen for a normal heartbeat with no murmur. She would then have the child walk across the room to observe his or her gait. Afterwards, she would talk to the parent, usually the mother or grandmother, and ask about the child's appetite, bladder, bowel and sleep habits, and she would inquire if there were any other issues she should know about. If something seemed irregular, the attending physician would be informed, and the child would be referred to a specialty clinic. All of this needed to be done within half an hour. It was a tremendous amount of responsibility for a young doctor, and she embraced it.

Julie was relieved to not be on call that evening, and when the workday ended, she sped home to change and get ready for the dinner. She quickly showered and slipped into a short black dress, fishnet stockings and black heels, and reapplied her dark eye makeup and red lipstick.

When Doug came home, she waited to hear him remark how sexy she looked, since the men she'd known always flipped over red lipstick and fishnet stockings. But he said nothing. A bit let down, she noticed he did not have a bouquet or candy box or, in fact, anything. *It's probably in the car,* she told herself.

"We are going to go to a dance club," he announced.

"A dance club? But it's Valentine's Day! I thought we would be going to one of our favorite quiet restaurants."

"Nah," he said dismissively, "clubs are much more fun."

Here we go again, she said to herself. *He made a unilateral decision, ignoring my wishes.*

They drove into the city and parked on the street. Doug reached into his pocket and pulled out an envelope.

"Here, I have something for you," he said.

She opened the envelope to find a handmade card on which he had drawn a boy and a girl sitting on a blue moon. Inside, he had written, *Once in a blue moon someone special comes along.*

"Oh, how sweet!" Julie exclaimed, and waited. When

nothing happened, she chewed on her bottom lip to stop from crying.

"Something wrong?" he asked.

"Well, I was kind of hoping for some flowers or candy."

"Well, what did you get me?" he asked. "Flowers and candy are a waste of money. They charge so much on Valentine's Day. I made you a great card and that should be enough," he stated with annoyance.

Julie had to wonder, *What kind of a red-blooded guy does not know about giving his sweetheart candy or flowers on this holiday? Did he have no role model? Doesn't he know that this is what normal guys do?* But she kept quiet.

They went into the noisy club, and Doug ordered a glass of wine for Julie and a cocktail for himself. She drained the glass too quickly in hopes of elevating her mood. Quietly seething, she asked herself if it was wrong to feel she'd been shortchanged. Doug's Valentine efforts were really inadequate. Once again, she had to admit to herself that she'd known better treatment. Worse than that, though, she knew there was no sense trying to talk things out with him. He'd only start to scream and certainly would not acknowledge her disappointment.

And so they danced to the deafening music, but Julie did not have her heart in it. *What are we doing here, anyway, grinding against each other on a crowded dance floor with sweaty people? And not one word of 'I love you' said to each other.* They got home around 1:00 a.m. Julie was exhausted and dissatisfied. Knowing that the next night she would be on call, she promptly undressed and fell asleep.

The clinic was quiet the next day. Her fellow resident Sue came to work donning a dainty gold bracelet her boyfriend had given her. She told Julie that it had come with a bouquet of red roses. Inevitably, Sue asked Julie about her own Valentine's celebration.

"He made me a beautiful card!" she said, with a forced smile that faded quickly.

"And…??"

"That's all. Oh, yes, and we went dancing."

"Oh," said Sue.

The day may have been quiet, but the on-call in the emergency room was brutal. Flu season was upon them, and there were plenty of sudden cases. Julie felt tired and depressed and wondered if she was overreacting to what did or did not happen on Valentine's Day. When her shift was done, she drove home slowly. The traffic was stop and go, which was tedious, so she kept the window open, letting the frigid air keep her awake. Finally arriving home, she fiddled with the lock, but the door to the apartment wouldn't open. Frustrated and overwrought, she sat down on the floor in the hallway and burst into tears. The super happened to come down the hall and looked at Julie.

"Ms. Kent," he said softly, "this is not your apartment. You live on the *second* floor."

"Oh? Where am I?"

"This is the third floor. Here, let me help you get up." She just burst out laughing, nodded to the super and went down a flight of stairs. Finally in the correct apartment, she pulled off her clothes and collapsed on the bed.

In the morning, as Julie hurriedly dressed for work, Doug handed her a mug of coffee and a small box of chocolates. He said nothing, just hugged her quickly and left. She looked down at the pathetic little red box with its silly bow. Had she made too much of a fuss over Valentine's Day? She was too tired to think about it anymore. *He's trying, she conceded. I don't know why he doesn't know any better. But he's trying.*

CHAPTER 18

As the springtime advanced, work-related tasks that had once seemed daunting to Julie were now becoming routine. She was about to start her next rotation, pediatric psychiatry, treating young, developmentally challenged children and adolescents struggling with depression, anxiety and eating disorders.

Julie's late spring birthday fell on a beautiful weekend in May, when the sun shone brightly. She had been looking forward to both the day and evening because Doug told her he set up grand plans for the occasion.

"Where are we having dinner tonight?" she queried.

"Some place you'll like," he replied, "not noisy and trendy."

Doug, in a celebratory and upbeat spirit, joined Julie for the morning shower. He brought a glass of Champagne for her and one for himself, which he playfully poured onto her breasts. This lighthearted, spontaneous gesture set off an erotically-charged lovemaking session. As the hot water streamed over the two of them, they enjoyed the silky feel of each other's bodies and prolonged the sex play until they reached a mutual peak of satisfaction.

"Oh, amazing!" she gasped.

"Yeah, good," he agreed.

"Say it's great!" Julie protested. She needed to hear him say that sex was more than just good.

"Oh, it's great!" he said, wanting to please her.

We're making progress, she mused. They wrapped themselves in bathrobes and sat down at the dining room table. Doug refreshed their Champagne flutes and then chose that moment to make an important declaration.

"So, Julie," he said, "I think we are perfect for each other in so many ways. We look great together, we're smart, both doctors and Jewish. We love the arts and animals, we want to travel, and we're good in bed. So, will you marry me?"

Julie was glad to hear these words from Doug, but she thought it was an odd sort of proposal, more like a list of qualifications that they both met. He didn't include words like, "I love you" or "You make me feel complete" or "I can't live without you." Doug was always more practical than romantic, perfect in his own way, but not mushy.

"Yes!" Julie nevertheless exclaimed, "Of course I'll marry you!"

Doug took her hand and slipped a delicate sapphire and diamond ring on her finger. Then he held her in his arms and covered her face with kisses.

"Well," he said, "good! Let's go to the city and celebrate your birthday and our engagement."

"We have to tell the moms," she said.

"Later. Let's go now."

They started by walking through Central Park, observing the people out for the day, the dogs greeting each other and the tourists looking around in awe. Eventually, they reached the carousel, and Julie jumped on a white horse adorned with vibrant colors. As the music played, her horse rose and dipped. She waved at Doug and saw her new ring glittering in the sunlight.

Later that evening, dinner was at Café des Artistes, a softly-lit dining room whose walls were covered in murals of lush gardens where nymphs frolicked. They sipped Champagne at a corner table and excitedly touched on the first plans for their wedding. Noting the luxurious pastry display in the middle of the room, Doug remarked, "I'd like a dessert table like that at our wedding." It made Julie's heart sing to know that Doug wanted to be involved in the arrangements.

Their magnificent dinner of duck *à l'orange* with wild rice and vegetables was topped off with chocolate soufflé and apple tart. Over coffee and liqueur, they once again toasted the double celebration, feeling the sweetness of both the birthday and engagement. Smiling, they relished the thought of everything they now had to look forward to. It had been a wonderful day, full of youthful energy and anticipation of the future and the life they would enjoy in the years to come.

At home, they brought those loving feelings to their bed, and then, completely at peace in body, mind and spirit, they snuggled beneath the covers.

"Oh, it feels good," Julie sighed with contentment.

"Yes," Doug replied. "It feels great."

For Julie, the next couple of months was a race to the end of internship. Her head was spinning with choosing electives and filing applications for a dermatology residency. She wanted so badly to focus on her wedding plans, but work overshadowed that desire. Doug tried to put her mind at ease.

"Don't even worry about the wedding," he told her. "I'll take care of everything."

Much as she had always loved to hear a man say that, she did not want to be standing on the sidelines for her own wedding plans. "But I'm the bride! I want to have a say in things."

"Listen, Julie, let me handle this. You're so busy with the residency applications. I'll look at country clubs in Westchester. I think I can get us a good deal in January."

"But it's OUR wedding!" she protested. "Aren't we going to do this as a team?"

"I'm trying to make it easy for you. What do you know about those kinds of plans anyway?" As always, there was no arguing with Doug. He meant well, and although Julie felt he was riding roughshod over her, she could see that he was trying to free her up to concentrate on work.

Doug and his mother, Helen, made plans to visit country clubs the following afternoon while Julie would be at the hospital. Lately, Doug had been consulting his mother instead of Julie, and Helen gladly took on the task of offering her opinion and giving advice. This irked Julie, and while she knew Doug's intentions were good, she could not help but feel left out.

"You know," she started, "this is the beginning of our life together. We should be making joint decisions."

Doug cut her off at the pass.

"Stop it! You're not appreciating how easy this will be for you!"

Somehow the notion of this "being easy" did not seem like an advantage to Julie. Did she necessarily *want* it to be easy, or did she want to have the experience of planning their wedding together? The phrase "How you set it up is how it's going to be" reverberated in her mind. She winced as she saw Doug exchanging some of the wedding gifts he judged to be "too traditional," like candlesticks and candy dishes, because he preferred modern décor. But disturbing as it was to see him making decisions without her input, Julie chose to avoid confrontation. It would only create more stress between the two of them. *Well*, she mused, *at least I'm going to pick my own wedding gown.*

As the days and weeks went by and plans became more concrete, Julie felt more and more as though she was standing on the outside looking in. Doubts rose in her mind and haunted her sleep. Doug was Rick all over again, demanding, controlling and critical. What is it with me that I'm drawn to this kind of man? she wondered. *On one hand, I am relieved to have so many decisions and tasks taken care of. It gives me the time I need for work and studies. But on the other hand, I am not an equal partner. Have I sold my soul to the devil to become a doctor? Is this the kind of life I have to have in order to achieve that goal? It's as though I have been forced to abdicate control of my personal life.*

The road Julie had chosen was an arduous one, requiring tremendous sacrifice, and she had already come far. But she was still not convinced that in the end she would be good enough. Perhaps if she were more confident and less fearful of failure, she would not shy away from confrontation. One day, she reckoned, her own voice would be heard. But that day was still far off.

CHAPTER 19

Feeling as though she'd climbed Mount Everest after finishing her internship, Julie was now confident that she could handle the increased responsibility of being a resident. She looked forward to her new position, when the interns would be asking her advice.

The extra responsibility was offset by an easier schedule. Her on-call assignments, which used to be every third night, would now be every fourth night, which would make a considerable difference in her personal life. And best of all, there'd be no more "scut" work. She certainly had done her share of drawing bloods and running to the lab in the middle of the night.

She entered Jacoby Hospital on a hot day in July, walked through the crowded lobby and took the elevator to the pediatric ward. Meeting with the interns this morning, she shared some techniques that had worked for her during her internship. She advised them that the simple practice of keeping handy that metal ring with an index card for each patient was useful and expedient, as was keeping *The Harriet Lane Handbook* within reach at all times. Teamwork, she told them, was paramount. The pediatric ward could be a high-tension place to work, and without team spirit, young lives would be at risk. Interns, residents and attending doctors were all interdependent.

There was a wide range of maladies in the ward. Children would be admitted with asthma, juvenile arthritis, juvenile diabetes and leukemia. On this first day of Julie's residency, a three-year-old girl with a number of symptoms was brought in. Her eyes were bloodshot, and her lips were severely chapped. Her tongue resembled a strawberry, and her tiny hands and feet were puffy. The very high fever and swollen lymph nodes under the neck and in the groin indicated an inflammation of the blood vessels known as Kawasaki disease. The danger of the disease, in addition to the high fever, was that the coronary blood vessels could be affected, and that could cause myocarditis, an inflammation of the heart. Even worse was that there could be an aneurysm of the coronary arteries. Julie and the intern checked the blood tests, searching for changes in the platelet count. They consulted the cardiologist and started the patient on a course of aspirin and intravenous immunoglobulin. Julie would later reflect that her first day as a resident was a full-on challenge that called upon her education and ability to judge and act quickly. Wasn't this exactly how she had hoped her training would play out?

Doug and Julie were living in Riverdale now, but their work took them to two different parts of New York: Julie to the Bronx and Doug to Greenwich Village. As he had planned, Doug was now doing a private practice in ENT and was already starting to perform cosmetic procedures. He knew it would take time to develop a cosmetic surgical practice, so to supplement their income, he worked in an emergency room, stitching up lacerations and repairing hand fractures. Julie and Doug, both hardworking and optimistic about their chosen paths, were forging ahead.

One crisp autumn day in October, Doug, as always, drove Julie to work. But that evening when he picked her up, he arrived in a new sports car. Julie heard the repeated honking of a horn but did not know where it was coming from. Then she saw the sleek, shining car and realized it was Doug behind the wheel.

"Oh, my Lord!" she shrieked.

"Hop in!" he shouted. "We're going to go get pizza!"

"But...this car...? she asked.

"My boss just leased it for me!" he said with glee. They sped off to Arthur Avenue, the only place in the Bronx to get the best and most authentic Italian food.

They sat at a table with their pizza and two glasses of chianti. Doug looked as though he was about to burst.

"What is it, Doug?" Julie asked. "You look like you have a secret."

He grinned as he handed her an envelope. She opened it and saw the letterhead: The Chairman of New York Medical College. It was an acceptance letter to the Department of Dermatology.

"Yes!!!" she exclaimed. "How did you know it was an acceptance?"

"The envelope was thick. Rejections are paper thin," he said with a smile.

"You know everything!"

"Tomorrow we'll celebrate in that French restaurant you wanted to go to," he said, taking her hand tenderly. At that moment, Julie felt completely happy. This was the part of Doug that she adored. He wanted the best for her and was there to share her joy. And he did so with panache, more than any other man she'd known.

That night when they made love, Julie's body and mind were swooning. At long last, she had arrived at the place of her dreams, both personally and professionally. She had the man she loved, and he cherished her. She was succeeding at work, seeing her efforts bear fruit. There was so much to feel good about now and in the months to come. In January, they would get married, and then in July she would start her dermatology residency. Her last thought before falling asleep was, *This must be what is meant by having it all.*

Now it was time to go to Kleinfeld's Bridal Boutique. Julie's budget was limited, but she still had a clear idea of what she wanted. That had never changed. As she sifted through the racks of wedding gowns, a voice came from behind her.

"Can I help you, Miss?"

"Oh, yes! I'm looking for a bridal gown for this January!" she told the saleswoman.

"This January? Hmmm…it's already October."

"Yes, I know. Do you think you can find something for me?"

"Of course, of course. What did you have in mind?"

"I'd like something classic, a fitted gown with long sleeves and a sweetheart neckline. You know, satin and a little lace."

"That sounds easy enough. By the way, my name is Sylvia."

"I'm Julie."

"Julie, I think I have just the dress for you. Come here."

Sylvia brought Julie over to the perfect gown, complete with the tiny buttons down the back and the large bow at the waist. Plenty of satin and lacy sleeves.

"I love it!" Julie beamed. "How much is it?"

"About $2,000, plus the alterations."

Julie's eyes filled with tears. "I can't afford a fraction of that," she said, discouraged.

"I have an idea," Sylvia said. She walked over to a mannequin that was wearing the same dress. Removing it from the display, she nodded toward the fitting room and said, "Let's have you try this on."

Julie let her everyday clothes drop to the floor of the fitting room, and Sylvia helped her step into the sweeping yards of satin. She stood up very straight as Sylvia buttoned the close-fitting bodice. As if by magic, the dress matched Julie's body the way the glass slipper fit Cinderella's foot. Julie stood before the three-way mirror and smiled through her tears. "I love it," she said. "Thank you so much. And the price?"

"You can take it for $400," Sylvia said.

Julie's eyes glistened with gratitude. Having found her dream dress, she chose a rhinestone tiara and a long veil. Sylvia carefully placed the tiara on Julie's head and spread the veil out so that it flowed down Julie's back and spilled onto the floor.

"Just look at yourself, dear," Sylvia said with a smile. Julie took another look in the mirror and breathed deeply. She felt like a queen.

She left the bridal salon with the gown, veil and tiara in a box and drove back to Riverdale as dusk was falling. This was her favorite hour, the bridge between the busy day and the quiet of evening. At home, she made herself a cup of tea and lit a lavender-scented candle. Relaxing on the couch, she inhaled the lovely aroma, sipped the tea and nibbled a chocolate cookie. She sat back and reflected on how well plans for the wedding were proceeding, and although she was involved in none of them, she had made peace with that. Chuckling to herself, she recalled how she'd told Doug that their wedding was going to be a surprise party for her!

Yes, she thought, *this is happiness.*

CHAPTER 20

January 20th, a cold, bright Sunday, was Julie and Doug's wedding day. Julie awoke that morning, smiled at Doug in anticipation and then sprang into action. She had a quick breakfast, showered and slipped into comfortable clothes, knowing there was much to do before the festivities that afternoon.

At 10:00 the hairdresser arrived. At Julie's direction, she blew out Julie's long, dark hair into a straight, glossy sheet and made a diagonal side part. The effect was striking. Julie opted to apply her own makeup, creating a warm, natural look that included her pink lipstick. For extra good feeling, she added a spritz of Chanel No. 5.

The couple packed up the wedding gear and drove to the country club where, in separate, small but comfortable dressing rooms, they got ready. Julie, remarkably relaxed for a woman on her wedding day, got into her magnificent gown by herself, but she needed Lara's help with the long column of buttons. Then she placed the tiara and veil on her head, picked up her bouquet of red roses, and stepped into the club's central room.

Doug and the families of the bride and groom were assembled there, and upon seeing Julie in her full regalia, took one long, collective breath. The couple looked stunning. As with any happy occasion, there was lots of hugging and kissing and gushing over the bride's beauty. The photographer then lined everyone up for some formal photos. This being the middle of winter, Julie had wanted a snowball wedding, so her bridesmaids were dressed in white gowns and held bouquets of white roses. Standing next to the ushers, the entire party looked like something out of a royal family portrait.

While the photo session was in progress, the guests gathered in the next room, where the ceremony would take place. Chairs had been set up in rows, and there was a beautiful *chuppa* decorated with white flowers. The rabbi signaled that it was time to start, so guests took their seats and the bridal party, parents, bride and groom took their places.

A string quartet began to play Pachelbel's Canon, and Julie's two matrons of honor, Elizabeth and Bibi, began the procession. Then came the rest of the bridal party, and as they made their way down the aisle, snow flurries could be seen blowing across the window. *Did Doug arrange that too?* Julie thought with a secret smile. The groom, between his parents, walked down to Massenet's "Meditation," a soft violin solo from *Thaïs*. The musicians then switched gears when the bride was about to appear. Hearing the opening notes of Mendelssohn's classic wedding march, everyone stood up to see radiant, joyful Julie walking between her parents.

The ceremony was brief and heartfelt, and after the couple exchanged rings and took their vows in both Hebrew and English, Doug, in the Jewish tradition, smashed a glass with his foot. The rabbi pronounced them "husband and wife," bringing on a wave of enthusiastic applause from the guests. As the new Dr. Doug and Dr. Julie Stone turned and walked back down the aisle, they nodded and smiled at the many beloved friends and family members who had come to see them married.

The doors to the reception room were opened, and everyone went into the elegant space, where small tables were tastefully set with white tablecloths and vases of tulips. The cocktail hour featured a smorgasbord of caviar, lox, herring, turkey, lamb chops, ribs, Swedish meatballs and chicken marsala. Champagne flutes were passed around as the band performed a medley of Broadway tunes, some Cole Porter, and a bit of lively Latin music. Julie and Doug danced to Frank Sinatra's "Under My Skin," their wedding song and a bit of an inside joke, she being a dermatologist and he an ENT surgeon.

Julie looked around the room and saw all the faces of the people she loved, people who wished her and Doug well and had come to celebrate with them. She felt overcome with gratitude in the fullness of the moment, one she would never forget. Whatever would happen in the future, she knew that nothing could change this pocket of time, this memory of being with so many cherished people in this enchanting setting.

After everyone noshed, chatted, danced and admired each other's clothes, they sat down for more fantastic food. The appetizer of poached salmon and mixed green salad was followed by prime rib, Chilean sea bass and potato baskets garnished with vegetables. In between courses, people got up, danced and made toasts to the new couple.

Doug's best man was his childhood friend, Todd, who was dating Julie's sister Elizabeth. Todd toasted the couple, saying how perfect they were for each other and how thankful he was for them setting him up with Elizabeth.

Julie smiled widely at Doug and congratulated him. "Well, my husband, you really planned a great party!"

Doug nodded. "This is nothing! Wait until the desserts arrive! Remember Café des Artistes?"

After all the eating, drinking and chatting, the Viennese table was unveiled with something for everyone: apple pie, carrot cake, lemon meringue pie, strawberry shortcake, eclairs, cookies and puddings. On its own little table was a magnificent

Black Forest cake, complete with whipped cream and cherries. There was coffee and tea and continuous music, with everyone dancing the afternoon away. Suddenly it was 6:00 and the party wound down. People started to kiss each other goodbye and say "mazel tov" one more time before they got their coats and left. There was no denying that the event was a success in every way. Lavish, well-planned and generous to the guests, it left everyone, especially the new husband and wife, feeling pleased and happy.

Just as Doug had arranged almost everything about the wedding to be a surprise, he wanted the honeymoon destination to be a mystery too.

"Just pack some light, casual clothing," he had told Julie.

On the way to the airport, she could not stand the suspense any longer.

"Well, Doug," she asked, "where exactly *are* we going?"

"You'll see soon enough," he said. "I promise you'll like it."

Back then, in a world of travel that did not include security checks and all kinds of hoops to jump through, a passenger could get all the way to the gate without knowing where their plane was headed. So it was only after Julie and Doug checked their bags and walked through the long corridor that Julie saw the sign at their gate: St. Maarten. She beamed.

"That's just where I wanted to go!" she squealed.

"I knew that," Doug said with affection.

They boarded the aircraft and buckled themselves in. Before long, the plane roared off the runway and into the skies. Julie grasped Doug's hand, feeling the thrill of being on their honeymoon, a midwinter vacation on a tropical island with the man she loved.

In a matter of a few hours, they landed in St. Maarten, a lush and colorful West Indian island with both French and Dutch influence. The newlyweds caught a taxi to the hotel, and after checking in, went straight to the beach. Within moments, they were floating on gently undulating waves in the clear aqua sea. They let the warm water flow over them, and as it did, all the tension and weariness of city life disappeared. The weeks of frantic planning and keeping track of everything that had recently characterized their life just dissolved, and they surrendered to the pure relaxation of their Caribbean retreat.

Back in their room, they began to make love. Julie had packed both her black and white lacy bras and panties to add spice to the sex play. But Doug didn't really care.

"It's all about the skin," he said. "The underwear comes off in a second."

"Will sex be different now that they were married?"

"Nope," he laughed, "just official."

St. Maarten had numerous small, hidden beaches and coves, and each day, they drove or took a motor scooter to one of them to swim, snorkel and read books. As they sat on chaise lounges, friendly servers brought cold drinks and snacks. Julie and Doug luxuriated in the ease and comfort of this divine honeymoon island. It seemed as if everyone there was on their honeymoon or having a well-deserved break from the northern climate. The evenings were mild and allowed for candlelight dinner outdoors. There were many tiny restaurants that offered fresh fish and seafood, ripe fruit and locally made desserts. And under the moonlit sky, one could hear the unending, soothing sound of Caribbean waves lapping on the shore.

After one week they flew home, refreshed and ready to begin the next phase of their lives.

Soon enough, June arrived, and on the last night of Julie's pediatric residency, they went out to their favorite Asian restaurant to celebrate the completion of yet another milestone. When the ice cream and fortune cookies were brought to the table, Julie broke her cookie open first.

"He who listens to his heart will be happy," she read. Silently, she recalled how she often listened to Doug instead of her own heart. *Has that done me any harm?* she asked herself.

CHAPTER 21

D iagnosis?" A voice could be heard thundering
down the hall of the dermatology clinic at South
Bronx Hospital. It was Dr. Stern, a brilliant, devoted but high-
strung physician who demanded perfection of his residents.

Julie entered the clinic on a Monday morning in the
first week of July 1986, ready to start her residency. She had
been studying dermatology for the past six months and was
intrigued by the fact that field encompassed many facets
of medical care. Rashes and lesions could indicate a wide
range of problems, such as infection, underlying medical
systemic disease, a tumor, a reaction to a drug or a primary
dermatologic disease. In the course of this residency, she would
learn how to pinpoint exactly what the symptoms meant.

Her first contact at the hospital was with a fellow
resident. "Hi, I'm Julie Kent," she said, and held out her hand.

"I'm Angela Barrett," replied a pretty young woman
with a warm smile.

"I'm so excited to begin residency," Julie said. "I did hear
Dr. Stern could be a bit strict," she whispered with a nervous
laugh.

"We will soon see," Angela said, nodding.

The two young women hit it off from the start, and their kinship would be helpful to them during the high-pressure residency. They had chatted a bit and learned about their similar backgrounds, and were then joined by three more senior residents. Introductions were made, and a casual conversation ensued, when suddenly a cloud of cigar smoke billowed through the clinic. A voice barked, "Are we ready?" It was Dr. Stern, looking like a professor in his "uniform": blue shirt, tan chinos and horn-rimmed glasses.

He led them into the clinic, a series of very small rooms lining the sides of a narrow corridor. With a multitude of patients and only five residents to see two hundred patients a day, to say the environment was challenging would be a gross understatement. The doctor and Julie entered the first exam room to find a female patient with a rash consisting of purplish bumps and white scale.

"Diagnosis?" He gave Julie no more than a few seconds to respond.

"Lichen planus."

"Good," he clipped. "What might you be concerned with?"

"I would look in the mouth to see if there were lesions. I'd order a lab test to check if the patient might have hepatitis, liver problems or HIV. I'd also check what medications she's on as there could be lichenoid drug reactions," Julie answered.

"Good! What drugs would cause this?" Dr. Stern asked.

"Beta blockers, seizure medications, diuretics and antimalarials." She surreptitiously took a deep breath and felt both relief and pride at having answered correctly. No matter that her hands were ice cold and her heart was racing.

The next patient was a one-month-old baby girl with a red bump on her back.

"Diagnosis?" the doctor blasted.

"Infantile hemangioma."

"Are you concerned?"

"No," Julie replied. "It is on the baby's back, not compromising her vision or ability to swallow. It will continue to grow rapidly, probably for the first four months until she is one year old."

"Are you concerned with Kasabach-Merritt syndrome?"

"No, because that would occur if there were a rapidly enlarging lesion and would present with a tufted angioma, not with an infantile hemangioma."

"That's excellent," Dr. Stern replied.

Julie was elated, as she seemed to be impressing her professor.

Throughout the rest of the day, there were some routine cases of acne, eczema, syphilis and verruca. Julie felt a sense of accomplishment at the completion of her trial by fire with Dr. Stern. She met up in the hall with Angela.

"How did it go for you today?" Julie asked her.

Angela shrugged. "It was going well until I didn't know the name of the allergen in nail polish and he went on a rampage. We're in the program one day and I'm supposed to know paraphenylenediamine. He wanted to know if I cared about my patients!"

"My turn hasn't arrived yet," Julie reassured her. "He is so intense, and I can see that his mood changes on a dime."

Meanwhile, Doug, too fiercely independent to work for anyone, was starting his own cosmetic surgical practice, performing rhinoplasties, commonly called "nose jobs." He chose Long Island, where he and Julie had sworn they would never move to, because a good opportunity for a practice presented itself. At the same time, he was running the emergency room in a local hospital, taking trauma calls and treating ENT infections. Starting one's own practice, establishing a client base and working a second job was a huge undertaking, but Doug was undaunted. He knew that with excellent and ethical work, it could be done.

Julie drove home, stopping by the market to pick up a roasted chicken and vegetables for dinner. After stowing them in the oven to keep warm, she did thirty minutes of exercise and sat down to study. Doug would get home in about two hours, and she planned to study vigorously, reading about each case she had treated in the clinic. Her goal was to get through the entire textbook by the end of the first year.

Her concentration was broken when she heard the door open and Doug call out, "Hi, I'm home!"

"Hi!" she shouted back. "How was your day?" Before he could answer she said, "Mine was great! I think I impressed Dr. Stern."

Doug came into the room, kissed her and smiled. "Well, you see, Dr. Bookworm, all your studying has paid off."

Julie put the dinner on the table and watched Doug wolf it down. Between bites, he told her, "I saw a few referral patients from the local pediatricians and booked a surgery."

"Great. What's the surgery for?"

"A deviated septum and a cosmetic reconstruction."

"It's going to be terrific!" she said, encouraging him.

After dinner, Julie sat down to read for another hour. The dermatology curriculum, she realized, was quite extensive. Her other interests would have to wait for now, and she made the commitment to give her all to absorbing the material. *There goes my pleasure reading and piano playing,* she told herself, with just a twinge of envy as she glanced at Doug relaxing in front of the TV.

The next morning, Julie arrived at the clinic ready for a good day. She entered the exam room and saw her first patient, a man in his thirties with an ulcer on his penis. When she touched the lesion through gloved hands, the man didn't flinch. A moment later, the door was flung open and cigar smoke wafted into the room.

"Diagnosis?" Dr. Stern said, in his usual barking tone.

"It's a painless ulcer," Julie replied. "I believe this could be syphilis. We should get laboratory tests and a dark field microscopic smear."

"Excellent. How do you know it's not a chancroid?"

"That would be a painful ulcer with discharge," Julie answered.

In the next room, Angela was examining a young woman with blisters on her buttocks.

"What do you think?" Dr. Stern asked brusquely.

"Probably herpes simplex," replied Angela.

"That's right! Why do you think it's on the buttock?"

Angela paused. "I'm not sure."

"You're married, aren't you?" he spluttered. "Haven't you ever spooned with your husband?" Angela turned a bright shade of crimson. "Oh, forget it!" he exploded. "You're a real Catholic girl! Obviously, the infection spread from the penis onto the buttock!"

Never did Julie and Angela expect the clinic to be a version of Masters and Johnson sex therapy. Over lunch, the two friends burst out laughing.

"My nerves are shredded," Angela wailed. "He's so rude!'

"I know," nodded Julie. "I feel like I've been through the wringer."

The afternoon clinic was fairly tame, just some cases of eczema, acne, and secondary syphilis. Then suddenly Dr. Stern broke the calm, screaming because one of the residents didn't have the lab tests for a patient with lupus.

"Did I not say same way every time?" he shouted. "Look up the test in the logbook!" The resident tried explaining that he was going to get the book, but Dr. Stern was furious because he wasn't moving quickly enough. Each resident had his or her turn.

When the day came to a close, Julie and Angela were mentally exhausted, and this after only two days of rotation! Julie drove home, picking up dinner on the way. The two-hour interval before Doug got home left her time to work out and study.

Over dinner, she asked, "What should we do this weekend? East or West Side?"

"Let's do the park," he said. "We can have a Mexican brunch and catch an exhibit at the Met to make you happy."

"I'm kind of nervous about tomorrow," Julie confessed.

"Oh, stop worrying! You'll do fine," Doug assured her.

Julie was referring to the weekly Wednesday patient presentation, where the residents would examine patients with unusual diagnoses. The resident was only allowed to ask if the rash or lesion was itchy or painful. With that small bit of information, they would have to write down a presumed diagnosis on the card and hand it in.

The residents would then be made to sit around a large conference table like knights in Camelot, with Dr. Stern presiding as the king. Seated around the circumference of the table was a voluntary attending staff, there to observe each resident. The doctor would call upon a resident, asking for the presumed diagnosis. The first-year residents looked ashen and fidgety as they waited to be randomly called on, but although their stomachs were in knots, they usually performed quite well. Dr. Stern would grill everyone as to other diagnoses the patient might have, various treatments and everything that could possibly be associated with the disease. If a single fact was omitted, he would burst out with criticism.

Running a close second to the Wednesday conference was the Friday morning slideshow. Squeezed together like sardines in a can, the residents would view slides on a projector. Again, Dr. Stern would randomly call upon them for the diagnosis. On one hand, it was a plus that the attending doctors weren't present to view a resident's embarrassment, but on the other hand, Dr. Stern didn't have to tone down the volume of his rampage about how inadequate a resident's fund of knowledge was.

On a particular Wednesday morning, Julie was feeling nervous. The slide showed the classic butterfly rash of a case of lupus. Dr. Stern called out, "Julie, diagnosis? What lab tests will you order?"

"An ANA, double stranded DNA, CBC, metabolic screen, anti-Ro and anti-La," she replied.

"What about anti-Smith antibody?"

"Ummm…" Her mind went blank as to what anti-Smith antibody was.

"How could you not obtain the anti-Smith antibody?! Did you go to medical school?" he roared. Julie felt her cheeks flush with humiliation. How could he turn on her when she was performing so well in clinic?

"Yes! I remember!" she stammered. "Smith antibody is associated with systemic lupus and kidney disease."

As the students left the conference that day, Angela remarked, "Boy, is he brutal! You're so bright and informed and he goes wild over one thing you missed."

Julie nodded. "He is volatile. But I always remind myself that we're lucky to be in a dermatology residency. It's such a coveted position."

"That's just the reason he should be more charitable with us!" Angela countered. "We're really good students."

"Well, at least we have Friday clinic this afternoon to look forward to!" they joked with each other.

Friday clinic was usually frenetic, with many patients to examine before the weekend. Fortunately, this day was an easy one, with a range of cases of syphilis, genital warts, acne and eczema. There was not a lot of time to devote to each patient, and residents had to treat them quickly with penicillin or topical creams. Time and again, the resident tried to impress upon patients the importance of using condoms but doubted if the thirty-second explanation was effective.

When Julie arrived home that evening, she vented her frustration by describing the entire slideshow incident to Doug. He didn't understand why she was upset.

"You have to tough it out! It's nothing compared to what goes on in a surgical residency," he stressed.

"But I'm not in a surgical residency! Can't you just comfort me? Why does everything have to be a lecture! I just want you to soothe me right now."

Doug reached over and put his arm around her. "I mean, it's for your own good. The stronger and more knowledgeable you are, the better doctor you'll be."

"OK, maybe you're right. I just have to keep my goal in mind and be less sensitive," she conceded.

The hectic atmosphere in the clinic had a paradoxical effect on the residents. As Charles Dickens had said, "It was the best of times, it was the worst of times." Some residents developed deep, close friendships, while others alienated themselves from the group.

"Did you ever think you'd study this hard during residency?" Angela asked Julie.

"No, never," she replied. "That's all I seem to do."

"And you're the Brainiac of all the residents!" she said with admiration.

"I'm not so sure about being a Brainiac, but I admit I'm OCD with my studying. I feel like the trick pony in the ring."

"More like a cockfight!" Angela laughed.

Julie shook her head. "You and I support each other, but sometimes when Dr. Stern screams, it seems like some of the residents are gloating."

"Well, everyone has their own way of dealing with the torture, even if it's just rejoicing that someone else is getting yelled at. That's true everywhere."

Julie sighed, thinking of how very narrow her life was at the moment.

"Angela, I admire how well-balanced you are, cooking, making brunch, gardening," Julie said. I haven't done much else but keep my head in the books."

"I wish I had more stamina to study like you and could know everything!" Angela countered. "And you are a culture buff, even if you're not pursuing that right now. You *will* one day, when everything is settled."

The first year of the residency was coming to an end, and the students took a mock American Board of Dermatology exam. Julie scored in the 99th percentile, and Dr. Stern actually gave her the satisfaction of expressing his amazement and pleasure.

Julie and Doug celebrated at the same French bistro where they dined the night she was accepted to the residency.

"Here's to my Brainiac!" Doug toasted as they clinked their Champagne glasses.

"Thank you, Doug! You helped me so much!"

Doug shook his head. "You did it all by yourself, Julie. I saw it with my own eyes."

She smiled. "I could never have the opportunity to study as much as I did if you didn't take care of everything for me."

"We're a team," Doug said, taking her hand.

CHAPTER 22

The following July, just as everyone else in the world was going on summer vacation, Julie started the second year of her dermatology residency. She entered this new phase with confidence, having performed so well on her exams that she was now regarded among the residents as the fair-haired child.

The new rotation was in the Public Health Hospital on Staten Island, just beneath the Verrazano-Narrows Bridge. The dermatology division was headed by Dr. McQueen, a young married woman with a toddler. She was bright and energetic, and Julie felt an instantaneous connection with her. In addition, it felt great to be out of the line of fire of Dr. Stern.

"Good morning, Julie," Dr. McQueen greeted her, with a warm smile. "Let's get a cup of coffee and review your schedule." Julie could not believe the difference in the demeanor between Dr. Stern and Dr. McQueen. It was a refreshing change.

As a second-year resident, Julie's job would be supervising first-year residents. Not until the third year would she be performing surgery and laser treatments. In the Public Health Hospital, there was an entire clinic exclusively for the treatment of skin cancer, which included malignant melanoma, as many of the patients were military veterans who had been exposed to toxins or harsh sunlight during wartime. Especially vulnerable were the fair-skinned Irishmen. Until treating these patients, Julie had never actually seen skin studded with cancer caused by excessive sun exposure.

The signs of melanoma were ominous: lesions with irregular or very dark coloration and roughly contoured borders. As with any diagnosis bringing bad news, it was difficult to share the results with a patient. They always considered it to be a death sentence. Fortunately, many patients did well if the lesion was caught early and was not too deep.

Of course, during the day Julie saw patients with the usual cases of eczema, psoriasis and syphilis, but she handled these easily because of her first-year experience. By the end of the day, she felt she had accomplished a lot of meaningful work, and although tired, she'd drive home singing along with the radio.

◊ ◊ ◊

Doug's practice on Long Island was beginning to take hold, and, to be practical, he and Julie rented a small apartment in the Five Towns, an upper-middle-class enclave on Long Island, abutting the Atlantic Ocean. Their plan was to buy a home somewhere in the area before too long.

On the evening of her first day of rotation, Julie came home and called out to Doug, who was in the study.

"Hi, Honey! How was your day?" Too excited to wait for his answer, she said, "Mine was great! I really love this clinic, and the head of it is a lovely woman, only thirty-five years old. The place so busy and I knew what I was doing—on my own!"

"That's good to hear. You see, Dr. Stern really prepared you!" said Doug. "Let's go out to eat tonight. You've done enough work for one day."

They went to small Italian restaurant and dined on

good old meatballs and spaghetti, finishing up with homemade cannoli.

Each day for the next few months, Julie mastered more aspects of dermatology, including the treatment of leprosy. Although she assumed that leprosy would occur only in patients from developing countries, to her surprise, she had one patient who was raised on Park Avenue and had contracted leprosy from his nanny. This experience taught Julie that diseases know no boundaries and that one should not formulate a diagnosis based on stereotypes.

In the early spring, when pink and white buds were beginning to blossom, Julie and Doug, in the spirit of renewal, decided to start a family. Ideally, Julie wanted to become pregnant immediately and give birth in her last year of residency.

During lunch, she confided in her co-worker, Angela, and Dr. McQueen. Angela blushed.

"I'm already there! I was waiting until I was three months pregnant to tell you girls!"

"Oh, my God!" Julie squealed so loudly that everyone in the cafeteria turned around. "When are you due?"

"Early December!" Angela beamed.

"Any advice on how to get pregnant quickly?" Julie asked.

Angela laughed. "Just *do* it!!"

Dr. McQueen offered more exact advice. "Do it every other day, even if you think you're not ovulating."

Julie was on a mission. When she arrived home, she took a warm bubble bath with lavender salts to relax her body. Then she put on one of her most fetching negligees and relaxed on the bed. When she heard Doug enter the apartment, she called out to him. He appeared at the threshold of the bedroom, and she beckoned him toward her. He was right on board.

At the start of July, Julie noticed she was feeling tired all the time.

"Could you be pregnant?" Angela winked.

Julie froze. "I did miss my period and lost track. I might be about six weeks pregnant."

The two women ran to the clinic to grab a pregnancy test kit. Julie dipped the stick in the urine and then waited only to see the line turn blue.

"Yes!!" she shrieked. The two friends hugged each other, crying out, "Next year we will both be moms!"

Julie drove home feeling at once gleeful and pensive, anticipating the joy but also contemplating how she would blend being a doctor with being a mom. She stopped by the market to pick up dinner and a bouquet of flowers for the table. This was a special night for both of them.

When Doug arrived home, it did not take long for him to figure out that something was different.

"Something new at work?" he asked.

"Something new, but not at work," she smiled.

"What?" he probed.

Julie handed him the paper stick with the blue line. "Pregnancy test," she said. "What's special is that we're going to be parents!"

"Great!" he shouted, leaning over to kiss her.

"We're fast workers!" she laughed.

The summer began, hot, humid and sticky, and Julie, now two months pregnant, was back at Bronx City Hospital. The commute was an hour and a half each way, which was daunting in itself, but to add to the mix was the nausea, normal for the first trimester.

Doug decided that he wanted them to move into a house before the baby was born.

"Do you think we will be happy in the suburbs?" Julie asked.

"Yes and no," Doug replied.

"What do you mean?"

Doug paused. "We'll miss the pulse and ethnic mix of the city and Brooklyn, and neither one of us grew up playing tennis and soccer. But on the other hand, it'd be nice to have a yard for kids to play in and for a dog to romp, and we'll have more room."

True to his take-charge nature, Doug arranged for them to look at a few houses in the town of Lawrence. His plan was to buy a house and be moved in within the next few months, before the baby was due. He was determined to make this happen.

CHAPTER 23

Two months pregnant and tired most of the time, Julie was happy that Doug was managing the house-hunting project. The scope of the search was the Five Towns area, whose population was mixed, with Jewish, Italian, Irish and a smattering of Protestant residents, many quite wealthy. It was a somewhat insular community, as the multi-generational families knew a lot, or wanted to know a lot, about each other.

Julie was relieved that Doug was doing all the legwork and would listen to his description of the houses he'd seen, but there was a fly in the ointment. His mother decided to participate in the search, and if she went with him to view a house, it was sure to be nixed. There seemed to be a problem with every property he showed her. The one with the duck pond probably had rodents, the slanted ceiling made the bedroom asymmetrical, and on and on it went. Finally, Julie told Doug to take her only to the homes that had been "approved" by his mother. She didn't want to waste time seeing any that were going to be eliminated from the list.

In the oppressive heat of late July, Doug took Julie to a house in Lawrence that he had his eye on.

"You'll love this house," he said as he ran down the list of features. "It has a fireplace, a great spot for your piano and three bedrooms."

And she did love it. It was a charming, white Cape Cod with black shutters and a red door. The front yard, obviously well cared for, had a border of multicolored impatiens and begonias. On the ground floor there was a small living room and an adjoining dining room. There was a large den, and next to it that would be a study and house Julie and Doug's book collection. Tucked in back of the dining room was a cozy kitchen with a built-in breakfast nook and a window that looked out on a yard that had room for a patio, barbeque and swing set.

They walked upstairs to find a master bedroom and two smaller rooms.

"One of these rooms will be the nursery," Julie mused aloud, "and the other will be for our second child."

"We don't even have *this* baby yet!" Doug laughed.

The house had a basement, too, ideal for a playroom and gym.

"It's perfect!" Julie exclaimed. Always a bit impulsive, she was ready to buy the house that day. The realtor, seeing the couple's enthusiasm, talked up the other benefits: the lovely neighborhood, excellent school district and the town's proximity to Manhattan. As Doug delved into the serious topics of price, taxes and down payment, Julie was quietly decorating the rooms in her head.

The deal went through, and in October, when Julie was almost five months pregnant, they moved into their new home on Fox Drive. The whole place needed to be redesigned, something Julie was looking forward to.

"I can see a Chippendale dining room table and chairs covered in jewel tones. What do you think?" she asked Doug.

"Absolutely not. I hate hunter green and burgundy. We'll do neutral beige, earth tones and more modern furniture."

"Well, let's compromise," Julie suggested. "You design the living room, dining room, kitchen, den and bedrooms. I'll choose the colors and furniture for the nursery and the study!"

"It needs to all be in the same style!" Doug snapped. "If I leave it up to you, I'll have wallpaper with a border of ducks and a burgundy leather sofa!" Which was exactly what Julie wanted.

Julie shrugged. "You're being inflexible. I'm talking about two rooms." She sensed that this step, which was supposed to be fun, was going to be a thorny issue. Her hand reflexively rubbed her belly. She was grateful that her pregnancy was so easy, and she didn't want to cause stress. All she could do was hope that Doug would bend a little bit to her wishes.

Julie's third and final year of residency was relatively easy. She wondered, though, how she was going to manage work and motherhood, knowing she was so assiduous and thorough with anything she undertook. She thought about her own traditional upbringing and how her mother had concentrated completely and exclusively on her family and home. Would it be possible to do as good a job with *two* distinct roles? She laid out a plan in her head that included part-time work in the hospital or for another physician. A nanny would be hired to assist her, although she would assume most of the responsibility for the child care. She looked at the example of Dr. McQueen, who juggled two roles, and assured herself that she would do so also. *If you need something done, ask a busy person,* her professors used to say. This would be her motto now.

Julie found pregnancy to be the most beautiful experience. With each passing day she watched her waist expand and felt a new energy and sense of peace. The fatigue that had plagued her in the beginning was gone now. Driving two hours each way to and from work, she would talk to the baby while classical music played on the radio.

"You're gonna love music!" she would gently coo, feeling the baby move inside her.

"Today we have the pediatric dermatology lecture!" Julie said to Angela as they made their way into the lecture hall. Julie was five months pregnant, and Angela was due to give birth in two months.

Angela smirked. "This is just perfect for us two worriers, seeing all the congenital syndromes."

"I know," Julie laughed. "We haven't even had the babies yet, and we're Nervous Nellies!"

This day in clinic would prove to be an onerous one for the two young doctors and mothers-to-be. They both knew that the risk of a baby being born with a congenital abnormality was very low, but at the moment it loomed large in their minds. The skin could serve as a gateway for a myriad of systemic diseases. The first slide in the lecture showed a baby born with a large nevus on her back, putting her at risk for melanoma of the skin and underlying spinal cord. Other cases included patients with large hemangiomas (blood vessel growths), vascular birthmarks and port wine stains, which could signify Sturge-Weber syndrome, which could lead to seizures, glaucoma, developmental delay and brain hemorrhage.

"I feel like choking," Julie whispered.

Angela nodded. "I wish this lecture was over. We studied all the stuff for years, and now it's just frightening."

Julie sighed. "We are in the motherly protective state."

The next afternoon, Julie was sent to see a patient admitted for high fevers and infection. He was a drug addict with full-blown AIDS. Initially, Julie felt sorry for the man as she viewed his wasting body. He had a huge abscess on his back that needed to be drained, so she donned a gown, mask and gloves and prepared to incise and drain the infected mass. The patient was rolled onto his side, and as Julie gently pressed on the abscess, he jerked, turned around and glared at her with yellow, bloodshot eyes.

"Leave me the fuck alone!" he screamed.

"I know you're in pain," she softly told him, "but I have to treat this, or you will get very sick and might not live." A nurse came into the room to assist, and they rolled him back onto his side. Julie numbed the skin slowly with a syringe of lidocaine, and for a moment, the patient seemed to be tolerating the procedure. After a few minutes, she pricked the skin, ensuring that he was numb, and then made a small incision into the cyst. The pressure of the blade caused the patient terrible pain.

"Get the fuck off me!" he shrieked, as he grabbed her wrist, bending it away from him.

Julie clung to the blade handle, petrified that she would stick herself with his infected blood. She dropped the blade from her hand.

"You bastard!" she screeched. "I'm pregnant and you could've hurt me and my child!"

"Fuck you!" was all he said.

The nurse looked at her with tears. "Let the bastard die. No loss for the world."

They called a few more nurses to strap the man down and then continued draining the abscess. Julie left the hospital in tears.

"It's not just about me anymore," she said aloud. The thought that he could have hurt the baby was unbearable. She drove home rubbing her belly and whispered, "I'll always protect you."

October flowed into November. All of the baby furniture and layette had been ordered, but in the house on Fox Drive, the nursery would remain empty until the baby's arrival. This practice was in keeping with the Jewish superstition even concerning joyful occasions, known as *keinehora*, or "no evil eye." On the day of the baby's birth, everything would be delivered and set up.

Julie and Doug were invited to the city to attend the bar mitzvah of a friend's son. Julie, now almost seven months pregnant, looked as chic as ever in a black velvet maternity dress. She and Doug enjoyed the celebration, and afterwards, as they were walking on Lexington Avenue, they passed a pet store.

"Let's look at the puppies!" Doug exclaimed with delight. They stared through the window, laughing as they watched the puppies tumble over each other. "Look at that little golden retriever!" Doug said, pointing to an exuberant ball of fur.

"She's amazing!" Julie gushed "Let's go in and play with her." They entered the store, and before long they were petting and holding the puppy as she licked their faces.

"I think she wants to come home with us," Doug remarked.

Julie widened her eyes. "But we're having a baby in two months!"

"Puppies and babies blend nicely," Doug said with a wide grin.

"No, not at this time," Julie said, shaking her head. "How will we manage a baby *and* a puppy?"

Doug insisted that they were up to the task, and an hour later, unable to ignore the tugging on their heartstrings, they were on their way home with the tiny golden, along with bags of food and chew toys.

"She is a doll!" Julie giggled. "But we are crazy!"

During the drive, they talked about how they would set things up for their new arrival, whom they named Samantha. She was a lovable puppy, and they were sure she would live up to the reputation golden retrievers have for being excellent companions to children.

At home, they set up the crate in the bedroom next to the nursery and spread out some newspapers in the hope that Sam would soon be housebroken. They assumed they would wake up every few hours to take her out in the backyard but that in time, Sam would wait until early morning to do her business. And Doug planned to come home in between patients to let her out to run around in the yard.

That night when they went to sleep, it only took a few minutes for Sam to start howling, missing her littermates. The crate was transferred to the master bedroom so that Julie or Doug could stick a hand into it to comfort the dog. Yes, goldens were smart, but Sam was still a puppy. Doug lived up to his promise to come home from his nearby office to let her out, and if he couldn't, he would send a secretary. They were going to make it work.

The next project would be to hire a nanny. Julie planned on working three days a week for a total of thirty hours and drew comfort from knowing that she would be home for much of the time to observe the nanny and the baby. She put together a list of agencies, called them and sorted through applications. Having chosen a few that looked like possibilities, she composed a list of interview questions, including years of experience, background and references.

At work the next day, she asked Dr. McQueen, "How do you do this? I mean, how do you really know whom you are hiring?"

"You really don't," Dr. McQueen told her, "unless it's a direct referral from a friend who hired the nanny in the past."

"I hope I can handle this," Julie said.

"You *will* because you have no choice. You'll strike a balance between career and motherhood. Some women are fortunate enough to have the grandparents who babysit, but we don't have that option."

After interviewing a few applicants, Julie hired Nia, a warm, friendly woman from Trinidad. Her good track record, contagious laugh and kindness toward Sam were selling points. Julie wanted her to start two months before the baby arrived, which was coming up soon. It was a relief to know she would have help running the house and caring for Sam.

December arrived, and the holiday season was

underway. Shops in the Five Towns sparkled with Christmas tree ornaments and Hanukkah menorahs. On a Sunday night after a day of shopping, Julie came in the door and heard the phone ring.

"I had a boy!" cried Angela. "He's incredibly adorable!"

"That's wonderful! What's his name?"

"Mark," Angela gushed. "There's nothing in the world that can compare to this! I can't wait for you to see him. And Julie, you're next!"

Angela was so warm and loving that Julie knew she would be a fantastic mom.

Meanwhile, Julie continued to prepare her nest. Demonstrating on a doll, she taught Nia how to perform CPR on a baby. She wrote lists of instructions for her: never open the door for anyone or for a package delivery, never bring the baby near an oven or a pot of boiling water, and pick up the baby whenever he or she cries. Julie didn't believe in character building during infancy.

"The baby is not even born yet, and you're already a worried mom!" Doug laughed.

Julie nodded. "I've always been so intense with my schoolwork. Now I'm getting intense with motherhood."

Angela was given a two-month leave of absence, and during her weekly phone conversations with Julie, she recounted every detail about baby Mark. She especially loved breast-feeding and rocking him to sleep.

"How much are you missing work?" Julie asked.

"Not one drop!" replied her dear friend. "Julie, what are you having?"

"A boy. I'm thinking about names. Maybe Drew?"

"I love it!" Angela exclaimed, as her baby cooed in the background.

CHAPTER 24

Early one February morning, Julie was awakened by severe back pain.

"Doug," she nudged him "It's happening!"

He awoke, bleary-eyed. "Really? Get the stuff together."

The waves of pain would start slowly and then disappear, like a rollercoaster edging up a wooden track—creak, creak—and then suddenly...*whoosh*, the labor would go into full force. Julie and Doug slipped into comfortable clothes, grabbed the overnight bag and sped off to the hospital.

The doctors told Julie that she was not fully dilated and that she could expect lots of labor pain ahead. Using the Lamaze techniques she had learned, Julie breathed rhythmically between contractions. Sometimes the sensations were ridiculously intense, but Julie insisted on going through with natural childbirth and declined the epidural. In time, she fell asleep as the monitor hooked up to her belly registered peaking contractions. The doctor and Doug stared in amazement as she slept through labor.

At noon, Julie was whisked into the delivery room with extremely deep contractions.

"Push, Julie!" the obstetrician coaxed. "You don't want to be pregnant anymore!"

She made one final great effort, and a small head emerged from the birth canal, followed by a tiny, perfect body. For a moment everything went quiet, then came the piercing cry that is music to parents' ears.

"Here's your baby boy!" the nurse said joyfully.

Doug leaned over to kiss Julie. "You are amazing," he whispered.

"What color is he?" Julie asked.

"Darling," the doctor asked, "what color were you expecting?" Everyone in the delivery room laughed.

"No, I mean, I hope he's pink and breathing well."

"Yes, yes, he's breathing like a champ."

"Does he have a cleft palate?" asked Doug, hovering over the pediatrician, who was examining the baby.

"Are there any congenital birthmarks?" Julie asked.

"You are some pair of new parents!" the obstetrician said.

Finally, the beautiful newborn was placed on Julie's belly. Tears streamed down her face as she held Drew's tiny hand in hers.

Two days later, Julie and Doug took their son home to Fox Drive. Nia greeted them at the door. As Julie walked into the house, Sam brushed against her legs, softly whimpering, sensing that something special was happening.

They went up to the nursery, now set up with baby furniture, a navy-and-white comforter in the crib and, above it, a mobile of two hundred animals spinning to classical music. A rocking chair was draped with a navy-and-white throw, and a small toy chest decorated with multicolored balls was tucked in the corner. A wallpaper border of a train with little animals popping out of the cars lined the nursery walls.

Julie, who would have liked six weeks of maternity leave, was granted four. She was disappointed but decided to enjoy every minute with baby Drew. Totally enchanted by motherhood, she didn't want to leave the nursery.

Nia was a great nanny and taught Julie how to swaddle the baby and how to burp him. Sam would sit quietly at Julie's feet as she held Drew in her arms, rocking him back and forth. Whenever Drew was napping, Julie would catch some sleep or relax on her bed with a book. Nia, who was more than just a nanny, would bring Julie tea and biscuits. When Drew was fussy, Nia would rock him in the baby swing.

Every evening, Nia would cook delicious dinners: spicy jerk chicken or the traditional roasted chicken that Lara had taught Julie to make. All of this smoothed the way for Julie to ease into her role of mother and reduced what could have been a high level of stress. Julie felt fulfilled with all the blessings: her new home, her husband, her baby, Sam and Nia. She had everything she had ever wanted, and more.

And then, like Cinderella hearing the clock strike midnight, she had to go back to work. Missing her baby, she wept as she drove to the Public Health Hospital.

Dr. McQueen and Angela, who was now back at work also, assured Julie that everything would be fine.

"You'll finish residency, work part time, and the nanny will take good care of Drew," Dr. McQueen said. Those words helped a little but were small comfort for a new mother who had to make a huge adjustment.

In the emergency room, a one-year-old girl had just been admitted for high fevers and an inflamed tongue. She had developed scarlet fever as a result of strep throat. Before antibiotics, the child would have died, but now the girl could be treated and would recover. Julie saw the agony in the parents' eyes and understood, really for the first time, that her own life would never be the same now that she had a child. She would always worry about his health and well-being, even more than their own. Motherhood had given her a deeper dimension of compassion. That night, she rocked baby Drew in her arms, kissing his little hands and head, whispering, "I'll always be here for you."

It was April, and everything was in bloom, this time on the front lawn of Doug and Julie's house. The flowers appeared in stages—first the fluted heads of the daffodils, then the tall, straight tulips, followed by the colorful azaleas. On weekends, Julie would take the baby out for a stroll and would admire the gardens of other houses in the neighborhood. There were many different architectural styles in town: colonials, ranches and Cape Cods. Some were like her and Doug's, small and cozy, while others were large and stately. The wide, shady streets curved and sometimes led to a pond or harbor. As she walked along with Drew in the carriage, locals nodded and smiled, in the spirit of the close-knit the community, and she was completely content.

As residency was coming to an end, Julie was considering her options. Questions ran through her mind. *Should I take a full-time position at the hospital working with residents? Should I work in a private practice? Maybe I should start my own practice.*

Doug favored the last option, which offered Julie the flexibility to create whatever schedule she chose.

"But I don't know the first thing about running a business," Julie told him.

"You'll learn. I did."

"But I don't even know how to write a check!" It was true. At age thirty, she had never written a check. Her father or Rick had taken care of that. She had even managed to have Kevin write all her checks, and then Doug inherited the role.

"I don't want that responsibility!" she insisted.

"But, Julie, if you're not your own boss, you'll have to do whatever the boss tells you to do," Doug countered. "And when it's your business, you can take write-offs. And even better, you can refer your patients to me!"

Julie felt her level of frustration rising. "Doug, you are not listening to me! I do not want that much responsibility! Running your own practice is an extra job. I'm a one-trick pony. It will be more than enough for me to see patients and take a teaching position with the residents, which I really want to do. Most important, though, I want to have lots of time with the baby. And what about when we have our second child? Anyway, how do I start a practice? Just hang out a shingle? Find employees? Billing? It's all overwhelming!"

"I'll help you with billing and supplies. You find an office to rent from another physician, and I will help you place ads for employees," Doug offered.

"But the patients. Who will send them?"

Doug wouldn't back down. "You'll introduce yourself to doctors in the area. You'll give lectures to the local community hospitals and give out your cards."

Julie rolled her eyes. "That's an awful a lot of work to do when I just want to see patients. I want to just go in with an established group and not worry about staff or rent or supplies or where to find patients. I want to work and come home and be with the baby."

"Julie, I'm telling you, financially, having your own practice is a much better option."

"Why're you only thinking about finances? What about lifestyle?" She started crying.

Doug became impatient. "Stop being so emotional! I'll support us in the beginning, and I'll help run the practice. Just find a rental space and give some talks."

"But that is not what I want!" she screamed. Doug left the room. There was nothing more to say.

The next morning Dr. McQueen approached Julie in clinic. "Let's have lunch together," she said. "I want to talk about next year."

As they sat in the cafeteria and had tuna sandwiches and coffee, Dr. McQueen broached the topic. "Julie, how would you like to be a part-time teaching attending doctor at the Public Health Hospital?"

"*Really?* Oh, Dr. McQueen!" Julie was thrilled. "That's my ideal scene! I would like nothing more than to combine academics with residency training!"

"You could work at the hospital two days a week. I think that'd suit you, right?"

"Yes, yes! I'll take it!" And they toasted with their cups of coffee.

Driving home that afternoon, Julie was elated. She had accepted Dr. McQueen's offer and planned on finding a position in a private practice for two days a week, which would provide a four-day work week. She started her search by asking the drug reps if they knew of anyone needing a part-time dermatologist. Her timing was great. One of the reps knew of a Dr. Astor in Manhasset.

"She's an elderly dermatologist, probably approaching eighty, with a very small practice. She wants a young associate," the rep explained.

Julie had not even considered working for a retiring dermatologist. She had been thinking more of something along the lines of a large group practice. However, maybe this would be a compromise. She'd be joining an existing practice, and in time it could be her own, if that is what she decided would be best for her and her family.

She went to see Dr. Astor. Elegant, with platinum blonde hair swept up in a French twist, she had piercing blue eyes, an aquiline nose and a tight-lipped smile. She wore a matching set of large pearl earrings and necklace, and a tailored knit suit that flattered her slim silhouette. Julie was equally elegant in her short navy-blue suit, white silk blouse and black Ferragamo flats.

Julie greeted Dr. Astor with a warm handshake. The doctor looked her up and down and then asked Julie to sit down. Wasting no time, Dr. Astor blurted out, "I'm eighty years old and I'm ready to retire. My practice is very small, but I've been in Manhasset for fifty years." Then she paused. "Are you Italian?"

Julie was taken aback by her bluntness. "No, I'm Jewish." she responded.

"Well, you probably won't be welcome in the country club, but the community loves Jewish doctors, lawyers and accountants. Besides, you have the right look—slender and polished, and you don't look Jewish! Plus, you'll be the only female dermatologist around here, and that works well."

Julie did not want to get into a discussion about what "looking Jewish" was. Dr. Astor's comment seemed indelicate, but Julie considered that she was retiring, and the office was only thirty minutes from her house. She paused and cautiously asked, "Are you looking to sell the practice or have an associate?"

"There's nothing really to sell. I just want to work for year or so. You can build up the practice to your liking."

Julie then explained that she could work only two days a week because she was finishing up her residency and also had a teaching commitment. Dr. Astor was fine with that.

"I suggest that you work two half-days a week to begin with. One morning for the ladies, and one evening for the acne brats," she said. "Maybe you want to do a Saturday morning once a month for the few working women. I'll pay you 50 percent of whatever you bring in."

By the look of the office, it had not been updated for quite a while, but still and all, it was in a medical building. Julie felt that with some networking, she would be able to gradually build up the business, and in the meantime, she wouldn't have any overhead.

That night at dinner, holding Drew in her lap, she reviewed the plans with Doug, explaining that she would work two days a week at the hospital and two half-days and one Saturday morning a month at the practice. There would also be time set aside for making contacts. She reminded Doug that she also had to study for her board certification exam coming up in November. Even with all of this, she assured him, the schedule would allow her plenty of time with the baby.

Doug didn't seem to have the guilt that Julie had over the time *not* spent with the baby.

"Stop counting the hours," he told her. "Drew will be fine." Julie was catching on quickly that new moms and dads experienced parenthood differently.

So even though Julie had protested loudly about not wanting to have her own practice, she acquiesced to Doug's coaxing and planned to work with Dr. Astor. But privately, she felt overwhelmed by the prospect of working in the hospital, starting her own practice, studying for the boards, and being with the baby. *I'll take it one day at a time,* she reassured herself. She cuddled with Drew in the rocking chair, telling him that while she might develop herself as a doctor, he was now, and would always be, her most special love.

In June, the residency was coming to an end. The days were long and warm, and Julie was eager to get home and take Drew and Sam for their early evening walk. Afterwards, she would give Drew a bath and would sit in the comfy chair and rock him. As Sam licked the baby's toes, Drew would giggle. His large hazel eyes would open wide when he heard the singsong sound of the nursery rhymes. Then, soothed by the cadence and rhythm of his mother's voice, he would snuggle his perfect little head into Julie's neck and fall asleep. To Julie, this evening ritual, which she looked forward to all day, was nothing short of heaven.

CHAPTER 25

July 4, 1989, felt better than any Independence Day ever. Residency was over! The ensuing months would serve as a bridge connecting two pivotal phases of Julie's life: academic and professional work and studying for the board exams in November. With all of that going on, she would also be starting up her private practice. It was quite an intense schedule for anyone, especially for someone raising a young child.

She and Doug were spending the holiday at the Atlantic Beach Swim Club, where they were members and had a cabana. Julie unpacked their beach gear, *slathered* sunscreen on the baby and plopped him in the stroller in a shady spot. Smiling at the woman in the neighboring cabana, Julie said hello and introduced herself.

"I'm Susie," replied the slender, attractive woman as she eyed Julie up and down.

"My little one is five months old," Julie volunteered, "and yours?"

"This one is six months old, but I also have a three-year-old boy. Are you new here?"

"Yes," nodded Julie.

"I never see you during the week," the woman commented.

Julie opened up. "I work during the week. Just finished my residency in dermatology, so I couldn't get here. But I'm so looking forward to this break now."

"How will you be a doctor with a baby?" Susie asked, as if no woman with a baby had ever worked before.

"I'll be working part time, and we have a really wonderful nanny."

"Well, I decided to give up my career when I became a mom. And trust me, I had a big job in marketing."

Perhaps not wanting to lose a potentially cordial relationship, Julie found herself almost apologizing for becoming a doctor.

"Well, it's only part time," she uttered meekly.

"Try it, and let's talk in one year," Susie replied and laughed in a know-it-all kind of way. *I can never get away from this type,* Julie mused. *I went through this in grade school and college and now in the grownup world. These intimidating types seem to follow me.*

Julie told Doug she was ready for a walk on the beach. He carried the baby, who giggled as they dipped his chubby little feet into the surf. The smell of the sea water and the blue-green of the ocean exhilarated Julie, but she could not shake Susie's comment. It had struck her Achilles' heel. *Will I have enough time for my little boy?*

On the way home, she recounted the whole conversation to Doug.

"I'm already being judged as being an undevoted mom," she spluttered.

"The woman is a nasty, insecure bitch!" Doug replied. "She's jealous that you're a doctor."

Julie shook her head. "No, that's the way they think out here in the suburbs. It's not like the women in the city, who have careers."

"You'll find a group of intelligent women, either

professionals or some who are not catty. Don't let it get to you."

But it did. Julie felt a gnawing in her stomach. She didn't care what this woman thought of *her*, but she wanted Drew to be a part of a play group as he got older. She knew life was very cliquey in the small communities and didn't want to be excluded right from the start. She planned to go to the beach club during the week and would try to be friendly with the women. Certainly, they couldn't all be as rude as Susie, or at least she hoped so.

Following through on her plan, Julie was able to meet a few pleasant women. One had previously worked in finance, and another was a lawyer who had chosen to stay home with her child. The first one was thrilled to be a stay-at-home mother, but the lawyer was terribly conflicted. She admitted that her kids were adorable, but what would happen to the skills that had taken her so many years to acquire? Two other women, one a doctor and the other a dentist, were also trying to blend motherhood and careers.

Julie appreciated everyone's struggle. Most of them acknowledged that their mothers had not worked, and those who had were either teachers or nurses with regular hours, and they certainly were not the boss. In the movies and television shows of the 1960s, the female characters were either career women with no children or stay-at-home mothers and wives. For this current generation of highly-educated women, there were no role models, requiring them to pave a new path.

Adjustments would have to be made in Julie's approach to work. She had always strived for perfection, but now her work had a major competitor named Drew. And the problem was that she loved both kinds of work. She was zealous in her role of doctor, but she also relished all the facets of caring for her child: watching him grow, exploring the world with him and reading to him at bedtime. Even as she began studying for the boards, she would read through her notes at her desk while Drew sat in her lap, crumpling papers in his tiny but strong hands. He would crawl to the bookshelves and pull books onto the floor, gurgling as he flipped the pages. Julie somehow managed to concentrate, knowing her little boy was occupied and safe.

The schedule was fully packed. As she had planned, two days a week Julie was at the Public Health Hospital, and two afternoons a week she worked with Dr. Astor. In November, once the boards were behind her, she'd be able to focus more fully on developing her practice.

Of course, she had a lot to learn about running a practice. Whereas Dr. Astor ordered supplies without any regard for price, Julie, with Doug's help, got set up with medical suppliers and negotiated fair prices. She needed to order instruments, compose billing forms and create stationery and business cards. In the back of her mind, she was aware that once Dr. Astor retired, she would have to find new office space. But for the moment, there was plenty to do.

The contrasts between the diseases treated in the clinic and those in the private practice were eye-opening. Since patients in the clinic didn't have easy access to medical care, the skin diseases were severe, whereas the private patients would come to the doctor for a pimple or mild rash. Julie saw this as "survival of the wealthiest," and vowed that she would always be involved in treating all patients, whether they were wealthy or poor.

Finally in November, with the boards completed and her mind clear, Julie started her new routine, combining the private practice and her work at the teaching hospital. Simultaneously, she would be building her own practice on top of the small existing one.

As per Doug's advice, she joined the staff of three community hospitals and obtained a list of their doctors. Systematically and methodically, she introduced herself to the doctors, handed them her CV and politely asked if they would refer patients to her. The delicate part was establishing herself in a community where most patients already had dermatologists. Her strategy was to say, "I know you must have wonderful dermatologists that you refer patients to, but if for any reason the patient would like to see another doctor, I'm available."

And it worked. Julie she began to see patients who were pleased with her service and referred family members and friends. But while she was achieving her desired goal, she was often alternating between elation that patients liked her and the worry that if they did not, she would lose the referral pattern from the physician.

Over the following months, Julie's head spun with the rapid growth of her practice. She boosted it by giving lectures to local community physicians and offered talks to OB/GYN physicians on dermatological disease during pregnancy and on other skin and genital conditions. She addressed pediatricians on acne, eczema and viral infections and lectured to family physicians on skin cancer, psoriasis and vascular diseases. The lectures were successful and resulted in an increased number of patients. Some female patients invited her to speak at local community chapters of the American Cancer Society, women's charity groups and recreation centers. She also had a grass roots approach to networking, distributing her cards at the hairdresser, nail salon, tailor and dry cleaners. Every effort increased her patient base, and the office was soon humming with business.

Next came the issue of which insurance plans to accept. As her old boyfriend Rick had once predicted, medicine was changing. The long-established pattern of fee-for-service was being replaced by insurance plans that would dictate the fee for a given visit or procedure. Some doctors resisted being in-network providers who had to accept the insurance plan payments, but Julie felt that as a new physician she would have to be on many insurance panels. Some of the payments were dreadfully low, less than one would pay for a haircut at a fancy salon. Some physicians compensated for the decrease in reimbursement with an increase in patient volume. But that had its downside. How many patients could one see in an hour and still deliver meticulous care and present a good bedside manner?

The fear of a malpractice suit was always in the back of a doctor's mind. As a physician, one couldn't just make an error and apologize for it, as in many other professions. One of Julie's colleagues put it aptly: "If a doctor diagnoses a melanoma, they get $75 from an insurance company. But if they *miss* the diagnosis, the lawyer will sue them for millions." And so, accuracy was paramount.

Another colleague noted, "Patients want excellent care in an unrushed environment, no wait time in the office and a caring physician." That certainly made sense to all physicians, but how would one maintain a decent income without seeing a huge number of patients? It was a dilemma: work longer hours to earn more, or work regular hours and earn less. As a mother with a young child, Julie chose the second option.

In February, Drew was a year old, and Julie and Doug threw a big party. Fifty people piled into their home on a sunny, frigid Saturday. Little Drew, looking like a miniature college boy in his navy-blue sweater and corduroy pants, got lots of attention from the guests. Julie and Angela hugged each other long and hard and then traded their baby boys, cuddling and admiring them. Many good friends, among them Julie's good friend Sara, arrived with gifts.

After the guests gave themselves a tour of the house, Sam scampering alongside them, they gathered in the dining room, where there was plenty of food: platters of turkey, roast beef, corn beef, chicken and an array of salads, along with finger foods like franks in blankets and tiny knishes. Then out came a spectacular chocolate birthday cake topped with an entire small-scale circus: a Ferris wheel, merry-go-round, lions, tigers, elephants and trapeze artists. It was a satisfying, love-filled event.

In the evening, after the guests left and Julie and Doug sifted through the gifts, Julie smiled at Doug sentimentally.

"We're so blessed!" she said. "We are in our own private practices, we have a gorgeous home, and most important, a beautiful, healthy son!"

Doug hugged and kissed her, but then suddenly he looked at the floor. There were cookie sprinkles on the carpet, wrapping paper and odd cups and plates everywhere.

"Let's clean this up," he said. "All the wrapping paper, it's really a mess."

"OK," Julie answered. "Let's clean up the sprinkles now but do the wrapping paper tomorrow. I'm exhausted."

"No! Now!" Let's clean up the entire mess now!" he shouted.

Julie was angry. Why couldn't they just relax and clean up the next day? But this was Doug. He wanted a perfect environment, whereas Julie could ignore the mess till morning. Julie was aware of this trait before she married Doug. She had seen it in Rick and walked away from it, but she didn't walk away from Doug. No matter how much his finicky nature upset her, she was not going to leave. She needed the order he created in her life, even though she resented it. Just like Rick, Doug took care of everything, but the price Julie paid was that he had to have everything his way. Could she have started her practice without his help and encouragement? Probably not. Could she have set up their home while finishing residency, starting a practice and having a baby? Definitely not. Doug was Doug, handsome, brilliant, exciting and urbane. Even though his perfectionism and control were oppressive, he provided a stable foundation so Julie could grow. She accepted all of this, but still, she had tears in her eyes. Cookie crumbs and wrapping paper. How important were they? *I'll change him,* she thought, trying to soothe herself. But she had said this a thousand times before.

—— PART 6 ——

AGE OF ANXIETY

CHAPTER 26

One Friday night in December, Julie and Doug, along with baby Drew, the new nanny and Sam, piled into the Mercedes and headed for a ski weekend in Vermont. Around 11:00, the snow finally stopped pelting down as they drove along the two-lane road, just outside of Killington.

Julie had dozed off but was suddenly awakened by a forceful, unnatural sensation. The car was spinning in 360° turns.

"I'm OK, I'm OK!" Doug kept repeating. Then suddenly it was dead quiet as he steered the car over the median to avoid a huge truck barreling toward them. The truck swerved on black ice, and as the driver slammed on his brakes, the trailer jackknifed into the Mercedes. It was eerily quiet as the car slowly rolled off the road. Then came a thunderous bang as it tumbled into a ditch. Steam started to rise from the snowy ground.

Julie screamed, "The baby! Is he OK?"

Nia just stared ahead of her. "He's not in the car!"

"What?" Julie shrieked

"He was crying, so I took him out of the car seat." Then came a faint crying from outside. Was the baby trapped under the car?

Doug tried opening his door, but it was stuck. He kept banging his head against the window and heaved against the car door as blood dripped down his forehead and cheeks. Julie continued screeching, "My baby! My baby!"

Local residents, hearing the crash, came running out and jerked the car door open. Then they saw him. There, on Route 9 in Rutledge, Vermont, baby Drew, clad in red pajamas, was standing on a mound of snow. He stood perfectly erect, his arms reaching up as he called out, "Mommy!"

Julie ran to grab him and saw the small bruise on his forehead. Sam was circling them wildly. As Julie scooped Drew up, she cried out, "Dear God, I'll never ask for anything again!"

Doug ran onto the barren road toward the truck driver.

"I really tried to avoid hitting you," the driver repeated over and over. "Damn black ice!"

Doug grabbed his hand. "Listen, we all did our best, and we're all OK."

The people who had come to their aid helped Julie stand up, as she was clutching the baby and crying hysterically. The nanny, who had admitted to taking the baby out of the car seat, just kept staring ahead silently. Julie's trust in her had vanished.

Everyone tried to make sense of what had happened, and when they did, it amounted to nothing short of a miracle. Apparently, the rear window had cracked apart on impact, and Drew had been catapulted out. As he flew through the air, his body had, amazingly, not touched any of the broken glass, and more amazing was that he simply landed on a mound of snow.

The locals called an ambulance that came and took the family to the hospital. After being examined, they were discharged with no injuries. Grateful to be alive and unharmed, they continued on by taxi to the condo they had rented for the weekend.

The next morning the sun was out, and the sky was a clear blue. Snow dripped from the branches of the evergreens as Julie and Doug skied a few runs. Julie, usually a timid skier, felt that after surviving the horror of the previous night, she could easily handle the slopes. She glided down the mountain, following Doug's smooth turns.

They came back to the condo, invigorated from the exercise and fresh air. Doug lit a fire in the fireplace while Drew played with his toy xylophone and piano. Not even two years old, he already showed signs of musical talent. He laughed loudly as his pudgy little hands plopped down on the xylophone's colored bars. Julie nestled into a large leather armchair with a glass of Chardonnay. Doug, knowing that Julie wanted to cuddle the baby, picked him up and placed him on her lap. A small stack of Drew's favorite books was close by, and Julie opened one and began to read in a soft voice. It did not take long for Drew's head to nod as his eyelids began to close. Julie inhaled the clean scent of his freshly washed curls, and then, completely at peace, she winked at Doug as the baby fell asleep.

CHAPTER 27

On the second weekend of a chilly April, Doug set off to Colorado on a ski trip. Julie didn't want to go, feeling that she was still mentally recovering from the car accident. She also valued her private downtime, as there was not that much of it these days. In Doug's absence, she could catch up on some things that had been waiting and would have some time to give Drew special attention.

The week went fast, and the following Thursday, Doug was home again. On Friday night, they went out to dinner with friends, and the guys drank their vodka as the girls sipped white wine.

The following morning, Julie left to put in her Saturday office hours. She and Doug had plans to go out again that night, while Macy, the new nanny, would babysit Drew. Julie arrived at work in an upbeat mood. In private practice for almost two years now, she had built up a clientele of local community patients and was enjoying her success.

At about 11:00 a.m. she was attending to a patient with a painful abscess on his back. She had prepared him for incision and drainage by injecting a local anesthetic. Just as she was finishing up the procedure, there was a knock at the door.

"Come in!" she called out.

Her receptionist slowly opened the door and whispered, "Dr. Kent, the nanny is on the phone. It's important."

Julie's heart began racing, instantly imagining that something had happened to Drew.

"I'll be right back," she told the patient. "Just lie still." She ripped off the bloody gloves and ran to the phone. Barely breathing, she managed to gasp, "Macy! Is the baby all right?"

"Yes," Macy said calmly. "It's not Drew. It's Dr. Doug. He's acting really strange, like he's having a nervous breakdown."

"Dr. Doug *gives* breakdowns, he doesn't *get* them. What's going on?"

"It's like he can't talk," Macy said.

"Put him on the phone," Julie said, thinking the man had had too many vodkas the night before.

Doug came to the phone. "Hi," he said softly. "It's weird."

"What's weird?"

"It's like I can't talk."

"What do you mean?" Julie probed.

"I can't find words."

"OK, what's your son's name?"

"I...I...don't know," he answered.

"Is it Mike?"

"No."

"Is it Tom?"

"No."

"Drew?" she asked, feeling panicky.

"Yes, yes! That's it!"

By now, Julie felt her throat tightening and her ears burning. "Don't go anywhere!" she told him. "I'll be there soon." She finished up with the patient, flew out of the office and drove home.

It was true. Doug *was* acting strange. One moment his speech was fluid, and the next, he couldn't find words.

"We have to go to the hospital," Julie told him.

"There's nothing wrong! I probably just had too much to drink last night."

"No, this is not a hangover. There's something off. Maybe you have an aneurysm. One minute you're lucid and then you're not."

With a little more cajoling, Doug agreed to go the hospital, where he was admitted for observation. His speech was getting worse, and he looked frightened. Julie was frightened too, but she tried to conceal it. She had always counted on Doug to be the strong one, but he was dissolving right before her eyes.

The doctors ran a series of tests that all came out negative, yet over the next few hours, Doug didn't improve. Finally, a young neurologist appeared with her senior attending doctor, and they concurred that he was experiencing an atypical migraine or stroke.

"What?" Julie exclaimed. "He has no risk factors! He's athletic, his blood tests are normal, as is the MRI."

"Even in the event of a TIA or early stroke, the initial MRI would be normal," the neurologist said.

Within the next twenty-four hours, Doug's symptoms, including aphasia, started to abate, but no one understood why. Doug's brother-in-law Todd, a cardiologist, visited him in the hospital. He told Doug that he'd recently read an article describing a new medical condition called "patent foramen ovale," which could lead to atypical migraine or strokes in young, otherwise healthy patients. Hearing this, Julie felt faint.

"This could be a *stroke*?" she asked weakly.

"I'm not sure," Todd replied, "but there's a Dr. Mohr at Columbia Presbyterian who is doing research on this, so let's call him."

The next morning, Julie telephoned Dr. Mohr's office and explained to the secretary that they needed to see the doctor urgently. Not surprisingly, there were no appointments open for at least one month. But Julie pleaded, and the secretary put her through to the doctor. After telling him Doug's age, perfect state of health, and the spontaneous nature of the aphasia, the doctor grew interested in the case.

"Bring him to the neurological unit in the morning," he offered.

An ambulance brought them to the medical center, where Dr. Mohr performed a transesophageal echocardiogram. It revealed an opening between the two atrial chambers of Doug's heart. These should have closed up after birth, he explained, but in some people, they remain open, creating a condition known as "a hole in the heart." This could account for a stroke in a young person.

Dr. Mohr went on to perform a Doppler exam of Doug's lower legs. It showed a clot that normally would have traveled to the lungs and be filtered or, dangerously, would have caused a pulmonary embolism. But since in Doug's case the two chambers of the heart were connected, the clot went the wrong way and ended up in the carotid artery and then the brain. It was not a stroke per se, but a "transient ischemic attack," or TIA. The doctor's best guess of the cause was that Doug developed a blood clot as a result of dehydration on the long plane trip home from Colorado.

"What now?" Doug asked. "Will this happen again?

"Well, you're fine now, and the chance of this happening again is about the same as two planes crashing in the Colorado Rockies," the doctor said with a smile. "So for the moment, no surgery is required. We'll put you on Coumadin to prevent blood clots, and you need to stay hydrated to prevent future clots. You know what that means—minimal amounts of coffee and alcohol." Doug seemed resigned, but relieved at the same time.

He was brought back to his room, and Julie stayed to talk privately to Dr. Mohr.

"What if this happens again?" she asked in a shaky voice, "and if it's a full stroke next time?"

The doctor took her hand, looked her in the eye and

said, "Don't worry about that. None of us are God. Please relax and assume we have taken care of it. I can't promise you anything, but the chances are that it probably won't happen again."

"I'm just so nervous! I feel like we are skating on thin ice!"

"Try not to think any more about it. If you focus on this, you're going to have a nervous breakdown, and then there'll be a *new* problem. Please, just try to relax."

Despite the doctor's efforts at soothing her anxiety, Julie left the consulting room in a state of emotional paralysis. She took a long, long walk down the corridor to Doug's room. Opening the door, she put on her best smile.

"What did the doctor tell you?" Doug asked. "Am I going to be all right?"

For the first time since she knew Doug, Julie told a white lie, using some, but not all, of what the doctor had told her.

"He said that you're doing perfectly, and with the Coumadin this is not going to be an issue. But you need to stay here for a little while."

That night, after the entire surreal episode, Julie lay in bed with little Drew sleeping next to her. He snuggled closely, and as she kissed his silky hair, she felt a degree of comfort. Just hours earlier, she'd heard the most frightening news concerning Doug. Four months before that, they'd had a horrible car accident. *Are we cursed?* she pondered. *Or is this just a of spate of bad events?* Cuddling in bed with Drew was a gift, helping to stop her mind from racing. She reminded herself that they had all survived the accident and that Doug had survived the TIA.

A week later, Doug came home from the hospital. He looked tired and weak. To avoid complicated and revealing conversations that they did not want to have, they told everyone that Doug had had a skiing accident and was now convalescing. Within two weeks, Doug's speech returned to normal, and though somewhat psychologically vulnerable, physically he felt as strong as ever and insisted on returning to work.

At home, though, Julie detected a frailty in Doug that she had never seen. One evening during a quiet dinner, he confided that his body and mind had failed him. His strongest attribute, he felt, was his razor-sharp intellect, and now he feared that it had been compromised.

"I keep thinking, what if this happens again?" he said with dread. "And if it's not *minor*? What'll we do *then*?"

"Doug, Dr. Mohr said the chances of that happening are really slim. You're strong now, and we were very lucky. It's been a tough year, really tough with the car accident and now this. But let's focus on the amazing miracle that we are safe." It took a lot of acting to hide her fears, which were exactly the same as Doug's.

Feeling depressed and defeated, Doug said, "I'll never ski again now that I'm on Coumadin."

"You will ski," Julie said softly. "You'll teach Drew to ski too. And by the time he's old enough for the advanced slopes, they will have come out with a device to close the hole without surgery." She was trying hard to convince herself of her own prognostications.

That night, as they made love for the first time since the TIA, Julie sensed Doug's hesitancy. She knew he was afraid that the vigorous sexual activity would dislodge another clot. But she encouraged him, knowing he needed her body to tell him he was still strong. Afterwards, as she closed her eyes to sleep, she felt a sense of dread, one that would be with her for a very long time.

CHAPTER 28

By the time summer arrived, Drew, now two-and-half years old, was a healthy, curious, beautiful little boy. Julie rearranged her work schedule in an effort to spend more time with him. She put in ten-hour days at work on Monday and Thursday, and half-days Tuesday and Wednesday. That freed her up to take Drew to Mommy and Me classes at the library and music classes for toddlers. Those afternoons were the highlight of Julie's week.

Drew was remarkably alert and astute for someone his age, and definitely marched to beat of his own drummer. There was a certain intensity in his hazel eyes, and it was clear that the wheels of his mind moved rapidly. An independent thinker, Drew had no hesitation about doing his own thing in class. If every child ran to the right, he ran to the left. As other toddlers stared vacantly during music class, he banged rhythmically on the toy drums and piano. Julie took all this as a positive sign of his intellectual and physical growth.

On weekends, Doug and Julie drove out to the East End of Long Island, which was known for its pristine coastline. The Hamptons had always been the summer paradise for affluent families, where they could enjoy the wide, sandy beaches and brisk waters of the Atlantic. On the way to Southampton, they stayed at small hotels, where they could cycle with Drew in his own seat on Doug's bike. The roads leading to the beaches had a peaceful magic about them, with the bay on one side and the ocean on the other. Tall, swaying grasses rose from the dunes. and seagulls and egrets dotted the marshlands.

A favorite spot to stop was a small lobster shack that offered lobster rolls, fries and iced tea. Drew picked at chicken fingers, throwing little bits into the bay as he watched the swans dabble for the food.

Feeling the soft, warm sand underfoot and hearing the lull of the ocean soothed Julie and Doug's souls. It was good medicine, and Julie observed that Doug had gradually regained his physical and emotional strength. The TIA, which they now referred to as "the event," was behind them now, and they took comfort in the simple pleasures of nature, content to just feel well and happy. Seeing their son's tiny footprints in the sand reminded them of the many blessings they had enjoyed so far.

"I'd like to buy a house out here," Doug mused, as they walked on the beach.

"What? You're kidding!" Julie responded. "We are working so hard! Our practices are blooming, and we just got around to finishing our home."

"It's a good time financially," Doug insisted. "There are lots of new developments out here. Just think—a swimming pool, tennis court and a large backyard. We could never afford that in Lawrence." In his usual way, Doug was thinking in practical terms. And in *her* usual way, Julie was concerned with the social and emotional aspects of the situation.

"But Doug, if we leave our neighborhood on summer weekends, I'll never get to socialize with the other women."

"And???"

"Don't you understand? I need to be friendly with them for Drew's play dates."

Doug sighed. "As usual, you're overthinking and obsessing. Julie, I'm telling you, this would be great for all three of us!"

Julie smirked. "You just don't get how cliques function in the suburbs. Most of the women don't work, which makes me the pariah. Either they think I'm not a good mother because I *work*, or they are intimidated *because* I work. Most of these women grew up together. They act like they're rich, but their money is coming from their parents."

"Look, there are a lot of people to choose from. Just find a group that suits you and thinks like you. I know this: We are buying a summer home," he stated.

There was not going to be any further discussion. The next week, they lined up appointments to see a few houses in the Hamptons. The first one, in Hampton Bays, was a model of a wooden house with a large front yard and backyard. It had a modern feel, with light, stained floors and high ceilings. The realtor was emphasizing the pool, tennis court, yard, four bedrooms and living room with a fireplace. By the end of the week, Julie and Doug had gone to contract to purchase a similar house that would be built by the following summer.

Julie didn't know what to say. She should have been elated, but instead she was just overwhelmed. Back in Lawrence, with more than a hundred patients a week and a toddler at home, her main concern was to integrate herself and her child into life in the neighborhood. She had no real friends yet and now would have two homes. She felt totally frazzled.

But then there was a breakthrough. Joining a tennis group, Julie met Emma, a young lawyer who shared many of Julie's interests. Julie felt an instant connection with this woman who grew up in the Bronx and was bright, cultured and elegant. Emma loved classical music, theater, ballet and dogs, and so the two women bonded quickly.

"I've met a friend!" Julie announced gleefully to Doug over dinner.

"What friend?" Drew piped up. They both laughed out loud.

"I met a woman during a tennis drill. We want to go out as couples," Julie gushed. "Her husband is a pediatric dentist, and they live in the Five Towns."

"Great, Julie. I am glad for you. See, I knew it would happen."

"She's so bright! She loves piano music, and we're going to do a book club!"

"I hate to say I'm always right, but I *am*," said Doug with a nod. "I told you to give it time and you'll find friends that you can relate to."

For the first time since the event, Julie felt relaxed. There was a lot to look forward to.

CHAPTER 29

Within the next year, Julie and Doug's beach house was completed and fully outfitted for year-round use. In keeping with contemporary styles, they had designed and furnished the interior in light, neutral hues, with sleek, Scandinavian furniture. The house had a serene, modern look, yet it was child-friendly and safe for their three-and-a-half-year-old son.

Julie was delighted to have her own tennis court in the backyard, as she was now a tennis enthusiast. She especially enjoyed playing with Emma. Tennis was almost a form of meditation for Julie. The rhythm of the ball going over the net and the alternating change in body position were therapeutic and cleared the mind of all extraneous and trivial concerns of daily life.

In the meantime, both private practices were flourishing. Doug had been in practice for six years now and had treated many neighborhood residents. He wanted to expand the business to include cosmetic surgery, as many ENT doctors had done, and felt impatient to get to that goal.

"Just give it time," Julie assured him. "You're plenty busy, and you're helping people. Don't let your ego influence you." She knew Doug was driven by the prestige of the specialty.

Julie worked part time, but even on the half-days she would return from work completely exhausted. On her short days, she'd see about thirty patients, and on the long days, close to fifty. Always a victim of her own rigorous standards, she required her staff to be assiduously attentive to patient needs. If she received any negative comment, be it about booking an appointment, not being properly greeted, or encountering rudeness on the phone, she went into a tizzy.

"I have control over the doctoring," she'd tell her employees, "but I cannot control what goes on in the front and back of the office. You are a reflection of me. Please keep that in mind." Nevertheless, it was always a challenge managing staff. If they didn't book an appointment, Julie worried that the patients were not being accommodated. If they *overbooked* patients, she'd be upset when people complained about a long wait in the office. She remembered how, in the years back in Brooklyn, patients might wait for hours, but would never complain to the physician. Well, it was not like that now, at least not with *her* patients. She worried constantly that any unhappy patient would make a disparaging remark about her to the referring physician or the community, potentially damaging her reputation.

Julie had done well these last five years and never expected to be as busy as she was, but that gnawing insecurity about not being good enough was always there. Perhaps it was a good thing, something that compelled her to keep to her high standards. She knew it would take all her energy to see as many patients as she did, and so it was only a matter of time before she would have to hire an associate. This was not something she looked forward to, as it meant dealing with yet another personality. But how long could she go on being so fatigued? And what about the quality of her time with Drew?

When Drew turned five, he was brighter and more curious than ever. Julie felt that he needed the stimulation of an all-day kindergarten program and found one that seemed suitable. He liked his teacher, Mrs. Bell, so for the moment, that piece was in place.

Drew's latest interest was dinosaurs and everything about them: their names, the era in which they lived, whether they were carnivores, vegetarians or omnivores, and every other possible detail. Julie encouraged his interest by reading dinosaur-related stories and would play games in which the two of them took on the roles of mother and baby dinosaur. Drew jumped around the house hunching over and curling his fingers as he pretended to be a T-Rex.

Julie enjoyed their afternoon activities and assumed Drew was doing well in school, but there was still that unresolved piece: she was concerned that because she wasn't interacting with the other mothers, Drew wasn't asked to go on too many play dates. The answer was for Julie to be more social with the local women. But with her schedule, when would she have time for that?

Everything came to a head at the parent-teacher conference. Mrs. Bell asked Julie to sit down with her. Somehow, Julie sensed she was going to hear unpleasant news.

"Is Drew OK?" she asked, knitting her brows.

"He's a remarkably bright child. He loves science and music and is quite animated," Mrs. Bell said with a smile. "But Dr. Kent, he's an intense child. He doesn't always know how to engage with other children. He's way more intelligent than most of them," she confided in a hushed voice. "He quizzes them about dinosaurs, or circles around them, pretending to be one. It frightens them and when they run away, his feelings are hurt."

Julie's eyes welled up with tears. "Mrs. Bell," she said, stifling a sob, "maybe this is all my fault. Drew doesn't have many play dates during the week, probably because I have no time to mix with the other mothers. They all meet for lunch while I'm working, and when I get home, I'm exhausted. In the city, it's the nannies who take the children on play dates," she continued, her voice cracking.

"Listen to me," Mrs. Bell said, taking Julie's hand in hers. "The problem is *not* that you work. Drew is a very bright, wonderful little boy. His mind is working so much faster than the other children's. It's good that he enjoys science, but he needs to do silly, fun things and just be a little kid. Teach him to play at simple activities like throwing a ball and blowing bubbles. That will relax him, and you'll see—he'll interact better with the other children."

"Thank you, Mrs. Bell," Julie answered, grateful that the teacher had been honest with her.

Who knew how strategic one had to be with such young children? It was time to encourage Drew to be plain silly, and Julie knew that it didn't come naturally to him. She devised a plan. First, she took Drew to the toy store and let him choose some toys. To her surprise, he grabbed a set of Legos and a Slinky. Julie added some balls to toss, a few jars of bubbles and a small tennis racket. Next, she arranged some lunch dates with a few of the mothers in the hope that it would result in making play dates.

The lunches, now a necessary part of Julie's life in the community, were a tedious bore for her. In the limited amount of time she had off from work, she would have preferred to relax with a book or catch up on odd tasks at home that always seemed to be awaiting her attention. Instead, she was sitting with overly pampered, suburban housewives whose main concern was who gave the best haircut or had the best cleaning woman. Julie feigned interest in their mundane topics, but all the while she was thinking, *This is only a means to an end.* She was not even sure these women liked her or would have chosen her for a friend, were the circumstances otherwise.

Yes, the play dates were of the utmost importance. Julie was even willing to host some of them at her house on Saturdays. Despite desperately needing her day of rest, she would commit to taking the kids to the jungle gym or the movies.

The plan seemed to work. Drew was getting some invitations for play dates, but if Julie heard him quizzing the children with science questions, she would call him aside and gently say, "Drew, remember what we spoke about? Science is for some times, and silly fun for other times."

Drew would look her at her and say, "But Mommy, learning is fun, and science is fun!"

"Yes," Julie would say, "but some of us like science more than others do. Let's do what *they* like now, and later you and I can play at dinosaurs, OK?" Drew understood and nodded. In the subsequent weeks, he became better at interacting with others. It took effort on his and Julie's part, but all seemed to be going well.

CHAPTER 30

During February, Julie and Doug took Drew to Disney World. He was five years old, and it seemed the perfect time to for him to have the experience so many children long for. They knew he would be especially delighted to see Epcot, which had a huge dinosaur exhibit.

Every day for five days, they visited a different theme park and did everything on the list: Fantasyland, with the famous "It's a Small World" boat ride, the Dumbo the Elephant ride, the roller coasters at Frontierland, and the scary Snow White's Adventures ride, complete with dwarves and witches. They also visited the Hollywood MGM park and Universal Studios, but for all three of them, Epcot was the best. Drew was fascinated by the large, mechanical dinosaurs with their swaying necks and loud roars. Dinners were fun at the fish restaurant, with the huge aquarium to enchant the children. And there was also Epcot's international theme park, where individual countries each had a pavilion showcasing their history, culture and cuisine. During the day it was delightful walking down Main Street America, hugging the Disney characters, and at night Drew's eyes widened when he saw the fireworks display over the promenade. It was a spectacular, perfect trip.

Onboard the plane heading home, Julie was reading the inflight magazine and noticed an ad for a product that she thought might interest Doug.

"Look at this," she said, "It's ladders for your home in case of a fire."

"Don't you ever stop worrying?" he said, annoyed. "We just left Disney World. Relax and get a glass of wine." He went back to reading his novel.

I was just being practical, Julie reflected.

As they disembarked and walked toward the exit, they spotted Doug's mother Helen and their friend Mike. They had strange expressions. Doug's face stiffened. "Is everything all right?" he asked them.

"Just terrible!" Helen kept repeating.

"What? Did the house burn down?" Julie snapped sarcastically.

Mike took Julie's hand and gently said, "Yes, Julie, your house did burn down."

"What the hell?! What happened?!" Doug asked.

"They don't know," Mike answered. "It started while you were flying home."

They drove home to Lawrence and saw fire trucks lined up in their street. The smell of smoke wafting through the neighborhood was the burnt odor of destruction. From the outside, the house appeared to still be standing, but the front door was bashed in. Helen sat with Drew in the car as Julie and Doug walked into what was once their home.

The mirrors in the hallway were shattered, and glass was scattered across the floor. The ceilings were ripped open, with tangles of metal cables and coils hanging down like twisted snakes. The furniture in the living room and dining room was covered with soot, and the kitchen cabinets were missing. All of the china and glassware were smashed on the floor.

They slowly walked into the den. The large aquarium was gone. Totally evaporated. All the electronic equipment, the giant television set, the leather couch and chairs were gone. Everything had been consumed by the fire and burned to ashes. Then they slowly walked into the library. Somehow miraculously, the wooden cabinets survived, and all of the photo albums were intact. On the floor were Drew's bronze baby shoes, blackened but still attached to the base.

They went upstairs to find their bedroom covered in soot. Julie opened her closet door and saw her beautiful clothes, not burnt, but covered in ash and reeking of smoke.

And then they walked into Drew's room, and that was when Julie became hysterical.

When the fire destroyed the den, the flames travelled through the ceiling to Drew's room. There was nothing left—no furniture, no toys, no clothes. Julie could not help thinking that had they been at home, their son might have been in his room and would not have survived. Waves of nausea washed over her, and she collapsed momentarily on the floor.

Doug, stoic and practical, called the insurance agent, who came over promptly. He assured Doug that all of the policies were in order, and that all the damage and loss would be covered. The fire marshals deduced that the fire had started in the den. A leak in the roof allowed water, snow and ice to seep through the ceiling and onto the wires of the fish tank, causing it to catch fire and explode. The fire snaked its way up the walls to the Drew's room as billowing smoke filled the house. The fire alarm had malfunctioned, and so only when the flames burst the windows did the neighbors call the fire department.

That night, suitcases in hand, they all went to a local hotel. *Keep calm,* Julie kept repeating to herself, while sensing the fear in Drew's eyes.

"I am so sad for the fish," he said.

"They are in heaven," Julie said, comforting him.

"And my dinosaurs?"

"Don't you worry, my love. Remember, they were toys and can be replaced."

The blessing was that neither Macy nor the dog were in the house when the disaster occurred. Julie kept affirming to herself that this was their miracle. No one was harmed, and even their pictures were saved. That did not mean that it was not harrowing, but Julie could live with it.

The next step was to meet with the insurance agents to itemize everything that was destroyed or ruined. They kept multiple lists categorizing their possessions, and the damaged items had been photographed. In order to get reimbursed, Julie and Doug would have to replace an item and produce the receipt. What stunned Julie was the irony of the insurance policy: you could not get reimbursement unless you replaced the destroyed or damaged item. But what about poor people who couldn't *afford* to buy new items? They had paid for insurance and could not collect on it without spending *more* money. Just one more loss of faith in the world. Julie had already seen the increasing premiums for health care insurance and, for some patients, denial of access to health care and prescription coverage. Now she was cutting her teeth on the world of fire insurance reimbursement. It was disillusioning.

As a stopgap measure, Julie and Doug rented a small house in one of the neighboring towns and started the process of rebuilding their home. Doug took full control of the project and would complain that everything fell on his shoulders. Then Julie would whine that he didn't care about her opinion. This was their usual way. Doug would have the benefit of having everything his way, and Julie would have the luxury of extra time for herself. And so it went on and on like a ritual dance of pecking, posturing and mating.

After meeting with the architects and builders, they decided that they would design a colonial style house with high ceilings and multiple floors. Julie had no idea which kitchen cabinets Doug selected, which type of ceiling moldings or door frames, or which bathroom tiles were being installed. When friends asked about the home, she just shrugged and said, "Ask Doug!" And when they protested that she should be equal in the decision making, she shrugged again.

"What should be is not always what is." She decided to take the path of least resistance. If Doug needed to be in control, she was going to benefit by having time for herself and Drew.

The first task was to replace Drew's entire collection of dinosaurs.

"Oh, Mommy, they've returned from heaven!" Drew exclaimed.

Julie smiled. "I told you, they are toys and not real, remember?"

As the project progressed, Doug did assure Julie that they would furnish the house together, down to the last spoon and fork.

Yeah, she snickered to herself, *we'll see about that!*

CHAPTER 31

J ust at the time that the house burned down, Julie was in the midst of negotiating for a larger office. Her practice was so robust that she decided to hire an additional associate, and she knew she would need more space. Dressed in a conservative, navy-blue suit and Ferragamo flats, she started her quest by walking into five medical buildings in the area. The search was successful, and she found a suitable office space to rent.

Doug accompanied her to the final meeting with the realtor. His ideas were bigger than Julie's, and he suggested that she *buy*, rather than rent, her own office and hire additional dermatologists.

"Doug, I hate business," she whined. "I'm overwhelmed enough with just my current practice, and now I'm hiring an associate. I don't want to run a small business. Now you're talking *three* associates, more staff and more personalities."

"Oh, come on! You can do it!" he persisted. "You'll get extra staff, and your office manager will coordinate everything."

Julie felt her cheeks flush with anger. "Doug, you have to hear me. I know you think I'm capable, but this is not what

I want. Running a bigger office means more networking, more meetings with staff and lots of loose ends to tie together. I'm just not interested. You know that I really didn't want to own a practice to start with. I only wanted to work for another doctor, so this is good enough. As it is, I constantly feel the pressure of running an efficient office."

"Julie," Doug said with some frustration, "it's just all-around better to be your own boss."

She sighed loudly. "Some people want to be the chief, and others want to be the Indians. You're just not listening to me. I'm OCD. Everything I do matters to me. I *have* to do well. It unhinges me if I'm not running my practice efficiently. I feel like I'm getting a C or a D in a course where I should be getting an A, but to get an A requires work that I prefer not doing, at least not now with a young child."

"Julie, listen…"

"No, *you* listen. I don't like confrontation, and to be a good, effective boss, you have to enforce the guidelines. That's not my strength. A small practice, I can control. A large practice is not what I want. I truly only want to be a doctor. I've compromised enough by being a boss, so stop pushing me! You know what Shakespeare said: 'Uneasy lies the head that wears a crown,' and it's true for me!" There was nowhere for Doug go to with this.

Julie nevertheless ended up renting a space that was larger than what she planned. Doug worked with the architect and designer to create a beautiful and streamlined office. There were enough exam rooms to accommodate two physicians working simultaneously, as well as an aesthetician. Julie worried about the increased overhead and was irked by the fact that all of this was exactly what she had planned NOT to do.

She turned to her mother for emotional support. "I'm worried, Mom. I think this will be too much responsibility for me. I now have to concern myself with two physicians in addition to my patient load and have an aesthetician to keep busy."

"Julie, you're always worrying," her mother remarked sympathetically. "Listen, if the new doctors don't work out, you'll just fire them."

Julie shook her head. "No, I hate confrontation. I was raised by *you*."

Lara laughed. "Yes, I remember how you always wanted your schoolwork to be perfect. That's just you," she said. Julie knew that this was true.

By and by, the Stone family's new house was built and was quite perfect. Julie's new office was beautiful, and the associates she had hired were lovely people. All was flourishing, except for Julie's nerves. Like an iced cake on a hot summer day, the cake was fine, but the icing was melting all over the plate.

Springtime was particularly beautiful that year. As in years past, the flowers were blooming in succession: first the daffodils, then the tulips. Rows of tiny purple grape hyacinths sprouted, and the dogwood tree exploded with white and pink blooms.

Julie decorated the new office in jewel tones, with paisley prints on the banquettes and burgundy leather chairs. A large Asian urn atop the center table held silk flowers, and there was a wreath of silk lilacs, pansies and roses on the interior office door. Soothing classical music played continuously in the treatment rooms.

Julie began adjusting to working with the two new associate physicians, whom she privately referred to as "the Bobbsey Twins." Seeing to every detail, she wrote extensive lists of responsibilities, such as calling back referring physicians, writing referral letters and checking the biopsy logs weekly. Now, with more staff, she also wrote lists for the front desk and nurses. At home she wrote lists for Macy. Drew was finishing first grade, and she wanted him to have more nutritious meals, not just chicken fingers. She also wanted him to practice the piano, and of course play dates had to be supervised, so she scheduled them only on days she was home. She had Macy take Drew to tennis and karate lessons, and before long, she was getting calls to tell her that he was doing his own thing and not focusing on the lessons. This was not so much because of Drew's personality, but Macy's. She was sweet and easy, but she just let Drew do as he pleased.

Julie had the haunting feeling that wherever she was, she was in the wrong place. She was always smiling and appeared calm and well put-together in her smart clothes, but inside she was all knotted up. If she spent too much time in the office, she felt guilty about not supervising Drew, and if she cancelled patient hours, she felt the practice would suffer without her supervision. Forget talking to Doug. He thought she was overreacting and just making too much out of everything.

"Why do *you* have to take him to karate or tennis? Are you taking the lesson? Isn't that why we have Macy?"

"You don't understand," Julie insisted. "When I'm there, he focuses. Macy doesn't want to be strict with him, and you know he likes to walk to the beat of his own drummer."

"Big deal," Doug retorted. "He's not going to be the class athlctc!"

"But I want him to have the exposure, and without practice, he won't be good at any of this. Boys bond through sports."

Doug thought Julie was crazy, and on and on the discussions went. Team sports were not a priority for him, and he simply didn't think any of this was important. But Julie wanted a vehicle for Drew to be social, as he was naturally shy.

And then it came to a crisis point for her. As she came to the school one day to pick Drew up, she saw the mothers congregating and chatting about the day's activities. They turned and looked at her as if she didn't belong there. One of them, a skinny blonde, walked over and asked, "How come we never see you?"

Julie retained her composure. "You know I work. I'm a doctor, but I'm here every Tuesday, Wednesday and Friday," she smiled, defending herself.

"Oh, so your housekeeper is the mom on Monday and Thursday?"

"Macy is not the housekeeper. She is the babysitter for Drew," Julie answered.

Not to be deterred, the skinny one laughed and said, "A *black* au pair?"

Julie felt like she was going to lose it. "I think this conversation is over," she said sharply. She met up with Drew and decided that, like it or not, she was going to have to get friendly with some of the nicer women in the group. She would avoid the petty, nasty ones, and although she understood intellectually that these women were insecure and not terribly intelligent, she felt guilty that Drew might suffer from their clannishness.

Over the next month, she encouraged Drew to have play dates with some of the children who had working moms. She would take the children for a pizza dinner and have great treats at home. She arranged Saturday lunch dates with the mothers as the children played. To her surprise, she actually enjoyed the company of these women, who shared her conflict about being a working mother. She also befriended some very nice stay-at-home moms, but she vigorously avoided the "mean girls."

Macy went to school one afternoon to pick up Drew and came home noticeably upset. Drew and his play date zoomed into the play room as Macy and Julie set out cupcakes and juice.

"This woman is terrible," Macy said shaking her head.

"What?" said Julie.

"In front of Drew, she called me Mrs. Stone."

"Don't worry about it. I'll take care of it. Which one?"

"You know, the skinny blonde," Macy responded.

The next afternoon Julie went to school and walked straight up to the woman. "Excuse me," she said. "I am Mrs.

Stone, or Dr. Kent. Take your choice. But Macy is not Mrs. Stone."

"Oh, I was just being funny," the woman replied with a nasty grin.

"You're not smart enough to be that funny," Julie snapped back.

And at that moment, Drew came running up to her with his little friend, asking for ice cream from the truck. Julie walked away with her shoulders straight and didn't look back.

CHAPTER 32

When it was time to furnish the newly built house, Doug wanted to be completely in charge of all the decorating. He had a vision for the place being done in tones of bone, beige and gold and was all set to go ahead with making that vision a reality. He did not want or need any input from Julie. When she protested, saying that she'd like to be part of the design team, he answered her thus: "You don't have a sense of spatial proportions, and your taste is provincial. You weren't involved in the construction of the house, so why are you coming in at the ninth inning?"

"Well, here goes a catch-22!" Julie said, as she stomped around. "I let you do everything you wanted concerning the design of the house, and it's truly beautiful, but I may have done some things differently. I just thought I'd let you have free rein because it would be simpler. Now you're throwing that back in my face as the reason I shouldn't be involved with the decorating."

In truth, Julie wanted to decorate only the library and guest room. She loved the traditional Federalist and Chippendale styles, the rich palette of burgundy, navy, deep green and gold. She had envisioned the library as a warm, inviting place with a dark red leather Chesterfield sofa and a Persian rug, huge wooden bookcases and lots of luxurious paisley and plaid pillows.

"Doug, we're only talking about my decorating the library and the guest room, both of which you will probably never set foot in," she pleaded.

But Doug would not relent. "It's just a control thing with you."

"That's *not* the way it is," she screamed as she threw her hands up in the air. "Every time I want something, it's a *control* thing, but if *you* want something, it's because you know better."

In the end, Doug acquiesced to her wishes, but he complained bitterly that she selected wallpaper with a border of ducks, calling her taste "unbelievably provincial."

Hearing about the debate, Lara herself became frustrated, as did Julie's friends.

"This is incredible!" they bemoaned. "You work so hard and earn more than most men! And it's your home too!"

"Why not just pick out the furniture you want, and have it delivered?" Elizabeth suggested. "What's he going to do, send it back?"

Julie tried explaining her situation. "He won't stop lamenting and complaining. It's not like I'm afraid of him, but he'll sulk around, and that upsets me. You know I hate confrontation and the negative mood it creates, and anyway, sometimes I think I'm being petty. After all, it's only furniture."

Elizabeth balked. "It's more than furniture. It's your self-expression, your home, your environment, your nest. It should reflect you and your style!" Her face was turning red as she uttered, "Who died and left him king?"

It came to a crisis the following week, when they took a day off and went to the design center in Manhattan, a huge building laid out with rooms done by all the major designers. A client could wander from one room to the next and make choices from a wide range of styles. As with all shopping expeditions, Doug brought along his mother because, as he said, he "liked her taste."

As they entered a gallery with large glass ornaments, Julie picked up a hexagonal piece and exclaimed, "Look at this! Isn't it great?"

"May I help you, Madame?" a polite voice asked. Julie turned and saw a salesman standing there.

"Uh, I was just showing this to my husband."

"Oh?" he asked, looking puzzled.

Julie looked around, and sure enough, there was no one in the room but the salesman and herself. Doug and Helen had wandered off without telling her. She put down the ornament, tightened her lips and quickly walked into the next room, finally locating the two of them admiring some modern art objects.

"Don't you think you should tell me when you're walking away? I was just talking to myself in the other room and the salesman must have thought I was crazy!"

Helen laughed out loud. "Why do you want to be involved in this, really?" she asked. "You're so good at dermatology. Why don't you just stick with what you know?"

Julie flashed her eyes at Doug. "Are you going to say anything?" She couldn't believe he didn't defend her to his mother.

"Well, she has a point," he retorted.

Julie was flushed and teary. Being left out of all decisions was last thing she imagined when she got married. She realized that it wasn't about just the decorating. A marriage was supposed to be two separate individuals blending their values, interests and needs. While it was inevitable that they would not agree on everything, weren't they supposed to learn from each other and compromise? Passion was wearing thin these days as they were tired from work and angry with each other. But passion ebbed and flowed in a marriage. The one constant had to be respect and trust. Doug wouldn't compromise, and that indicated a lack of respect. He didn't stop his mother from criticizing her and *that* was a lack of respect and created a loss of trust in him. Sure, he liked the way she looked, he was proud that she was a doctor and he was delighted that she earned an excellent living. But that wasn't enough. He didn't defend her.

Doubts lingered in her mind as she went to sleep that night. She tried to snuggle close to Doug, but he kept rolling away, shutting her out, as he always did when she disagreed with him on anything. She didn't want to think about this. Everything on the outside looked great. Her patients loved her, the practice was growing, Drew was darling, bright and talented, and she didn't want to rock his boat.

She thought about Kevin and Rick. Where were they now? Would it have been different with them? Both of them would've wanted her to work less and have a bigger family. She knew Kevin wouldn't have given a damn if she'd wanted the house done up in polka dots and stripes, and although Rick was demanding, if she was sexually eager at night, it would nullify any friction they'd had. And if she cried, well, he just melted.

Was I thinking straight back then? she asked herself. *Was it the stress of Dad's drinking? The pre-med studies? Well, here I am with Mr. Perfect, who thinks that only his opinion counts, and I'm feeling lonely, unappreciated and criticized.* Did it really matter now that Kevin didn't know Chopin, or that Rick insisted on cakes from the German bakery? They'd both adored her. Doug didn't. She closed her eyes, tasting salty tears.

CHAPTER 33

After that day in the design center, Julie knew something had to change. As she wasn't going to leave Doug while Drew was still so young, she comforted herself by saying that in time, he would change. She considered that perhaps they would go for marriage counseling. Doug was a terrific, devoted father. He worked hard and took care of so many things. He didn't drink, take drugs, or cheat. *Yes,* she thought, *it could be much worse.* Somehow, she had to convince him to give up control and occasionally discuss issues when they disagreed, rather than take disagreement as a personal affront.

Julie knew that taking part in activities that were fun would definitely restore everyone's spirits, and to that end, she made a lot of plans for the summer. The Hamptons were idyllic. Julie loved driving to the country house and seeing the lavender and blue hydrangeas, the tree on the front lawn bordered by impatiens in wild shades of orange, red and purple. It was an enchanted garden, and their time there was blessed.

Each Saturday they started the afternoon with a long bike ride, rolling through the various towns on the East End.

Drew peddled his bicycle fiercely on the trailer attached to Doug's bike as they rode along Dune Road with the breeze in their faces. They would stop at a favorite beach and walk along the shore, staring out at the calm blue waves or fierce whitecaps. Back home again, they would jump in the pool with Sam. Then Doug would prepare an abundant barbecue of steaks, burgers and grilled vegetables. After dinner, they would stroll into town for ice cream, stopping off at the toy store for Drew.

On some evenings, they would drive into the towns of Bridgehampton or East Hampton, where the large windmill was always a welcoming sight. Small shops, ice cream parlors and bakeries lined the wide streets. Julie and Doug would meet up with friends and slowly walk and chat as the children scampered ahead of them.

The Hamptons provided an escape to the pristine beauty of white beaches, coves ideal for kayaking, bike roads abutting beaches, and the lore of the Peconic Bay. Doug bought a powerboat to take onto the bay to use for water skiing. He took them boating on most Sundays, weather permitting. The bay could be smooth as glass or choppy and bumpy, but with Doug at the helm, Julie felt safe. They always went boating with other couples. Doug was an excellent captain, and as he stood there with his tall, thin frame and sinewy, muscular arms, he looked very handsome. They would sail to Sag Harbor, originally a whaling town and now a quaint, quiet enclave.

Many of these towns were settled during colonial times, and they retained a charm of days gone by. Each town had its own personality. Southampton was reserved and proper with boutique stores. Now, in summer, the windows of women's clothing shops dazzled with garments in hot pink, lime green and orange. The men's clothes were always conservative: khakis, blue pinstriped shirts and navy blazers. Easthampton, once very artsy, was now becoming hip, with upscale restaurants and trendy shops. Bridgehampton had a slew of antique shops and terrific restaurants. Sag Harbor was laid back, with fish restaurants, small shops featuring bohemian clothing and bookstores chock full of candles, chimes and books on spirituality, meditation and Buddhism.

The harbor housed huge yachts as well as much smaller crafts. Somehow a trip to Sag Harbor always included two stops. The first was a huge toy store featuring multicolored kites, Legos and dollhouses. The second stop was for lunch at a local seafood restaurant on the water with huge burgers, fries, lobster rolls and ice cream cones. They enjoyed walking by the boats and glancing at the various names, some of them picturesque or amusing, such as *Seascape, My Toy* and *Recovery Room.* Some boats were named for women, such as the *Elizabeth Joy* or the *Goodbye, Liz.*

"Must've been some divorce!" Julie laughed. Doug named their boat *Skin Deep* as a nod to their professions.

They also took the boat to towns on the North Fork of the East End. Greenport had a beautiful carousel set in the town square and, of course, a commercial street with antiques, collectibles and beach clothing. Claudio's was a large restaurant on the edge of the dock, where one could order huge platters of lobsters, steamers, clams and shrimp, reminding Julie of Lundy's in Brooklyn. Greenport itself was a hub for ferries to Shelter Island and Connecticut. On Sundays, one could see the bikers with their leather vests and tattooed arms, their women wearing short shorts and black ankle boots with chains. This was definitely a different scene from that of the South Fork, especially East Hampton, where people got dressed up just to buy milk.

Shelter Island was its own haven. There were rolling hills and marshes and small coves for kayaking. Accessible only by ferry or boat, it was a bit remote. And, of course, there was Montauk. As the last town on the South Fork, it was called, "The End." It had a sense of a sturdy seafarer's destination. The Atlantic Ocean loomed forever, reaching the horizon. Gosman's Dock was a square at one end of town, with small stores and a huge restaurant featuring every type of seafood. Montauk had its famed lighthouse, the Montauk Point Light, where one could climb the tower and just stare at the vast expanse of the Atlantic.

On occasion, they took a ferry ride to Block Island in Rhode Island. A charming New England island, Block Island was its own special world. Large stone fences ringed grassy lawns in front of houses dating from the 1600s. They rented bicycles and rode up to its lighthouse. Julie reflected that most women loved lighthouses, as they were very romantic. Beacons in the storm to ships on the ocean, they connoted a safe harbor. How many women fantasized about making love in a lighthouse with a secret lover?

As a result of going boating, Julie lost her fear of water and felt exhilarated. It was a bonding experience for her and Doug. Sometimes she would just stare out at the wake and the prismatic color display created by the sun's rays on the waves, and she was mesmerized by the sparkling dots of light. At moments like these, the world seemed perfect.

Fall arrived, and once again came the tangle of colored leaves and a new school year. Time was passing quickly as Julie and Doug worked hard and played hard. It was now two years since the fire, and they were back in their home and their routine. Drew was seven years old and was ever brighter and more curious. On Sundays, they would take him to museums, especially the Museum of Natural History. Drew knew everything about dinosaurs, reptiles and mammals, and loved talking about rock formations, lava and volcanic eruptions. He never tired of peering at the dioramas displaying the flora and fauna in the different regions of the world.

Theater and music were the passions that Julie shared with Drew, and on Saturdays she took him to Young People's Concerts at Lincoln Center. He had started piano lessons at age three and was now playing classical music. As a spectator,

Drew was fascinated by the orchestra, its musicians and their instruments.

Doug started taking Drew skiing when they went to the Berkshire mountains. Drew glided down the gentle slopes, taking to the sport unlike to any other physical activity. He had no fear and truly had a spirit of the outdoors, loving biking, hiking and running on the beach. Julie loved that father and son had such a wonderful bond. The slopes at medium pitch (blue slopes) were just fine for her, but Drew and Doug skied much deeper, ungroomed terrain. Julie had to stop worrying about the Coumadin that Doug took daily and the risk of falling. She had to let it go or she would never be at rest. The scent of the evergreens, the glistening white snow, the smell of logs in the fireplace and the plop of marshmallows in hot cocoa were an eraser, clearing her mind of all tension and worry. And when Drew came back from the slopes with his cheeks flushed and his hazel eyes sparkling, Julie's heart swelled with satisfaction.

That night in the lodge, she snuggled up to Doug. "I think we are giving Drew the childhood that we would've loved," she noted, laughing. "He's exposed to everything. We are such good parents. Shouldn't we have another child?"

"It's too late," replied Doug without hesitation. "You'll be thirty-eight. If we started trying now, we might not actually have a baby until you're forty."

Julie shrugged. "Many of my patients have babies at forty. That's not a problem."

"Julie, you're always concerned about not having enough time. You can barely keep your stuff in order now. How would you manage work and two children?"

"I've thought it out carefully. I will cut back work to two-and-a-half days for patients. I'll manage the office six hours a week, and I'll hire a separate cleaning woman for the house, so Macy can focus on Drew and a new baby. I'll see fewer patients, but I'll manage everything."

"Great," said Doug. "You'll earn less, and we will be spending more on childcare."

Julie cried, "Is money all you ever think about?"

He screamed louder, "Oh, excuse me! I didn't know you came from royalty and don't have to worry about money!"

"We have enough. I earn enough. What if I were a teacher?"

"I didn't marry a teacher," he snapped. "I wouldn't have married a teacher!"

"Clearly not," she hissed. "I'm earning a good living, and I'm still not allowed to pick out a pillow. People like us should be parents!"

He sighed loudly. "Don't you see that we just about keep it together as it is? If we keep on as we are, eventually we will be very comfortable and have the security we both want."

Julie rolled her eyes. "You don't get it. I want a brother or sister for Drew. I want another child. So we will have less! That's OK. If anything, I'll work longer."

"The house will be just more confusing. You're very overwhelmed. You're cut out to be a professional woman."

"I can be *both*. If I wasn't managing a practice but only working as a doctor, this would be a breeze." Julie was not going to let this go. "We are a married couple, and we need to discuss this. It's very important for me." She felt as if she was going insane. She never wanted to run a practice or be the boss, and now her success was punishing her! "I love being a mother."

"You *are* a mother. Topic is dropped," Doug said, as he got up and walked out of the room.

Doug was adamant. He didn't want more children, and unless Julie became pregnant by another man it wasn't going to happen. She felt angry and resentful. Why couldn't she have a second child? Professional success was blotting out her personal happiness. Doug was more concerned with the additional income she earned by running a practice and not working for someone else. He didn't care that she was overwhelmed or that she desired another child. She could've sold her practice and worked for another doctor. But as always, she acquiesced. Something inside her frightened her into not listening to her heart. Was she afraid of being abandoned by Doug? No. He wouldn't leave. But he would withhold love. And she needed his love and approval.

She was a ball of confusion. Her life was perfect on paper. Beautiful homes, wonderful practice, terrific child, fun trips, theater, museums and concerts. She felt ungrateful. But on the other hand, what was so wrong with wanting another child? Most of the women she knew had more than one child. Yes, her external life was perfect. But the compromise and respect for her needs and opinions was missing from the marriage. Yet, she felt safe and secure. How many times would she tell herself that Doug was brilliant, hard-working, a great father and didn't drink or cheat? But what about her needs as a woman?

Julie went to sleep depressed and didn't even want to cuddle. She went into Drew's room and kissed his cheek. "My little love," she whispered. She knew her seven-year-old son wouldn't always be so affectionate with her. She sighed. Something was missing. She needed to feel the deep love of a man. Not sexual love, but ultimate love.

CHAPTER 34

The day Julie turned thirty-eight, she went to work wearing a pretty red suit with matching shoes and a dash of bright red lipstick. She was feeling upbeat, which was good, because the office was very hectic that day. With three physicians and a support staff of more than twenty women, the place was buzzing. As the practice had grown, so had the weight of Julie's level of responsibility and management. The crown on her head was getting heavier with each passing day. She made a habit of delegating as much as she could to Bibi, her sister-in-law and office manager, but the final decision was always hers.

Julie thought constantly about how this situation had come to be. On quiet days, the associates complained that they weren't busy enough. On frenetic days, they complained that they didn't have time for lunch. Julie was beyond frustrated and concluded that all of this was her own fault.

She knew that somehow she would have to learn how to deal with confrontation and be OK with not pleasing everyone. Ideally, instead of listening to the complaints about scheduling, nurses not performing and general bickering among the staff, she would just tell them that nothing is perfect, but it was good enough. She tried to keep a brisk flow of patients for the associate doctors, but it was really their responsibility to increase the size of their individual practices. Constantly trying to make everyone happy was draining Julie's battery, and she needed to conserve her energy for her patients, not for disgruntled employees.

Most of the patients were lovely, but there were a few who always groused about the wait time. Some complained about the increase in costs of medication and co-pays, which Julie could not control. Some reported that the nurses and staff were rude, and although Julie knew this was not the case, she tried to placate them. In short, it was really quite stressful being a doctor, heading up a practice, and being a mother all at the same time.

Julie could remember precisely the moment when the first feeling of panic came over her. She was at the Estée Lauder counter in Lord & Taylor, looking at lipsticks. The store was quite warm and very crowded, as Mother's Day was approaching. Suddenly, out of nowhere, she was lightheaded and unsteady on her feet. Her pulse started to race, and she felt her throat tighten. She felt an intense level of terror, as though a Siberian tiger were chasing her around the store. *What is going on?* she asked herself. Within five minutes, the whole thing passed as though nothing had happened. She ran out of the store and into the quiet of her car.

That evening she waited to tell Doug when he came home from work. "I'm sick," she told him. "Something's wrong," and she recounted what happened.

"You look fine," Doug answered. "You must've been dehydrated or hypoglycemic. Did you have lunch? Were you rushing?"

"No, I wasn't rushing at all. I had eaten lunch and I was at the makeup counter, looking at lipsticks." Doug had no answer.

In a few days, she returned to the store, which was lively with women rifling through racks of spring clothing. Julie

picked out a few lipsticks and then went to the ladies' dress
department. She was choosing a few dresses to try on when the
awful sensation started to return. First, the flush in her cheeks
and ears, then the unsteady feeling as though she were floating.
She looked down on the floor to see if her feet were touching
the ground. She took her pulse. Normally sixty to seventy, it
was now in the nineties. A feeling of dread and panic overtook
her.

"Are you OK?" a saleswoman asked her.

"Oh, I'm fine. It's just so warm in here."

The saleswoman brought her into the dressing room
to sit down and then went to get her a glass of water. Julie
was already planning on what day she could visit her doctor,
but by the time the saleswoman returned, the symptoms had
disappeared.

At night she asked Doug if he thought she might have
thyroid problems or issues with her heart and brain. He told
her to go to the doctor. "It's probably nothing but anxiety," he
commented.

Julie knew she felt somewhat nervous her entire life, not
insecure about who she was, but frightened of the world being
a dangerous place. She thought back to the time when she
had a terrible neck spasms and anxiety attacks when her father
was drinking. *Maybe it's the same thing,* she told herself. In the
morning, she would set up an appointment with Dr. Green.

A few days later Julie was at the doctor's office. All the
blood tests, EKG and x-rays showed nothing. The MRI of
the brain was negative; fortunately, there was no evidence of a
tumor. The stress test and a cardiac sonogram both came out
negative.

Kind, strong and insightful, Dr. Green assured Julie that
there was nothing physiologically wrong. "Are you upset about
anything?" he gently asked her.

"Well, I'm always overwhelmed," she confided in him.
"I'm embarrassed. This must all be just my nerves."

"I do agree that you're having panic attacks, but that's nothing to be embarrassed about. You're a sensitive woman with a lot on your plate. Try to exercise, avoid caffeine and make your schedule easier," he advised.

Julie was grateful that there was nothing physically off, but the panic attacks were extremely uncomfortable. She read everything she could on the topic. Panic attacks involve sudden feelings of terror that occur without warning. Patients feel that they are having a heart attack, fainting or just going crazy, and the attacks aren't in proportion to the situation. Symptoms are a racing heart, feeling weak, having a constricted throat, dizziness, feeling faint, tingling in the hands and a sense of terror and impending doom. Usually the symptoms persist for ten minutes to an hour. Julie read that the disorder could run in families and that the symptoms are like those of generalized anxiety disorder (GAD) but to a more severe level. In GAD, patients might feel edgy and irritable and have multiple spasms, but panic disorder make patients feel out of control. The attacks take on a life of their own as the anticipation of the next one coming on leads to an avoidance of places where the first attack occurred.

Soon enough, Julie started to feel uncomfortable most of the time except when she was at home or in the office. She avoided crowded and noisy places whenever possible. Her delight in shopping was now diminished, although Doug suggested that she buy clothes to put herself in a better mood. The fear was spreading to any noisy place, including the auditorium at Drew's school, the supermarket or bustling restaurants.

One Tuesday afternoon after work, Julie ran to do a few errands before picking up Drew at the tennis clinic. She was in the local market deciding which salad dressing to choose when it seemed as if the jars and cans on the shelves were dancing up and down. She took a few breaths, as she had been told to do, but it didn't help. This attack, like those before it, came and went. Afterwards, she started worrying about passing out in front of others. *I'm a doctor in the community. How will this look?* she kept asking herself. *People will think I'm nuts!* She put one foot in front of the other made it to the checkout counter, focusing on the magazine display nearby. She drove home and asked Macy to accompany her to pick up Drew.

The next day she needed to be at Drew's school for a performance. Each grade was presenting skits to honor various countries. Drew's grade was representing China, with panda bears, costumes of the Imperial Dynasty, dragons and dances. As Julie entered the hot, crowded auditorium, the panic came upon her. She held on tightly to the bleachers for fear of toppling over and creating a scene. She smiled falsely at the other mothers, just hoping they couldn't see her terror.

After the performance, Drew, dressed as a dragon dancing and trolling with a big head and a long tongue, ran up to her. She fought hard for him not to see that she was in a terrible state. The parents were all taking the children for pizza, and Julie had to go too. She was jumping out of her skin as she sat in the restaurant, barely able to eat a slice.

After she took Drew home, she went to Foodtown to pick up milk, juice and snacks, but instead sat frozen in her car outside. She just couldn't enter the store, as the feelings of dread were overwhelming. Instead, she drove to the local Red Barn, which had a drive-through and ordered $100 worth of groceries for the week. The young clerk looked at her in disbelief, and she kept ordering milk, juice, ice cream, bread, snacks and cheese just to get through part of the shopping.

"It" was getting worse. She began to call the anxiety attacks "It" or "The Beast." It was affecting every aspect of her life. Late each Saturday afternoon after Drew's play date, she usually went to The Beauty Spot for a manicure and a hair blowout. Normally, she loved the relaxing feeling of being groomed. But this day, sitting in the crowded salon, she began to feel lightheaded. She reassured herself that she wouldn't fall down as she sat with her throat feeling dry and her palms sweating. She smiled as the hairdresser chatted away but had no idea what the woman was saying. She finally told the stylist that she had a migraine and needed to close her eyes. By the time her hair was blown out, she told the appointment desk that she had a patient emergency and couldn't stay for the manicure. She tossed money at the receptionist and fled.

She arrived home in a total state of despair. "I can't go out with friends tonight," she told Doug. "This is ruining my life. I hate going into stores. The supermarket feels like a lion's den, and I dread the salon."

Doug looked at her with sheer annoyance. "Just control yourself. It's your nerves. Toughen up!" Why did she expect him to console her?

They did go out to dinner to a small Italian restaurant. It went well enough. She got a glass of wine down, and that gave her a bit of an appetite. Lately, she had been losing weight, and patients were beginning to ask her if she was OK. She just told everyone that she was training for a marathon. As bad as the symptoms were, it was worth trying to hide them from others. The shame of being so nervous was demoralizing.

Monday morning rolled around. Julie wasn't sleeping well, waking up in the wee hours and worrying nonstop. So far, no attacks had happened at the office. She started to get dressed for work when, sadly, a wave of nausea overcame her. In the bathroom, she tried to vomit, but nothing came up.

"Can you shut the door?" yelled Doug. "You're fucking inconsiderate and waking me up!"

Julie slammed the bathroom door. Did he get up and hold her head or comfort her? He was bothered by her anxiety! It didn't fit his image of an ambitious, capable woman.

When the nausea finally passed, Julie pulled her hair into a ponytail and dabbed on lots of blush and lipstick. She put on a black turtleneck with a slim skirt and black tights, telling herself that her too-thin body would be considered fashionable and not anorexic.

On the way to work she started worrying about the food shopping she would have to do on Tuesday. Macy would certainly accompany her to the market. Julie confided in Macy about the panic attacks.

"I think I need a psychiatrist," she said.

"I think you need a different man!" Macy laughed.

Maybe both, Julie thought to herself.

The summer came, and Drew was off to day camp, enjoying all the activities. On the weekends, they went out to the East End, but now Julie dreaded eating out in all the nice restaurants, as the noise would trigger the panic.

What's bugging me? I'm losing my mind! she said to herself. She wouldn't take Valium because of what happened to her father with alcohol. When they went out with other couples, she would inhale a glass of wine. Normally chatty by nature, she felt herself to be quieter now. As of late, she had started worrying that she wasn't a good enough mother. *Drew must never sense my anxiety!* she promised herself. The blue waves of the ocean failed to soothe her, and with every day that went by, the sense of fear and dread drained her more. Her best time was nighttime, as she could lie in bed reading with no responsibility. In those few isolated hours, she didn't have to perform as a doctor, a mother, a friend, or a member of the community. *Maybe this is what it's like to be a vampire,* she mused. *They come to life at night.* But it truly wasn't funny. Feeling totally lost, Julie felt as if she was sinking in quicksand.

"'I can't do this without help!" she cried to Doug, "I'm having a nervous breakdown. I'm going to go seek psychiatric help."

"Psychiatrists know nothing!" Doug boomed.

Julie just stared at him. "I don't care what you think! I need this whether you agree or not."

That night, after deciding to do what she needed to do for herself, Julie slept, for the first time in a long time, like a baby.

CHAPTER 35

For some time, Julie had been feeling that she was falling deeper and deeper down a rabbit hole, to the extent that she barely recognized herself anymore. She did not discuss with anyone her decision to consult a psychiatrist.

Dr. Donner, who had been recommended by a close friend, had an office in her home on the North Shore of Long Island. Julie felt relief just making the appointment, and within a few days, she was sitting in Dr. Donner's waiting room on one of the comfortable chairs, surrounded by green plants. Just as she picked up a magazine to leaf through, the door opened. A petite, middle-aged, dark-haired woman with a warm smile stepped out to greet her.

They both walked into the consultation room, and Julie took a seat on the couch. The doctor gazed at her and quietly asked, "What brings you here today?"

"I'm a mess," said Julie. "I'm suffering from severe anxiety and panic attacks. It's affected every aspect of my life, except for my work and my child. Lately I can't sleep. I've lost ten pounds and I'm constantly nervous, and unless I'm with a patient, I have trouble concentrating. Sometimes my heart races and I feel lightheaded, and a complete sense of terror and doom comes over me."

Dr. Donner nodded. She asked Julie about her childhood. Had she had panic attacks as a young girl? Julie explained how she was anxious as a child, being raised to be frightened of everything, to depend on a man and to resist change, but she also said that her childhood was magical until she was eighteen. She recounted how her anxiety attacks began when she was engaged to Rick, which was the same time that her father began drinking heavily and was verbally and physically abusive. But then the attacks subsided. She didn't experience any severe anxiety in medical school or during her residency, even though she worried and was anxious about her performance.

Julie told the doctor that she'd had a wonderful pregnancy, had no postpartum depression and had never felt more relaxed. She enjoyed her work, but it had become overwhelming, even though the quiet environment suited her, and her treatment rooms were small and cozy. She enjoyed being with patients but frequently ran late. If a patient got angry because they had to wait longer than expected, Julie feared that it would have a negative impact on her practice, which it never did. She went on to say that the office with three physicians working at the same time was very busy and that she was always keenly aware that everyone was relying on her.

"I really don't know how I ever developed this," she confided. "Me and business—that's an oxymoron. I didn't even know how to write a check before I started this business. I just wanted to be a doctor in a clinic, working for another doctor. I wanted to spend most of my time with my son."

"Why did you start your own practice?" Dr. Donner pointedly asked.

"My husband thought it would be better financially and envisioned that we would link our two practices, which would result in more referrals. When I told him this would be too much for me, he said he would run both practices. I would just be the dermatologist."

"Why did you agree?" Dr Donner asked.

Julie paused. "Actually, I didn't. Just bringing up the topic caused terrible arguments between us. He would say I wasn't being practical or financially responsible. I didn't want to continue arguing with him, so I just gave in."

"So," Dr. Donner said softly, "you preferred sacrificing your needs for his needs?"

Julie reflected upon this. "Yes, I was raised to be a people pleaser and was conditioned to be frightened of just about anyone who could be intimidating. I was taught that confrontation in and of itself was harmful. I was told to always ask a man what he thought, as if my opinion were secondary." She paused. "Doug didn't push me to have a huge practice. In fact, he told me to work at a relaxed pace. It was I who felt that if I didn't accommodate the patients, I'd destroy the practice. Then I took in two associates and created more confusion for myself. I don't want to be the chief. I want to be the Indian!" she blurted out.

"You object to ultimate responsibility," said Dr. Donner, carefully treading on the issue.

"Yes, I do. I hate it. I only wanted to see patients. I don't like being the conductor of the symphony. I just want to be the pianist and let someone else conduct."

"Why do you think that is?"

"I don't know if I'm lazy or resentful, but to be truthful, I don't like the extra work. The money means less to me than it does to my husband. And, again, I don't like confrontation. When you're in charge, all the problems come back to you. I know that some people thrive on that, but I don't. This extra responsibility is a dirty word to me."

"Uneasy lies the head that wears the crown," said Dr. Donner, echoing a thought Julie had had so many times.

"I don't know. Maybe I think that if the practice were small, there would be no chance of failing. I'm always afraid that I could have the same reversal of fortune that my father had when I was young."

Dr. Donner knew she was onto a lot with Julie, and she pushed further. "So, if you don't achieve too much success, you won't fail?"

"Yes, exactly!" said Julie. It was the end of the session, and they had hit on the crux of the problem. Julie felt both exhausted and relieved, having talked to someone. "When will I see you next?" she asked.

"Well, because you are having severe symptoms at this time, I think we should see each other twice a week," the doctor suggested.

"Excellent," said Julie. "Will you be able to help me?'

"Of course I will! You will be fine. You will open up, and we will discuss everything. I see you are not afraid to be in touch with your feelings, and that is excellent." Julie left the office feeling somewhat better. She liked Dr. Donner's probing yet thoughtful, gentle manner, and she would make time to see her as often as necessary.

On her next visit two days later, she spoke at length about her work and fear of responsibility. She didn't even get around to discussing her conflict about working and having a child, or her anxiety when Doug was ill, or the fire.

"What is a panic attack?" Julie asked. "Am I having a nervous breakdown?"

"No, Julie, you're not having a nervous breakdown. You have no break with reality. You were just burning the candle at both ends. Some people have a genetic propensity for anxiety. They're just more sensitive to their environment, whether it is fast-paced, noisy or crowded. So, think of it as a pail half-filled with water at the start," Dr Donner explained. "Now you add in stresses, like juggling too much too fast or not getting enough sleep or down time. Then you can add in psychological stressors: your fear of failure, fear that you will lose the practice like your father lost his business, fear that you will disappoint your husband, that you're not a good mother if you work. You add these to a half-filled pail and voilà! you have an anxiety or panic attack. Now to add to the mix, once you have had an attack, your body goes into a protective mode to shield you from danger. But this protective mode has gone awry. We have to break the cycle because now you're fearful of another attack. Your brain is associating certain places as danger zones to avoid. If you were facing a tiger, your reflexes would be appropriate to get you out of harm's way. But your brain is now associating the supermarket as a dangerous place, because you had a panic attack there. It becomes a vicious cycle caused by overactive fight-or-flight hormones in your brain."

Dr. Donner discussed that anxiety comes from the shortage of GABA and serotonin compounds in the body. She told her that they would approach the panic attack from three vantage points. Together, they would discuss stressors in Julie's life, both physical and emotional. They would review relaxation techniques and lifestyle changes, and if need be, Julie would be prescribed medication to adjust the serotonin levels in her brain.

During the next few sessions, Dr. Donner helped Julie delve into family issues. What was her relationship with Doug like? Did she feel unconditional love and support from him? Julie answered honestly about her appreciation for all that Doug had done but also spoke about her areas of discontent. Her son, she said, was the light of her life, and she felt terribly guilty about being so absorbed in work. She started to cry when she told the story of the fire and how it might have killed Drew. She described Doug's TIA and how petrified she was that he wouldn't be well again, even though he was so healthy.

Reaching back further into the past, she then spoke about her father's drinking. William, she explained, was an incredibly hard-working man and good father except during his bouts of drinking, which brought about the loss of financial stability. She confessed that she never came to terms with the ravages that alcohol created because William had been her hero, her buddy, with whom she shared her love of poetry, literature and science.

"I felt betrayed by him when he drank, and he was so vicious," Julie sobbed. "I never fully digested this. And soon after he stopped drinking, I went to medical school and had no time to think—you know, to *process* it. I felt somehow that my father's recovery was linked to my being a medical student." She was breathing very hard, gasping for air as she ran her hands through her hair. Dr. Donner came over to her, took her hand and gave her tissues. "I fear," Julie continued, "that I may fail, like he did. Like Humpty Dumpty who took a fall, and nobody could put him back together again." Tears were streaming down her face, and she was shaking.

"You needed this catharsis," Dr. Donner told her gently.

Julie paused. "I pretty much went through this alone. I never even told my fiancé at the time."

"Oh, you were engaged then?"

"Yes, to a young medical student who had encouraged me to become a doctor. We broke up because I just couldn't trust men at that time." Julie caught her breath and continued. "Rick—that was his name—was very supportive of me, as my dad was. He could be demanding and liked to have his way, just like my dad and my husband, for that matter. But Rick also had a zany streak, and that reminded me of my father, who was never totally comfortable in his skin. My dad was a jeweler who wanted to be an English professor or a doctor. Rick was also searching to be different from the typical medical student. And so I drew a parallel between the two men and started to worry that Rick would betray me like my father did. I was so stressed out, and Rick was so demanding that I didn't even let him know how bad the drinking situation was at home."

Dr. Donner nodded. "Did you feel Doug betrayed you when he was ill?"

"Yes. I was terrified that I might have to be in charge. I don't really like to be in charge. Maybe it goes against the way I was raised, that I felt it was scary to be a boss, which is exactly what I am now. My mother always emphasized that being a homemaker and taking care of children were the priorities. Work—whatever kind of work—was secondary. She also encouraged me to depend on a man for the final say, as if my opinion didn't count. And so as a result, you see, I don't truly believe in myself, even though I'm really quite successful."

Dr. Donner continued. "Julie, it sounds like you're afraid and maybe resentful of responsibility. I think that you might associate responsibility with not being feminine, or you think that having responsibility will harm you."

Julie kept shaking her head up and down. Dr. Donner was striking a chord. "Why do you think that crowded places make me anxious?" she asked.

"At this point, you have associated panic with crowded and noisy environments simply because you're anticipating the panic. Probably, the panic initially occurred because you were so emotionally keyed up, and the stimuli of noise, heat and crowds added to your baseline anxiety. Remember how we discussed a pail of water brimming to the top? Additional water caused the overflow."

"Yes," said Julie. That sounded exactly right.

She loved her therapy sessions, feeling totally herself and absolutely unashamed to tell the doctor anything. Dr. Donner suggested that in addition to the talk therapy, she should exercise, meditate and resume hobbies such as piano playing, reading and tennis. These would help her to relax. She also prescribed a low dose of Zoloft, an anti-anxiety and antidepressant to increase the level of serotonin in her brain.

Julie took the proactive step of readjusting her work schedule to make it, as Dr. Donner suggested, "user-friendly." She loved her work, but the stress of seeing many patients and running the practice with multiple associates was just too much.

"I'm on the right train, but it's on the wrong track," she told Dr. Donner. She dropped some insurance plans to keep the practice smaller and decided to have only one associate once the second one left to start her own practice.

"You don't have to throw the baby out with the bathwater," Dr. Donner advised. "Keep the practice small so you don't feel overworked and resentful about it. It's your decision to run the practice the way you wanted it to be."

Julie accepted that she was a sensitive person who needed more down time than Doug did. She set aside time for meditation and imagery, picturing herself sitting by the ocean or in a garden or imagining the sound of the waves, the color and scents of flowers and the touch of soft fabrics. She even bought a machine that produced the sound of the ocean, crickets in the garden and waterfalls.

All of the steps she took were effective. Within four weeks of therapy, changing her lifestyle and taking her medication, Julie began to feel better and less susceptible to another panic attack. Dr. Donner also insisted that she work on changing those negative thinking patterns that added to her anxiety. They were myths from her past that had to be dispelled. Creating a more positive outlook was essential to good mental health.

Julie devised a list of the negative ideas that she would let go of and a list of positive- thinking mantras that she would now embrace.

1) **The Humpty Dumpty Myth:** *If something goes wrong, it will be a disaster, never to be put back together again.* This may have happened to Dad, but he was not an instantaneous failure. It took many mishaps and poor judgment, along with his false pride, for his business to fail. He refused to reconcile with his brothers, and when his new business failed, he wouldn't attempt to work with them again. It is catastrophic thinking to assume that anything that goes wrong will lead to disaster.

2) **I must please all of the people all of the time:** *If someone in my personal or business life is displeased, then everything good that I have accomplished won't be valued or*

recognized. Going forward, I will focus on the good that I can do, make changes when necessary and accept that sometimes, someone will not be satisfied.

3) **Stop catastrophic thinking:** *If someone is running late, it doesn't mean that he or she is in grave danger.* If one month, the practice is slow, it doesn't mean it is disappearing. Don't assume negative outcomes; they only heighten anxiety. Most of what I worry about never comes to pass.

4) **Black/White and Either/Or Thinking:** *In life, one can assume many roles and blend them together.* I can be both a mother and a professional woman. Guilt is a wasted emotion. Many working mothers schedule their time very efficiently and are just as, if not more, devoted than non-working women. It's the woman herself, not whether or not she works.

5) **The leopard doesn't change his spots:** *Totally untrue. If people want to expand their skill set and abilities, they could do so with hard work.* If people do not change, it's because they are not sufficiently driven to do so. I can be independent and can rely on my own good instincts.

6) **Pencils have erasers:** *This is true.* Most errors can be changed. Not all, but enough.

7) **To thine own self be true:** *I must do what I feel is right for me, even if others tell me not to.* I may have been on the right train, being a doctor and a mother, but on the wrong track, when the pace of life was incompatible with my goals. Family members might be impressed with my accomplishments, but they aren't the ones suffering from extreme anxiety.

8) **Just do it:** *If you want something badly, go for it.*

9) **Stop and smell the roses:** *I need time to regularly recharge my batteries.* Some people just need more rest and relaxation than others. Everyone needs some down time to appreciate the good things in life.

10) **Carpe diem—Seize the Day:** *Every day is a gift, and negative thinking is a waste of time.*

For the first time in a long time, Julie felt completely healthy and happy, and she was having no more panic attacks. She caught herself if negative thoughts clouded her mind. She even discussed her positive-thinking mantras with her patients. So many skin conditions and diseases, such as eczema, psoriasis, hives, itching and hair loss, were a result of chronic stress. Dispelling anxiety would help the patients.

Another wonderful insight Julie gained from her journey was that true friends didn't judge her when she was at a low point. Emma had gone with Julie to the supermarket when the panic was unbearable. Her friend Michelle insisted that she accompany Julie to the beauty parlor and clothing boutiques when Julie felt too anxious to enter these places. Michelle kept assuring Julie that so many very sensitive people, herself included, were prone to such attacks. Her sister Elizabeth and sister-in-law Bibi kept cheering her on to achieve the goals she wanted for herself and at the same time encouraged her to slow things down.

Ironically, when Julie confided to Emma, Michelle, Elizabeth and Bibi that she was embarrassed about her anxiety attacks to, they laughed.

"What?! You're amazing!" they all were quick to exclaim. "Don't you think you're entitled to be overwhelmed at times?"

Julie also rekindled her friendships with her doctor buddies, Angela and Sara. Being so busy, she had lost touch with them. When they met up, she confided how unhappy she had been and how ashamed she was of feeling weak. All three women went to lunch at La Grenouille and reestablished their everlasting friendship and support for each other.

Sara toasted, "Doctor, heal thyself!" and they all clinked their glasses of Champagne together. With a wonderful doctor, effective therapy and the strength of dear friends, Julie felt healed.

—— PART 7 ——

CRISIS AFTER CRISIS

CHAPTER 36

$\mathbf{A}$nd so it was that Julie triumphed over her identity crisis. Dr. Donner helped her find her way out of the maze of anxiety and despair, and with that, her zest and fervor for life and learning were restored. She no longer felt that she had to be Super-Mom and Super-Doctor because she realized that as a woman, she could have everything, just not all at the same time. She could be a devoted physician with a huge, successful business, but it would come at the price of time spent with her child. Likewise, she could be a mom who was involved in many committees at school and attend every baseball game, but then couldn't efficiently run a large medical practice. So considering all of these new-found truths, she listened to her heart and rearranged her work schedule to be the way she needed it to be.

Doug did not take the news well. "What's with you?" he asked her when she informed him that she was going to reduce the size and volume of the practice. "What's wrong with a having large practice?"

Julie shook her head, her eyes ablaze with fury. "It's just never enough for you, is it? I work hard. I am involved with Drew. And now that I want to scale back my work, you're annoyed." This time, she wasn't going to give in to Doug's opinion. "You know, Doug," she ranted on, "sometimes you just have to say 'enough!'" In his characteristic style, Doug turned and walked out of the room. As he did, Julie stared at his perfect butt. *Butt man,* she murmured to herself, feeling that she was always talking to his back. "And you know, Doug," she railed on, "I still have not put the rest the issue of a second child. I just turned forty and I'm healthy! We can still have another child!"

There was a stony silence. Doug's blue eyes glared at her. "Julie, you can't even handle *one* child. How could you possibly raise two children?"

Julie felt that she had been dealt a blow to her stomach. "What?" she shrieked. "Are you saying that I'm not a good mother?"

"You're too old to have a child! The incidence of birth defects increases at your age."

Julie shook her head in dismay. "It's almost the year 2000! Testing is performed routinely now to check for major birth defects. But you're right! Any baby can be born with a defect. It's a chance we all take!" She knew she was getting nowhere. So many of her Irish Catholic patients had their sixth or seventh child at age forty or even forty-five, but Doug had made his decision and wasn't going to change his mind. Julie felt lifeless. She so wanted to have a second child. "It's as though I'm being punished for working as hard as I did," she said softly. "If hadn't worked so much, there would've been no issue with my being stressed," she added.

"I wouldn't be married to you if you weren't an ambitious career woman," Doug said.

"Good to know," she added, between clenched teeth. "What if I was working in the emergency room and not a private practice?"

Doug stared at her for what seemed like an eternity. "You have to know who you are, what you're good at and what you're not good at. You love Drew, but you don't provide enough structure for him. With two kids there would be total pandemonium!"

Julie knew the conversation should end there, but she persisted. "What if we adopted a baby girl from China? You know the issue there with female babies. Then you wouldn't be worried about my being too old to have another child. It would be a blessing! Wouldn't that be a solution?"

Again, Doug stared at her. "You don't get it, do you? It's not only that I have no interest in adopting a child, I don't think you're capable of working and taking good care of two children. I don't want to start now with another baby!"

Julie felt the tears welling up in her eyes. "It's clear to me that you want me to work as hard as I can and function like a man, with a man's priorities. You want an equal partner when to comes to work, but not an equal partner when it comes to big decision making. You won't even discuss the baby issue with me. You just keep saying no. I'll drop my dream of having a second child, but things will change around here. Either we are equal partners in *all* aspects of life, or I'm not going to work as hard as I do."

As a result of this painful exchange, over the next few years Julie completely changed her approach to life. Especially with Drew growing older, she decided that she was going to take better care of herself, doing more of the things most women she knew did: manicures, pedicures, time with hair stylists, personal trainers, yoga instructors, tennis coaches, etc. If Doug chose to live in an affluent suburb and wanted only one child, Julie was going to pamper herself in a manner she felt she deserved.

Julie and her friend Emma met regularly every Friday morning to have breakfast and play tennis. They discussed the arts, music and politics. Emma was extremely informed about current events and prompted Julie to keep abreast of the news. But on this morning, Julie needed to talk about her personal crisis. She expressed her disappointment over Doug's reaction to having or adopting a child.

"I never wanted to see this side of him," Julie muttered between sips of coffee.

"Are you kidding me? He's always been a control freak," Emma responded.

"I know," Julie replied, nodding her head in agreement. "but he's an amazing father."

Emma paused before answering. "Look, Julie. Mike and I have known you and Doug a long time, so I think I can speak plainly. It's true, Doug is an amazing dad, but it looks like he's decided that his whole life has to be in balance, with him at the control panel. If you have another child, he knows he won't be able to go to the gym and do what he wants in his spare time, because there will be more responsibility. But more important, he thinks you'll be overwhelmed again and will want to cut down your hours or work for another doctor. And we know he does *not* want that!"

"I never thought about it that way. I'm his wife," Julie said in despair. "Don't *my* feelings count? I adore Drew, and I want him to have a sibling. And anyway, I would love to have other children."

Emma agreed. "No question about that, but Doug is not big on compromise."

Julie was tearing up again. "I have such gratitude, having a wonderful child, but my dream was to have more than one. We're good, ethical, intelligent people. and we should have more kids," she emphasized.

Emma took her hand. She appreciated that Julie was struggling. "You're not going to get anywhere with this issue. So either accept it, or divorce and have another child with another man. And we both know that you're not going to do that."

They finished breakfast and went to the tennis club, running each other from side to side of the court during a singles match. Dripping with perspiration, they laughed as they left the court. "I needed this so much!" Julie confessed to Emma. "Friends definitely fill the many voids in life," she said with a bright, wide smile.

◊ ◊ ◊

During the days of her panic attacks, it was difficult for Julie to even walk into a store, let alone spend time browsing through racks of clothing. How that had changed! Every Thursday now, Julie met with Michelle, her petite fashionista friend. Michelle had decided that Julie was a neglected Barbie doll. They met at the mall, and Michelle would handpick items of clothing she felt were perfectly suited for Julie's frame. The two women both loved jewelry and would visit the small boutiques and try on various pieces, feeling like royalty.

"You have no idea how pretty you are," Michelle told Julie. "You have been so busy working that you haven't focused on your femininity and style." She was being a true friend, as another woman might have been competitive and wouldn't want anyone to share the limelight. Michelle beamed with admiration as Julie, wearing a sexy outfit, walked confidently into a restaurant, her long, lustrous hair flowing behind her.

The women spent Thursday afternoons shopping for household accessories. At first, Michelle thought that Julie was exaggerating about Doug's resistance to her selecting anything for the home without his consent. But she quickly absorbed that her friend was not being dramatic. The only silver lining was that Doug was so impressed with the choices Michelle made with her discerning eye that he didn't protest.

Over lunch with Michelle one afternoon, Julie admitted, "I was just too focused on my training and then my practice to even care about my style, which was so important to me when I was younger."

Michelle smiled. "That's what friends are for!" she said. Then in a serious tone, she added, "We've got to take care of ourselves. If we don't, no man will do it for us."

With her newly-crafted lifestyle, Julie was happily busy. She enjoyed her days off, looking after her own needs and satisfying them. Now, at age forty, she was feeling younger and sexier than she did in her thirties.

The only problem was that she felt herself drifting away from Doug. What she found tolerable in the beginning, she now found absurd. She was an accomplished doctor, and yet he expected her to agree to everything that he wanted. He vetoed every suggestion she made, from traveling to Maine in the summer, to picking out wallpaper, to keeping canisters on the kitchen counter. It seemed that she was screaming at him with fury all of the time.

"You can't have it both ways! I can't be independent and ambitious at work and then totally passive at home!" Julie argued. There was less discussing and more arguing daily, and soon Julie began to doubt her sanity. She tried to implement the self-knowledge she had acquired during therapy, and to that end, she asked herself some pointed questions. Why was she even *listening* to Doug? She would scream and throw things in frustration, but still she was paralyzed and unable to do what she wanted. Why was she still so frightened about confrontation? Was she fearful of Doug's conditional love? She knew in her heart that he would never leave her, but she also knew that he was definitely capable of withdrawing attention and affection, which she always needed.

With a little more delving into the conditioning of her childhood, Julie recalled how she had gotten this message over and over from her mother: Marriage requires compromise. If it means not having your voice heard to avoid conflict, then so be it. *Well,* Julie thought, *compromise is excellent, and so is having a happy marriage with minimal arguing, but not at the cost of self-esteem and respect from a partner!* Perhaps because of the old belief that the world was dangerous place, Julie was still afraid of being rejected and alone. Some unrelenting, nagging voice whispered that she couldn't survive on her own. Would she collapse or have a nervous breakdown or fail if she were alone? Or maybe she just had a need to avoid confrontation, because by its very nature, confrontation is dangerous. This issue would plague her for years to come.

She thought about why she married Doug. Was it his

confidence that attracted her to him? Once again, she recalled how he took care of everything, and how his doing so had freed her to study. His uncompromising nature, as opposed to her timorous approach to life, had once made her feel secure. But what price had she paid? What felt like security at the outset was now stifling.

Feeling increasingly resentful, Julie found herself now openly criticizing Doug. She told him he was an unyielding, inflexible control freak. His constant berating had gotten to her, and she wanted to pierce him. One night, she went for the jugular. "You know, Doug," she commented, "you think you're so perfect. Well, my previous lovers in some ways were maybe better than you."

The moment she spoke those words, she saw Doug's eyes freeze. Following that remark, neither of them spoke for a couple of weeks, just passing each other in the house. Finally, Doug broke the silence.

"What did you mean by that comment about your old lovers?" he asked, glaring at her.

Julie paused before answering. "Those men really adored me. They cherished women. They wanted to take *care* of them. You only put me down and call me neurotic. You're angry at me because I depend on you and I need you."

"So, you're saying your other boyfriends were better lovers?"

"You don't get it!" she continued. "I wasn't talking about sex. I was talking about being more understanding and kind. You do take care of so many things, but you're resentful, dissatisfied and angry. I want tenderness and comfort. You're always annoyed with me. I want to be adored! I deserve that!"

Julie knew that no matter how much she explained, pleaded, screamed or ranted, in the end she wasn't getting through to Doug. She hoped desperately that he would change. Some people fought out loud to the bitter end, and others got even in silence.

Maybe, she reflected, *this boat is heading into dangerous waters.*

CHAPTER 37

When it began, Julie couldn't really say, but something was occurring in Doug's life that was causing him to behave differently. She had read enough women's magazines and listened to enough confessions from her patients to know when a man was straying. What were the clues? Well, one was going to the gym for the first time. This was not the case with Doug, as he was a gym rat from day one. Another was dressing differently. Hmm…Doug had started wearing clothes that were inappropriate for a man in his late forties, like cargo pants, flip-flops and short T-shirts. Was he kidding? Then there were the constant phone calls from "patients" during dinner hours and during weekends. Doug had been in practice for about twenty years. and there had been only a few phone calls from patients. Besides which, he'd talk to them in front of Julie. Now suddenly, he had to scurry outside the restaurant or leave whichever room they were in to communicate with them.

"What's going on?" Julie asked him one evening after he had surreptitiously left the den to take a phone call.

He looked at her and shrugged. "A patient phone call. What now?" *Ah, the best defense is a good offense.* He was annoyed that she was questioning him.

"Since when can't you talk in front of me?"

He shook his head and sarcastically replied, "Did you ever hear of HIPAA laws? I can't talk to patients in front of anyone!"

"Really, now!" she replied tartly. "I know nothing about HIPAA, I mean, what do I know about being a doctor?" She seethed with anger. Did Doug think that she was that stupid? "I never talk to you when you're on the phone with patients! And why all the phone calls?"

He paused and sighed loudly. "I'm seeing more patients. You like the money, don't you? So, more patients means more phone calls. Why this constant interrogation?"

"It just doesn't make any sense," she harped. She had his attention and was not going to let him dodge the topic. "You just seem so different. The way you dress, the phone calls, leaving the room all the time. Yes, you're busy, but you always were. No privacy for patients. Do you think I'm an idiot?" Julie heard her voice rise two octaves.

"What do you think is going on?" he queried.

"Honestly, Doug, I don't know. And after 5:00 p.m. I can't reach you in the office."

"Did it occur to you," he questioned slowly, "that we have a new phone system, and after five the phone goes into voicemail? If I hear it's an emergency, I call back immediately. If it's a routine question, I call back after the last patient leaves."

"So," she persisted, "I guess I'm not an emergency. Now you don't call back, even to tell me when you're getting home."

Doug was now totally red-faced and screaming. "I don't get what you're implying! I'm busy! If you said it was an emergency, I would call you back. I don't have time to just shoot the breeze!"

Julie was like a dog with a bone. "So calling me back for two minutes is too long? Just too weird," she continued. "Why not man up and tell me what's going on? Are you having an affair?" she asked bluntly.

"No! You're crazy!" he shouted. "When would I have the time? I think you're getting paranoid. Maybe you should go back on Zoloft. Maybe you're overstressed with work!"

Julie paused. "I can't help questioning this situation. Suddenly, the phone system is changed. Suddenly, you don't have two minutes to answer my phone calls."

She began to doubt her judgment. Could she be imagining all of this? Had she listened to too many stories about infidelity from her patients? They all started sounding alike. The husband always denied that anything was happening. That was the strategy: deny, deny, deny! Midlife crisis was a reality. Men wanted to feel young and sexual after decades of being in a relationship. Wasn't a new woman more exciting? A man could feel like a young guy with renewed vigor. And because men are wired differently from women, at least most women, they could more easily separate their emotions from their sexual behavior.

Julie never thought of Doug as a player or the unfaithful type. But it was midlife, and they had been married almost twenty years. Maybe he wanted to experiment with someone new. She could probably handle a one-night stand if it occurred occasionally, especially if she didn't know about it. But this was different. Doug seemed detached and angry. He was resentful about Julie's newly-acquired independence, and the comment about her ex-lovers being better than him "in some ways" had cut him to the quick. Things were never the same between them since that comment. They rarely had sex, and it was almost mechanical, with no affection. She blamed their lackluster sex life on the arguing, but wasn't that a red flag that Doug might be unfaithful? She tallied up all the clues: change in clothing style, change in availability at the office, constant phone calls, change in their sex life, and their lack of communication. All that with a midlife crisis was the perfect recipe for an affair.

But with whom? She didn't have to think too long about the answer. It was probably Morgan, the drug rep working for all of the big pharma companies. She was always hanging around the office, and as of late, Julie perceived frostiness in her demeanor whenever they met. Morgan was always dressed provocatively, usually in a short, black skirt, tight jersey blouse and super high heels. Doug had commented on how ambitious and intelligent she was. *Really?* thought Julie. *All she does is promote already popular medications. I guess being a doctor fails in comparison to pushing the newest antibiotic.*

Julie came to the office unannounced one afternoon at the end of the day. Doug and Morgan were in his consultation room, and Julie could hear Morgan laughing boisterously at something Doug must have said. When Julie walked into the room, they froze.

"What's the joke?" Julie questioned. Doug stared blankly at her while Morgan looked out the window. Julie felt that she could cut the tension with a knife and knew she was clearly interrupting cozy time between them.

She knew very little about this young woman except that she had been raised in a troubled family. Doug had confided this to her one evening when they were having dinner. Apparently, Doug was an important client to her, as he prescribed large amounts of medicine. He related that Morgan was very ambitious and that her family didn't provide her with any assistance when she was growing up but that she had wanted to have a good life.

"Where are her parents?" Julie asked.

"Her father left with another woman when she was six years old," he answered. "Her mother was always running around with different men."

At the time, Julie thought it was a perfect setup for young woman to be attracted to an older man who could serve as a father figure. The fact that Morgan's father left her mother for a younger woman was another trigger for an affair with an older man. History often repeated itself, with younger family members replicating the behaviors they had seen, even if those behaviors were unhealthy or harmful. It was what they were accustomed to. Sometimes one wanted affirmation from a neglectful parent, so the older lover fulfilled all that was denied by the father. Or it could just be a simple case of a gold digger spotting a wealthy man who could be a sugar daddy and could give her an easy life. *Maybe I'm analyzing this too much,* pondered Julie. *I'll stop comparing my patients' experiences to my own and start taking Zoloft again,* which she did. Only it didn't help. Each day, she became more suspicious.

Drew was now a young teenager, occupied with his own schedule and friends, giving Julie time to observe and reflect on what was occurring. In order to keep her sanity, she decided to focus more on productive activities that would clear her mind. She and Emma played tennis twice a week, and Julie decided to increase her skills by taking a series of private lessons. The pro at the tennis academy was a vibrant, energetic young man named Marcus. Julie loved watching his technique and tried mimicking each of his movements. Maybe, she thought, she and Doug could play tennis together.

Over dinner at the local burger spot, she surprised Doug with a gift of series of private tennis lessons with Marcus. "Maybe we will get into playing doubles on the weekends," she suggested. Doug seemed genuinely interested in the lessons, to her delight and her shock.

"I think that's a great idea," he agreed, and added that he was going to call Marcus and arrange for his weekly lessons.

Over the following months, Doug left every Tuesday night for his lesson and would grab a slice of pizza on the way home. One Wednesday morning during Julie's lesson, she asked Marcus about Doug's progress with tennis.

"Your husband is not as disciplined as you," Marcus laughed. "You don't miss a single lesson and he's skipped three of them already. He's just too busy at work."

Julie felt the color rising her cheeks and a knot forming in her stomach. Doug had been leaving the house dressed in tennis garb, and saying his lessons were fine when he got home. "Oh yes!" Julie replied. "He is way too busy!"

She left her lesson, feeling despondent. She was going to approach Doug head on, giving him no time to conjure up an excuse. She waited till they had finished dinner, and then casually, she asked him if he was enjoying his lessons.

"They're going fine," he replied.

She sat quietly and quickly blurted out, "Marcus told me you missed half of your lessons! Where were you?"

He remained silent and then retorted sharply, "Now you're monitoring my free time! Of course I missed a few lessons! I got called back to the office a few times. I operate, or did you forget that?"

"Then why didn't you just tell me the truth?" Julie persisted. "I asked you how the lessons were going, and you answered that they were fine. Why didn't you tell me that you had to miss some of them?"

Doug was not going to back down. "Some weeks I went, and others I didn't. I never realized that I had to account for each minute of my time! If I had to leave the lesson or didn't make it to the damn lesson, what the fuck did it matter to you? I said the lessons were fun. I didn't mean that on a specific night they were fun."

Julie realized she was getting nowhere. He was sticking to his story. "You know, Doug," she said slowly, "maybe it would be easier to take the lessons on an evening when you don't operate. Then you wouldn't be called back or be delayed at the office."

"Oh, now you're arranging my schedule?" he said bitterly. "Mondays I work late, and Thursdays I try to have dinner with Drew. Do you want me to take lessons on Saturday nights?" he continued, pushing his dinner plate to the side. "This is some relaxing dinner conversation isn't it?"

She looked at him squarely in the eye, paused and barely murmured, "Forget the topic. It's just bizarre that you don't tell me that you're missing lessons." She knew the facts were irrelevant. He was turning the issue back on to her, accusing her of being inconsiderate. Was there any use in continuing the conversation? No, she told herself. She'd have to monitor him more closely, but discreetly. She was no fool and knew that something was amiss. It was so like Doug nowadays to get angry at *her* for *his* deception. Dinner ended with the two of them barely saying a word to each other.

Over the next couple of months, Julie noted that Doug was needing more private time than usual. In the past, he would spend Saturday afternoons running a few errands or watching a movie on television. He always said the films cleared his head. Now he wanted to go to a local men's shop to "sharpen his wardrobe." He told Julie that as a surgeon, he required a "special image." The strange thing about it was that he kept going to the men's shop but came home with no purchases. Julie actually called him out on it, but he had a quick rebuttal. He claimed that the tailor in the shop was not expert enough at the fine details of fitting the clothes, requiring multiple return trips to the shop. He also complained that the owner was not buying the latest styles and the merchandise was not up to snuff. When Julie suggested that he shop elsewhere, he looked askance, not dignifying her comment with a reply.

Julie realized that for sure, something was terribly wrong. Doug was avoiding her. But not sexually. This was the odd part of it. Almost all women said that if their husband was having an affair, their sex life changed. But Doug still wanted to have sex, though only weekly. Julie rationalized that maybe he was *not* having an affair, but just avoiding her because he was angry or conflicted about their marriage. She decided to just observe and say little, grateful that she could work as hard as she did because it was the most stable part of her life.

For the fifteen years that Julie had been in practice, medicine had continued to evolve. There was a new wave of cosmetic rejuvenation with Botox and fillers that could be injected to treat wrinkles and lines. Julie attended seminars and workshops to learn the latest techniques and became absorbed with studying facial anatomy. She had not looked at an anatomy textbook in more than two decades, but there she was, sitting at her desk, poring over diagrams of the facial and angular arteries and the branches of the facial nerves.

Injecting could be daunting when the injector was aware of the potential complications. It was like any other endeavor: the more you knew, the more you were aware of the risks involved. Yet, how wonderful it was to see lines vanish, eyebrows lifted, and cheeks and lips made fuller after injection.

Julie had again expanded her practice to include two other physicians, a step that increased the amount of paperwork and office management. She had weekly meetings with Bibi, her office manager, to see about curtailing the costs of running the practice. It was a constant juggling act to maintain impeccable standards yet run a cost-efficient office. The government and insurance companies seemed to have no problem with lowering the reimbursements to physicians, while not imposing any restrictions on the increasing cost of supplies. In addition, the directive to implement mandatory data reporting systems increased the requirements for the number of employees. This also added to the cost of running the office. Yes, it was a juggling act to maintain the bottom line while balancing the employees' raises, the doctors' demand for 50 percent of the gross revenue and all the extra work involved in keeping everyone happy.

"How do I increase their salaries while the insurance companies decrease our payments?" Julie lamented to Bibi as they went through the bills and expenses.

Bibi shook her head. "You can't give them raises unless you drop the insurance plans that are not paying you properly and join plans that pay better."

"What to do I do with all of the patients?" Julie said with exasperation., "Drop them like hot potatoes?"

Bibi, less emotional and more practical than Julie, continued, "You can't have it both ways. The only good thing is that you love cosmetic dermatology, and its fee-for-service basis will increase the revenue. That compensates for the decrease in reimbursement. And tell your doctors to be more conservative with the supplies. They don't need to use wads of gauze to clean out acne."

"Yes, you're correct," Julie replied, "they don't care about the expenses. They get their 50 percent, and it doesn't matter what the cost of running this practice is."

"You know," suggested Bibi, "you could lower their percentage to forty or forty-five percent of the revenues. Times have changed."

Julie, who abhorred confrontation, just shook her head. "Yes, I know I have to do this, but it makes me uncomfortable."

Julie sighed out loud. She was feeling stupid all around. It seemed that many people in her life were taking advantage of her. She knew that she was very bright, ambitious and ethical. Why did she allow people to take advantage of her? Though Julie had accomplished so much, she was still emotionally arrested at an age where she was frightened and insecure. She knew that was why she hadn't hired a private detective to follow Doug. Anyway, what would she do if she had found it to be true that he was having an affair? She would have to confront him again. And she wasn't ready for the truth.

As time passed, Doug's behavior became increasingly suspicious. He had now made a habit of taking the dog for long walks at ten o'clock at night. Julie told him to just put the dog out in the backyard as they always had, but Doug insisted on this new routine. In addition, when he traveled for business, Julie could never reach him. He had a variety of explanations: his cell phone battery was low, the lectures went longer, he was having business dinners in places with no cell service. Julie also noticed that his secretaries give her strange looks when she came by his office. If he left work early, they said they did not know where he went. When she tried calling him, he didn't answer his phone.

One Friday afternoon she called the office and demanded that the secretary call and tell him she had an emergency at home. When Doug called back he sounded worried.

"What's the emergency?"

"I couldn't reach you," she responded defensively. "I assume you'd answer the phone when your secretary called. Why won't you answer my calls?" she persisted. He ignored her questions, choosing to focus on why she had the secretary call him urgently.

"Where *are* you?" she shouted. The answer was a click on the phone. He just hung up.

Julie was furious and decided that it was finally time to have him followed. She called a private investigator and arranged to meet her. She'd had it. It was time to throw down the gauntlet and not tolerate Doug's evasive behavior. No matter how much she buried herself in work and spent hours reading medical journals, no matter how much she shopped and golfed, no matter how many hours she devoted to meeting friends, she could no longer suppress the nagging suspicion that Doug was involved in something or someone he was hiding.

CHAPTER 38

The next pivotal event occurred right after the Christmas vacation on a cold January morning. Snowflakes drifted through the gray skies as Julie moved from room to room, busily seeing patients. She was just about to enter an exam room when Bibi ran up to her, pale and upset.

"Come and take this call," she said breathlessly. "It's Drew's school. They say there's an emergency!"

Julie ran to her office, feeling faint. She grabbed the phone and said, "What happened to Drew?" Her voice was desperate. The voice on the other end, however, was steely and cold.

"This has nothing to do with Drew. This is Morgan. I knew I'd get you on the phone by saying it was emergency at school." Morgan laughed haughtily, then continued, "Doug and I have been having an affair for the past year. I just thought you should know about it."

Julie stood frozen, feeling the blood draining from her face. "I do, and I always did know about it," she said calmly. "I really only wish one thing for you, and that is that one day you'll get a call from someone insensitive enough to use your child as an excuse to get you on the phone. You don't have a child now, so you might not really appreciate the cruelty of your actions." With that, she hung up.

She walked into the next exam room, flashed a warm smile and asked the patient what brought her into the office. And from there she continued, listening to her patients' litany of complaints. Robotically, she completed her day's work.

Later that afternoon, she called Doug's office and spoke to the secretary. "I need to speak to Doug. Tell him it's an emergency." She decided to employ the same cheap tactic that Doug's paramour had used.

"Hey!" he said, "Is everything OK?"

Julie paused and continued in a quiet voice. "Earlier today I was told that the school was on the line. Supposedly there was an emergency."

"What!" he exclaimed. "Is Drew all right?"

Julie waited and let that sink in for a moment. Then she said, "Yes, he's fine. You see, the call had nothing to do with Drew. In fact, it was your friend Morgan telling me that you two have been having an affair for the past year." Silence. "Doug, how could you lie straight to my face when I *knew* you were having an affair with her? How??"

Doug's voice rose two octaves as he replied, "I don't know what she's talking about!"

"Really?" Julie said wryly. "Where would she come up with that story? I have been accusing you for one year now. You've been pulling a gaslight on me, telling me I'm nuts. I guess now it'll be deny, deny, deny!" she shouted.

Doug was audibly concerned. "Look, ., she's nutty. We all know that. She and I were friendly, and in her distorted mind, she must think that by concocting this story, you'll be furious and leave me, and I'll be available for her." His voice was shaking "I know you must be angry, but do you really think I'd have an affair with her? She's twenty years younger than me and crazy. You know that!" he pleaded.

Julie was not to be deterred. "I know that I suspected you were having an affair with her. It's not as if this comes as a shock. I not only knew you were having a dalliance; I knew the woman! Can I get any better?"

"She's nuts!" Doug protested. "You only assume something was going on because she gave you dirty looks. She's jealous of you. Somehow, she became obsessed with me. Who knows? Maybe she saw me as a father figure."

Julie was exasperated. "Man up, Doug! Why don't you come clean? This lying and denying is just plain deceitful. I've had suspicions all along."

Like many men, Doug was not going to confess. "You were only suspicious because we were fighting, and so I was avoiding you. Then you saw her, she looked at you, and you assumed we were involved with each other."

Julie was losing patience with him. "No, that's not it at all! It was so obvious to me that you were fooling around behind my back. First, your schedule totally changed. I could never reach you after work or on a Saturday afternoon. In fact, your whole demeanor changed. Suddenly you took on this juvenile way of dressing. It was ridiculous, almost desperate. My God, Doug! You met the criteria that all the women's magazines list to signal that your man is cheating. You were scoring 100 percent! On top of it, Morgan was not subtle. Every time I saw her, she was killing me with her eyes!"

"You're just not going to believe me!" he cut in. "It was horrendous for me to be friends with her. OK, look, I will certainly request that she be replaced as the drug rep. And I'll tell her never to call you again."

"Well, isn't that just dandy?" Julie interrupted him. "We can go on playing house just as if nothing ever happened! Did you ever kiss her?"

"Maybe once," he replied.

"Maybe once!" Julie shrieked. "You don't even remember?"

"I meant," he stuttered, "maybe once to say happy birthday. I... I... I don't remember."

Julie was frozen. He couldn't remember if he ever kissed her? Not an affirmative *no*? What was she supposed to do now?

She questioned all her friends as to whether they had seen or heard anything. One said that she had seen Doug having coffee with a woman at a Starbucks in the neighboring town. Another had said that she thought she saw Doug rollerblading with a woman near Jones Beach. Julie asked each of them why they didn't tell her. It seemed some friends didn't want to get involved. They assumed, as in most marriages, the affair would blow over and everything would return to normal. But Julie's dearest friends swore they hadn't seen or heard anything. She believed them, but she could not believe Doug. She would never know for sure if he'd had a full-blown affair or just an obsessive flirtation. Tragically, in the dark places of her heart, she felt Doug had been unfaithful.

The issue was, what she was going to do with her life now? Drew was a teenager, on track to an Ivy League school. Did she want to disrupt the family? Should a wife give her husband the benefit of the doubt, as her mother had done with her father? She wondered if the phrase "Once a cheater, always a cheater" applied to her husband. But Julie abhorred change as much as deceit or unethical behavior, so for better or for worse, she decided to give Doug and their marriage another chance. Things were going to have to change, though. There would be no more lying, and equally important, Doug would have to be more giving, accessible, respectful and considerate of all her needs and wants. Maybe, she told herself, he would appreciate her more if he feared losing her.

To get through the rough aftermath of the confrontation, Julie needed to distract herself. Drew was almost seventeen years old, and he certainly didn't need her doting attention any longer. She joined a golf course and became delightfully obsessed with the game, taking two lessons a week. She also hired a personal trainer and a Pilates teacher. It was a bit extravagant, but she didn't care. She had certainly worked hard enough and had earned enough money to justify her extra expenses. She signed up for a women's theater group to go out with on her day off. When there was no theater, she would go to the museum with a friend and have a long lunch.

Doug was like a dog with its tail between its legs. It was going to be a new beginning, Julie reassured herself. They were in their late forties, and whatever might have happened was written off as a midlife crisis, she rationalized. Before long, Drew would start college and they would be empty-nesters. Part two of their marriage would begin, and like the sun shining brightly after a storm, their marriage would be even more beautiful than before. Julie told herself that all of it had probably been just a ludicrous infatuation, and with that, she allowed her mind to obliterate all the sordid data she had assimilated. She may have been deluding herself, but her goal was to maintain the status quo and not cause total upheaval in her life.

Over the next few years, Julie and Doug did live a quieter, more peaceful life. Drew left for college, and although he came home often, they were now face to face with each other most of the time. There was no doubt that things were different without their kid in the house. Now they had to form a new kind of relationship. They made the adjustment by traveling extensively, spending more time in museums and playing golf together. Everything seemed to be going back into balance.

Julie made some personal adjustments too. She became more assertive in managing her staff and associates, finally learning the difference between assertive and aggressive. Still having a long way to go with the dreaded issue of confrontation, she adapted her behavior more to reflect the woman she had become.

For some couples, the empty-nest stage of life was an absolute affirmation of their love. No longer burdened by the dual responsibility of career and childrearing, they could now refocus their attention on each other. Many couples began to re-explore their early mutual interests and passions. For some couples, Julie observed, without the distraction of children, the husband and wife discovered they really had nothing in common, and so the marriage went into decline. Julie was determined that this would not be the case with her and Doug.

With Drew away at college, they were free to travel to Europe more frequently. They went to the Dalmatian Coast, exploring Croatia and Montenegro by car and scooter. The aqua blue and emerald green waters of the Adriatic sparkling at the foot of the mountainous roads were mesmerizing. At night, they enjoyed the fresh catch of the day in small restaurants perched on the cliffs above the sea. They roamed around Dubrovnik, the walled medieval city in Croatia, with its central castle and small tourist shops dotting the perimeter. They rode bikes through lavender fields on the island of Hvar and visited Split, admiring the classical architecture of the Diocletian palace built in 305 AD. The trip was the perfect combination of walking through history and exploring nature. Throughout the trip, they found themselves holding hands as they wandered through a labyrinth of narrow cobblestone streets with piazzas, churches and restaurants.

The next European adventure was Munich at Christmastime. What could be more delightful than being in Bavaria with snow fluttering down as they admired shop windows replete with toy trains coursing through miniature mountain tunnels and tiny villages where teddy bears ice-skated? They stood in the cold at a beer stall and munched on huge pretzels and drank beer from tall glass mugs. They wandered into bakeries boasting an assortment of cookies, eclairs and fruit tarts, and, of course, Black Forest cake with whipped cream and cherries. The whole place was a true winter wonderland.

Traveling brought Julie and Doug closer. They had always shared a passion for history, architecture and art from every civilization and movement. Because of their shared European heritage, they felt at home in Europe, and this period of healing and rejuvenation was much needed in their marriage. Their lovemaking was revived and was warmer, as they felt once again that they were both friends and lovers.

Over the next few years, they continued focusing on their careers, maintaining their robust practices. Julie became enthralled with cosmetic dermatology and was enthusiastic about how it could revolutionize the aging process. She learned the delicate art of refreshing and enhancing a patient's appearance while being realistic about her expectations: a sixty-year-old woman was not going to be turned into a thirty-year-old woman. Julie knew that some patients would be woefully disappointed if they were not properly educated. That was a skill in itself.

All in all, it seemed to be smooth sailing for Dr. Kent and Dr. Stone. Julie breathed a sigh of relief each morning. Until the other shoe dropped.

CHAPTER 39

Four years after the end of the questionable affair, things began to unravel. As Julie sat in her office on an early October morning, she began to feel anxious and insecure. Once again, she was observing a change in Doug's behavior and attitude. He was irritable and short-tempered with her. To add fuel to the fire, a few friends noticed that a forty-something Russian divorcee was hanging around him and his friends at the gym. Galena was a very attractive woman and, according to Julie's friends, would meander over to Doug, smiling and chatting with him while he was working out. This time, Julie was not going to question Doug. She was going to quietly watch what was going on. She decided to join the gym and see for herself.

It was a Saturday afternoon when Doug left the house to run errands. He forgot his new phone on the bathroom counter. Julie was applying makeup when she heard it bling with an incoming text message. A notification banner appeared across the phone screen: MWAH, from Galena.

At first Julie didn't know what MWAH meant, and then she realized that Galena was blowing Doug a kiss. She was stunned as she stared at the screen. About an hour later, when Doug came home, Julie just handed him the phone and watched the blood drain from his face.

"I know this looks bad," he muttered. "It's just some woman who hangs around the guys at the gym and it's meant as a joke. I'll introduce you to her."

Julie stared at him. "Joke. Very funny. Why is she hanging around you guys? You never work out with me."

"It won't happen again. Seth is friendly with her. They're both in finance."

Julie shrugged. "Does she text *them* "MWAH"? And by the way, my friends have seen her at the gym with you. I heard about her flirting with you. Galena. Russian and divorced. Perfect! Is she reviewing Finance 101 with you?"

Doug stammered. "It looks bad, I know. I promise I won't let her hang out with me. I'll tell the guys she's being too aggressive, so I don't want her working out near us."

Julie decided that this was it. She just responded, "Sounds good," but she was already planning to get a private investigator. They had dinner plans with friends that evening, and though she wanted to cancel, she certainly didn't want to be alone with Doug.

She dressed for dinner, and they drove to the restaurant without saying a word. Doug tried to take her hand, but she pulled it away. At dinner, she was introduced for the first time to Doug's colleague and friend, Leo, and his wife. They ordered drinks and then dinner, and everyone asked each other about their backgrounds, where they grew up and that kind of thing. Julie turned to Leo and asked where he was from.

"I grew up in Bayside, Queens," he said, with his strong borough accent.

Julie paused. "How old are you?"

"Fifty-six," he replied.

Julie knitted her brows. "Fifty-six? From Bayside, Queens? Did you know a guy named Rick Wind? Your age? From Bayside?"

"Are you kidding?" he exploded. "He's one of my best

friends! Lives in North Carolina now. He's a general surgeon. I grew up with him. Do you know him?"

Julie laughed. "Sort of. We were engaged way back. But I never met you."

"Holy shit!" Leo continued, "Rick and I lost contact during his med school years. But we met up again about ten years ago."

Julie nodded. "That's why you and I never met. I was with him during his med school time."

Leo was visibly interested. "So what happened with you guys?"

Julie shook her head. "Leo, it's a very long story. Bad personal time for me back then. My father was ill, and things fell apart. It wasn't him. The problem was me. But when you speak to him, please send him my very best." With that, they continued with their evening. Julie put on her best act not to show her disgust for Doug.

That night when they went to bed, she kept thinking about Rick and their long-ago romance. But foremost in her mind was hiring a detective to follow Doug. No one would make a fool of her ever again.

—— PART 8 ——

REKINDLING

CHAPTER 40

The disturbing weekend was over, and a new work week had begun. Julie was just finishing up with the last patient of the morning when her secretary let her know that a Dr. Wind was waiting to speak to her on the phone. She excused herself and hurried to the phone, her face flush with excitement.

"Hello," she said calmly. "This is Dr. Kent."

"Julie, it's Rick," the caller said in a familiar husky voice.

"Rick! "How are you? You sound the same!"

He laughed softly. "So do you. So how are you, Julie? I heard we have a mutual friend, Leo. He called me last night saying you saw him on Saturday."

"Yes, we do have a mutual friend! What a coincidence! Where in North Carolina do you live now?"

"I live near Duke University. Actually, Leo and I ran into each other one weekend in New York. We hadn't spoken for years, but it was as if time had never passed. He was my best friend from grade school through college." He paused. "Julie, I was nervous about calling you. I remember how it ended between us. I thought you were angry at me. But Leo said that you told him to send me best regards."

"Rick," she said quietly. "It was me, not you that caused the break-up. There are things you didn't really know about. I was out of my mind with pre-med and my dad being sick. You were good to me, Rick. I just couldn't give you the attention you needed. You were demanding, but I have always thought that we could've worked it out if the circumstances were different."

There was just silence, then Rick continued. "What are you up to these days?"

"I'm a derm in private practice on Long Island. Never thought I'd end up here," she said with a laugh. "Remember I wanted to live in a brownstone in Park Slope?"

"I do remember," he paused. "I wanted to leave New York."

"Well," she said softly," Leo tells me you're very successful, have a huge practice, and that you lecture all over the world."

He laughed again. "Yeah, things have worked out well for me. I was always a workaholic except for the short time when I goofed up in medical school when we first met. You helped straighten me out."

"I remember," she agreed. "I talked you into staying in med school, and you talked me into going to med school! But I'm not as esteemed a physician as you are. I'm a dedicated community physician, and I teach residents at Stony Brook Hospital."

"Do you have kids?" he asked.

"Oh yes! I have a wonderful son, the light of my life. And you?"

"I have two daughters."

"I remember when you came to my apartment in Queens and you were married to a Chinese woman. Mayling. Are you still married to her?"

"I divorced Mayling a couple of years after I saw you. My second wife is from Mexico. Her name is Rosa."

"Oh!" Julie laughed. "Seems you married anyone but a Jewish woman after me."

"Julie, are you happy?"

"Yes, I'm happy. There are many different kinds of happiness. Right now, though, I'm not exactly thrilled with my husband. I'm pissed at him."

"Why? Did you find out he's having an affair?" Rick asked. Julie found it odd that Rick nailed the situation. But maybe not that odd. He always did know what she was thinking.

"Oh, I don't know. I saw a provocative text from a woman on his cell phone," she confided.

"Hmmm," he murmured. "Cell phones can be a problem. But before you saw that, were you happy?"

"Rick, why do you keep asking me if I'm happily married?"

"Because you were once my baby. I want you to be happy," he replied.

Julie felt her heart skip a beat. "Doug is a good man. He's brilliant, hard-working, a great father, and very accomplished. But right now I'm disappointed in him. And you? Are you happily married?" she asked.

Rick chuckled. "Yes, I am."

They continued chatting for about twenty minutes more. He told her about his work, and she filled him in about her private practice, and they spoke about their families.

"How's your mom?" he asked, with a note of nostalgia. "I always loved her."

"She's great. She would love to know how you're doing." Julie remembered how Lara loved Rick and would cook special meals for him.

He grew silent. "Don't say anything to your mom or anyone about us talking. Let's keep this between us. My wife is Hispanic, and those women tend to be jealous," he added.

Julie had to go back to work. "Oh, Rick!" she said sweetly, "It's been so wonderful hearing from you."

"Julie," he said, "I would love to speak again and catch up some more."

She didn't know what to make of his sudden interest in her, but she decided to go along with it. Was he coming on to her, or just curious to see how she was doing? She really didn't care. All she knew was that Doug was busy texting with this Russian gal at the gym. Now she, Julie, was now going to pursue this renewed friendship.

Over the next few weeks, Rick's fascination with Julie flourished. He called her daily to ask about her work, her hobbies and her marriage.

"So, do you still have sex with your husband?" he asked during one of their daily conversations.

"Yes, I do," Julie stated honestly. "And you?"

"Shit, yeah," he stated emphatically. "It's just boring. She lost her libido, but I didn't."

Julie began to suspect that Rick was unfaithful, with his comments about libido and sexuality. She decided to be really clear.

"Rick, did you cheat?" He evaded the question.

"Julie, I'm married. Very married. I just play around a little. When I'm with my wife I'm with her. I compartmentalize."

She responded slowly, "It sounds to me as if you do cheat."

"You know, Sweetie, men are different from women. We're like a different species. You know why men cheat?"

"Yes, I do. I have thought a lot about this. Either they are not happy or they don't feel appreciated or adored, or maybe they just lost their attraction to their wives, or their wives are preoccupied with children and they want more attention," she rambled on. "I have heard it *all*. A million excuses."

Rick laughed again. "There you go, analyzing away. Sometimes men cheat for those reasons, but sometimes they cheat just because they can."

Julie didn't want to believe him. Even though he said he was happily married, she remembered Rick as a very loyal boyfriend, and she wanted to maintain that image. *He must be unhappy and he's just afraid to admit it,* she told herself.

Rick asked, "So, you have sex with your husband. But is it good?"

She felt herself flush as she replied, "Sometimes yes, but not right now. I'm fuming at him."

Julie began to tell Rick that she suspected that Doug had had an affair a few years ago but never really knew for sure. They had come to a rapprochement and things got better, but now this texting really freaked her out.

Rick laughed sarcastically. "You don't honestly believe he *didn't* have an affair the first time? And that he's not having an affair now with the Russian? Julie baby, you can't be that naïve!"

"Rick," she protested. "I want to believe that my husband is faithful. Marriage is not a sprint. It's a marathon with ups and downs. Doug is a very special man. I admire him and appreciate how hard he works. He's the best father, and we have the same values."

"Oh, come on, baby!" Rick interrupted her. "Sounds like you're convincing yourself. What about passion?"

"Passion ebbs and flows in a long-term relationship. One must be mature about that," Julie persisted. "And what about you? Is there passion?"

"No, it's boring as hell!"

"Well, there you go," Julie said firmly. "I knew something was off. You're just another horny married man."

"I am horny, but my wife is a good woman. I'm happy here. It's not perfect, but it's very good. True, my wife complains nonstop that I'm a workaholic, but it's still good."

Julie knew at that moment that she should wish him well and say goodbye, but she didn't want to end it. She was angry at Doug, and she still refused to believe that Rick was as happy as he claimed to be. *The man doth protest too much,* she thought.

She hung up the phone after the conversation and called her sister. "Hi, it's me. Let me ask you something: do you remember when Rick came to our apartment in Forest Hills after I graduated from med school?"

"Yes I do, I think," Elizabeth said. "That was so long ago. Why are you bringing this up now?"

Julie did not want to reveal to her sister what was transpiring between Rick and her. "Oh, I ran into someone who knew him. I hear he is doing well. Remember when he asked me if I would go dancing with him and he said he'd call and never did?"

Elizabeth went silent for a moment. "Well, not exactly. He *did* call, Julie. And he told me that he was confused about his marriage. I was newly divorced, and I didn't want you getting involved with a married man, so I never gave you the message."

"How could you do that?" Julie gasped. "Things might have been so different for me! Rick and I might've gotten back together then."

Elizabeth remained firm. "Like I said, I didn't want you to get involved with a married man."

"Well, guess what? He divorced that woman and remarried soon after!" Julie retorted. "I should've been the one to make that decision, not you!"

She felt herself flush with anger. What had Elizabeth done? Doug was certainly not a bright star at the present time. Maybe Rick would have been a better husband for her. Rick needed to be needed, and Julie was emotionally needy. It was a major conflict between Doug and herself, as Doug didn't like emotionally needy women. She began fabricating a romance about ill-fated starstruck lovers. She was disappointed with Doug, and Rick was unappreciated at home. That was one way to justify her desire for him.

During the next few conversations, Rick focused on his travel lectures for work. He was going to be in New York and wanted to see Julie.

"Why don't we meet in the city with our spouses?" Julie suggested.

"I want to meet you alone," he said bluntly.

Julie hesitated. "Rick, do you think this is a good idea? We had strong feelings for each other. What if they come to the surface again?"

"Julie," he replied calmly," what's wrong with our rekindling a friendship?"

"Do we tell our spouses?"

"No! Absolutely not!" Rick insisted. "This is just between us. They will not understand."

She was flustered. "But, Rick, we were once lovers. I don't feel guilt right now, I'm so angry at Doug. But what about you?"

"Baby," he said smoothly, "I've been around the block once or twice before. I'll handle this for us."

Julie felt nervous but exhilarated. "Rick you've been around the block, but I've never stepped out the door."

"Sweetie," he said in his soothing voice," I have taught you many things in life. Now I'm going to teach you how to be *bad*." He laughed loudly. "Speak to you tomorrow."

CHAPTER 41

Sure enough, Rick called daily to remind Julie that he was coming to New York. He said repeatedly and with no hesitation that he couldn't wait to see her and hold her again. Julie had tremendous trepidation and was ambivalent about getting together, but Rick was relentless, and so she agreed to meet him.

Doug was away giving a lecture in Dallas, and Julie took a room at the W Hotel in Midtown. She must have changed her outfit ten times before settling on an all-black ensemble: velvet jeans, silk top, heels and a leather jacket. She applied eye makeup, blush and a light pink lipstick, blew out her hair and tousled it up a bit.

Julie sat in the lobby of the hotel, tapping her foot as she waited for Rick. Her cell phone rang, and she saw his name on the screen. Her heart was beating quickly as she answered.

"Hi. I'm outside," he said.

She dashed out of the hotel to see Rick stepping out of a cab. Their eyes met for the first time in twenty-five years. Rick looked the same, except that his hair was gray, and his face had grown slightly thinner with age. Wasting no time, he grabbed

Julie, hugged her and pulled her into the cab. Immediately, his hand was on her thigh.

"You look great Julie! You haven't gained a pound."

"How do you know?" she asked demurely.

"You know me, Sweetie," he continued, "I could tell if you gained an ounce."

They arrived at the Algonquin, a classic New York City bar and restaurant. As they entered, Julie looked around, appreciating the red leather chairs, couches and crystal chandeliers. The hostess led them to a secluded corner of the bar, where they sat side by side on a small, plush, leather couch. Rick ordered a vodka on the rocks for himself and a Chardonnay for Julie.

"You still like Chardonnay?" he asked, "or do you want a cosmo?"

"Yes, I still like Chardonnay. I don't drink hard liquor," Julie replied. She liked that Rick remembered her drink of choice.

He moved close to her, and they started talking without a moment's break. It felt as if a day hadn't gone by since they'd last seen each other. He told her about his work, his surgery, lecturing and living in Raleigh, North Carolina. Things were good now between him and Rosa, but again he stressed that Rosa had lost her libido. He also confided that he and Rosa had fought viciously over the years, as they had such different upbringings. He characterized himself as very dramatic, structured and precise, whereas Rosa, being Mexican, lived by "*mañana* time," as he called it. He said he was too organized for her, and she said he was a workaholic who didn't spend enough time with the family. She resented that she'd pretty much had to raise the children by herself because Rick was always working or traveling to lecture.

"That's weird," Julie declared. "Doesn't she like the money that you earn and that she doesn't even have to work? You give her and the kids such a wonderful life. Doesn't she appreciate that?"

Rick shook his head. "I would have to have married a Jew for that," he replied. "Jewish women understand work first and foremost. They don't mind workaholics," he continued.

"Don't mind it? We love it!" Julie exclaimed.

Julie told him that Doug was demanding, and it was ironic that she seemed to always be attracted to perfectionist Germans.

"Nah, you never got over me!" Rick added, in his usual arrogant tone.

"Maybe I just like structure," Julie protested. She related how impressed she always was with Doug but that he was very controlling. As she had gained self-confidence and independence, his controlling nature had become more of an issue. She also told Rick how hurt she was when she suspected that Doug was having an affair. For a few years it seemed as though they had healed that hurt, but now this recent dalliance with the Russian woman had re-opened the wound. She paused and looked at Rick, then quietly asked, "I think you fool around. Why?" She had to know. "You were monogamous when we were together, so loyal. Did you change with success, or are you really happily married?"

He peered at her. "Julie, being with the same woman for more than twenty years—you know, sometimes you just want to change your shirt."

"So you're just horny and bored," she retorted, aware that her tone was judgmental. Instead of answering her, Rick leaned over and flicked his index finger down her nose. Then he leaned forward and kissed her hard on the mouth. Julie was stunned. "Please, Rick, we are in public. We can't." But instead of pushing him away, she kept kissing him back.

"Let's get out of here," he said. "I have a hotel room a few minutes away. Let's go!" He was in a fury to be with her.

"No, Rick," she gasped. "We can't. We're both married."

He looked her straight in the eyes. "It's what we both want, isn't it?" He kept pressing his lips firmly on her small mouth, swirling his tongue around hers. "I'm on fire! I want you, Julie, so don't play hard to get. What's with the shy shit? You never were shy with me."

"I'm not playing hard to get. We weren't married back then. Right now I'm not happily married but *you* say you *are*. I'm confused. I never had an affair, but it's clear that you've had many. What do you want? Just some fun, fuck and forget?" She felt her cheeks grow red with anger. "You're just bored. That's it, right?

"Baby, not for nothing, but I can fuck anyone I want. I don't need to go back to an ex-fiancée. Obviously, there's something between us. I felt it the minute you walked out of the hotel."

Julie smiled. "I feel like when we first met and you told me that you wanted to have sex not for you, but for me."

They left the restaurant. Julie was determined not to sleep with Rick, despite her desire and the thrill of being desired. *Screw this*, she thought to herself. *Wonder how Doug would feel if he saw "MWAH" on my cell phone?*

Rick took her back to the W. "Come on, Sweetie," he pleaded. "Let me go upstairs with you."

"No, Rick, I can't. It's not only that I'm married. I'm so confused by all of this. If you told me that you were miserably married, it would be easier. I don't want to be with a married man, let alone a *happily* married man. Right now I'm angry at Doug, so I'm easy prey."

"Stop the craziness! I feel so attracted to you. We once really loved each other," Rick persisted.

She shook her head. "Sounds like you're a player. I don't want to be involved with a player."

"Maybe I am, but it's different with you. Don't judge me, Julie."

"Oh, yes, I forgot," she said sarcastically. "The libido issue."

He stared her down. "Don't be cute. Again, everyone has their needs."

It was hard resisting Rick's advances. It felt so natural being with him, as if the twenty-five-year gap were a mere hiccup. But she kept her ground and wouldn't spend the night with him. He kissed her good night long and hard and said he'd call her soon. He wasn't joking.

Over the next few days, Rick poured out a torrent of texts that Julie responded to. They would reminisce about the trips to the Frick and museums in the city when they were young lovers. They laughed about all the sex they had and how they never tired of doing it in different places, including a restaurant bathroom. Rick certainly loved sex, as did Julie. She reminded him of the penguin mug he bought her years back that showed penguins having sex in every position. Remembering her definite sense of style, he asked her what she liked to wear now.

"Did you still like fishnet stockings?"

"I don't wear fishnets," she said. "Doug is not into the stockings or sexy lingerie or the 'Come fuck me shoes' that you liked so much."

Rick laughed out loud. "What do you mean *liked?* I still do! You're so fucking beautiful, Julie. Save that stuff for me. I appreciate your beauty."

Julie let herself be flattered by him, and she loved the sexy banter. But she had to hold back, she kept reminding herself. He was happily married, just sexually dissatisfied at home. He had turned into a player. It was hard for her to accept. Actually, she didn't want to. It just couldn't be. Rick, her Rick, must be unhappy, or he wouldn't cheat.

A few weeks later, on Thanksgiving weekend, Julie texted Rick to say that she was so thankful that he had come back into her life, even as a friend. He texted her back a strange message. "Baby, you don't have to come on so strong. I love you anyway."

"I'm not coming on strong," she texted back. "I just appreciate your interest in me and everything you did for me as a young woman. Rick, you're very hard-working and ambitious," she continued texting, "your family should appreciate that."

"You're so right, my sweetest," he texted back.

They don't appreciate him, she thought to herself. That explains his cheating. She needed to justify why Rick had strayed from his marriage. *No!* she told herself firmly. *He is not a player!*

CHAPTER 42

I t was a pleasant December afternoon in New York City, with brilliant blue skies dotted with fluffy, billowing clouds. The temperature was in the fifties, perfect weather for walking around the city. Julie agreed to meet Rick in one of the parks on Sutton Place that he called "his park." He had played there as a child when his immigrant grandmother was a nanny to a well-heeled family. In those days, many of the educated immigrants escaping the terrors of Nazi Germany found positions as nannies and butlers to wealthy New Yorkers. It was a tremendous asset for the American families to employ educated, refined people who themselves used to have their own staff in Europe. Rick and Julie used to frequent the park back in their dating days, and today they were going to meet there and go for lunch in a nearby French bistro.

True to her own style, Julie wore a black turtleneck sweater with tight blue jeans. She clipped on long, dangling, gold earrings and threw on a black pea coat. Her makeup emphasized her long lashes, and she highlighted her cheekbones with blush and her lips with a pale pink gloss.

Feeling like a teenager again, she drove to Sutton Place, left the car in a nearby lot and walked to the park.

They approached each other after the month's absence, their eyes locked in a gaze. Julie felt the same familiar fluttering in her chest as Rick reached out and held her in a tight embrace. His mouth quickly found hers, and he kissed her fervently.

"Rick," she murmured, "I missed you."

He smiled. "I always miss you, Sweetie."

"Do you remember this spot?"

"Of course I do, silly. I took you here the first time."

She smiled sweetly. "We were going to live on Sutton Place, remember? But then you wanted to leave New York, so maybe we wouldn't have lived here," she added.

"You would've made me come back to New York," he reminded her, grinning broadly.

"Maybe, But then we would have lived in Park Slope."

"As they say, you can take the girl out of Brooklyn but, well, you know the rest," he chided her.

They stared out onto the East River, watching the lapping waves and the passing ships and boats. They held hands as they reminisced about their joint pasts and how much in love they once were. Rick reminded Julie about their bickering at the end of the relationship.

"You were a brat," he emphasized.

"Yes and no," she replied slowly. Even to this day she kept from Rick the extent of her father's drinking and the shadow it had cast upon her at that time. "Do you believe we're both doctors? And in the coveted fields of surgery and dermatology?" she added.

"Of course I believe it!" he said emphatically. "We're both OCD, and we work to get what we want!"

"Well, you are OCD major and I'm OCD minor, like musical notes," Julie joked.

He gently pushed her. "Always in my shadow, huh?"

"Yes, and I like it that way," Julie said with a nod.

They walked to a bistro on Second Avenue. The restaurant mimicked the ambience of a French country inn, with unpolished wooden tables and chairs, and wicker seats in the French provincial style. A huge bouquet of flowers adorned the entry table. Rick ordered a bottle of white wine, and they chose French onion soup, roast chicken and pork cassoulet, which they enjoyed as they sat by a fireplace in a quiet alcove. Rick leaned over and kissed Julie's lips—a long, sensuous kiss. He began rubbing her thigh and moving his hand up her long leg. He grabbed her hand and placed it under the table onto his bulging erection that she could feel through his jeans.

"Let's get out of here," he insisted. "I need to touch you."

Julie was confused, but she let herself feel the surge of her emotion. "Let's take a walk," she suggested. Rick paid the bill, and he started walking with her in the direction of his hotel.

"I'm not ready!" Julie blurted out. The day was getting colder, and she felt the wind against her cheeks.

"Why not? What's wrong?" he asked, frustrated.

She sighed. "You know, it's not that I'm not attracted or that I don't want this, but we have to talk."

"OK, we'll talk in my room. It's damn cold out here."

Always one to please, Julie agreed on the condition that they talk first over coffee in the hotel lobby. Cappuccinos arrived with lots of froth and cinnamon sticks. Rick watched as Julie's tongue circled the foam on the stick.

"OK, shoot," he laughed. "I'm ready to talk," said, edging closer to her on the small velvet couch.

She paused and then came right out with it. "I'm confused about why you want to see me. You told me that you love your wife. You even told me that in many ways you were not worthy of being with her. You tell me she's a best friend and that she has amazing insight into people. So far, she sounds great. So what are you doing here with me? If it's just for nostalgia, I get it. But you obviously want to get into bed with me. Why? Are you bored or just horny?"

Rick smirked. "Always analyzing everything, aren't you?"

"Rick, this is important to me. I just don't get it. I remember you as extremely loyal. Is this the new you? Did you change with age or success? I could understand if you were in my situation, angry, frustrated, on the verge of leaving. But you're not! And you say Rosa is wonderful. Big deal if she lost her libido! Get it back for her! Does she know you've had affairs?"

Rick grew very stern. "No, and she's never to know. Some men want to be found out. I don't. It would be a mess. The money is all in her name to protect it from malpractice cases and business. I mean," he wavered, "if we did get divorced, I expect that she'd split it, but who wants all that mess?"

"Uh-huh. So let me get this straight. You're happily married, your wife is wonderful, but you like to play around and, shall I quote you, 'to change your shirt.' Your wife is not as sexy as you'd like her to be, so you just compartmentalize your dalliances just to have a little spice in your life. Is that it?"

He nodded emphatically. "Exactly!"

"And," she continued, "you like to keep things very quiet?"

Again he nodded. "No emotions, no feelings. A phone call once or twice a month maybe, to get together every few months for a nice lunch or dinner and some sex. No one gets hurt. You see, when I'm with you I start to *feel* things. I want to spend time with you, do things with you, travel with you. But we know we can't. So we have to keep the schedule. Get it?"

Julie was stunned. She barely knew what to say. Then she finally murmured, "So you want a mistress or a concubine, but without the payment? Whoever heard of a couple that was once engaged meeting occasionally for dinner, sex and no feelings? You know that's not for me. Go with the other women you meet on business trips and have your one-night stands or casual hook-ups or booty calls, but not me. That will never work."

She felt both hurt and disappointed. She could barely believe that Rick expected this of her. Who did he think she was? That she was that lonely that she would settle for occasional sex? Boy, had her opinion of him changed! He was more arrogant than ever.

"Look, Rick," she said politely but firmly, "I don't want to break up a marriage. I thought you were going through similar things as I'm going through, maybe confused or disillusioned with your marriage. Like when you visited me in Forest Hills and you were married to Mayling. You did leave her then to start an affair with Rosa. So I thought it was probably a similar situation. I didn't start up again with you back then because you were married. This feels similar, like déjà vu. But because you've been married a long time, I just assumed that you wanted a special relationship with me, even though I didn't count on your leaving Rosa. But you've made this crystal clear that you don't even want an affair. You just want a casual fling now and then." Julie was fuming. She felt her face grow hot with anger.

"No, Julie," Rick protested, "it's not like that at all! I just know if we don't keep our distance, we are going to fall in love again, and we can't."

"Then we must end this now," she stated. "It was wonderful seeing you, but we can't give each other what each one needs. I don't want to be a quickie for you, and you can't have a conventional affair. That would mean that you'd treat me as a woman you care about and need in your life for whatever reason. Thanks, but I'm not one to be compartmentalized." She got up and he followed her.

"Call me if you change your mind," he said, and leaned over to kiss her, but she offered only her cheek.

On the way home to Long Island, Julie had tears running down her face. She had so wanted things to be different. In her imagination, she thought that she and Rick would rekindle a special friendship. She didn't want to disrupt his life, and she so wanted to believe that something was missing from his marriage as it was missing from hers. She refused to believe that Rick was a player, and happily married, but that he just liked variety. Sort of wanting to have his cake and eat it too. What had happened to her Rick? He now felt entitled to extracurricular activity? Was it his success? Or was he just that bored? She felt a wave of nausea pass over her. Her sadness was changing to anger and repulsion. Hadn't Rick said, "What's wrong with rekindling?" Clearly, he did not want to rekindle! He wanted a roll in the hay, not even a love affair! He was too busy setting restrictions and guidelines as to how to keep his distance. Who did he think she was? The schoolyard whore? Did he think she was some bored and lonely housewife?

She arrived home fuming with anger. She was not only angry at Rick, she was angry at Doug. Had he not started this thing with Galena, she knew that she would never have allowed herself to get involved with Rick. She made a resolution that if Doug was not totally transparent and if he continued flirting or whatever, she would end the marriage. It was as simple as that.

The winter was long and cold. Julie focused on her work, and Doug, although distant, didn't seem to be preoccupied elsewhere. Whatever had occurred with Galena was clearly over. Julie got busy with her tennis and lunch with friends and was making time to shop and satisfy her fashionista needs.

In April the daffodils were starting to bloom, along with the dazzling array of tulips. Julie felt the burst of energy that spring always delivered. She came into the office wearing a navy dress and had tossed a navy and kelly-green scarf around her neck. Her bright pink lipstick accentuated the glory of springtime.

She entered the room to see Ina, the first patient of the day, and gave her a broad smile.

"Hi, Ina!" she exclaimed. "How was your grandson's bar mitzvah?"

Ina was beaming. "Just beautiful, an amazing day!"

"So what brings you in today?" Julie asked her.

"My skin exam, and I have a spot on my back that itches," Ina replied.

Julie looked over Ina very carefully and then, with a sharp curette, removed the growth from Ina's back. She reassured her that it was benign growth that had erupted with time. She never like to say "age spot" but rather a "time spot." Aging should be revered, she told her patients, not disparaged.

Ina took her hand as she was saying goodbye. "I'm happy to see you looking so well. Always keeping yourself looking so pretty. How's your hubby?" she inquired with a quizzical expression.

"All good," replied Julie.

Ina stared at her for a long moment. "OK. You're very special, Julie. Don't ever forget that," she said as Julie hugged her and left the exam room.

For the next few hours, Julie continued seeing patients at a busy pace. After a productive morning, she was famished. She sat down with Lisa, one of her nurses, for a quick lunch.

"You know," Julie said as she quickly nibbled on a sandwich, "Ina seemed worried about me. She looked at me with a puzzled expression and asked me about Doug." Lisa became sullen and looked away. "What's wrong, Lisa?" Julie asked.

"Nothing," Lisa said, as she looked quickly down at her sandwich.

"Something is off. I see it in your eyes," Julie said.

Lisa paused and then quietly continued. "Ina actually asked me if you were getting divorced," she murmured.

"What?" Julie exclaimed. "She lives in my neighborhood! What is she hearing?

Lisa continued gently. "I was going to tell you after hours that she was hearing rumors that you were getting divorced. In fact, Julie, I don't want to tell you this, but in the past month two other patients asked me the same thing."

"Why didn't you tell me?" Julie snapped.

Lisa looked sad. "I didn't want to hurt you. People

gossip. You know that. I figured this would pass. Maybe they saw you arguing with Doug when you were out to dinner. Who knows? It's a small enclave."

Julie felt her throat tighten. "Maybe Doug is still hanging out with Galena at the gym, or maybe doing more!" she retorted. "My neighborhood loves soap opera drama, and this is just enough to put fuel on the fire. I'm going to ask Doug later tonight exactly what is going on."

That evening over dinner at a local eatery, as Doug gulped down French fries and a burger, Julie picked at a salmon-topped salad.

"You know, Doug," she stated quietly, "there's gossip going around that we're getting divorced. Why do you think that is?"

Doug shrugged. "How would I know? Probably just idle women with too much time on their hands."

"Have you been seeing or talking to Galena at the gym?" Julie asked.

Doug flared up. "Do I have to account for every second of my time? Sometimes she's at the gym when I'm there. I can't tell her not to go to the gym, can I?"

Julie lips tightened. "Doug, you're avoiding my question. Are you talking to Galena at the gym? That would be enough to instigate this gossip."

"I'm done with this conversation!" Doug said loudly. Julie was done, too. She decided that she was going to have Doug followed by a private investigator and get to the bottom of all this. On the two evenings when she worked late, Doug was able to go to the gym and talk to Galena and do who knows what else? If he was lying to her, even just about chatting at the gym, she was going to find out.

The following week, Julie got the names of a few detectives and made appointments with them. On Wednesday evening after work, she got a text which read, "What's doing? It's been too long. Thinking of you." It was from Rick.

Perhaps in different circumstances Julie would've

ignored the text. Rick was off her list of friends. Was it loneliness, curiosity or spitefulness toward Doug that made her text back? "All good, just busy. And you?" she texted.

Rick texted that he was coming to New York in May and wanted to meet her for coffee. He understood that she was upset with him, but he missed seeing her smile. Just coffee or a drink, nothing more. Before she knew it, she texted back.

"Fine. Would love to meet and catch up."

During the next few months, Rick texted her often about how happy he was that she agreed to see him. He suggested that they meet at the Frick and go for lunch. Julie was so engrossed in her thoughts about Rick that she put the appointments with the detectives on hold. She told herself that she couldn't be bothered with Doug's antics. She was going to take care of herself. Maybe, just maybe, Rick really wasn't so happily married. Otherwise, why did he reach out to her again?

CHAPTER 43

Once again, it was a glorious May, the height of springtime in New York. On a beautiful warm morning, Julie set out to meet Rick at the Frick Museum. The trees were in full bloom, and the planters on Manhattan's side streets were full of pansies and impatiens. As Julie approached the museum, she spotted Rick. *Always punctual,* she thought. She felt confident in her tight blue jeans and snug leather jacket, and by the look on Rick's face, he approved of her outfit—that is, until he noticed her ballet flats.

Knowing exactly what he was thinking, Julie said, "Don't worry, I have black heels in my pocketbook to wear at lunch," and she laughed lightly. Rick kissed her on the lips and escorted her into the museum.

"Our place," she whispered in his ear.

"Always," he agreed.

They walked around the softy-lit rooms, revisiting their old favorites by Turner, El Greco and Degas. Rick's hand kept swinging around Julie's waist, and she kept reminding him that they were in public, although she wished they could relax and be openly affectionate with each other.

"Remember how much we loved this place?" Julie

said, looking wistfully into Rick's eyes. Her anger over what transpired at the last meeting had dissipated, as she decided that Rick was deceiving himself about being happily married. After an hour or so, they left the museum and went into Central Park and found their familiar hiding place, the secluded, leafy area where they could recline on the large, smooth rocks. With the same fervor of their youthful years, Rick kissed her and brushed his hands across her breasts. Re-enacting the movements they knew so well, Rick slid his hand slid under her sweater and stroked her nipples as she reached down to find his firm erection. Intertwined in each other's arms, they kissed endlessly. Using Julie's jacket as a blanket, Rick unzipped her jeans and found her private spot. It had been years since he had touched her, but she had never forgotten how he'd bring her to ecstasy with his fingers. A part of her thought she should resist, and she gasped and tried pulling away, but he held her tightly, and she was powerless. They were panting heavily when Rick stopped. "Let's get out of here," he said in a hoarse whisper.

They left the park, laughing, and started walking down Madison Avenue, gradually regaining their composure. They gazed at the beautiful clothes and jewelry in the shop windows.

"Rosa likes Etro dresses," he commented as they passed the designer's store.

Julie froze. It had only been moments since their tryst in the park. She didn't expect him to talk about his wife. But she said nothing, and they continued walking.

When they stopped to look in the window of a high-end jewelry store, Julie spotted a magnificent diamond bracelet. "That's so beautiful, isn't it?" she commented.

"Yeah, that is amazing. I'd buy that for her."

Julie could barely restrain herself from telling him to fuck off. He had been kissing and fondling her for about an hour, and now he was telling her what he would buy for his wife? She could not believe her ears, but she said nothing and just bit her lower lip.

After five minutes of complete silence, Rick asked, "Julie, are you OK?"

She would like to have told him to get lost, but instead said, "I'm OK. It's just that I have a headache. I think I need something to eat." They stopped in a chocolate shop and picked up a sweet, but Julie could barely taste a thing. She just wanted to go home.

"Rick, I'm not feeling well," she lied. What she should have told him was that she was feeling disgusted and totally turned off. "It's my birthday tomorrow, and I don't want to be ill."

"Oh," he said, looking disappointed. "I was hoping to spend some alone time with you."

She shook her head. "I don't think so."

"Want some coffee or a cold drink?" he suggested.

"I think I'd better get home and rest for my birthday," she answered. He still hadn't even uttered a "Happy Birthday." Unable to contain her annoyance, she chided, "How about saying 'Happy Birthday' to me?"

He stared at her. "Stop fishing, will you?" Julie knew he was probably annoyed because she wasn't going back to his hotel.

"Fishing? Because I asked you to wish me a happy birthday after you had your hands down my pants? Are you kidding?"

Still not giving in to her request, he walked her back to her car and he kissed her goodbye, long and hard. She kissed him back, feigning affection, avoiding confrontation. *This is it! Three is the charm. First, he's all over me in November, and then he tells me how happily married he is. December he's all over me, then tells me how he needs his distance or he's going to fall back in love. Now it's May and I almost sleep with him and he's bragging about what jewelry he'd buy for his wife! He's either insensitive, desperate to put up a wall between us or just nuts. Whatever it is, I'm done! I'm going to concentrate on Doug and get our marriage to work,*

or I'm leaving. But I'm not going to be involved with this nut job!
Julie told herself.

　　She drove home, dismayed but not crying this time.
She took a long shower to wash off any scent of Rick and to
literally "wash him out of her hair." Summer was coming, and
she and Doug always loved being at the beach. Her focus was
going to be on their relationship. Rick was no longer going to
be a distraction, as he had been for the past six months.

　　At least she thought so.

CHAPTER 44

Early June arrived, and Julie was focusing her energy on creating a new website for her practice. Social media had entered the medical world. Doctors could be researched on Facebook, and medical sites such as healthgrades, Vitals and RateMDs, in addition to Yelp, had ratings for doctors as if they were restaurants. Plain ridiculous. And to make things even more ludicrous, some online sites posted only negative reviews unless the doctor had an account with them.

Most of Julie's new patients were still referrals from other patients and doctors, but one had to keep current with the trends. So Julie contacted an internet marketing company specializing in creating and managing websites for doctors. This was the absolute last thing she ever pictured herself doing when she first received her M.D. degree. Doctors were supposed to heal, keep up with the latest information and be compassionate. But it seemed that online, humility was out of fashion, and instead, a doctors were supposed to bolster their achievements and shower themselves with accolades. Bob Dylan's words rang in her ears: "The times, they are a changin'."

Any lingering thoughts of Rick had been obliterated from her mind, as he had so disappointed her. But Julie's plans to concentrate on her marriage and make it work were not panning out. As of late, Doug was acting more detached and just plain obnoxious. She did hear rumors of his ongoing "friendship" and flirtation with Galena, which she had dismissed temporarily because of her fascination with Rick. But now that she was focusing on Doug's behavior again, she did not like what she was seeing.

Doug and Julie started going out east to the summer home again. Arriving after the long drive, Doug would plop down in a lounge chair, check his phone and start texting. Julie decided not to confront him, but to just observe. She noticed that as she walked over to the chair, he would quickly put his phone down and pick up a book. He vetoed any suggestions to go to the beach or take a bike ride. When Julie finally told him she was bored, he snapped that he was exhausted and just wanted to relax.

"You know, Doug," she complained, "I'm not getting this at all. You're always a ball of energy. Since when don't you like to bike ride?"

"You like our lifestyle, don't you? Well, I'm tired. Try operating yourself."

"That's ridiculous, and you know it! A walk on the beach or riding our bikes or kayaking is invigorating. You're just obsessed with that damn phone, and you sit around lounging. You are not being good company!" she fumed.

Hadn't she had enough of this during the episode with Morgan, the drug rep? When Doug went inside, Julie picked up his phone but saw that it was locked and required a password. *Here we go again, she thought.*

When he came back outside, she confronted him. "Doug, what is going on? Are you seeing Galena in the gym or, better yet, are you having an affair?"

"Why don't you get off my back?" he retorted. "Your stupid, idle friends are creating havoc again! Furthermore, no one owns anyone in a marriage! If I feel like talking to someone in the gym, I will!"

"Really?" Julie seethed. "No one owns anyone in a marriage, but they owe each other loyalty and honesty! I want to know what's going on!" Once again, she knew she would not get anywhere this way. It was time to reactivate her plan to have Doug followed.

A week later, Doug told Julie that he would be coming out east on Friday instead of the usual Thursday night, as he had to finish putting together a lecture in his office. Julie knew that this was peculiar, but nonchalantly told him she understood. That Thursday night, she called him at about 8:00 p.m. He answered the phone but sounded distracted.

"Where are you?" she asked quietly.

"I'm in my office writing up this lecture, like I told you," he answered.

Julie paused. "Doug, if you really want me to believe you, then call me from your office phone, not your cell phone, OK?"

"Fuck you, Julie!" he shouted and hung up.

Julie quickly called her friend, Amy, who lived close to Doug's office. She breathed a sigh of relief when Amy answered.

"Amy?" she said in a rushed voice, "could you please drive by Doug's office? I can't reach him and I'm worried. Today he said he felt weak and I'm concerned he might be sick at the office," she lied. "Just please tell me if he's in the office. Check the parking lot. Thanks so much, Amy."

"No worries, Julie, I'm on the way!" Amy said.

In about ten minutes, Amy called her back. "Julie, I don't see his car, and there are no lights on in his office. I even knocked on the door. No one is there. What should we do?" she asked anxiously.

"I'll just keep trying. If I don't get him, I'll call the police in about twenty minutes. Thanks so much!"

Julie felt her throat tightening, and her head spinning. She took a few deep breaths and steadied herself. She knew something was terribly wrong and that her worst fears were being confirmed. *That's it,* she told herself, *Monday morning I call the detective!*

About thirty minutes later, her cell phone rang, and she recognized Doug's office number. She was tempted not to answer the phone but decided to play along.

"Well, have you calmed down?" Doug asked her in a husky voice. "I don't like your accusations."

Julie took a deep breath. "I don't know what makes me suspicious, but I see you're calling from the office. How's the lecture going?"

"Pretty good. I haven't stopped for a minute. Almost done. You are creating such tension with your doubts," he continued.

She felt wave of nausea pass over her. "Yeah, you're right," she said as sweetly as she could. "Well, now I'm going to just chill and read. I'll see you tomorrow."

She hung up, knowing Doug had blatantly lied to her. She poured herself a glass of white wine and picked up a book when she heard her phone ring. It was a text from Rick that read, "Please text with me. I miss you so."

She wanted to ignore it or at least not answer for a day, but she was so despondent over Doug's apparent lying that she texted right back: "What do you want?"

"I'm coming to New York in July. Please see me."

"For what? Horny? Bored?"

"I know you're upset. I'm not going to fight this anymore. I miss you. I need you. I really care about you."

"So, I should meet you to hear about how great your wife is, that we can have no emotions, just a lovely evening to rekindle, and of course, you'll want sex, but NO EMOTIONS. Then, of course, you'll tell me what you want to buy your wife, and it's not my birthday, so at least I don't have to fish for a happy birthday. Do I have it all straight?" she texted, knowing the text was oozing with sarcasm.

"I'm an ass," he texted back. "You're right. But maybe I did all this to protect my feelings. Please, please see me."

She couldn't believe she was doing this, but she texted back: "OK, you'll get another chance to redeem yourself. If you are rude again, I'll just spit in your face."

Why? Why am I giving him another chance? she asked herself. *Is it that I am fuming at Doug and need comfort from another man? Yes, but why Rick? No, she told herself, he's admitting to me that he's been fighting himself over this. Now he's ready to have that special friendship that I need. I will never break up his marriage. We will just give each other comfort. Maybe, just maybe, we were meant to be. And all the kids are grown. Who knows?*

And so, they made plans to meet. Julie knew she was lying to herself, pretending that she just wanted a "special friendship" and didn't want Rick to leave Rosa. She now convinced herself that he was unhappy with Rosa, just as she was with Doug. But deluding herself would soon complicate her life more than she could have ever imagined. If only she had heeded Sir Walter Scott's words, "Oh, what a tangled web we weave, when first we practice to deceive!"

CHAPTER 45

It was a hot, humid Thursday in July when Julie went to meet Rick in Manhattan. She had told Doug that she had tickets to the ballet and planned to drive out to the summer house late Friday night. Doug couldn't care less. He was so preoccupied with himself and whatever else was going on in his life. The saying, "What's good for the goose is good for the gander" was certainly à propos now.

Julie was nervous and excited to meet Rick again. It had been a few months since their last encounter, and he had assured her, through a series of texts and phone calls, that he was on board for their rekindled relationship and that he was not going to fight his feelings any longer.

The Plaza Hotel's Oak Room was as elegant and inviting as it had always been, with its rich brown, oak-paneled walls and plush chairs. The boisterous, crowded bar, swarming with well-dressed patrons, promoted a clubby atmosphere for New York's privileged class. Julie strolled in wearing an outfit she knew Rick would go for: a splashy, colorful dress and black patent heels that had a seductive red stripe along the sole. With her wavy dark mane and shiny red lipstick, she ignited Rick's smoldering emotions. He engulfed her with his stare, and she leaned over to meet his hungry kiss. Then he led her to a small table where they could talk.

"You look so beautiful," Rick murmured in her ear as he kissed her lips, her head and her cheeks. Julie did not fight him, nor did she care if anyone saw them together. All she cared about was how safe and excited she felt in Rick's arms. Over drinks, they chatted about everything—their work, the kids, their pastimes. Julie noticed that Rick was careful not to mention Rosa's name.

They left the hotel and went to one of their reliable French bistros and ordered their old favorites: onion soup with thick cheese and roasted duck with orange sauce. They each enjoyed two glasses of wine and nibbled an apple tart. They had shared many meals like this, which helped them to feel even more comfortable with each other.

"Let's not overeat," Rick suggested. "We don't want to get sleepy, as we have the entire night ahead." It was quietly understood that Julie would spend the night with him. She called Doug to say once again that she was going to the ballet and she'd stay over in the city, and added that in the morning she would be attending a dermatology lecture. She knew the Doug wouldn't check up on her. Should she just disconnect her phone and say that the battery ran low? She certainly heard that excuse enough times from him!

Succumbing to reckless abandon, she headed with Rick to his hotel and up to his room. It only took a few seconds for him to pull her to him and run his hands through her hair, whispering, "Oh, baby, at last!" He discarded each layer of her clothes swiftly and smoothly—the dress, the bra, the lace panties.

"Julie, Julie!" he whispered breathlessly, as he fondled her breasts. Julie was breathing very hard, and Rick didn't take his mouth off her lips, except to exclaim, "Oh, baby, I can't get enough of you!" He started kissing her breasts slowly, one then the other, arching his tongue over nipples as he slid his hand between her thighs. He grasped her two hands and held her arms so she couldn't move as he locked her legs apart with his strong thighs. She felt totally possessed and adored. How she had longed for this, how she had dreamed of it, how she had missed it all these years. "Open your eyes," he demanded. "Look me in the eyes." Julie locked her eyes with him as he slid inside her, pushing her thighs over his shoulders. "Hmm, baby, those long legs do it for me all the time," he whispered. He rocked back and forth inside her, slowly, then quickly, as he orgasmed and released all the tension in his body and lay on top of her. "Tell me you love me, Julie,"

"I do love you, Rick. I always did," she cooed.

He sighed. "I love you back. What happened to us, baby? We are perfect for each other. Being with you just now reminds me of how deeply we loved each other."

Julie's heart was jumping with bliss. She felt that she had come home. Doug had hurt her so much over the past few years. She had felt so afraid, hollow and fragmented, but now she felt whole and fell asleep in his arms.

"You fit into me so perfectly," she said as they both drifted off to sleep.

$$\Diamond \quad \Diamond \quad \Diamond$$

Julie awoke on Friday morning and checked her phone. She saw that Doug had not tried to reach her late Thursday night. *Of course,* she thought wryly, *he was probably having a grand old time.*

Rick woke up, and as Julie padded around the room, he grinned at her. "I've got a business meeting this morning, and then you're mine for the rest of the day," he said.

Julie replied, "But I have to leave early tomorrow morning, so we will have all our fun before I turn back into Cinderella."

"My Cinderella," he said, as he clutched her tightly.

Rick went to his meeting and returned at one o'clock. They ordered room service, and after lunch they left the hotel and walked out into the steamy summer afternoon. After a stroll in Central Park, where they stopped at their trysting place, they headed to an afternoon movie at the Paris Theater. They were recreating their dating days. They always had a shared passion for parks, museums and movies. They held hands and kissed a bit during the movie, and at 5:00 they went back to the room to change for dinner.

Julie slipped into an Etro print top, with Rick's approval. "You always loved dressing me, didn't you?" she asked coyly.

"Yes," he smiled. "I love dressing and undressing you." And with that, the clothes came off. "I just can't get enough of you, can I?" he gasped. Julie didn't think. Her body just responded. It was sheer joy. Then shifting gears, Rick said, "Let's get dinner. I'm starved!"

Rick chose a small Italian restaurant with all the right stuff—the red-and-white checked tablecloths, the chicken marsala and meatballs followed by cannoli. What had been good so long ago was still good now. They were old friends who had forged a life together at one time and were reliving it now.

"Rick," Julie said softly, "I want to tell you something that I hid from you many years ago. It was a stupid thing to do, but it was my only secret from you." He peered over his wine glass as she continued. "Rick, you know my dad had a drinking problem, but you didn't know how bad it really was. I wanted to protect him, so I was not completely honest with you. Whenever you demanded things, and you *were* demanding, I felt as if I was going to crack up. Between pre-med studies and the need to get straight A's, and the alcoholic rantings, I thought I was going to have a nervous breakdown. That's why I couldn't handle your silly commands over where I bought cake or why I didn't wash a plate in the sink quickly enough. You see, Rick, I could've handled the pre-med easily," she was now speaking rapidly and breathlessly, "and I could've handled my dad's drinking, but I couldn't handle both." She started to sob quietly, as Rick took her hands in his.

"Why, Julie? Why, baby, didn't you tell me? I would've pushed to hospitalize him! I would've understood your moods, your tantrums. I know it wasn't easy, but you kept flying off the handle. You were the sweetest girl ever, and then you just turned on me. It all makes sense now, and here I thought you were just a pouty, spoiled brat."

Tears streamed down her face. "Rick, I had panic attacks when I drove from Brooklyn to Manhattan. I didn't want you to know. I thought you'd either be turned off by my family or think I was crazy. I just kept waiting for the situation to change. I didn't want to betray my father," she confessed. "The situation *did* change, but it cost you and me our relationship. I was wrong to keep the secret from you. When you tried to come back to me after I broke the engagement, we were just too angry at each other. Then you married Mayling."

Rick's eyes were glazed with tears as he mused, "I wonder what life would've been like with you. You know, Mayling was a rebound affair. It didn't last long. I felt bad about divorcing."

They ate slowly, mainly in silence, then Julie said, "Then you didn't call me, or so I thought, after you came to my apartment in Forest Hills."

"You know now that I did call, but Elizabeth never gave you the message. I thought you weren't interested, so I didn't call you again. Then I married Rosa and that was it."

They sighed out loud together. "Well, we have our rekindled bond now," Julie said, managing a smile. "This is our treasure chest."

"More like Pandora's box!" he said and laughed.

They went back to his room and made love again. He moved gently though fervently, and then he climaxed, calling out her name over and over. They lay in each other's arms, holding each other as if this would be their last night together. They fell asleep, and when they awoke, they looked lovingly at one another. Julie murmured, "So it's OK to allow yourself to feel for me?"

He shook his head. "Julie, so many things remind me of you. Songs, words, places. I have always been in love with you."

"Well," Julie said softly, "for the past few months,

whenever I heard Springsteen's 'Dancing in the Dark', I thought of you. You kind of fought this for the past six months. Remember the line, 'You can't start a fire without a spark?' You wouldn't let the spark ignite."

He got quiet. "Now what?" he asked. "I feel like being with you again. How is this going to work?"

"We will take one day at a time. So now we are 'right back to where we started from,' another one of our songs. Rick," she continued, "I have to leave early in the morning to go out to the beach house. I'll miss you."

"Baby," he crooned, "I miss you already."

Soon enough, the rays of sunlight poked through the curtains. Julie started to get up from the bed, but Rick pulled her back. "We are like Romeo and Juliet, Sweetie, for whom parting was such sweet sorrow."

She kissed his lips softly and hurried to get ready. Rick lay in bed, watching her dress. She bent down and kissed him goodbye, and quickly left. Outside, it was another hot, humid New York summer morning. Julie couldn't tell if it was the heat outside or inside of her that made her feel as though her blood was boiling.

She drove out to the beach and called Rick on the way. "Hi, baby!" she said as he picked up his phone.

"Hi, baby, back!" he answered. "So, you got your way, didn't you? Now I'm sweet on you. I'm feeling all the old feelings again. Julie, I so tried to prevent this, but it was not possible. Now we love each other again and I fear this."

"Fear what? Always the pessimist," she said, gently chiding him. "No one is going anywhere. Just think of this as a special friendship, OK?"

"Yeah, some friendship. Baby, we're not friends, we are lovers, Always were and always will be. That's our deal."

"OK, so just accept it then. I know you're feeling excited, but we're not going to make any rash decisions. So just let it play out."

Rick agreed with her, but over the next two months, he called her daily, telling her how conflicted he was. He loved her, he missed her terribly and he wanted more than a hidden romance. Now he kept complaining about Rosa. He couldn't tolerate that she was always late. He resented her resentment over his being a workaholic. "It's who I am," he told Julie. "You would have no problem with it. She's ungrateful for the life I've provided her."

Julie agreed that a hard-working man was an aphrodisiac for her. Rick loved Julie's intensity with work, the arts and exercising. He confided in Julie that Rosa seemed lazy to him. Julie felt validated in her suspicion that Rick was not as happy as he said he was. How could he say his wife was perfect, but then complain that she was lazy, tardy, critical of his work schedule, ungrateful and unexciting in bed? Julie wanted to believe that Rick's marriage was far from perfect so that she wouldn't feel guilty about being involved with a married man. And why was she with him? The situation between her and Doug was deteriorating daily. For the most part, he was on his phone for long periods of time each afternoon at the summer house. He didn't want to be with Julie. That was crystal clear.

In the earlier years of their marriage, Julie and Doug would take long bike rides out east along Dune Road. The cool breeze and the colors of the bay interspersed with the grasses and the brush propelled them to bike, despite the heat and blazing sunshine. When they reached the beach, they would collapse in the warm sand, staring out into the ocean, sipping iced tea and talking about their lives, ambitions, their child and just about everything else. But it was all different now. Doug had no interest in biking, walking around town, or even going for ice cream. He just wanted to lie on his lounge chair, staring at the pool or sleeping. Julie felt in her heart that although he was physically married to her, he was not emotionally married. The few times she tried talking to him, terrible arguments erupted, with him screaming that she was ungrateful and that he just needed to unwind.

"Why work so hard if you can't enjoy it?" she protested. "Are you waiting until you're in your sixties or seventies to enjoy your free time?"

Doug's answer was a simple retort. "I'll do what I want, and stop trying to micromanage me. I thought you were happy with our level of income! Well, aren't you?"

"Not if it means we have no life!" she declared.

Truth be known, Julie was so preoccupied with Rick that she was starting to not even give a damn anymore. She looked forward to Rick's texts and calls as a welcome distraction. She was honest with him about her situation with Doug and his zoning out. Rick insisted that Doug must be having an affair and expressed how much he wished he could be with Julie. He complained that Rosa was late for a corporate dinner as usual and that she needed to get out and do volunteer work. He was growing intolerant of her criticizing his work schedule. "Maybe if she wasn't so lazy and did some work, she would stop bitching about my schedule," he ranted. Julie resisted egging him on, but inwardly, she was happy that Rick was finally admitting that things were not so perfect in his marriage.

"We just belong together," he told her, sounding morose one afternoon.

Julie appreciated his candor. "I know that, but we can't be irresponsible," she told him.

She wondered whether, if she weren't so distracted by Rick, would she be tolerating Doug's vile behavior? She stopped trying to make things better. She simply stopped caring. To hell with the biking, kayaking, beach walks, or even sex! She and Rick were falling back in love, and things were going to be great!

Or so she hoped.

CHAPTER 46

The summer ended. The days became cooler and the nights longer. Julie and Rick missed each other terribly. "Baby," he insisted one afternoon, "you have to meet me on the road when I travel. I can't just come to New York now and then. If you meet me, we will get into a rhythm where we see each other on a regular basis."

Julie sighed out loud. "It's not like I'm married now, Rick. I'm not. Doug and I are just cohabiting. But you're married." Julie assumed they were both on their way out of trouble marriages.

"Where are you in October?" he questioned.

"In Boston at a dermatology conference the second week."

"You're kidding! I'm there the second week of October too, giving a lecture! Wow! We're going to spend some time together! Rosa and I will be coming home from Europe, and then I'm going to Boston. It's going to be perfect!"

In October, as planned, Rick returned from Europe. Julie could barely wait to see him. They made a date to meet in the Boston Commons. They would stroll to the park before going to a museum and having lunch. Julie packed three dresses and five pairs of shoes for their two-day rendezvous.

Rick texted her as soon as the plane landed. "I'll call you tomorrow," the message read. Julie eagerly awaited the sound of his voice, but he didn't call the next day or the day after. Four days later he finally phoned, and Julie knew there was a problem. Still, they set their date for two weeks later.

Julie perceived a change. Rick told her that he missed her but said he was really busy at work, so they probably couldn't speak until the day before their meeting. Julie was stunned and didn't know what to say. She surmised that Rosa had picked up on Rick's emotional distance and was now staking out her territory. Maybe she was not complaining as much about his work, maybe not arriving two hours late to events. Maybe she was playing up to him. Whatever it was, Julie could tell that something was off.

She didn't hear from Rick until the following Sunday, when he called with excuses about why he hadn't found a minute to talk to her all week.

"You know, Rick, I'm thinking," Julie said in a slow voice, "maybe we shouldn't meet in Boston. It might be too hectic."

He snapped, "What started this?"

"Your attitude," she replied. "You've barely spoken to me in a week. I know you're busy, but this is inconsistent. I think it's best that we don't meet," she stated.

Rick was persistent. "Please, I've been busy! I miss you, and I want to see you so badly!" Julie caved. She did want to see him, and she was very lonely at home. And so, despite her misgivings, she planned to meet him on Thursday morning in Boston.

Julie arrived in Boston Wednesday night. She took a long bubble bath and thought about what the next morning would bring. She awoke the next day and slipped into a hot ensemble: tight jeans, black turtleneck, leather jacket and black suede booties. A beige-and-black linen scarf added a touch of panache. She was just finishing applying her lipstick when her phone rang.

"Yes?" she answered tentatively.

"Hi, I'm here!" he said loudly. "What room are you in?"

They were supposed to meet in the park at noon, but Rick had come early. She told him the room number, and within minutes there was a knock on the door. She opened the door and fell into his arms. He led her to the bed, kissing her firmly on the lips and whispering, "*Je t'aime,* I love you, I adore you." Julie succumbed to his passion as he lifted her shirt and bra, bringing his lips to her breasts. He was wildly ruffling up her hair when his phone rang.

"Oh, wait," he said. "It's Rosa." He picked up the phone and Julie listened as he told Rosa where he put her new Prada heels. "OK, speak later," he said, and quickly returned to kissing Julie's breasts. Then the phone rang again. "Yeah, baby," he said. "I don't know where I put the insurance papers. Look in the drawer in the kitchen. OK, talk later." Now, again, he kissed Julie hard on the mouth. She felt her lips tense as he slid his hand around her shoulder, and for the third time, the phone rang.

"Don't answer!" Julie heard herself say. "Pretend you're on a conference call."

He didn't listen and instead answered, saying, "What, baby? What's up?" There was talking on the other end, and then Rick said, "So you think your mother broke her ankle? Take her to the ER and I'll have them send me the films and I'll get her admitted. OK, baby, I love you."

Julie was in shock. He was telling his wife he loved her within minutes of kissing and touching her. She finally mustered the strength to ask Rick exactly what was going on.

"I don't get this at all. You cannot answer the phone the second your wife calls!" she protested.

"I have to, or she might think something is up," he said. "She thinks I have a business dinner tonight, and I told her I was going for a run this morning. She knows I don't run for three hours."

"Wait," Julie said. "She actually times your runs? She knows your schedule to the last minute?"

Rick nodded. "Latinas are very jealous. She wants to know my whereabouts every second."

Julie shook her head in disbelief. "Oh, my Lord, you are so afraid of her! It's as though you're under lock and key with a prison bracelet. Rick, you are way too married to be having an affair or fling," she stated indignantly.

"No, it's not like that! I just don't want trouble at home. Besides which, the money is all in her name," he explained.

Just as Julie was turning away, the phone rang again. Rick spent about an hour discussing his mother-in-law's ankle surgery. Julie felt her face flush with anxiety and anger. How dare he be so inconsiderate? Julie had told him that she didn't want to meet him, and he lured her into coming to Boston. Now he was on the phone for the fourth time in one hour! He finally hung up, saying," Hispanics are so emotional."

"You know, Rick," Julie said in a clipped voice, "you like this emotion and neediness, or you wouldn't tolerate it. It must make you feel really important. Furthermore, again, you are way too married to waste my time! It's so disrespectful, both to your wife and me, to hear you say, 'I love you, baby' as you're literally kissing and touching me!"

Rick protested. "No, it's not that way at all. I'm just really torn. I like my wife, I do. I like her."

"And me?" Julie practically shrieked.

"Julie, I adore you. Just bear with me," he begged.

Julie insisted that they leave for lunch. To Rick's dismay, she was not going to be intimate with him. She didn't even understand why she was spending time with him instead of just leaving. Trying to get something out of the day, they headed to a nearby museum, appreciating the wonders of Impressionism, and then stopped by a café for a glass of wine. Julie talked about art and literature and smiled at Rick, but inside she felt a lump in her throat.

The afternoon passed, and they returned to their

separate rooms. *Thank goodness,* she said to herself, *that Rick insisted on each of us taking our own rooms, in case either spouse called the hotel.* He knew the ropes well from past experience. Julie wouldn't have even thought about Doug calling the hotel to check on her. She knew he would call on her cell phone. But Rick was worried that Rosa just might call the hotel to check if indeed he was where he said he was. Yes, he had been around the block many times.

In her room, Julie showered and changed into a knit dress and slipped into her black suede heels. She didn't understand why she was bothering to have dinner with Rick but thought, *What the hell?* They met downstairs in the hotel restaurant. Rick stared at Julie across the table.

"You look so beautiful tonight," he said as he poured each of them a glass of wine. Julie just smiled slightly. She felt dismayed but was committed to following through with the evening.

"So, how was Europe?" she prodded him.

"Well, really nice. We had a very good time. You know, it was Rosa's birthday, so I gave her a Tiffany necklace, and she cried."

Julie sat stone faced. She debated if she should just leave the table, when Rick continued, "We've had our problems, but I think we're turning a corner. Rosa does adore me, and lately things have gotten better between us. You know, Julie, when I crossed paths with you again, if things had been the way they are now between Rosa and me, I don't know if I would have called you. On the other hand, if something ever happened to Rosa, I'd marry you." He was pouring them each another glass of wine. Julie just stared into space and felt the room spinning. Rick leaned over and asked if she was feeling OK.

"I think I had too much wine," she lied. She wanted to pick up the bottle and toss the remaining wine in his face. "Rick, I must go back to my room. I don't feel well," she said. She stood up from the table and walked stiffly back to her room.

Rick ushered her to the door. "Let me stay with you and make sure you're safe," he said softly.

"No, it's better if I'm alone. I really need space. I'm so dizzy," she said.

"I so wanted to be with you tonight," he said as he leaned over and kissed her lips.

She pulled away. "No, I'd better sleep this off," she whispered, never wanting to see him again. She opened the door and walked into the room, feeling it was finally over. She quickly closed the door in his face and wondered if he had any idea as to how insensitive and self-centered he was.

Julie lay down on the bed and burst into tears. She had never been so humiliated in her life. This was worse than when, decades before, Robbie asked her out to get her friend Sara's phone number. Here, she'd met up with her ex-fiancé who was telling her how amazing his marriage was and yet wanted to be intimate with her. It would have been one thing if he was unhappily married and needed comfort. But now he seemed perfectly content with his wife and just wanted to walk down memory lane with an old lover. She promised herself she would never see him again. Why didn't she tell this to him? Why did she just sit at the table enduring the lack of respect? Was it her discomfort with confrontation that kept her from screaming at him? Did she think he was lying to himself about his marriage and would eventually accept that he loved her and that they belonged together? She didn't know. She didn't care. She just wanted to go home.

At 6:00 a.m., Julie awoke, still feeling dazed and teary. She threw her clothes in her carry-on, left the room and went down to the front desk.

"Can you help me arrange an earlier train?" she asked the concierge. "I must get home."

"Yes!" he said enthusiastically. "There's a train from Back Bay to Grand Central at 8:00 a.m." Julie thanked him, left the hotel and hailed a cab. She wanted to avoid running into Rick.

She boarded the train and slumped into her seat, sipping

coffee and wiping tears from her eyes. She was staring out the window, gazing at the passing scenery of all the autumn leaves, when she heard the familiar message alert on her phone. She knew it was Rick. "Baby, where are you?" the message read. "I knocked on your door, but no one answered. The concierge told me you checked out."

She felt nauseated and angry at the same time. Was he trying to have a morning quickie before he went to his lecture? Right. Then he could go home to his perfect wife and his perfect life. She wanted to ignore his text, but needing closure, she responded, "I left."

"Are you OK?" he texted. "The thought of you hurting is killing me. Please tell me that you are OK."

Her next text was curt. "I'm OK, I just want to get home. It is what it is."

He persevered. "I know you're upset. I'm not exactly sure what happened. I just can't give you everything you need. Please understand that it's too hard for me to leave my marriage."

Julie swallowed hard to avoid vomiting. Was he that clueless? He now thought that she was upset because he was not leaving his marriage, which she never expected or wanted. He had no idea how rude he was, wasting her time talking to his wife multiple times on the phone and then saying 'I love you' right in front of her. This was the stuff of television daytime drama. He was so conceited that he thought his grand presence was enough. Did he even remember the previous night's dinner conversation when he extolled his wife's virtues and boasted how wonderful their marriage was? For the moment, Julie began to doubt herself. Did *she* not hear the conversation clearly? Did he really say all those things about his wife and their marriage?

She realized that she was so disappointed and hurt that she couldn't really believe that anyone could be as selfish and rude as Rick was. But he was. Whether it was his being conflicted with his life or just being a narcissist, she had had enough.

"I don't have much to say," she texted for what she hoped would be her final communication to him forever.

"Please calm down," he replied. "I didn't mean to upset you. Please let me call you."

She acquiesced. "I'll call you when I arrive in New York." And she did. "Rick," she said slowly, "I never expected you to leave your wife. I don't know what your true deal is, but your needs are different from mine. I'm upset that we met and all you did was tell me how great your marriage is. That's terrific really, but where do I fit in? I don't. So I'd like to end this. I know when it's time to leave."

Rick persisted. "Why can't we just keep this casual and see each other occasionally?"

"Because I'm not a Geisha girl or French mistress!" Julie exclaimed. "I don't need this with you, and I won't tolerate your insensitivity. Why meet me and tell me how great your marriage is? What's wrong with you? If you need a fling and something new and different, then pay for it!"

"I guess you're right," he replied. "I'll miss you and I love you."

"I know I'm right," she answered. "It's for the best. Be well, and I wish you the best," she lied. She didn't really wish him the best. She hung up and burst into tears. It was better to feel the pain now and move on. She was angry at herself for being naïve, angry at Doug for being the trigger that allowed her to be vulnerable and angry at Rick for being so selfish.

For a week or so, Julie walked around in a daze, feeling as if she was slowly coming apart at the seams. She went to work and robotically saw her patients, forcing herself to smile and act if as if nothing in her life had changed. She replayed the scene in the hotel room in Boston listening to Rick go on about how perfect things were in his marriage. She was happy that she managed to tell him how awful his behavior was that evening, but she was angry at both of the men in her life. They had both hurt her. If Doug hadn't started that absurd flirtation with Galena, she never would have met up with Rick. It was as if the two guys were bookends, crushing her spirit. She decided that starting now, she would refocus her energy on positive things in her life, like the coming winter, her piano, reading, tennis and the arts, anything but thinking about Rick and Doug and their narcissism.

Thanksgiving was approaching, and it was always a joyful holiday for Julie. She loved having the family gather for a huge meal and then sit by the fire in the living room with the women while the men sat in the den watching TV. She vowed that this holiday would mark the beginning of a peaceful year ahead.

Work finished, Julie went home, poured herself a glass of Chardonnay and began perusing recipe books to plan a great holiday dinner. She decided there would be butternut squash soup, turkey with cranberry and walnut stuffing, broccoli au gratin, marshmallow-encrusted sweet potatoes, roasted potatoes and asparagus. Doug would prepare most of the food with her, as he was a talented chef. She wanted to bond with him again and needed her anger toward him to dissipate, as it was tearing into her.

The days passed slowly, but she managed to admire the brilliant blue November skies as she peered out the blinds of her treatment rooms. Something about the crisp November air caused the sky to appear a deeper blue in the late morning, and this never failed to thrill Julie. She felt her spirits starting to lift a bit.

Julie was always very busy seeing patients the day before Thanksgiving. The college kids were in from school and needed their acne check-ups after being away for three months. She affectionately called the visits "the turkey appointments" and knew she was in for a long day before going home to start preparing for the holiday.

On the way home from work, she heard the familiar chime on her phone. Rick. She hesitated before reading

the message but knew that her curiosity would win over
her caution. The text was seemingly heartfelt. "I can't get
you out of my mind. I have to figure out some way to
compartmentalize this. Please let me know that you read this. I
understand if you don't want to speak to me, but please let me
know that you read this. I miss you."

Julie felt her heart pounding beneath her winter coat.
She didn't know how to interpret this. Hadn't they agreed
to let this whole thing go? Was he now truly regretting his
behavior? Was absence making his heart grow fonder now that
he realized it was over? Or was he just bored and horny and
making sure that she was an option, should he come to New
York alone? She texted back a simple response. "Stop playing
with me."

Her sadness was now morphing into anger. How dare he
keep tugging at her heart strings! He just liked different flavors
of ice cream now and then. She continued to text, "You're a
happily married man, by your own admission. We tried this.
You had me at a very weak moment of my life. You're not
interested in a meaningful friendship or affair. You want a
fling. Again, I'm not fling material."

"Not really," he texted. "I'm so conflicted. Please talk to
me."

She knew she shouldn't, but she couldn't resist hearing
his voice. The phone rang within seconds. "Hi! Please listen to
me, Sweetie, please!" he pleaded. "I'm not playing with you.
I'm so confused. I never expected my feelings to come back the
way they did. In the past I could always compartmentalize my
feelings, but now, with you, I can't."

"And that is exactly why we can't do this," Julie
emphasized. "I can't be a toy you take out of the drawer to play
with and shove it back in when you're done. I'm free. You're
not. My marriage is hurting me. Yours is glorious, according
to you, or if it's not perfect, it's very good. I don't want to be
involved with a happily married man! Anyway, Rick, your
time is not your own. You need to be accountable for every

moment. You pick up the phone like a dog running for a treat. It's awkward. It's humiliating, actually, for both me and your wife. I thought you were unhappy, like stuck there, and I was your escape, like you are mine. Rick, you're a player, and I despise players." She felt breathless, but she couldn't believe how honest and firm she was being with him, and it felt really good.

"I'm not a player with you. I adore you, Julie," he murmured, with his voice cracking. "I'm getting emotional, and I'm sorry."

She wanted to believe him, but even if she did, what good was it? Nothing would change. She paused and asked, "And how will any of this change? Let's be friends, maybe speak once in a while. Who knows what the future will bring?"

"OK," Rick said, sounding hopeful. "As long as I know you're still in my life." He probably assumed he would work his way back to her.

"Have a great holiday. I need to go home and start cooking," she added.

"Later," he answered. "We'll speak soon."

She went into the house feeling totally drained, yet hopeful that there was still a possibility that maybe one day it would work out between them. She held onto a romantic notion of an enduring, special friendship, even if it was totally emotional, without any sex. Just their thing, for a lifetime.

December arrived with a biting chill in the air. Holiday parties and festivities occupied Julie's thoughts. She had always loved New York during the holiday season. She had never lost her enthusiasm for seeing the Fifth Avenue store windows with their displays of colored lights, puppets and mechanical figures. The Christmas tree was in its usual place, overlooking the skating rink. Julie ran from store to store, buying gifts and meeting friends for lunch at Saks and Bloomingdale's. The end of the year meant bonuses and holiday parties for the staff. She made sure to always be generous to them, as they worked hard and looked forward to their party and extra salary.

On New Year's Eve there was going to be a small dinner party at home with just Emma and the guys, and they would cook up a feast. The menu was planned perfectly, and Julie vowed that it would be a good year ahead for her and Doug. It was just over one year since she had seen Rick, and although she missed him, she was relieved that they were only going to be friends at most. They just couldn't have more than that.

Julie was busy cooking holiday delicacies with Emma when she heard a ping from her phone. She debated whether to answer the text, but like Pavlov's dog, she read it.

"Just wanted to wish you a happy holiday. Always thinking about you. I haven't texted for a few weeks, as I think that's best."

She smiled to herself. Well, I guess he does think about me, she thought smugly. She responded, wishing him a very happy and healthy year ahead. He wanted to know what her evening plans were. She told him about her dinner party, and he reminded her that he knew her when she couldn't even boil an egg and said how proud of her he was. He seemed sentimental, as holidays always did that to people.

Julie told him she would text him after the holiday, although she couldn't quite understand why she was opening Pandora's box again. She assured herself it was just friendship and that her recent infatuation was a result of Doug's having hurt her with Galena. It was not unusual, she thought, to seek comfort from an old boyfriend. Somehow, she didn't want to totally disengage from Rick.

Julie was confused. She couldn't understand if she just wanted to feel the thrill of a secret affair or enjoy the comfort of someone who rescued her in the past. She had given up trying to understand Rick's motives. It seemed he did not understand his own behavior. It wasn't worth the effort to analyze him. She needed to understand her own actions and emotions. It was time to return to therapy.

CHAPTER 47

J ulie decided that she and Doug were going to start
a new life together. It was Valentine's Day weekend
and their anniversary, and to celebrate, they planned an escape
to Florida. They would to stay at a boutique hotel in the
center of town and have their first night's dinner at an upscale
restaurant. She hoped it was going to be a romantic getaway in
hot Miami.

But somehow Julie had a premonition about the entire
weekend. Doug complained on the flight down that he really
didn't want to go away, citing his busy work schedule. He
was distant on the plane, barely holding her hand, but rather,
reading a book on his Kindle and listening to music.

They arrived at the hotel and settled into their room.
Immediately, Doug suggested that they have a drink and then
take a walk on the beach. They sat at the bar in the hotel lobby
sipping their drinks when Doug got up, saying he'd forgotten
his wallet and was going back to the room to get it.

"We don't need a wallet," Julie insisted, "Charge the
drink to the room."

Doug snapped at her. "Don't tell me what I need!"

Julie sipped her Chardonnay, staring at the bottles

behind the bar. Doug came back twenty minutes later. Julie didn't question what he was doing for that twenty minutes. They set out to the boardwalk, strolling silently as Julie watched Doug's mood darken. She suppressed her tears as she observed other couples holding hands, laughing and kissing. A brilliant blue sky above and a turquoise blue ocean should have set the scene for a joyful stroll, but instead they were miserable.

When they got back to their room at 4:00, Doug collapsed on the bed and fell asleep immediately. *How romantic,* Julie thought. Finally, at 7:00, she gently tapped him on the shoulder. "Doug," she whispered, "we should shower and start getting ready for dinner."

"I'm too tired!" he shouted. "Why are you waking me up?"

She recoiled at his harsh tone. "We need to get ready."

"Why would you wake me?" he retorted, his voice filled with anger. "You're just so inconsiderate!"

Julie wanted to leave right then and head home. She could not read the situation. *What was going on?* And then, out of nowhere, Doug stared at her and said, "Julie, I don't know if I want to be married to you. It's just not working for me anymore." It was as though he had stabbed her with a knife.

Doug fell back asleep. Julie picked up her clothes, walked to the front desk and requested a separate room for herself. This little trip was turning into a nightmare. As she slumped into the bed, she started to cry. Then somehow, she managed to compose herself and called the concierge to help her arrange a flight home.

At 2:00 a.m., Doug awoke from his sleep. Realizing he was alone, he called Julie's cell phone. "Where are you?" he asked.

Julie calmly informed him that she was in another room and was taking a flight home in the morning.

"What room are you in?"

"None of your business! And if you come to this room, I will call security!" She already informed the front desk that he was not to be given a key, as she was nervous about being with him alone. That didn't stop him. Within minutes, he was knocking on the door and yelling at her to open it. Julie contacted security, and they escorted Doug back to his room.

In the morning, Julie fled to the Miami airport by taxi. She settled into her seat and drowned her pain with a bloody Mary. Just before takeoff, she sent out two texts. The first was to Doug. "I'm on the plane home. Not exactly the best anniversary!" The second was to Rick. "I miss you."

The plane touched down, and Julie's phone started ringing with messages. Doug texted that he was sorry, he was out of it, and didn't really remember what happened. A few friends had sent texts, and then Julie's eye caught Rick's name.

She slowly read the text. "Baby, I miss you, too. Can I call you on Monday?" Julie texted back a simple "Yes." She knew this was wrong, yet she couldn't stop herself. *Maybe things will be different now,* she told herself. *Or maybe not.*

Doug finally arrived home late Saturday night. He muttered that he was sorry but also said that Julie overreacted by leaving and flying home. Julie said nothing. She was disgusted and depressed, but she was privately excited to have heard from Rick. She told Doug that she needed space. He insisted that he had too many drinks, and she persisted by saying that the truth comes out when people are drunk. They had a cursory dinner together on Sunday, making small talk about politics, but Julie's mind was back on Rick.

Monday was a frigid February day, but Julie tingled inside, waiting to hear from Rick. Sure enough, at 4:00 p.m., the message alert came in: "Can I call now?"

"Sure," she texted back, and within seconds the phone rang.

"Hey!" Rick shouted.

"Hi," she whispered.

"So you miss me, do you?" Rick inquired.

"I guess so," Julie answered.

"Well," he said in a drawn-out voice, "I'll be in town in April. So...?"

"I'll meet you," Julie said coyly, barely believing that she was making plans with him again. He was winning again, but she didn't care. She was lonely, scared and hating Doug. Rick, the knight in shining armor. Hope was playing a rude trick on her, and she fell back into the trap, believing it was all going to change.

Every few days, Rick texted her, flirting and acting concerned about her work. She shared details of her practice and bounced her ideas off him. Rick told her how to structure the office management, and she followed his instructions. It was like being college students again when he had advised her on what to do. She loved it. She felt safe and coddled. It did not matter that she had accomplished so much in her life. She liked this kind of attention, and the need for it had never left her.

They avoided talking about their spouses. Rick had finally caught on that Julie would freak out over that. She told him nothing about her trip to Florida. She and Doug were giving each other space. They still went out occasionally, with friends serving as a buffer, but they barely spoke to each other.

Without Rick, there was not much to look forward to. Work was routine, Doug was off doing his own thing, and Drew was busy at college. Julie counted the days until April.

CHAPTER 48

It was a cool April evening when Julie and Rick met at Adour, a fancy French restaurant on the Upper East Side. Always dressed to the nines, Julie wore a starkly simple but chic black dress, nude stockings and black pumps. Her hair was slightly curly, which added a hint of softness to the look. She slowly sauntered to the table in the corner where Rick was waiting for her. He looked her up and down, and she bent over to kiss him. She cozied up next to him, and in moments his hand was on her thigh.

"I've got to tell you," he commented without taking his eyes off of her, "you look so beautiful. I can't believe how much I've missed you."

A small candle flickered on the table as they talked about everything but the taboo topic of their spouses. Rick didn't take his hands off of her, holding her hand, rubbing her thigh, stroking her cheek. After a few glasses of Champagne and a light meal, he cuddled her, kissing her wildly on her lips.

"You're part of me," he whispered. "You get me. You understand me, baby. We are the same. Always were." Julie felt her heart surge with joy. The pain that Doug had inflicted evaporated as she devoured Rick's words.

"Julie," he paused, "can you imagine if I lived in New York?"

"We would see each other weekly," she suggested.

"Daily," he said firmly. "You have no idea how lucky you are that I'm controlling the situation. This thing between us could spiral out of control if not for me, and we would destroy two families."

"And," she teased, "if ever we were ever alone by ourselves?"

"We wouldn't be alone. We'd be together," he said definitively.

Julie felt happy and sad at the same time. "Rick," she asked, "why do you always say we are the same?"

"Because we are. You crave affection, like I do. You admire my accomplishments. You love to work, and you're full of energy. We are exactly the same as we always were, but now we have money. Of course, I'm married now, and Rosa is a good woman. I think you'd actually like each other." Julie grew sullen and Rick pulled her close. "Let's enjoy the evening," he whispered. But Julie couldn't. Not after that last comment about Rosa. Why did he have to say that? She feigned a migraine.

"Rick," she said, I'm going back to my room."

"But…but…I was hoping we would spend the night."

"Not this time," she said, and got up and left.

The next morning, Rick texted her that he was leaving to go home to North Carolina but that he missed her already. He said that he was flying to Brazil the next day to give a lecture and that he would text her from there. She knew she was at the end of her rope. The comment about Rosa being a good woman cut her to the core. *Look at what I have been doing!* she said to herself. *I am still so stupid and naïve, totally addicted to this man who repeatedly mistreats me! I did this to myself. I put myself here! By now I should know better.*

Ten days later, when Julie still hadn't heard from him, all her demons surfaced: depression, anxiety, anger, loneliness and sadness. Finally, he contacted her.

"Hey, you!" read the text. "How are you?"

"Fine."

"Fine, wow, awesome!"

Clearly, he doesn't get it, she thought. "Listen, Rick," Julie wrote, "we need to talk. I can't text what I want to tell you."

A moment later her phone rang. "What's up, baby?" he asked in a concerned voice.

She took a deep breath and composed her thoughts. This time she would tell it all.

"Rick," she began, "I'm tired of this roller coaster I'm on with you. The ride is rough, too up and down. I need consistency and a steady pace. I'm into merry-go-rounds— you know, a slow, easy, continuous ride. One minute this relationship is up and exciting, building to a crescendo, and then it plummets till the next time, when it builds to a crescendo again. It's just not working for me."

"But baby, that's exciting! I love your metaphor about the roller coaster. It gives us a thrill and something to look forward to as a treat!" he exclaimed.

Julie paused. "That's exactly the problem. I'm not a treat. I'm not the kind of woman you have a casual fling with. This whole thing has been on your terms, as if only your needs count." She felt a rush as she finally let her feelings out. "This is not a love affair; it's a lame affair. For you it was a blast from the past, letting you relive your youth. I don't need this. You can't handle a real relationship. And for me it's just too much work to restrain my real feelings."

Rick was stunned. There was total silence. Then he cleared his throat. "Julie, I'm in conflict. When I see you, I go back to the past, and I love it. But then I feel guilty. I love my wife dearly, and I'm happily married, but then there's you and you're an unfinished chapter in my life. You are like comfort food."

Julie felt anger swell inside of her. "An unfinished chapter? I see. I'm a thrill. It's the excitement of a new woman infused with the familiarity of an old lover. Like cocaine and chocolate chip cookies. Is that what you are implying?"

"No, Julie, calm down," he pleaded, "I'm telling you about my conflict."

Julie was enraged. "I am so tired of hearing about your conflict!" she blurted out. "You have more than most. Have some gratitude for what you have and learn to live with whatever you're missing, but for heaven's sake, accept that you are not entitled to have it *all*. Maybe, Rick," she hissed, "it's time for me to have a chat with Rosa. Perhaps she should know just how much you love her but that you need to revisit the 'unfinished chapters' of your life. Maybe you and she can enjoy an exciting roller coaster ride when she learns about this. I know how much you love thrills!"

"Julie, please," he begged, "don't call her. Please. She would never understand."

"So then why, Rick, knowing that she would be devastated, would you put your marriage at risk, going—how did you say it?—around the block many times?"

"I have demons, Julie. We all do," he said contritely.

Julie felt pity for him. "Relax, Rick. I'm not going to ever call Rosa. But your next conquest might. So learn from this, Rick," Julie stated in a low, firm voice, "I'm done. I don't wish you ill, but I don't wish you well."

Julie thought of her favorite Andrea Bocelli song, "Time to Say Goodbye" as she hung up the phone. She felt numb but also felt tremendous relief as tears poured from her eyes. She knew she would now have to come to terms with her own marriage. There would be no more distractions. It was time to move on.

—— PART 9 ——

RESOLUTION

CHAPTER 49

As the months passed, Julie worked on rebuilding her relationship with Doug. She thought about how there could have been a variety of scenarios to play out, and how the situation could have turned out differently. She might have run off with Rick, picking up where they left off as teenagers. Or she might have descended into an abyss of anger and rage, perhaps even calling Rosa to tell her about Rick's infidelities, a choice that would have left her finished with both Rick *and* Doug. She chose a third option: forgiveness. She decided to focus on Doug's strengths and the loving aspects of their marriage. Once again, she reminded herself that without Doug, she never would have achieved what she had professionally. His taking charge of everything left her free to concentrate on work, their son and her avocations. Yes, she admitted that he was controlling, but the irony was that because of that, life was actually easier.

She reflected on her relationship with Rick. It was like one of Seurat's pointillist paintings, better viewed at a distance. He was an exciting partner when they were young, but if she had to judge his character as a mature man, there was no doubt that he had become an entitled, selfish person.

Yes, forgiving everyone was her choice. She decided to forgive Rick's self-serving nature, Doug's rigidity, and most of all, her own insecurity that had allowed her to cling to unhealthy partnerships in order to feel protected. Children of displaced immigrants living in an unfamiliar world, the three of them, she recognized, had been exposed to whatever insecurities their parents felt and either succumbed to them or overcame them.

The secret insecurity that Julie had harbored her entire life began with the shame she felt about her father's drinking and infidelity, and continued with the attempts to obtain confidence from the men in her life. At last, it was time to expose her secret and acknowledge the fears within herself. She could have applied the well-known adage, "What doesn't kill you makes you stronger," but Julie found something better: "Time heals what reason won't," and forgiveness and acceptance provided the answer she was seeking.

ACKNOWLEDGMENTS

As I reflect upon the process of creating this book, many significant people come to mind. Firstly, I would like to thank my patients for entrusting me with their medical care, and my staff for their devotion to me and the people we have treated. Being a doctor requires a special type of patience, a commitment to maintaining a high level of ethics and compassion. My staff has consistently carried out my numerous requests and has met my demands for excellent patient care and the efficient running of a practice.

Many thanks to my publishing team: editor and friend Elizabeth Uhlig of Marble House Editions paved the way for me with this first novel. She edited the manuscript and coordinated all the aspects of bringing it to life; Mim Eisenberg of WordCraft, for proofreading the manuscript and for doing such meticulous fact-checking; Janet Atkins of Hinterland Design for creating the look of the book.

I have been blessed with so many family members and friends who truly assist me with the practicalities of my life, and at the same time support me emotionally during difficult periods. Sister-in-law Benay Katz was my office manager and confidant for over twenty-five years and ran the practice as only a devoted sister would. My sister Cynthia Leopold has been at my side since, at age three, she pushed me in my stroller. Always an available source of support, Cynthia will pick up the phone at any hour of the day to offer comfort and sage advice.

I have so many dear friends, but a special thanks to

Dr. Shelley Wertheim, Wendy Levine and Lori Gunn, who have been consistently loyal, loving and encouraging. I'd like to give a huge thanks to Dr. Barbara Deutsch who has been my lifeline when anxiety reared its scary head in times of crisis.

Finally, there are three family members who mean so much to me: my mom, who offered her unconditional love and taught me to respect others, to value education and to be a loving mother myself. And the two men in my life: my husband, Dr. David Funt, who has taken care of just about everything pertaining to our personal life. A perfectionist, he can be challenging at times, but I reap great rewards from his efforts. For decades, he has guided me to be the best possible physician. Lastly, my son Daniel, who has so many facets. Like a diamond, he glitters brightly, adding light and beauty to my life. Always the jewel in my crown.